WITCHFINDER
The Last Nightfall

The first ever Rabicus was created by Summer Furniss of Queen Elizabeth's Grammar School, Alford.

OXFORD
UNIVERSITY PRESS

Great Clarendon Street, Oxford OX2 6DP

Oxford University Press is a department of the University of Oxford.
It furthers the University's objective of excellence in research, scholarship,
and education by publishing worldwide in

Oxford   New York

Auckland   Cape Town   Dar es Salaam   Hong Kong   Karachi
Kuala Lumpur   Madrid   Melbourne   Mexico City   Nairobi
New Delhi   Shanghai   Taipei   Toronto

With offices in

Argentina   Austria   Brazil   Chile   Czech Republic   France   Greece
Guatemala   Hungary   Italy   Japan   Poland   Portugal   Singapore
South Korea   Switzerland   Thailand   Turkey   Ukraine   Vietnam

Oxford is a registered trade mark of Oxford University Press
in the UK and in certain other countries

British Library Cataloguing in Publication Data

Data available

ISBN: 978-0-19-273192-0

1 3 5 7 9 10 8 6 4 2

Printed in Great Britain
Paper used in the production of this book is a natural,
recyclable product made from wood grown in sustainable forests.
The manufacturing process conforms to the environmental
regulations of the country of origin.

WITCHFIRE

The Last Nightfall

The future of humankind rests on Jake's shoulders.
His only hope is to close the demon door for ever by
harnessing the power of the witchball. But the demon,
Pinch, holds it in hell. He waits for a witch with enough
darkness in their heart to summon him back to earth.

Jake must travel to hell and back to stop the demon and
save a stranded soul. All the while, a strange voice that is
his, but not his, is getting louder in Jake's head. A truth
as old as time has been hidden deep within him and
it is slowly forcing its way to the surface.

The Age of Man is over.

Vampires stalk the streets.

Dark creatures wait to be unleashed.

The Demontide is here.

... my love to

Marilyn and Bill Hussey.

My parents.

My heroes.

WITCHFINDER
The Last Nightfall

WILLIAM HUSSEY

OXFORD
UNIVERSITY PRESS

Contents

THEN circa 29,000 BC –
Where Demons Dwell

'She's just a child, a baby—why must you do this?'

'Because I am hungry.'

'I have meat in my shelter. All the reindeer flesh you can eat.'

'But I have told you, I cannot live in this world on animal meat alone. I must have my fill of human flesh or I will fade back into the shadows. Is that what you want?'

'No, my child!'

'Then let me eat in peace.'

The baby in the demon's arms started to cry, a high-pitched mewling that set his teeth on edge. He ought to silence her. Snap her frail neck and then feast, but the demon wanted the blood to be as hot and as fresh as possible.

Perched on the bank of the wide river, the demon lifted the baby to its jaws. So weak, so fragile. How could these pitiful mortals hope to survive in such a cold and ruthless cosmos? To destroy them—to *eat* them—was really a kind of mercy. The woman squatting beside the demon shivered; a delightful tremor that made him smile. Not only were they weak and fragile, they were sentimental!

The baby flailed her plump little limbs. Her hand latched on to the demon's lower lip and turned his smile into a grimace. His tongue slavered and his needle-sharp teeth grazed her fragile fingers and moved up to her tiny wrist. He would soon strip the meat from this young carcass. Then, when the feast was over, he'd fling the bones into the great river: a watery graveyard that had already washed away the leftovers of six sumptuous meals.

The demon crammed the baby's arm into his mouth, ready to bite down . . .

'I SEE THE MONSTER! HE HAS THE CHILD!'

Three men crashed through the trees on the far bank. Spears raised, they glared at the woman and her demon.

The monster reacted with lightning speed. He dropped the baby onto the soft earth and darted into the forest. Behind him, he could hear the fading cry of the infant and the woman's breathless pursuit.

'Where are you, my child? Answer me! The hunters are crossing the river!'

And now her words became ragged with fear—

'*Please*, my little Pinch, they are going to kill us!'

The demon hurtled on into the lush green depths of the forest. A low-lying mist lapped around the trees and the creature's powerful body cut through it like the prow of a canoe through still waters. Foraging animals scattered before him and the insects hidden in the long grass ceased their chirrup-song.

Gradually, the forest began to thin out, the trees became more stunted and patches of cold sunlight broke through. Up ahead, he could see a landslide of immense boulders that had smashed its way into the forest, felling small redwoods and providing a rugged slope to the foot of the mountain. Within seconds, he had reached the first boulder and scrambled over the scree. At the base of the mountain, Pinch craned his neck and tried to gauge its height, but the summit of the red-rock giant disappeared into a crown of wispy white clouds.

Pinch filled his lungs and began the climb. His talons found niches in the rock and he swung himself from crevice to crevice, moving with monkey-like agility. The demon was beginning to tire when he caught sight of a ledge jutting out from the rock face like a petulant lip. Exhausted, he clawed his way onto the little plateau.

Birds nesting on the ledge took one look at the demon and exploded into the sky. They climbed high, wheeling and shrieking. Anyone in the forest valley below would be certain to notice their panicked flight. Pinch scampered back to the edge and peered over.

The river blinked up from between the trees. Somewhere down there the womenfolk had herded the children into the safety of their reindeer-skin huts. Pinch imagined them sitting in circles, holding hands and praying for the safe return of the hunters. Those fearless men had tracked and killed every danger that had ever threatened their camp: hungry wolves and ravenous cave lions, even the cannibal tribe that had made its home in the next valley. All the same, Pinch knew that they had never faced a creature such as he.

A dark spirit summoned forth by one of their own.

The demon's gaze swept around the plateau. It was a wide ledge bound on three sides by the mountain *Ayyuk*, named in honour of the falling night and of the 'Great Giver'. At the centre stood a beautiful statue almost as tall as Pinch. Carved from mammoth tusk, it depicted the Great Giver in the form of a tribesman—a tall, long-limbed figure, his bone-white hands pressed against the earth.

Pinch snorted and shook his head. By some accident, he had reached the place most sacred to the tribe. They called it the 'Watching Eye'. From here, so the legend went, the Great Giver saw all of creation and judged everything in his view, good and evil.

A sudden fury took hold of the demon. He snatched up the idol and threw it with all his might into the forest below. The white god shimmered in the late-summer sun before vanishing into the whispering ocean of redwoods. *Down you go*, Pinch thought, *out of the light and into the shadows*. He allowed himself a brief smile before turning back to the mountain. The sheer walls were impossible to climb, even for the dexterous demon. What was he going to do?

'Pinch? Answer me!'

At the sound of the woman's voice, Pinch sought shelter in the only place he could: a rough collar of juniper bushes that ran in a semi-circle around the plateau. He snuffled, breathless as that strange emotion—fear—ran through his little body. For a short time, he had known freedom and, more importantly, the sense of being whole again. No longer a thing of shapeless shadow, he had felt solid earth beneath his feet and the sharp mountain wind against his face. He had breathed the air, drunk the water, eaten the flesh. After eons in the airy darkness, he had been grateful for his liberty and his crude form, but now Pinch sensed that his time in this world was almost up.

The hunters were coming.

'My little child, where you?'

The woman clambered over the ridge, a whisker away from Pinch's hiding place. Her words were rough but he had been her companion for almost a year and had developed an understanding for the tribe's brutish speech. Now he automatically translated it into his own, more refined demon-tongue.

Half-crouching, his mistress wheeled around the ledge, eyes alert, ears straining. As tough as a rhino's hide, her bare feet padded across the rocky ground. She swept her head low and the reindeer horn pendants hanging around her neck grazed the earth like limp fingers. She called out again, spittle flying from her lips, the indecision plain on her face—should she continue the hunt for her beloved 'child' or should she flee? Already she could hear the thunder-step of her pursuers and the clack of their spears.

'Where? Where?' she cried. 'Cannot lose him again. Cannot. But where my child? Where my little man? Where my son made alive again?'

Pinch drew back, the bracken folding around him like a bearskin blanket.

The hunters arrived in a wave. They broke over the ridge and fanned out around the sacred plateau. With a shriek of terror, the woman stumbled back against the cliff wall. Fifteen faces stared at her, square eyes narrowed, high foreheads crumpled. The men were dressed in reindeer hides decorated with bright feathers and painted shells. Blue thunderbolt tattoos blazed across their cheeks and rippled down their powerful forearms. Each hunter held a spear, a formidable weapon fashioned from a mammoth's thighbone.

The leader of the tribe came forward. He walked with calculated grace, every muscle in his battle-scarred body turning and tensing. He wore a diadem of bones around his head—the crown of a seasoned warrior. His sad eyes looked from the woman to the mark in the dust where the idol had stood.

'Where the Great Giver?'

The woman shivered. 'Don't know.'

A leathery squeak as the hunters' hands tightened around their spears. Some cried out in grief: this traitor to their tribe had desecrated the Watching Eye, their most sacred place.

'Where the monster?' the leader said, stepping to within striking distance of the woman. 'Where the dark child?'

'Don't know,' she whispered.

'You are wise-woman. Daughter of the daughter of the daughter of she who first saw the Great Giver. You are teacher and worker of the sacred gift. You are speaker and mover of Oldcraft.'

'Oldcraft is for good,' one of the tribe barked. 'Not evil, so said the Great Giver.'

'Our people were told, warned,' the leader nodded, 'not to let evil into our hearts. Not to let it turn the magic dark. Why you bring the monster here?'

'Not "monster"!' the wise-woman shrieked. 'My child!'

The leader pressed his fingers to her lips.

'All knew you missed your Pinch. When starving wolves found him alone in the woods, we grieved with you.'

He turned to one of his hunters, took the warrior's weapon.

The hunter bowed and stepped back, away from his leader and the killing ground.

'Cried with you, prayed with you, even begged the Great Giver to look after the boy's soul in the grey beyond, though He told us He had no knowledge of that place. That none of his kind did. We felt your pain, my sister, and saw how it made you bite and snap at us like a crazed dog. How it turned your thoughts to bleak winter. But this thing you brought to our camp—'

'Not thing! Please, brother, hear me: his face and form was made ugly by my poor magic. He told me that I had bad skill and could not shape him. But this "monster" *is* my little Pinch. My child. Your sister-son. He heard my crying in the grey place where all our ancestors go. Heard the prayers of his mother for him to return. My strong Oldcraft brought him back to us.'

'No, sister. What came to you was a thing of lies and death. Would your good child Pinch have returned here and made his mother's magic like poison? Would he have murdered so many of our little ones? No. It is the thing the Great Giver warned us of. It is *demon*.'

'I do not believe——!'

'Your belief does not matter. Now, tell us where the demon is.'

The leader brought the tip of the spear to rest against the throbbing artery of his sister's throat. A rustle of feet as the hunters gathered round. Anticipating the kill, some of the younger tribesmen smiled, but the older ones, weary from a lifetime of blood, merely nodded in acceptance. Although she was sister to the leader, her crime was the gravest their people had ever known and execution the only punishment. Chosen children of Oldcraft, they had a duty to stop this evil before it spread throughout the known lands. If not, then how many more demons might come out of the darkness?

'Guide us!' The cry was taken up by the tribe. 'Guide us to the demon!'

'Not demon,' the wise-woman said, her voice as barren as winter. 'Son. He told me, promised me—*son*. Please, brother, he said he was my Pin—'

The leader struck home. His spear pierced flesh, grazed bone, split rock. Pinioned against the mountain, the wise woman kicked and wriggled, her hands loose around the bloody spear. The younger hunters roared their approval, a victory call that was soon silenced by their leader's bellow.

'SHE WAS MY SISTER!'

He turned back to the woman.

She was trying to speak.

'Pin . . . Pin . . .'

The wise-woman pointed a shaking finger. In her dying

moments, she had glimpsed the shape in the juniper bushes.

'Pin-ch. M-my Pin-ch . . .'

The demon had been summoned by this woman and his life force was tied to hers. Now Pinch felt the last flickers of that force die out. Fire erupted around his body. He was going home. In a final act of cruelty, the demon locked eyes with the witch who had given him his form and freedom, and slowly, slowly shook his head. A gesture that meant only one thing—

I lied.

The scene before him—the furious hunters, the grief-stricken leader, the betrayed and slow-dying witch—flickered and vanished. As the fire faded, Pinch felt himself being drawn through the dimensional rift and back to the demon prison. Leaving the solid world of the tribe behind, he had expected that his body would melt away to its old shadowy form, but here he was, on the cusp of the demon realm, still possessing the crude shape that the witch had conjured for him.

The creature now known as Pinch smiled. He would go straight to the Shadow Palace and beg an audience with the Demon Father himself. He would tell of his adventures: of the woman whose bitter cry had pierced the walls of the demon dimension and drawn him to her. He would tell of the tribe's magic, of its superstitions, of its 'Oldcraft', and then he would outline his plan.

These mortals had the power to release demonkind. If their hearts were dark, if they hated and envied, if they lusted for power and vengeance, then their minds would be open to demonic influence. Let us prey upon their weak natures, Pinch would suggest. When they cry out in pain and fury, let us answer them and pretend that it is only through *us* that they can work their magic . . .

He arrived in the murk and silence of the demon realm and hurried to the palace gates. Without sun or moon or stars in the empty sky it was impossible to gauge time here, but it could not have been many minutes before Pinch was standing in his master's presence.

Once, long ago, the Demon Father had possessed a form, wondrous and terrible. Then the war had come, and the trap had been set, and demonkind had been relegated to things of shapeless shadow. Even the Demon Father had managed to maintain only the crudest of forms: a pair of heavy, blood-soaked eyes that hovered above his insubstantial throne.

Breathless, Pinch bowed before his master and began his story.

The Demon Father did not possess a mouth, but when Pinch reached the end of the tale, a deep, booming voice echoed around the chamber.

'Oldcraft . . . Is it possible that one of the Three could have gifted the mortals their magic? They called the mountain *Ayyuk*. Nightfall.' A brief silence, and then the terrible eyes focused on Pinch. 'Your plan is admirable, my child, but your ambition is too limited. Temporary freedom will do for now, but my eyes see far. The mortals you have described are a primitive breed, but gradually they will evolve until their knowledge and their magic reaches a pinnacle. There are clearly weak points in this world of theirs, portals into our dimension, otherwise the woman's magic could not have reached here and drawn you to her. One day, when the time is ripe, the mortals will use their magic to open a great door into our prison. A door large enough for all of demonkind to pass through.'

'But that may take centuries!' Pinch cried.

'Thousands of years,' the Demon Father corrected, 'but we have been imprisoned here for millennia and we have learned patience. I promise you, my child, one day the Time of Demons will come. One day the Demontide will dawn!'

NOW

'If the doors of perception were cleansed
everything would appear to man as it is, infinite.
For man has closed himself up, till he sees
all things thro' narrow chinks of his cavern.'
The Marriage of Heaven and Hell, William Blake

Chapter 1
Blood and Ash

Jake plunged into the darkness, reached into the cold, cosmic emptiness, searched every corner of the black and barren void. *Dun-dun, dun-dun, dun-dun*, the jackrabbit beat of his heart gave a kind of time to this timeless place. Time passing, slipping away like stardust through his fingers. He did not have long to find her. He must hurry.

Invisible in the dark, his hands groped and met no resistance. She was not here. She was never here. Despair even deeper than the darkness whispered to him: *Don't you realize how hopeless this is? Don't you know that you will* never *see her again?* Jake felt his dream-self nodding, as if, on some level, he agreed with these desolate words. He was about to draw himself back, to abandon the search and surface from the dream, when he saw a distant glimmer. There, at the very edges of the nothingness, a light shining like a beacon. He dared to hope.

'Is it you? Are you there?'

The light swept forward. Haloed in a burning aura as brilliant as any sunset, she reached out to him.

'Eleanor.'

The girl smiled, and in that hopeless, deathless darkness the light of her soul warmed him. She was just as he remembered—the golden hair, the cornflower-blue eyes, the once-perfect skin now marred by a demon's claws. Like a priestess offering up tributes to her god, Eleanor stretched out her hands. In her left she held a glass ball, its surface glittering and green; in her right an object which, try as he might, Jake could not make out. It was like looking through a wall of ice, the thing beyond a hazy and yet familiar form.

These were the powerful and mysterious Signums which had once belonged to Josiah Hobarron—objects that long ago had inspired the formidable magic of Jake's other self. The first, the glass 'witch ball', Jake had seen with his own eyes; the second he had sensed but never seen. He had once been told that the Signums were like brothers that could never meet. Not until all hope was lost . . .

'Here is the Orb.' Eleanor looked from the ball to the mystery object. 'And here is the . . .'

The word was one of the first a child might learn: short, simple, only three letters long, and yet he could not understand it.

'Brother Signums. They must be brought together, Jacob, but only when the time is right. Until then, you must resist their lure. Keep them at arm's length until the darkest shadow has fallen. Be strong, Jake, be true . . .' Eleanor's smile faded and her expression became wary. She glanced behind, into the black reaches of the void. 'I hear his step upon the stair. *He* is coming. You must hurry, Jake, you must find me. Find me before he—Oh God, *NO!*'

Jake bolted upright in his chair, and the hand that had been tugging gently at his shoulder flinched away. Shaking off the ghost of Eleanor's scream, he blinked at the girl who had woken him. For a moment, he believed that Eleanor herself had emerged from the void, that somehow he had plucked her clean out of the nightmare. He felt the warmth of her soul-light—that inner radiance of a person that only he could see—touch his heart again. Then the vision fell away and he recognized the girl standing over him.

'There's that look again,' Rachel said. 'You're happy to see me, overjoyed I reckon, then you realize who I am and the glum face kicks in.'

'Time is it?' Jake mumbled.

He rolled his shoulders and worked out the creaks in his weary bones. Lying open on the desk in front of him was his makeshift pillow—a mouldy-smelling book entitled *A Short History of Starfall*.

It had been two days since Jake's return from the seventeenth century, and he had not yet slept in a proper bed. Almost every hour had been spent here, in the room at the Grimoire Club that his father had used as a study. Most of that time had been occupied in researching the fate of the girl he had left behind. Eleanor of the May, who, last time he'd seen her, had been recovering from the demonic Mr Pinch's attack. Despite consulting hundreds of history books and registries, Jake could find no mention of Eleanor nor any record of her daughter, Katherine. Nevertheless, he knew that she must have survived Pinch's assault or the girl who stood before him, pulling at his hand and avoiding his gaze, would simply not exist. Rachel Saxby was a descendant of Eleanor and the Witchfinder, Josiah Hobarron.

'Sorry, Rach, what were you saying?'

She let go of his hand.

'It's midnight, Jake. It's time.'

He swallowed hard and clutched the edge of the table. Then he swung back from his father's desk and walked over to the small china urn that stood on a pedestal by the door. He picked it up with all the care and reverence it deserved. So light in his hands, so insubstantial: a great treasure reduced to almost nothing.

Rachel led the way out of Mr Murdles's luxurious apartment and through the candle-lit corridors of the Grimoire Club. From behind closed doors came the usual cacophony of shrieks and bellows, raucous laughter and strident screams. As Jake passed, the chaos within subsided. Keen ears and psychic senses had alerted the club's clientele to his presence and to the burden he carried. At their approach, Razor, dog-headed guardian of the Grimoire, pushed open the spike-studded door. The Cynocephalus's huge jaw sank against his chest and he touched a claw to his forehead in salute.

Further evidence of the respect that the dark creatures of the borderlands bore for Jake's father waited outside. A sea of flowers, beautiful and bizarre, covered the ground. Some of the larger plants had risen up onto creaky root-legs and were ambling along the arcades that ran around the square. Sinister specimens, they clustered together, their bulbous heads bent as if they were engaged in deep conversation. Jake suppressed a shiver—were those things really floral tributes, he wondered, or were some of them actually mourners?

Close to the centre of the square the remains of the funeral pyre lay toppled together like a jumble of burned matchsticks. The sight brought back memories of the ceremony that had taken place the night before: hundreds of fantastical creatures packed into the plaza; Brag Badderson climbing the ladder and placing Adam's body gently on the pyre; Pandora's heartrending speech as she committed her friend to the flames; the corpse itself, wrapped in finest silk and doused with petrol. Jake flexed his fingers. He could still feel the weight of the torch in his hand, the warmth of it against his face as he bent down to light the kindling.

Rachel said, 'Jake, if you're not ready we could postpone the—'

'I'm fine. Come on, the others are waiting.'

An archway led out to the vast desert of the borderlands. On the brow of a distant sand dune, three figures waited, their silhouettes murky against the starless night. Jake and Rachel ploughed through the desert and trudged up the dune. By the time they reached their friends, they were both sand-smothered and breathless.

Jake lifted the lid of the urn. As white as bone and as fine as powder, the ashes shimmered in the light of the borderlands' twin moons. He looked at those gathered around him: handsome Pandora dressed in her stylish black robes; Brag

The Last Nightfall

Badderson, fearsome troll of the north, wiping away a stray tear; Simon Lydgate, part-human, part-Cynocephalus, managing a smile of such heartache that it made Jake love him all the more; and Rachel Saxby, beautiful, strong, kind, and so like the girl he had lost. Jake lowered his gaze.

Six pounds of ash. That was all that remained of the wise and compassionate Dr Adam Harker. Jake had not cried during the funeral, for the thing that burned on the pyre was an empty vessel, no more his father than the carbon crumbs encased in this glorified vase. Even now, on the cusp of their final goodbye, tears would not come.

With the wind at his back, he stepped forward and threw the ashes into the air. He felt something inside, his soul perhaps, lurch with the urn. It seemed to fly away from him and follow the sweeping, swirling, swooping dance of the ash. Jake took strange comfort from the dance: vigorous and free, it echoed the spirit of his father. He knew, however, that it could not last. The wind would fall and the ash would be folded into the desert, hidden there for ever. He didn't think he could bear that, it would be like losing his father all over again, and so he stretched out his hand and conjured a strong blue flame. A flick of his fingers and the Oldcraft magic chased away into the night. With Jake as its conductor, the spell took over from the wind and cradled the ash into fresh formations.

'That's enough, honey,' Pandora said in her sweet Louisiana drawl. 'You have to let him go.'

'Let him go?' Jake echoed. 'It's been two days. Two days since I lost him.'

And her, said a little voice at the back of his mind.

'Jake, these are the hardest words I've ever had to say, but you haven't any more time to grieve. After the fight is over, after we've won this war, maybe then.'

'*If* we win,' Brag grunted. 'And if you ask me, that's a big "*if*". Seems our only way of stopping the Demon Father is to follow Jake's plan, and I gotta tell ya, that plan's just about the craziest thing I've ever heard.'

The plan. Two nights ago, Jake had suggested a way in which the Demon Father's campaign to open a Door into his old realm could be stopped. After the vanishing of Mr Pinch into the demon dimension, the Demon Father's idea was to find a potential witch who could summon Pinch back to the human world. The creature would bring with him the witch ball, the first of Josiah Hobarron's powerful Signums. With possession of the ball, the Demon Father hoped to conjure a portal and release his dark children from their imprisonment.

Jake's plan was simple: somehow he would find a way into the demon world and snatch the Signum *before* this potential witch could be found. In reality, of course, the scheme was madness. Jake wielded strong magic, but nowhere near powerful enough to punch a hole through dimensional barriers.

'And even *if* the plan does work, most of us will probably die horrible, painful deaths before the end.' Brag paused and picked at his tusk-like teeth. 'Still, going out kicking some demon butt suits me just fine.'

Simon grinned. 'Me too.'

'And me,' Rachel laughed.

'What about you, boy conjuror?' Pandora asked. 'You with us?'

Jake followed the wave of ash as it wafted over the dunes. A single bright feather swept along beside it, a dance partner that had emerged from nowhere.

'Goodbye, Dad.'

A closed fist, a vanishing flame. For the briefest of moments the cloud of ash held, as if a fading soul bound it together. Then the desert wind picked up and the cloud fell apart, scattering the remains of Adam Harker across the borderlands.

'You're right, Pandora,' Jake said. 'We can't hang around any longer—we have to act. What have you heard from your contacts?'

'Most of the cowards won't talk to me any more,' Pandora snorted. 'Too scared of the "new situation". Can't really blame them, I suppose: the Father of Demons *has* possessed Marcus Crowden, one of the most powerful Coven Masters in the world. Plus he's in league with the Prime Minister of Great Britain, who just so happens to be a formidable dark witch . . . '

All eyes turned to Simon. He shuffled uncomfortably under their gaze: Cynthia Croft, Prime Minister and dark-hearted witch, was also Simon Lydgate's mother.

'On top of that,' Pandora continued, 'the DREAM agents are on every street, bringing in anyone even remotely suspected of having "unnatural" powers.'

'Does anyone know what these DREAM agents are exactly?' Rachel asked.

'No one's spilling any beans, though I have my suspicions.'

'And the camp? What have you heard about that?'

'It's a large Victorian prison on the Devonshire moors—bleak, isolated, perfect for the Demon Father's purposes. Its ordinary prisoners were relocated a month ago on the orders of the Prime Minister. There are already a few hundred new detainees being kept there, rounded up by the DREAM agents from every corner of the country. Officially they're being questioned about dark magic activities and demon connections, but that's only half the story. I've heard whispers about medical procedures: blood-screening, unorthodox injections, plus there have been several reports of . . . well . . .' Again, Pandora glanced at Simon, 'transformations.'

'She's using the same formula she used on me,' Simon nodded. 'Binding human blood with the Demon Father's so they'll change into Cynocephali-hybrids. She's building the slave race to serve the demons when they come through.'

He fingered the pendant given to him by Adam Harker. Encased in amber resin, the wolfsbane was the only thing that kept Simon's monstrous 'other self' from breaking free.

'So the plan remains the same,' Jake said. 'We have to smash our way into the demon world and get to Pinch and the witch ball before the Demon Father. OK. Good. Now there's only one question: how the hell are we going to do that?'

Brag lifted a massive finger. 'Um, I've been thinking.'

Pandora rolled her eyes. 'This is already sounding ominous.'

'Ignore her, Brag. What were you going to say?'

'Well, it's just a thought—you gotta understand, I've never met the guy—but why don't we ask the lo—'

'Shhhh!'

A cold shiver ran along Jake's spine. He spun round and looked back at the square.

'Something's here. Something—'

EVIL.

It slammed into Jake with the force of a sledgehammer. Before anyone could catch hold of him, he had lost his footing and was tumbling headlong down the side of the dune. Sand sprayed into his face, scuffed his skin and stung his eyes. He hit the bottom of the slope and scrambled straight to his feet. Responding automatically to the force emanating out of the square, two brilliant blue pillars of light erupted from his palms and lit up the night sky. It took all his self-control to concentrate the full force of his magic back into his hands.

Simon led the race down the dune. From the snarl rippling his upper lip, Jake could tell that his friend's Cynocephalus side had already sensed the new arrival in the borderlands.

'He's here,' Jake confirmed. 'The Demon Fath—'

BOOM!

The fury of the explosion swallowed Jake's words and knocked him to the ground. Dazed, he found his thoughts flying back to the last time he had experienced such a deafening roar. In the town of Cravenmouth, Sergeant Martin Monks had fired his pistol and blown Jake's right ear clean off. He had endured many torments during his time in the seventeenth century, most of them at the hands of Matthew Hopkins, the sadistic Witchfinder General. Later, Eleanor had used 'borrowed magic' to heal him, but the power had not been sufficient to mend his most terrible wound. Jake would carry the deformity always, and yet he did not resent it—the missing ear reminded him that his adventures had been real.

That *she* had been real.

A wall of phenomenal heat radiated across the desert. It bowled into Jake and shocked him back to his senses. Eyes streaming, he lifted his head and saw gigantic plumes of fire rise up from out of the square like a nest of angry red snakes. Another explosion—this one only a little less violent than the first—sent stone rocketing skywards. A hole large enough to accommodate an elephant stampede had been punched through the south wall of the square. As the ringing in his good ear subsided, Jake could hear screams coming from the other side of the wall.

Brag Badderson was the first to recover from the blast. Thumping past Jake, he marched fearlessly back to the square. Much as he was concerned for the troll, for everyone come to that, Jake couldn't help smiling as he saw Brag brandish his club and disappear into the hole. Whatever friends the Demon Father had brought with him, they now had their work cut out.

A hand locked around Jake's wrist and he was hauled to his feet.

'Thought the creep promised to leave us alone.' Simon's magnetic green eyes blazed. 'That letter he sent, didn't he say he wouldn't come after us as long as you played nice?'

'Can't even trust the Father of Demons.' Jake shrugged. 'What's the world coming to?'

The veins in Simon's neck stood out in thick blue ridges.

Beads of sweat formed on his brow and ran in tracks down the side of his face.

'You gonna be OK?' Jake caught his friend's sleeve. 'I can't fight him *and* worry about you. Remember what happened the last time you transfor—?'

'I remember.'

They looked back to where Rachel and Pandora were standing halfway up the sand dune. Deprived of her bow, Rachel was borrowing two of the ornate curved blades that Pandora kept hidden in scabbards at the back of her dress. The jagged scars on the side of Rachel's face glowed white in the firelight.

'I'll never forget what I did.' Simon grasped the wolfsbane pendant. 'You don't have to worry about me, Jake.'

'OK. Then let's get moving.'

The sand made it hard going but they slogged across the desert as fast as they could. Backlit by the fire, clouds of smoke belched out from the hole in the wall and acted like a kind of cinema screen, a confusion of shadows projected across its roiling surface. Screams cut the air and from inside the plaza came the frustrated roar of Brag Badderson.

Jake put on a fresh burst of speed. He thrust out his hands, pushed against the evil that tried to repel him, dug deep and summoned his magic. Now that he had learned the true source of Oldcraft it was easier to find the power. All he had to do was think of those people he loved, of the sacrifices he'd willingly make for them, and the flame would ignite. Two people were always foremost in his thoughts.

Dad.

A ball of magic appeared in his left hand.

Eleanor.

An identical orb in his right.

Still running, Jake looked down at the magic and his breath caught in his throat. There, at the very heart of each bright blue orb, the tiniest flicker of red. The telltale sign of a dark sorcerer. He remembered what the witch Tobias Quilp had said before he tumbled to his death: *What is the source of that righteous anger, Jacob? That merciless rage? Perhaps one day you will find out . . .*

The two friends reached the broken wall, and were about to step into the chaos, when something flew out of the smoke and landed at Jake's feet with a wet thud. Simon swore, and Rachel and Pandora, who had just arrived on the scene, cried out in grief and horror. For his part, Jake tried to suppress the fury that fed the dark part of his magic. He concentrated instead on the sadness that welled up in his heart.

The severed head of Razor, faithful doorman of the Grimoire, stared blindly across the desert. Blood trickled from the tattered stump of his neck and stained the snow-white sand. All the hair on the Cynocephalus's head was charred to a crisp and the lids of his right eye had been fused together by the heat of a hell-born hex. Simon dropped to his knees and touched Razor's blackened muzzle.

'He called me "brother". Then he'd laugh and say he was only joking, but I think he meant it. Jake . . . ' He rose to his feet. 'Let's do this.'

Jake lifted his hands—twin orbs of fire to light the way—and led his friends into battle.

Chapter 2
Buried Alive

Weeping wounds, charred corpses, screaming shadows: glimpses of horror that came to Jake through breaks in the smoke. Pools of blood sparkled on the sand-dusted steps of the square and from every side came the frightened calls of friends and family trying to locate each other.

Jake strode through the mayhem. Each monstrous face he saw was twisted with terror, each Grimoire guest desperate to escape the unseen menace. Only one group of creatures showed no fear. Dressed in robes that almost blended with the smoke, these tiny figures seemed to glide across the ground. When they reached the silver fountain at the centre of the plaza the leader of the troupe turned his head and looked directly at Jake. Fern-green eyes twinkled from inside the dark bowl of his hood—merry, mocking eyes touched with a tinge of seriousness.

Jake was about to call out to the robed men when Brag

Badderson emerged from the mist and almost lumbered straight into Rachel. The troll stopped himself just in time, regaining his balance by swinging his murderous club onto his shoulder. Brag's skin was torn in several places and green blood oozed from a gash at his throat. Jake knew of only one thing that could pierce that tough troll-flesh. As if reading his mind, Brag nodded.

'It's them.'

'Then I was right,' Pandora muttered. 'The Department for the Regulation, Examination and Authorization of Magic—or, in other words, Bloodsucker Central.'

'But how's that possible?' Jake asked. 'I thought the DREAM agents were out and about during the day. How can vampires walk around in broad daylight?'

'You haven't seen an agent yet, have you?' Pandora peered into the smoke. 'It was their peculiar appearance that made me suspicious in the first place. Of course, the government said they were dressed that way to protect them from evil spells, but that uniform could mean only one thing.'

'Quiet.' Simon held up his hand. 'Listen.'

The desperate cries had been silenced and a brittle stillness had descended over the square. Nothing to be heard except the creak of the Grimoire Club's door and the constant drip of fresh blood. The desert wind began to lift the smoke and tumble it over the roof of the arcades, silently excavating the slaughter ground.

Inch by inch, fifty or more bodies came into view. Like Razor, some of the creatures had been decapitated or burned alive while others had had their throats ripped out and their blood drained. A good few were not all in one piece. Various body parts had been piled upon the steps that led up to the door of the Grimoire Club, collected there like a macabre offering to a dark god.

'Attention, DREAM agents!'

Dozens of figures dressed in uniforms of deepest black stepped out from behind the arcade pillars. The agents' ivory-white faces turned to the Grimoire door and gloved hands snapped out a salute. And now Jake understood what Pandora had meant by the vampires' 'peculiar appearance'. Around each neck dangled a device that looked something like an old-fashioned gasmask, the round, vacant eyeholes covered with dark lenses. The mask, gloves, and head-to-toe leather uniform must be what protected them during daylight hours.

'Sixty or thereabouts,' Pandora murmured. 'I don't like those odds.'

Simon fumbled with his pendant. 'I could take out twenty or more if I . . . Jake, what d'you think?'

Jake was not listening.

The door of the Grimoire Club swung open and the Demon Father stepped into the square. He was dressed in an immaculate pinstriped suit with a crimson flower in the buttonhole. A little dash of blood on his crisp white shirt and a few red spots on his patent leather shoes seemed to complement the flower. The demon still inhabited the body of Marcus Crowden—a dead man whose face was almost as handsome as Jake remembered. There was the strong jaw, the sharp cheekbones, the delicate nose. Only the skin was different. As grey and weathered as old paper, it was peeling badly, especially in that area around the eyes that was not concealed by the demon's dark glasses.

'Dear me, Master Harker, did your poor dead father teach you no manners at all?' The musical voice rang out as if amplified. 'You know, it is considered very impolite to stare.'

'Yeah, well in the rudeness stakes killing innocent people trumps staring every time.' Jake forced a smile. 'You're wearing a bit thin, demon, you should moisturize more often.'

'True to form, Jacob. I'd heard that you like to make little jokes. That you stand and laugh at the darkness.' A sneer marred those angelic features. 'Well, you can fool your friends with that trick—who knows, you might even be able to fool yourself—but you cannot fool me. I see the fear behind the smile.'

'Wow,' Jake nodded, 'that's deep. You ought to go into the psychotherapy business.'

'Perhaps I should. I could specialize in patients suffering from identity crises; lost and lonely souls who have no idea who or what they really are.' The demon clicked his fingers. 'Here's an idea: *you* could be my first patient.'

Something inside Jake responded to these words. His vision seemed to turn inwards and he felt himself being carried through the twilight corridors of his unconscious mind, hurtling towards a destination that he had glimpsed once or twice before. He passed rooms crowded with memories, jumbled assortments made up from thousands of important and insignificant events and experiences. Most of them were his own, but a few belonged to his original self, Josiah Hobarron.

These were memories buried in the depths of his soul but there were deeper memories still. Up ahead, he caught sight of a light spilling from under the door of a forbidden room. He hurried towards it, reached for the handle, pushed against the door. Inside, the empty void of his dreams.

Here is the Orb and here is the . . .

Jake shook his head and the square came back into focus.

'You really have no idea, do you? It was a clue provided by my faithful Roland Grype that gave me the answer. The clue is in the Signums . . . ' The Demon Father's sneer developed into a smile. 'Pathetic creature, in your ignorance my victory is assured.'

He descended the steps, operating the possessed body of Marcus Crowden with the confidence of a master puppeteer. When he reached the level of the square, two vampire guards came forward to flank him.

'And so we come to it, my *young* friend. It is time now to put you to the test.'

'Fine by me.'

Jake's magic flared and he hurled a pair of Oldcraft hexes at the monster. Before the magic could strike, the Demon Father grabbed the vampire on his left and held the snarling, spitting creature before him like a shield. On impact, the magic blasted a hole in the bloodsucker's chest—a gruesome chasm filled with broken bones and bloodless organs. The Demon Father threw the corpse aside and dusted off his hands.

During the sacrifice of their comrade, the DREAM agents had not shifted an inch from their posts.

Buried Alive

'You just stand there and watch as one of your own is destroyed?' Pandora cried. 'What has he promised that could command such mindless loyalty?'

'Come the Demontide my friends here will wallow in scarlet oceans,' the demon shrugged. 'That is my solemn vow.'

'But what about when humankind is wiped out?' Jake looked from pale face to pale face. 'When there are only demons in this world, what will you drink then?'

'They may keep a limited number of cattle to sustain them.'

'He's lying,' Simon said. 'He'll destroy every human in existence and then he'll watch you starve!'

Did he see a twitch in one or two of those inscrutable faces? Jake could not be sure.

'The vampires are loyal to me, for I have promised them a feast like no other.' The Demon Father bowed. 'Still, it was a valiant attempt, my son.'

'I'm not your son! I was *never* your son. My mother just fed me your filthy blood.'

'Indeed she did. In over thirty thousand years, I have seldom met a more gifted dark witch. She murdered your father, you know? Once that worthless destitute had given her a child, she killed him without a second thought. As her demon familiar, I was at her side when it happened. I saw the flick of the knife, the dumb horror in his eyes, and afterwards . . . ' The demon licked his lips. 'She allowed me to suck the meat from his bones. Delicious . . . But you are quite wrong about not being my son. You may hide it away in that

33

bag of flesh, but the creature that rages inside you was born of my darkness. I will always be a part of you.'

'NO!'

The roar that tore its way out of Simon's throat had an inhuman quality that made Jake shudder. Ignoring the calls of his friends, he stormed across the plaza. Before either the boy could pounce or the demon cast its hex, Jake conjured a fistful of magic. It took the form of a crackling rope which lashed out from his fingers and wrapped around Simon's middle. Despite the formidable strength of his friend, Jake was just about able to hold him steady.

'You have no right!' Simon bellowed.

Jake strained at the leash. 'I don't want to see you hurt.'

'But I can take him!'

'No.' The love he felt for Simon, the need to keep his friend safe, strengthened Jake's magic. 'No, I'm sorry, but you can't.'

The lasso tightened and, with a drawing gesture, he pulled Simon away from the demon and back to Rachel's side. Simon continued to struggle, even as Rachel whispered to him, no doubt using one of the control techniques Adam Harker had devised to keep the Cynocephalus at bay. Gradually, the anger left him and Jake dismissed the magical leash.

'Whatever happens now, whatever you see, you have to promise me one thing.' He looked at each of them in turn. 'Don't try to help. This is my fight.'

'Noble Jacob,' the Demon Father laughed. 'You refuse to allow the "innocent" to die on your behalf. Well, now we will test that nobility to its limits. Bring out the prisoners.'

A pair of vampiric guards emerged from the teardrop doorway that led back to London. Between them, they held the leashes of three hooded figures. Hands bound behind their backs, the prisoners were lined up in front of the Demon Father and then turned so that they faced Jake.

'You are powerful,' the demon said. 'Just how powerful even you have yet to realize. If I am to defeat so mighty a foe I must take what advantages I can.'

He whipped off the first hood. Former head of the Hobarron Institute, Dr Gordon Holmwood wore a haunted, glazed expression and seemed unaware of the other people in the square. His thin hands trembled and his nicotine-stained tongue flickered over his yellow lips.

'Please forgive the good doctor,' the Demon Father said. 'I have been "experimenting" on him for some weeks now and the poor man has not responded well to my methods. You may also recognize my second guest . . . '

Another hood was tugged away. A square-faced woman with a jutting jaw and bright red hair peered into the square.

'Aunt Joanna.'

Jake had not seen his father's sister for several months. Joanna Harker was one of the Hobarron Elders, a senior member of that ruthless organization committed to stopping the Demontide, no matter what the cost. She had even been willing to sacrifice Jake in order to achieve that goal.

'Where's my brother?' Joanna asked, her voice as rough as gravel. 'This *thing* told me that Adam was dead. That's a lie, isn't it, Jake? Tell me it's a lie.'

Jake could not meet her gaze. While Joanna crumpled under her grief, the Demon Father moved along the line to the last prisoner. The hood was removed and a gaunt, tear-stained face revealed.

'Dad!'

'Rachel!' Malcolm Saxby cried. 'Rachel, I'm so sorry. I—'

'Enough.' The Demon Father clicked his fingers and Dr Saxby's lips snapped together. He turned to the DREAM agents: 'Three Elders of Hobarron, here to witness the end of all their grand schemes. Now listen well, if Jacob Harker's friends try in any way to assist him, I want you to kill the prisoners. If Jacob Harker makes any move to defend *himself* . . .' The demon gave Dr Holmwood's immobile face a playful slap, 'kill the prisoners.'

Jake wondered why the Demon Father didn't just secure them all with a binding spell. Then he realized the depths of the monster's cruelty: it wanted Pandora and the others to have the freedom to help him while also knowing that any move to do so would result in the prisoners' immediate deaths. This physical freedom would make it doubly unbearable as his friends watched Jake die.

'You'll kill them anyway,' Jake muttered, 'whether I defend myself or not.'

'Will I?' the demon smiled. 'My plans do not tend that way. After I have destroyed you, Jacob Harker, it is my intention to take these good people back to the prison camp. After all, why would I waste such fine and healthy specimens? They will serve their purpose as subjects in our Cynocephali experiments. I give you my word, Jacob, if you stand defenceless then your friends *will* live . . . in one form or another.'

'No, Jake, you can't trust him!' Pandora shouted.

But what if he is telling the truth . . . ? Jake looked back at his friends. They were clever, resourceful, strong. If he could buy them just a little more time then perhaps, en route to the prison or even inside the camp itself, they might find a way to escape. It was the slimmest of slim chances, but Jake's decision was an easy one. However faint the hope, he would gladly lay down his life for his friends.

The blue fire in his hands vanished.

'Come now, Jacob, don't look so mournful,' the Demon Father sighed, 'I'm going to send you home.'

The demon stepped around the prisoners and came to stand in front of Jake. Black magic danced in the reflective surface of his dark glasses.

'Defend yourself, boy!' Joanna shouted. 'You there, Rachel, Lydgate, do something—it doesn't matter about us.'

'Joanna's right,' Malcolm Saxby called to his daughter, 'you have to help him.'

Jake saw the indecision on the faces of his friends. Rachel's agonized gaze switched between Jake and her father.

'Stop torturing them,' he said. 'You want to kill me, kill me.'

'Very well.' The smile left the Demon Father's lips. 'Then let the pain begin.'

Jake closed his eyes and waited for death. The sounds around him—the hushing wind, the crackling sand, the whispers of his friends—all of it seemed to fade and fall away. He found himself thinking about what the demon had said—*I'm going to send you home*. Home. He had faced death before, on the gallows at twilight, and that same word had come to him then. Death meant that the light was waiting. Death meant that Jacob Harker was going home . . .

He heard a sizzle of energy but the impact did not come. Instead, he felt something lock around his middle and lift him into the air. He opened his eyes and saw a dark red lasso wreathed around his waist, just like the one he had used on Simon. He was suspended a few metres above the ground, arms pinned against his sides, drifting towards the hole in the wall. Below, the Demon Father held the end of the magical leash and conducted Jake's transport.

'Bring the prisoners, all of them. They must witness their saviour's end.'

Twenty or more agents closed in on Simon, Rachel, Brag, and Pandora.

'Lay one undead finger on us and I'll rip your fangs out,' Simon snarled.

Brag wheeled his club over his head. 'Stay back, vamps.'

The Demon Father called over his shoulder: 'Kill Dr Saxby.'

'No!' Rachel grabbed Simon's hand. 'We're coming.'

The agents and the prisoners followed the Demon Father through the cavity and into the purple-tinged desert. It had turned much colder since Jake had scattered his father's ashes, and now his breath fogged the air. Floating high above the party, he could see back through the hole and into the empty square.

Except it wasn't empty. A man in a shapeless grey trench

coat had appeared from one of the teardrop doorways and was picking his way through the rubble. He wore a sackcloth mask over his head, the gaping eyeholes of which gave him a faintly sorrowful expression. Each step he took was painfully slow, and Jake guessed that the stranger must have once suffered a terrible injury. Despite this, he moved with such care that not even the sensitive ears of the vampires detected his approach. Was this man here to help or simply to enjoy the spectacle of Jake's destruction? In the end, it hardly mattered—by the time he'd reached the desert the show would already be over.

The lasso vanished from around his middle and Jake fell to earth. His right arm twisted beneath him and his jaw snapped shut. Before he had time to catch his breath, a scarlet flare struck the side of his head and he found himself tumbling across the sand. Pain roared through his skull and turned his thoughts to sharp, molten flashes. Strong magic. Cruel magic. The twisted sorcery of Marcus Crowden made all the more brutal by the demon's touch.

Another hex slammed into his right shoulder and sliced like a rapier down the length of his torso. His body screamed and his mind burned. He was utterly defenceless. A creature with the knowledge and skills of the Demon Father could destroy him in an instant, but that was not what the monster wanted. Not yet. First it would play. Three successive hexes smashed into his face and Jake heard the dry crack of his nose. He lifted a shaking hand to his head and felt several deep lacerations running from forehead to throat.

'Did you think your death would be an easy one?' Two

fresh hexes were already brewing in the creature's hands. 'I am the Father of Demons, the Dark Desolation, the nightmare of ages. Your little boy-brain cannot conceive the depths of my cruelty but, before you die, I will show you a glimpse of the time before flesh.'

A firework of infernal magic exploded against Jake's left side. Another crack, thicker, deeper—the sound of a rib snapping in two. He had no time to scream before the second hex hit. This one blazed against his chest, a burning spell that set his shirt on fire and scorched the skin beneath. Rolling onto his front to put out the flames, his broken rib hitched beneath him, and Jake found his scream.

'We have to do something!' Rachel cried.

'Got to help him,' Brag growled. 'Can't let that thing just smash him to pieces!'

'We won't.' Simon took a step forward. 'Hold on, Jake, we're coming.'

The Demon Father waved to the DREAM agents.

'Kill the prisoners. Rip out their hearts and feast on their flesh. Start with Dr Saxby. Make his daughter watch.'

Pandora's gaze moved from Jake's crippled form to the Demon Father and back again.

'We can't let you die.'

Jake raised himself onto all fours. His lungs burned but he managed to draw three short breaths.

'You—have—to.'

'Enough,' the Demon Father snapped. 'The game is finished.'

He cupped his gloved palms into the shape of a bowl

and swept his hands over his head. From the depths of the earth came a leviathan grumble. The ground shivered and tiny white particles danced across the surface of the desert. Prisoners, guards and demon stepped back as a mighty geyser of sand exploded into the sky. The Demon Father reached out. For a few seconds, he held the hundreds of tonnes of sand aloft. Then he made a dismissive gesture and the great burden landed with an ear-splitting thud on the far side of the dune. Quick as a flash, he began to pour dark magic into the freshly made hole, crafting an invisible wall that shored up the sides of the chasm and prevented it from collapsing.

A crimson lasso snagged Jake's feet and he was hauled across the ground. Each divot in the desert jolted his snapped rib and sent out fresh waves of pain. Primal instincts began to stir: he didn't have to suffer like this, didn't have to die. Magic tingled at the tips of his fingers, begging to be released. It took all his willpower not to conjure a pure Oldcraft flame and hurl it at his enemy. If he missed, or if he only managed to wing the demon, his friends would die instantly. There would be no chance for them to escape, to live . . .

Jake reached the edge of the chasm. At least a hundred metres across, the roughly circular hole dropped down into utter darkness. Even sitting up and straining his neck he could not see the bottom. Another tug of the rope and his legs extended over the hole. He glanced at the Demon Father and saw the strain that the spell was taking on the monster. Holding back the colossal pressure of the sand was no mean feat.

Everyone except the demon was standing so still that a

sudden movement caught Jake's eye. The stranger in the trench coat and cloth mask had passed the broken wall and stepped into the desert. He wavered for a moment, as if he was about to collapse, but seemed to rally his strength. Reaching into his coat, he brought out a peculiar object that set the pages of Jake's dark catalogue rustling. The name of the gruesome talisman clicked into his mind and hope flowered in Jake's heart: whoever he was, this stranger was here to help.

The man fumbled, dropped the object, and Jake's hope died.

'I'm going to crush you . . . '

The Demon Father tugged the leash and Jake slid to within inches of the drop.

'Crush you beneath tonnes of sand.'

Another tug. Jake teetered on the brink.

'Bury you deep in the desert.'

Jake and the demon locked eyes.

'Bury you, just as my kind was buried in our shapeless shadow prison. Sweet justice, Jacob Never Born.'

The rope pulled taut, and Jake tumbled into the abyss.

His body snapped into a 'U' shape, his back arched, his hands and legs trailing behind him. Through narrowed eyes, he could see the granular walls of the chasm darken as he plunged ever deeper. Very soon now he would reach the bottom. Impacting at this speed, he doubted that there would be much of him left—just a wet mush of flesh and bone.

The climax of his journey was fast approaching. Jake just had time to register the strangeness of what he saw—instead of hard, compacted sand the hole ended in an archway, like the upper side of a stone tunnel. Then, rising up from the pit of his stomach, that instinct for self-preservation overwhelmed him. He pushed out his hands and conjured a stream of magic that blasted through the tunnel roof and began to cushion his fall.

But it was too little too late.

Sand rained down from above as the magic shoring up the hole vanished. With a sound like thunder, the walls collapsed.

Swallowed by the hungry desert, buried alive, Jake disappeared into darkness.

Chapter 3
Strange Voices

Simon watched as the crushing, suffocating sand descended on his best friend. The cry that burst through his lips came from a human heart, but it sounded more like the howl of a wolf. He could already feel the telltale signs of a transformation: blood heating up in his veins, bones and sinews straining, the prickle of hair all over his body. He clenched the wolfsbane pendant in his big fist and felt the corners cut into his palm.

Part of him longed to give in to the Cyno, to lose himself in the mindless joy that the creature took from rage and destruction. After he had attacked and injured Rachel in the Oracle's pit, his sense of guilt had almost banished the attraction of the creature, but recently he had felt it resurface. Now the beast called out to him . . .

The Demon Father stood on the little hump of sand where the chasm had been. His maniacal laughter drilled into Simon's brain and seemed to tempt the transformation. Simon eyed the vampire guards—if he was quick, he could snap the pendant, transform, and be at their throats before they had time to react. But could he control himself? What was to say he wouldn't turn on his friends and join the Demon Father's army?

'No.' Rachel prised his fingers from the pendant. 'We can't help Jake now, and if we try anything they'll kill the prisoners. My father . . . '

Simon glared at Malcolm Saxby.

'He was going to let the Elders kill you, Rach. He stood by while his own daughter was about to be sacrificed. He doesn't deserve your love.'

'Look at me, Simon.' She framed his face with her hands. 'Look at me. He's still my dad.'

The Demon Father craned his neck around. He had heard Rachel's words.

'And now, along with the rest of you chattering apes, Dr Saxby will die. My vampire brothers, it is time to . . . '

The demon broke off. He was staring at something just beyond the cluster of prisoners and guards. Simon followed his gaze and saw an oddly shaped man dressed in a long grey coat, thick woollen gloves, and a coarse sackcloth mask. As he lurched across the desert, the man leaned heavily to one side, his left arm trailing chimp-like to the ground. In his right hand he held out an object so bizarre and hideous that it sent an involuntary shudder down Simon's spine.

'By this dread artefact I command all evil things to leave this place.'

The man held the severed human hand aloft.

'*Be gone!*'

The gruesome talisman twitched. At the tip of each upright finger luminous green flames sparked into life and cast a ghoulish glare over the suddenly snarling DREAM agents. The vampires on all sides started to flicker in time with the light, vanishing and reappearing, phasing in and out of reality. One bloodsucker clearly did not want to leave the borderlands with an empty stomach and made a grab for Rachel. Simon went to block the vampire's hand and found his forearm passing right through it. With a final pulse of green light, the agents disappeared from the desert.

A frustrated cry brought everyone's attention back to the Demon Father. He too was phasing, but at a less rapid pace. Simon guessed that the demon's powerful magic was fighting against the influence of the severed hand. However, with the strain of recent hexes still etched on his face, it looked as if he was losing the battle. He reappeared once more, threw out a scarlet lasso and caught Dr Saxby around the throat. Saxby flew through the air and landed in a heap at the demon's side.

'Stop him!' Rachel shouted.

The demon gave a final, furious roar. There was a flash of green light, and he vanished into thin air, taking his prisoner with him.

Rachel spun round and marched straight up to the masked stranger.

'Where have you sent them?'

'Back to the prison. I think.'

The man spoke with a slight Scottish accent, his voice hollow and somehow small. He lowered the hand and blew out the flaming fingers.

'Bring my dad back.'

'I can't. Not without bringing the demon back too. I'm sorry he took your father, but there wasn't much I could do about it. I'm not a witch.'

'You do a pretty good impression of one,' Pandora said. 'Am I right in thinking that's a Hand of Glory?'

'A Hand o' what?' Brag frowned.

'You take a hanged man—preferably a murderer—cut off his left hand, dry it out, and make it into a candle.' Pandora rattled off the recipe. 'The resulting talisman can be used to immobilize your enemies or open portals.'

'You know your stuff,' the stranger wheezed. 'Now, I think you should all get some rest before your friend digs his way out of the desert and starts getting you into trouble again.'

'Jake.' Rachel looked back to the hump where the hole had been. 'But surely he's—'

'Not if I know a Harker.' The stranger managed a weak laugh. 'If he's anything like his father, that boy has more lives than a fully stocked cattery.'

'You knew Adam?'

'I was here for the funeral. Just another monster in the crowd.' He handed Pandora a chemical-stained business card. 'Next time you see the boy, give him this.'

As he twisted his head, the hem of his sackcloth mask hitched up a little and Simon caught sight of rust-coloured flesh, dark and diseased-looking. Thick yellow pus oozed out from the gaping sores that peppered the man's throat, but this was not his most repulsive feature. Sunken into the little well between his right and left collarbone there was a small hole shaped like a miniature human mouth. The lips were grey, the tongue behind them withered and wormlike, the tiny teeth little more than stumps. Simon couldn't help shivering as he thought of the stranger's small voice. Was *this* the mouth from which he spoke?

The man caught Simon's gaze and tugged the mask back into position. Then he touched the severed hand to his chest and vanished without a sound.

Jake groaned and blinked the sand from his eyes. Knocked unconscious by the fall, he had one foot still in the dream world and one planted firmly in the underground tunnel buried deep beneath the desert.

Buried . . . Something buried in the church, hidden away from prying eyes. The church of Starfall with its crooked walls that had once been struck by lightning. The storm-blighted church in which hyacinths grew beneath the altar, and beneath the hyacinths . . . *Bury the Signum deep.*

Jake gasped and sat up. Ever since he had returned from the seventeenth century his thoughts had been haunted by the death of his father and his separation from Eleanor. When he wasn't thinking about those he had lost, his mind was plagued by the idea of the Demon Father getting his hands on the witch ball and opening a door into the demon world. Two days of heartache and worry had blinded Jake to the solution staring him in the face.

The second Signum. What if it was still buried under the altar at Starfall? Of course, anything might have happened in the last three hundred years—the church could have been bombed during the war or demolished to build a new road or housing estate. The Signum might even have been un-covered by an archaeologist and now be the prize exhibit in a museum or some fancy private collection. But there was a *chance* it was still there, waiting for him to find it.

Although he had never laid eyes on the second Signum, he remembered well the draw of the object. How its power had called out to him, the low hum of its Oldcraft song pull-ing him in. With the Signum in his hand, Jake felt sure he could open a portal into the demon dimension and reclaim the witch ball. Then surely the time would be right to bring the brother Signums together and to use their combined power to send the Demon Father back to his infernal prison.

He glanced up into the darkness. Somewhere high above that monster might still be torturing his friends. Unless, of course, they were already dead.

He leapt to his feet.

'Ow!'

A sharp pain griped along his left side. Recalling the inju-ries he had sustained, he was amazed that he'd made it to his feet at all. He clicked his fingers and blue light flooded the tunnel. Unbuttoning his shirt, Jake found a ladder-shaped bruise running down his ribcage. The flesh was tender but, by some miracle, the broken rib appeared to have knitted itself back together. His fingers went to his nose—the bone was straight and firm—and roamed across his face. No cuts, no lacerations, no gaping wounds. In fact, aside from that ugly bruise, which was fading by the second, the only discomfort he felt was a dull ache around the shoulders. He had healed himself.

Jake remembered those injuries inflicted by the witchfinder, Matthew Hopkins. Then it had taken Eleanor's magic, borrowed from the second Signum, to restore him, so how the hell had he managed to heal himself this time?

A merry, mocking voice broke the silence and answered his question.

'Your powers are growing, boy conjuror.'

Jake swept the magical light around. The passage in which he found himself was the size of a large railway tunnel. Worn to dullness by centuries of passing feet, beautiful silver-white marble made up the floor while a slightly brighter version of the same stone clad the walls. Central columns supported an arched roof, gigantic spider webs strung between them like ghostly banners. Jake stared up at the smooth ceiling. He had used magic to smash a hole into the tunnel, so why hadn't the sand siphoned through and buried him?

Again, the puckish voice answered.

'Because this is an enchanted passage, Master Harker. Like you, it is fully capable of healing itself.'

Jake peered into the gloom. 'Who are you?'

'We cannot say. The time is not right. But we shall see you soon, young sir, old sir, lost sir, found sir. For now, follow the light and you shall find your way home. Not-home, home-for-now.'

He heard a scrabble of feet, a high-pitched titter, then what sounded like the boom of a heavy door closing. As the sound faded the orb of magic leapt out of his hand and swept down the tunnel. He had not worked the spell, and felt oddly resentful that his powers had somehow been hijacked. Nevertheless, he decided to the follow the light.

As he hurried down the passage, endless questions buzzed through his mind. Who was the creature that had just addressed him in the dark? More importantly, why did that word '*home*' continue to draw him back to a forbidden room inside his subconscious? A room that had been as dark as the dream void, but which now seemed to have a light burning within. For some reason those words of the Demon Father came back to him: *Lost and lonely souls who have no idea who or what they really are . . .*

The blue orb floated around another corner and stopped at the foot of a spiral staircase. Constructed from the same silvery marble as the passage, the stair corkscrewed away into shadows. Round and round, Jake climbed the spiral, lungs striving, legs burning. After what seemed like an age, he turned the final corner and reached the summit. By the light of the orb, he saw that hundreds of tiles or flagstones had been laid against each other to make up a chipped and gritty ceiling.

No. Not a ceiling, a floor. This was the underside of the square! And then Jake remembered the party of small, hooded figures that had disappeared during the Demon Father's assault. He glanced back the way he had come and thought again of that cheerful, mocking voice . . . . A memory stirred. His father on the balcony of the Grimoire Club, looking over the desert and telling him the legend of what might lie beneath the sand. He stored the memory away for future reference. Right now, he needed to get out of here. He drew the blue orb back into his palm, strengthened it with the love he felt for his friends, and placed his hand flat against the flagstone.

The force of the explosion surprised even Jake. He had intended to flip the stone from its fitting, instead he had blasted forty or more tiles into a hail of smoking shrapnel. Choking on dust and debris, he emerged into the square. Aside from the bodies of those killed by the Demon Father and his DREAM agents, the plaza was empty. He rushed to the hole in the wall. No sign of life in the desert beyond.

'Don't look so frightened, Jacob, they're waiting for you inside.'

Jake turned to find Mr Murdles, owner and manager of the Grimoire Club, floating behind him. In one hand the ghost held a large carpet bag, in the other a short, heavy club. Murdles caught Jake eyeing the weapon.

'It belonged to the brute. My poor, dear Razor.' The ghost's ectoplasmic face crumpled. 'We had our differences but, in my own way, I loved him. He was the very best of his kind.'

Murdles's voice hardened.

'I'm leaving this place. Maybe I'll start a new club at another borderland staging post. Maybe I'll just take off this suit and fade away. For the first time in my four hundred year existence, I feel tired of life. But I want you to do one thing for me, Jacob.'

'Of course.'

The cloth mouth set into a thin line.

'Destroy that demon. Wipe his evil from the face of this world. Then my Razor will be at peace.'

Chapter 4
Return to
Hobarron's Hollow

Jake's friends fell on him the moment he walked through the door of Murdles's private apartment.

'I don't understand,' Rachel said. 'Last time we saw you, you looked like a piece of pummelled meat, now here you are, handsome as ever.'

'He's still missing an ear.' Simon slapped Jake on the back. 'Not exactly mint condition Harker.'

'After being smacked around, flambéed, and buried under a desert, I don't think he's doing too bad.' Pandora fixed Jake with a studious stare. 'I'm guessing you healed yourself. That means your powers are growing.'

'Funny, you're the second person to point that out tonight.'

'Second?'

'We'll talk about it in a minute.' Jake's gaze swept the

lounge. 'Where's Brag? He survived, right? And the others—Dr Holmwood, Malcolm Saxby, Aunt Joanna, they're OK?'

Pandora placed a calming hand on Jake's shoulder. She explained that Brag was resting in one of the adjoining bedrooms. The troll had lost a lot of blood but the injuries inflicted by the vampires weren't life-threatening. Dr Holmwood and Joanna Harker were also resting.

'As for Dr Saxby, well—'

'Dad was taken by the Demon Father.' Rachel shuddered. 'Taken back to the prison camp.'

'We'll get your father back, Rachel, I promise,' Jake said. 'Now, tell me what happened.'

Pandora took up the story from the point at which Jake had been buried. When she got to the part about the masked man and the Hand of Glory, Jake stirred. He remembered seeing the stranger picking his way across the square. Pandora described how the man had used the talisman to banish the Demon Father and the DREAM agents.

'He spoke as if he knew your father. Asked me to give you this.'

She handed over a crumpled business card—

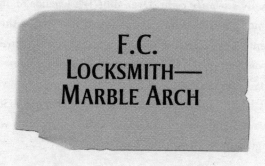

F.C.
LOCKSMITH—
MARBLE ARCH

'Doesn't tell us much,' Jake said. 'Still, I guess we ought to be grateful to the mysterious Mr "F.C.". He saved our lives.'

'OK, mate, now it's your turn,' Simon said.

Jake told the story of his underground adventure as concisely as he could. Then he turned to Pandora.

'I remember my dad telling me that there were forgotten cities hidden under the borderlands' desert. The homes of the ancient races. Demons, fairies . . . '

He pressed a palm against his forehead and felt sweat spring out on his brow. Eyes closed, he slumped back onto the luxurious leather sofa.

'Jake?'

'I'm all right.' He shook his head. For a moment, the door to that forbidden room had flashed into his conscious mind, the light within burning brighter than ever. 'Just tired, I guess.'

'You should get some rest,' Pandora said. 'We all should.'

'Soon. First, I want to hear about those forgotten cities.'

Pandora dropped into a chair and stretched her eight elegant arms.

'Well, this was one occasion where your brilliant father was only *partially* right. Over time the legends of the borderlands got mixed up until it was believed that the three ancient races all lived under the great desert. In truth, only the youngest of the Old Ones could make their home in this reality—the fairies.'

'Fairies?' Simon hitched an eyebrow. 'For real? So what are we talking about here, sweet little sugarplums who exchange baby teeth for cold, hard cash?'

'If you were ever foolish enough to upset them then the fairies might indeed take your teeth,' Pandora smiled. 'But they'll probably extract them with pliers, and they sure as hell won't pay you for the pleasure. Fairies are not the care-free critters you see gambolling about in picture books and on nursery wallpaper. Even those that tolerate humankind can become vengeful and mischievous if provoked. Basically, the fairy world is split into two camps—the Seelie and the Unseelie Court. The Seelie is more or less harmless, the Unseelie actively hostile. Both have their halls beneath the borderlands.'

'One of them spoke to me. Said they'd be seeing me soon.'

'Probably just trying to freak you out. The little swines enjoy spooking humans.'

Jake had the feeling that the voice in the dark hadn't just been playing with him; that behind its mirthful tone there had been a hint of seriousness, perhaps even respect. But right now there were more pressing matters to discuss.

'Murdles has left the borderlands, and I think we should do the same,' Jake said. 'This isn't a safe place for us any more.'

'Agreed, but where will we go? My contacts have dried up and—'

A booming voice cut Pandora short:

'There is *nowhere* you can go. His spies are everywhere.'

Joanna Harker emerged from one of the bedrooms. Grimy-faced and dressed in filthy prison clothes, she shuffled across the lounge and collapsed into the armchair opposite Pandora. With her big frame and spade-like hands, the prominent Harker chin and that shock of bright red hair, she was just as Jake remembered her, and yet a little of Joanna's forceful personality appeared to have vanished. Catching his gaze, she seemed to read her nephew's thoughts.

'First my darling Alice, now my brother.' Her sob was deep, guttural. 'Good people destroyed by the evil of witches and demons. I tell you now, there is no hope, no salvation, no chance of escape. This world will fall and there's not a damn thing any of us can do to stop it.'

Pandora sprang forward and slapped Joanna hard across the face.

'If you wanna run away and crawl under a rock, then we won't stop you, Joanna Harker. Just don't sit there and dishonour the memory of your brother with such talk.'

'But you haven't seen what the demon is capable of!' Joanna touched the angry handprint that flamed her cheek. 'You haven't been inside the camp. They're doing experiments there you wouldn't believe.'

'Turning people into Cyno-hybrids,' said Simon. 'We know.'

'Oh, you *know*, do you?' Joanna spat back. 'You've seen what happens to those prisoners who, for one reason or another, don't transform into perfect little Cyno-slaves? You've seen the mutants they wheel out of the operating theatres— freaks strapped down to gurneys, screaming like their souls are being torn apart? And it gets worse. Have you any idea what happens when demon blood is simply rejected by the host? Well, let me give you a clue—the prisoner's body turns into a pressure cooker. It burns and boils from the inside out, but there's no release valve, you see, and so—BOOM!'

Joanna rubbed her palms together.

'I was made to work in the laboratory. When an experiment went wrong, it was these hands that scrubbed the blood and brains off the walls. Men and women and children. So many failed experiments.'

Pandora leaned forward again. 'I'm sorry. I didn't know.'

'The demon was there some of the time,' Joanna croaked, 'but mostly it was *her*. She oversaw all the procedures and ordered the destruction of the freaks. It might have been a mercy, they were in so much pain.'

'My mother . . . '

Jake gripped Simon's shoulder, a gesture of reassurance, and went to kneel in front of his aunt.

'This is hard, I know, but I want you to tell us as much as you can about your time in the camp.'

'You've grown up fast, Jacob. There's steel in you now, I can see it.' She swallowed hard. 'It started on the night Cynthia Croft made her world-famous speech. It was funny, really: after all those years of the Elders keeping their secrets, this witch makes a ten-minute broadcast and everything is blown wide open. On every street corner, around every dining table, in every pub and office, ordinary people are talking about witches and demons like it's the plot of a soap opera! Even now they can't quite grasp the reality of it. You see them brought into the camp and it's like they're walking through a nightmare. Then they're dragged into the lab, shackled to a table, injected with demon blood, and suddenly the nightmare becomes very real.' She licked shaking lips. 'Sorry. Rambling. I didn't use to be like this.'

'It's all right,' Pandora comforted, 'just take your time.'

'They came for us the night of the broadcast. Of course, the Demon Father's universal coven had already destroyed much of Hobarron's Hollow. In a strange way, I think that gave us a false sense of security—we didn't think he'd attack again so soon. No one had heard from Holmwood or Malcolm Saxby for a while, but we just believed that they were busy working on the demon threat. We now know that, following his last conversation with Adam, Holmwood and Saxby were ambushed in Yaga Passage and taken straight to the prison camp. A few hours later, DREAM agents poured into the Hollow and took the rest of us.'

'What happened next?'

'We arrived at the camp and were "processed". All the Elders were interrogated and tortured for information.'

'Information about what?'

'About you, Jake, what else? You are the only weapon we have left. We told them what little we knew . . . Do *not* look at me like that, Simon Lydgate, I am not a coward and neither are my friends. If you ever have the pleasure of facing our interrogator then you might realize why we broke down.'

'Who was it?'

'*His* mother, of course.'

Simon lowered his gaze. 'I'm sorry.'

'It's not your fault.' Joanna shrugged. 'I only hope that Cynthia Croft hasn't passed her monstrous nature on to her only son.'

'Simon's a good person,' Rachel snapped.

'I hope so, for your sake.'

'Go on with your story,' Jake said.

'By the time we arrived, Gordon Holmwood had already been processed, only this time the demon had also been present. I heard whispers, most of it hearsay from the vampire guards. They said that somehow the old man had managed to stand up to the interrogation. Furious at his non-compliance, the Demon Father had conjured a nightmare vision of what the world will be like after the Demontide. From that moment, Holmwood's mind was broken.' Her eyes strayed to one of the closed bedroom doors. 'He was a great man . . . '

'Tell us about the camp itself.'

Joanna went on to give as detailed a picture as she could about the prison—its size and security systems, its internal and external layout, the number of guards and detainees.

'OK,' Jake breathed. 'So that's all the Elders in the camp, which means we're on our own. I think we should—'

'Not all the Elders.'

All eyes turned back to Joanna.

'Mildred Rice and her son Edward were never captured. Somehow, they escaped.'

* * *

Welcome to
HOBARRON'S HOL
'A VILLAGE WITH A HIS

Simon spied the uprooted sign from the window of Dr Harker's Volkswagen. When Pandora parked up at the outskirts of the village, he jumped out and strode to the roadside. Burned and broken, the signpost lay in a muddy puddle filmed with frogspawn. Simon pinched the top right corner between thumb and forefinger and lifted the post out of the slime.

'Not a good sign, eh?' he grinned.

Immediately, he noticed the way the others were looking at him, each trying and failing to hide the suspicion in their eyes. Not a single extra hair had broken through his skin and a probing tongue told him that his teeth were still small and blunt, at least by Cynocephali standards. And yet his otherself had crept up on Simon and given him the strength to lift the heavy post as if it weighed no more than a lollipop stick. He tossed it back into the puddle and, without a word, walked to the brow of the hill that overlooked Hobarron's Hollow. In his peripheral vision, he saw Rachel draw up beside him, the bow of Nuada and a quiver of arrows strung over her back. She did her best to keep up with his long, loping stride.

'It'll be all right.'

Simon grunted and picked up the pace. She might believe in him, but Rachel did not know the lure of the beast. The promise of its power that ran like electricity from the tip of his tongue down his throat and into his belly. It coiled there, impatient and hungry.

He crested the hill and, for a moment, all personal worries faded from his mind. The last time he'd been here, Hobarron's Hollow had been lashed by a violent storm. Tiles had been wrenched from rooftops and upturned telephone poles had blocked the roads, but such damage was insignificant compared to the devastation he now witnessed.

Jake and Pandora joined Simon and Rachel on the hillside. They stood in awed silence, each remembering the hazy video footage from the TV news reports. Sent out by the Demon Father, a hundred dark witches had fallen on this community, roasted its flesh and ripped out its living heart.

'Bodies in the streets,' Jake murmured. 'Lots of people didn't make it. That's what Eddie told us. It must have seemed like the end of the world.'

After a few minutes of respectful silence, Pandora spoke:

'We have to get moving, Jake. I told Brag to meet us in Starfall just after sundown.'

Brag Badderson had taken Joanna Harker and the broken Dr Holmwood across London to a safe house owned by one of the few dark creatures who would still do business with Pandora. The plan was for Brag to then return to his own people and see if his father Olaf could persuade the trolls to fight against the Demon Father. It was a long shot, Pandora had told them—trolls were creatures governed almost entirely by profit and self-interest. Still, Olaf had respected Adam Harker and, unlike his son, he had the gift of the gab. He might be able to persuade his people to launch an attack on the prison camp. From Joanna's description of the facility, it seemed that a large army was the only way to free Dr Saxby and the other inmates. In the meantime, there was work to be done.

'Are you guys clear on the plan?' Jake asked.

'I think I could recite it in my sleep.' Rachel nodded. 'You two amateur archaeologists are heading off to Starfall to go digging for buried treasure. The second Signum, whatever the hell that is. Once you've found it, we'll use it to open a portal into the demon dimension.'

'There's something I don't get,' Simon said. 'Why do we need to go looking for the witch ball? If you find this other Signum, why don't you just use that to send the Demon Father back to hell?'

'Where he'll find the witch ball waiting for him?' Jake raised an eyebrow.

'Ah. Good point, I guess.'

'While we're busy in Starfall, you guys have to turn over every stone here,' Jake continued. 'The Rices have probably already left the village, but Eddie was a smart kid, he may have left some clue behind telling us where they've gone. After you've done searching, give us a call and we'll come and pick you up.'

'Do we need to synchronize watches, Mr Bond?' Rachel asked.

'No need for that, Moneypenny. Just be careful.'

Jake looked down over the devastated village. From the way his body stiffened, Simon could tell that his friend was picking up on something: a sensory signal in the psychic ether that was invisible to the rest of them. And then Simon felt it himself—a cold chill prickled along his spine and made the hairs at the nape of his neck stand to attention. He turned to Jake.

'Whatever it is, it's hungry.'

'I know.' An agony of indecision twisted Jake's features. 'Pandora, there's something here. We can't leave Simon and Rachel alone. The Signum's been hidden for over three hundred years, another day can't matter much. We'll go to Starfall tomorr—'

'No,' Rachel interrupted. 'Before we left the Grimoire, you said that time was running out. That the Demon Father could find his potential witch at any minute. So we stick to the plan: you go to Starfall, we'll look for Eddie and Aunt Mildred.'

Jake frowned. 'Feels like a trap.'

'They can take care of themselves,' Pandora said. 'Jake, we have to hit the road.'

Swathes of cloud passed overhead like a flotilla of ships racing towards the horizon. Caught between them, shafts of weak October sunlight flashed across the deserted village.

Deserted? Simon shook his head—something was waiting in those silent, soulless streets.

Chapter 5
Catechism of
the Canvas Man

'It's a ghost town.'

'No. There's something here. It feels . . . ' Simon reached out and felt the crackle of psychic energy at the tips of his fingers. 'Bad.'

The tread of the Volkswagen's tyres on the road began to fade. Together, they turned and saw the car disappear into the fringe of trees that marked the edge of Wykely Woods. Then Simon took Rachel's hand and they began their descent into the village.

'This sudden feeling, it's some kind of sixth sense, isn't it?' Rachel said. 'That and the strength must mean your Cyno side is growing resistant to the wolfsbane.'

Simon didn't answer. Just stared dead ahead.

'Why won't you talk to me about it?'

'Because talking about it makes it real, and I don't want to believe that this thing has any power over me. If I do . . . ' He shot a glance at the three scars that ran down Rachel's face. 'You know what might happen.'

'So you want to starve the thing by ignoring it? Simon, I don't think it works that way.'

'Really? Well if you're so clever, tell me how it *does* work.' He wrenched his hand from hers. 'Tell me what I'm supposed to do.'

Rachel managed to keep the anger out of her voice, but only just.

'I think you have to accept that the Cyno is part of you, and that it's not going away. Perhaps it needs to be acknowledged, maybe even trusted.'

'Trusted! Jesus, Rach, after what it did to you?'

'I'm brave enough to take the risk, so why aren't you? Don't let it haunt you, Simon. Face up to it and you'll take away its power to frighten you.'

'Psycho-babble. We're not talking about a personality flaw here, Rach. I'm not suffering from depression or anger-management issues, this thing is a monster. If it's becoming resistant to the wolfsbane, I'll just have to find another remedy, that's all.'

'Whatever you find to replace the pendant, it'll just be a sticking plaster. Deep down you know that it won't hold for ever.'

Simon gave her a hard look. 'Do you want me to leave you again? Because this kind of talk is going to push me away. I won't hurt you, Rachel. I'd kill myself first.'

Tears swam in her eyes, but Simon had no words to comfort her and so they walked on in silence.

The main street of Hobarron's Hollow cut a charcoal-black path down to the village square. From there, a small road headed east until it reached the pale pink cliffs that formed the collar of the bay. Simon's gaze ran down the road, pausing at intervals to take in pockets of destruction. The bodies that Eddie Rice had seen littering the streets after the universal coven's attack had been cleared away long ago, but there were still telltale signs of slaughter: rain-faded blood trails that snaked from door to door; shattered windows with rusty-red smears on the frames; burned clothing caught in trees and odd shoes hanging by the laces from telephone wires. Some of those shoes so small that the sight of them made Simon want to scream.

The call of a carrion bird echoed across the dead village and a shadow passed overhead.

'I used to come here every summer,' Rachel whispered. 'I knew these people, played with their kids. Now they're either dead or being held prisoner at the camp. Tortured and experimented on.'

'Hey.' Simon put his arm around her. 'We're going to get him out, you know that, right? Soon as Brag's got his troll buddies on board, we're going in. The Demon Father won't know what's hit him.'

'Trolls on the rampage.' Rachel managed a smile. 'How come you always know just the right thing to say?'

She stood on tiptoes and drew him into a long, deep kiss.

The hunger coiled in Simon's gut seemed to fade as his

world narrowed and focused on the girl he loved. Ever since that night in the Oracle's pit, when his Cyno side had branded her with its claw, Simon had known that he would sacrifice everything for Rachel Saxby. He would fight any enemy, endure any torture, even destroy himself if it meant keeping her safe. But that was the nightmare. In his dreams there was another vision, one he longed for with all his heart: a life with Rachel; a family; happy, healthy children untainted by the dark creature that dwelled inside. The impossibility of the vision made him want to weep.

'Holmwood Manor seems the most logical place to start,' Rachel said. 'It was the Rices' home.'

'Come on then, I think I can smell rain.'

They left the road and headed along the overgrown footpath that looped like a mossy crown around the brow of the hill. To their right, Simon could just make out the burned-out shell of the Saxby residence peeping between the blackened trees of an orchard. Rachel tightened her grip on his hand and kept her eyes on the path.

In the field next to the orchard a haze of bluebottles droned over the rotting remains of sheep and cattle. Simon guessed that, after the DREAM agents had emptied the village, the animals must have simply starved to death. Now they presented a cold buffet for flies and foxes . . . *CAW CAW*. As if to remind him that these were not the only scavengers, the bird's bleak shadow passed again. Shielding his eyes, Simon glanced up. He caught sight of the old church spire, and stopped in his tracks.

'Ow! Simon, you nearly yanked my arm out!'

'Rachel, what the hell is that?'

Perched on the roof of the ugly grey-stone church of St Meredith an accumulation of rusty metal appeared to have been twisted together to form a kind of watchtower lookout. The structure was supported by five iron legs balanced on the slate roof with one side snuggled up against the church's spire. Roughly the size of Dr Harker's Volkswagen, the curious construction had a jagged starkness that struck Simon as almost beautiful.

'Maybe the dark witches crashed a pylon into the church,' Rachel suggested. 'Except it looks too—'

'Designed,' Simon said. 'Like it was built from the bottom up. Woven together by something . . . Come on, we've only got an hour or so of daylight left. I don't want to be here after it gets dark.'

Simon gave Josiah Hobarron's mausoleum a fleeting glance as they passed the graveyard. The heavy oak door still lay in the undergrowth where he had tossed it months before. Aside from this piece of vandalism, the crypt's roof, its walls, its faded frescoes were all still in one piece. It seemed that even the universal coven had hesitated before laying a finger on the great Witchfinder's tomb.

Holmwood Manor, dark and desolate, glowered at them from the end of the track. Shaped like a cow, the rusty weather-vane on the roof squeaked as a northerly wind slapped it around a good ninety degrees. The sky darkened, and Simon's prophecy of rain was fulfilled in a sudden, emphatic burst. Storm clouds snuffed out what remained of the day and ushered in an early nightfall. Simon and Rachel hitched their jackets into makeshift hoods and hurried along a path that was quickly dissolving into a muddy mire. Clattering up the steps to the covered porch, they took a moment to catch their breath.

'Ewww!' Rachel jumped back. 'That's just gross!'

Simon squatted onto his haunches and studied the mounds of bird dung that had collected on the porch. In some places it was more than ten centimetres deep.

'I don't like this.'

'No kidding. Who'd have thought this lot could've accumulated in just a few weeks?'

'It's not just that. Think about it, Rach—first the "lookout" on the church roof and now this. And there's something else: where are all the birds and foxes and rodents? Like you said, this is a ghost town, and the scavengers have free run of it, so why haven't we seen a single rat? You know something, I've got a horrible feeling that if we climbed up and looked into that *nest* . . . ' The very word made him feel sick. 'We might find a few more rotting sheep.'

'Something put here by the Demon Father.' Rachel's face turned as white as milk. 'But why? The DREAM agents had already rounded everyone up and taken them to the camp.'

'I don't know, but I think we should get the hell out of . . . '

AARK. ARRK.

ARRK. ARRK.

ARRK ARRK.

'Into the house.' Simon kicked open the front door. 'Move!'

He bundled her inside and slammed the big doors of Holmwood Manor behind them. He had just managed to draw the timber beam bolt when something from outside impacted with the force of a battering ram. Cracks appeared in the door but the strong, ancient oak held steady. Simon dashed across the hall, hefted a Georgian sideboard onto his shoulder and used it to barricade the entrance. Before a minute had elapsed, the rest of the great hall's oversized furniture had been stacked like a bonfire against the door. Simon stood back, swiped his brow, listened.

'Wow,' Rachel gasped. 'That was some serious lifting.'

'Shhh!'

He found a gap in the pile of furniture and pressed his ear to the door. From outside came a scratching sound, as if someone was running a long, ragged nail down the wood. Those lazy strokes had a teasing quality, like a predator making sport with its prey.

'What do you think?' Rachel whispered.

'Whatever it is built that nest on the church roof. Carried tonnes of metal all the way up there and then twisted it together to form a home. I'm not sure I want to meet anything that could do that.'

'Uh-huh. So what're we going to——?'

'HELLO?! IS SOMEONE THERE?!'

Simon and Rachel spun round. They could see no sign of Eddie Rice, but it had definitely been his voice echoing around the great hall. Rain-grey light shivered through the thin mullioned windows that looked out over the village and the bay beyond. The upside to these narrow openings was that the creatures pacing the porch were probably too large to even attempt to fit through. On the downside, they made the hall a place of gloom and shadows, which didn't help Simon and Rachel's search.

Eddie was so frightened he seemed unable to tell them where he was. He just kept repeating their names between fractured sobs and low moans. They circled around the hall, climbed the stairs, checked out a few of the rooms that led off the landing. The boy was nowhere to be found. Meanwhile, Simon's sensitive ears continued to tune into the long, languid strokes of the talon on the door. In his gut, he knew that the creature could easily break through the barricade, so what was it waiting for?

'Come on, Ed,' Rachel called, 'you have to tell us where you are.'

Rain rattled like bullets against the window and made it difficult to hear Eddie's words.

'In the cottage,' he gasped. 'I'm trapped in the cottage. You have to get me out of here. The dust chokes me and the sun in the morning makes my skin peel. Then at night it's so cold. I can feel the wall at my back and it's like a block of ice. My mum, I think she's in the room next door, but I can't move to get to her. Can't turn my head or even move my eyes. My mouth was open when the magic came, so maybe that's how I can speak, but hers was shut. Now I think it's just a line. What have I done, Rachel? I can't get us out of the cottage!'

Rachel grasped Simon's arm. He could feel the shudder that ran through her, could see the horror in her eyes.

'Oh God.' Her trembling finger pointed to the wall above the door. 'Please tell me I'm not seeing this.'

Simon shook his head in disbelief. 'That's impossible. Rach, it just can't be!'

'Hate to remind you, but there are monsters waiting outside the door.' Rachel towed a dumbfounded Simon behind her. 'So yes, this definitely *can* be.'

They came to a halt before the barricade and stared up at the painting that hung above the door. *Scratch, scratch, scratch*—the creature's claw on the panel, but this time Simon paid it no heed. His attention was fixed solely on the picture. Displayed in a dusty, gilt-edged frame, it was an oil painting of a countryside scene. In the foreground, a half-collapsed hayrick blocked a narrow dirt track. A pair of farmhands in straw hats and mud-splattered smocks stood at the roadside chewing stalks of grass and rubbing their chins. It was one of the dullest paintings Simon had ever seen.

Only the cottage and its occupants marked the picture as something unusual. At first glance, the small wattle-and-daub building with its whitewashed walls and thatched roof hardly stuck out from the rest of the painting. In fact, surrounded by a tumbledown fence and a drab garden, the cottage blended in well with the rest of the dreary scene. But then your eye was drawn to the figures at the downstairs windows. To the two horrified faces pressed against the glass.

Mildred Rice stood in the window to the left of the cottage door. With her fingers wrenching at her hair, she had the half-mad look of a snared animal. In the room to the right, Eddie's breath fogged the glass while his hands pressed against the misty pane like two pale spiders. His lips blurred as he spoke.

'You have to get us out of here!'

Simon recovered his wits. 'We will, but how did this happen? Was it the Demon Father? A dark witch?'

'It was me,' Eddie wailed. 'I'd been messing around with the spell books Tiberius Holmwood left in the library. You know, Rachel, the ones I used to change my appearance when I spied for Marcus Crowden. When I betrayed the Elders.'

'You were scared, Eddie. No one blames you for what you did.'

'But *why* did I do it? Why did I side with a dark witch against people I'd known for years? Against my friends? It can't have just been fear. Sometimes, when I'm alone at night, I feel this darkness and—'

'We all have our darkness.' Rachel glanced at Simon. 'What counts is how we deal with it. You're not a bad person, Eddie, I know that. Just tell us what happened.'

Eddie's painted expression did not change, but his lips steadied for a moment, as if he was considering his next words.

'The DREAM agents came to round up the last of the Elders. I've read thousands of vampire comics, Rach, but these things . . . I saw them from my bedroom window. They arrived like a swarm, hundreds coming over the hill and moving down into the streets. It wasn't as bad as the night of the universal coven. There wasn't as much screaming, less people died. But still, I saw . . .'

The boy's voice broke into sobbing.

'They packed them into vans, dozens of people squeezed in so tight they could hardly breathe. I couldn't move from the window, I was so scared. And then I heard Mum calling my name, screaming it to the rafters. By the time I made it downstairs and into the great hall, the vampires were at the door. We couldn't escape. Mum was crying, praying, just hysterical. I tried to tell her that Dr Harker or Jake would come to save us, but she wouldn't listen. She kept saying over and over that we were trapped and that we'd die here.'

She could still be right, Simon thought, and listened to the talon scratching on the other side of the door. What was the thing waiting for, an invitation to step inside?

'Vampires,' he said. 'In books and movies they have to be invited in.'

'I think those legends are right,' Eddie said. 'But if they couldn't get us to invite them in, they could always burn us out. I saw the glow of their torches at the windows and knew that we had only a few seconds left. Either we gave ourselves to the Demon Father or we'd be burned alive. It was death either way.'

Crrrk, crrrk, crrrk. The throaty voice of the thing behind the door.

'And then I saw this picture,' Eddie continued. 'I hadn't taken much notice of it before, it was just a boring old oil painting, but it gave me an idea. I remembered reading an incantation in one of Tiberius's old books. Something called "The Catechism of the Canvas Man"—a spell in the form of questions and answers. For some reason the words stuck in my head: *When peril comes, where shall I hide? Deep in the paint, where dreamers abide. How shall I get there, answer me, please? By speaking these words while down on your knees.*

Catechism of the Canvas Man

*Locked in the canvas, what shall I see? Your pursuers confound-
ed by this mystery. And when they have left empty-handed,
what then? On these vital words your freedom depends . . .'*

'And? What were the words?'

'I don't know,' Eddie said, his voice full of misery. 'The
page was torn, the rest of the spell missing.'

'But you used it anyway?!'

'What else could I do? At least this way we might have a
chance. So yeah, I made Mum kneel down and I spoke the
words. The next thing I know, we're trapped inside the cottage, looking out while the vampires sent in human helpers
to search for us. They looked high and low, even behind the
painting to see if there was a secret passage or something. No
one spotted us. I could tell the vamps were scared, they kept
whispering about going back to the Demon Father empty-
handed. After a few hours they left and we've been alone
ever since. Why didn't you come sooner?'

'I'm sorry, Eddie,' Rachel said. 'If we'd known you were
trapped, we—'

SSkkkrrrraaaaa!

SSkkkkkreeeeee!

KKRRRRAAAA!

A lethal talon ripped through the door like a hot knife
through butter. A dark eye, without white or iris, blinked in
the gap.

'That's why they're here!' Simon smashed his fist against
the wall. 'They wanted us to show them where Eddie and
his mother were hiding. And now they're coming to collect
their prize . . .'

Chapter 6
The Ghost Church

'Wake up, sleepyhead, we're here.'

Jake fumbled his way back from the dream void. Eleanor had been there again, stranded in the darkness, offering up the witch ball and the mysterious second Signum. *Here is the Orb and here is the . . .* And then that wary, fearful expression had crept over her features. *I hear his step upon the stair.* He *is coming. You must hurry, Jake, you must find me . . .*

Jake groped for the door handle, a movement that made him wince. Pain throbbed in his lower back but it was his shoulders that were really giving him hell. Maybe he hadn't shrugged off the Demon Father's attack as effectively as he'd thought. He got out of the car, stretched his arms over his head, and stared at the colossal concrete structure that sprawled out before him.

'OK, I'll bite: where's the old church?'

Pandora shrugged. 'I typed "Starfall" into the sat-nav and

this is where that creepy box of talking hoodoo brought us. Starfall Academy. It's a high school. While you were catching up on some much needed beauty sleep, I've Sherlocked my way around the premises. There's something you need to see.'

They left the Volkswagen, aside from an empty school bus the only vehicle in the car park, and approached the gleaming building.

'Looks brand new.'

'Unfortunately for us, it is.'

They reached the glazed double doors of the main entrance, and Pandora tapped a knuckle against a shiny brass plate screwed to the wall.

'Starfall Academy, built three years ago on the site of "a medieval church . . ."'

Jake's gaze swept over what had once been the little village of Starfall. All he could see was tarmac, concrete, steel, and glass—a pristine modern school isolated at the base of a wooded valley. Where was the church with its tottering walls and lopsided steeple? Where was the dirt road on which Pepper had once snuffled her nosebag and waited for her hapless rider? Where was the thatched house of the old Preacher—the place that part of Jake still thought of as home?

Rain clouds trundled across the sky and a hundred or more windows darkened.

'Where are all the kids?'

'I think it's a Sunday,' Pandora said. 'Always difficult to keep track of time when you've been in the borderlands.'

Sunday sermons in the church of Starfall; the Preacher asking the congregation to look deep into their souls and to find the goodness there. Look deep . . . A feeling, an instinct, a flicker of psychic energy took hold of Jake. He pushed his palms against the glass doors.

'It's here.'

'The Signum?'

'I don't know, but whatever it is, I think it's been waiting for me.'

Searing blue light, like the concentrated flame of a blow-torch, ignited at the end of his index finger. He pressed it into the gap between the double doors and the lock snapped. Jake was about to step inside when a high-pitched wail shook the rain-misty air. He pushed his way into the entrance hall and placed his palm against a small flashing box fixed to the wall. Sparks leapt from the control panel and the alarm was silenced.

'Better get moving,' he said.

Starfall Academy might have been a fine example of modern school architecture, but it still possessed those familiar school smells: overcooked canteen food, bitter staff-room coffee, sweaty gym kits, and cheap floor cleaner. As their wet shoes squeaked down the corridors, Jake couldn't help thinking of his old school. The new term had started in September, and he'd been due to repeat his final year at Masterson High with a view to taking his GCSEs the following spring. He wondered whether concerned letters from the headmaster were piling up on the mat at his old house.

School. New Town. The house he had shared with his

mum and dad. All those shelves of horror comics, all those stories he had written and stored in boxes under his bed. It seemed like the life of a stranger. He had not read a comic nor written a story since this all began, but one day he thought that he *might* write it all down. Make a story of his adventures and tragedies. A chronicle of everything that had happened.

'*Arrgh.*'

'Jake, are you all right?'

'Yeah, sorry.' He rolled his shoulders, shrugged off the pain. 'It's nothing.'

'Didn't sound like nothing.'

'It doesn't matter. We're close now, Pandora, I can feel it.'

He pushed open a set of swing doors. The smell of sweat and unwashed sports kits grew stronger as they stepped into a large gymnasium, its floor marked out with the geometric patterns of a basketball court. Through a glazed wall that looked out over the rain-lashed car park, Jake could just see the hazy shape of his father's Volkswagen by the gate.

Psychic energy tingled at the tips of his fingers. Acting on instinct, he moved his hands around like a dowser trying to locate an underground spring. The sensation led him to a point just outside the basketball court's centre circle. He dropped to his knees and placed his good ear against the ground. Muffled by layers of earth, he couldn't hear the words clearly but thought he recognized the voice.

'*Ja-cob . . .*'

He sprang to his feet.

'It's not the Signum. It's an old friend. Stand back, Pandora.'

Magical energy left his fingers and disappeared into the floor. He closed his eyes and pictured the spell as it drove deeper and deeper. Obeying his directions, the streams of Oldcraft formed themselves into two roughly-shaped hands which came together to cradle the hard-pressed earth. Jake mimed the action with his own hands before lifting them into the air. It occurred to him that this spell was not unlike the one that had been used by the Demon Father to bury him under the desert. The similarity made Jake feel uneasy.

Cracks slithered across the basketball court. Jake stepped back as the fissures widened and the floor broke apart. A shower of mud, concrete, and fat white earthworms flew into the air.

'Nice digging,' Pandora said. 'The hole goes right through to the foundations, and then some.'

'*Jacob?*' The voice echoed out of the earth. '*You must help me to rise.*'

'What the—?'

'It's Frija,' Jake said, excitement bubbling in his voice. 'Marcus Crowden's sister. She'll know about the second Signum. She'll know what happened to Eleanor.'

He sent a stream of blue light plunging into the hole. He sensed the magic latch on to something and begin to drag it to the surface. As it rose, Frija Crowden's voice became clearer and less spectral.

'I have waited so long, Jacob. Waited in the dank and endless darkness, but soon I will cut the tethers that bind me to this world . . . '

The magical rope emerged from the hole, its end looped

around a small wooden device. A bobbin, Jake realized: a bobbin from a spinning wheel.

'My soul will be set free.'

The bobbin rose by itself into the air, and Jake's magic returned to his hand. Once it reached the ceiling, the spool flipped upright and started to revolve. Soon it was spinning at such a pace that its hiss almost drowned out the thunder of rain on the windows. A ghostly white thread reeled out and floated across the gymnasium. Strand after strand was stitched together to form a fibrous screen that covered the walls and carpeted the floor. Jake stepped onto the soft material and motioned for Pandora to do the same. Within minutes, they found themselves inside a shapeless, billowing cocoon.

'This sure is something,' Pandora breathed.

'There is more to come,' said the disembodied voice of Frija Crowden.

The woven structure suddenly solidified and took on the appearance of timeworn stone. Complete with faded saints and holy martyrs, stained-glass windows pressed out of the medieval walls. Columns and wooden pews rose up from the ground while on the altar table a simply carved crucifix was knitted into being. The sight of Starfall church reborn almost overwhelmed Jake. Memories cascaded through his mind, some of them his own, most belonging to Josiah Hobarron. One image blazed above all others: Eleanor at the altar steps, burying the second Signum deep in the earth. He bent down and ran his fingers over a cold flagstone.

'The Signum is not there, Jacob. It is long gone.'

The figure of Frija Crowden stepped straight out of a crumbling pillar. She seemed solid enough, her long black dress rustling against the floor, her words stifled by the thick veil that hid her face.

'The spell gives my soul substance,' she said, answering Jake's stare. 'I am like the vision of this church you see before you, a memory made real by the art of magic.'

'Of course!' Jake turned to Pandora. 'It's ectoplasm—the same stuff Murdles's suits are made out of. Frija, you're a ghost.'

The phantom bowed her head.

'I have an important message for you, Jacob, and so, at the point of death, I used the last of my magic to bind my soul to the bobbin. I left instructions for the Preacher's wife to bury the bobbin underneath the church. I guessed that when you returned to the twenty-first century you would come looking for the Signum.'

'What's your message?' Jake asked impatiently.

'Simply this: Eleanor has taken the Signum, and now she needs your help.'

'What do you mean?'

'I mean that the old Preacher and I made a terrible mistake. A mistake that has endangered Eleanor's very soul.'

Fury burned in Jake's gut and a flame, more scarlet than blue, roared in his palm. Frija Crowden had helped to return him to his own time; she had destroyed her sister to save him, but none of that seemed to matter. If she had hurt Eleanor, then ghost or no, she would pay. He would show no mercy . . .

'You are right to be angry with me,' Frija said, 'but I am now beyond even your power.'

Silence in the church of magic and memories.

'What happened to her?' Jake said at last.

'The Preacher had intended to keep the second Signum buried under the church, trusting that, when the time was right, you would come to claim it. But after you left Starfall a vision came to him: centuries hence, a pack of vampiric beings would retrieve the Signum before you could find it. Their master, the Father of Demons, would feel its power and be drawn to it. And so we decided to use our gifts to open a portal into the future and to send the Signum to you directly. Eleanor volunteered to carry the burden.'

'So where is she?'

'We underestimated the intricacy of the spell. Believing you to be a relatively fixed point in time, we focused on your whereabouts. Then we opened the portal to your approximate location and Eleanor was drawn through. But she did not end up in your reality. For some reason she was catapulted into a very different dimension.' Frija cringed at the memory. 'I saw it in the flames of the fire: a dimension of fear and suffering, of terrible shadows and unimaginable torment. The demon world.'

Jake could hardly breathe. 'She's been trapped there for hundreds of years.'

'No.' Frija swept a hand through the air, as if to dispel the horror of the idea. 'The location of the spell was the part that went wrong. I am certain that Eleanor has arrived in your time. She has only been in the demon world for a few days.'

'A few days in the company of demons would seem like eternity!' Pandora cried.

'It is possible that she has evaded capture,' Frija said. 'I have seen a glimpse of the infernal landscape; there are places in which she might have found refuge.'

'Let's hope so,' Pandora said, 'because right now *both* Signums are in the demon dimension. It was bad enough when we thought the Demon Father might get his hands on one of them, but two!'

'We were going to use the Signum to get *into* the demon world,' Jake said. 'It was our only hope. How are we going to find her now?'

'I only know that you must.' Frija shook her head. 'Eleanor is counting on you.'

The witch looked up into the roof of the ghost church. She closed her fist and the bobbin materialized under the rafters. It fell to earth with a crack and broke apart on the altar steps. A single ectoplasmic strand that had been attached to the spindle began to wind itself up, gradually pulling the building apart, ceiling to floor. Colour drained from the grey walls as they flopped and fell like a curtain, revealing the school gymnasium and the rain-drenched car park outside. As quickly as it had been constructed, the church was gone, and Jake and Pandora found themselves in the midst of a great heap of white thread.

Frija Crowden was herself part of the same ectoplasm. As the magical cotton started to fade, so the witch began to vanish into the ether.

'You must make haste, Jacob. Eleanor carries with her the last best hope of this world . . . '

The brilliance in Frija's eyes dimmed. She appeared to focus on something invisible to Jake and Pandora. She reached, as if clutching at a spider web, stepped forward, and vanished.

Jake was about to ask Pandora what she thought of the witch's words when a glimmer beyond the glazed wall caught his eye. A large, lurching form had bounded over the school gate and was making its way towards the gym. As the thing careered across the car park it tripped one of the security lights. Darkness fell back and an orange glare sparkled through the deluge and shone against the creature's grey-green skin.

'Brag?'

Brag Badderson caught sight of Jake waving to him, and made his own frantic gestures. Understanding the crude semaphore, Jake dragged Pandora to her knees and covered their heads.

'Incoming!'

'What do you mean, inc——?'

An explosion of glass cut Pandora short. The whole building rocked as Brag landed feet first on the gym floor. Before Jake could shake off the powdered glass, the troll had pulled him to his feet and was busy bellowing in his ear.

'Whadaya want first, good news or bad?'

'Good, I guess. You all right, Pandora?'

'I'll live,' she groaned. 'You ever thought about using a door, big boy?'

'Good news it is,' Brag grunted. 'My dad's persuaded the trolls to go to war. They'll help us launch an attack on the prison camp.'

'That's great! And the bad news? I'm guessing it has something to do with the dramatic entrance.'

'They must've been tracking me for a while, but I didn't notice the sneaky gits till I was almost here. Honest to Odin, Jake, if there'd been twenty or thirty of 'em, I'd have taken 'em on meself.'

Beyond the broken window, an army of pale forms stepped into the dazzle of the security light. A hundred bone-white faces and, in the shadows behind them, perhaps a hundred more.

'Good evening, Jacob Harker.'

The vampire ranks parted, and a sinuous figure wearing a long leather coat stepped forward. The woman possessed a hard, strangely metallic face inset with a pair of electric red eyes. Beside him, Jake felt Pandora bristle and heard Brag's growl.

'I am acquainted with your friends,' the woman said, 'but we have not yet been introduced. My name is the Claviger.'

Chapter 7
Terror from the Sky

Another talon ripped through the solid oak door.

'Eddie, is there any other way out of here?'

Trapped in his painted prison, Eddie Rice called out to the living, moving world—

'When the agents came before they had every exit covered. There's no way out.'

'These aren't DREAM agents,' Simon said. 'Come on, Ed, think!'

SKRARRR!

'The cellar!' Eddie shouted. 'There's a coal chute down there that leads to a trapdoor at the side of the house. It might be padlocked, but—'

Agile as a monkey, Simon sprang up onto the jumble of furniture he had used to barricade the door. He unhooked the heavy picture containing Eddie and his mother and carried it effortlessly back to the ground.

'Padlocks won't be a problem.'

Another shriek from outside. Another avian shadow at the window. Rachel raced across the hall and opened a small door under the stairs. The smell of damp wood and mouldy brickwork rose up from below.

''S that the cellar?'

'Noooo, it's the attic.' She tapped a finger against her temple. 'It's a good job you're cute. Now get going, genius.'

Suitably embarrassed, Simon dragged the big picture frame through the door and down a narrow flight of steps. Cobwebs laced around his face and he felt the scuttle of startled spiders in his hair. Spiders had never bothered him. During his childhood locked in the basement of his old house, he had befriended many an eight-legged monstrosity. Hours, days, months, years: the prisoner of the witch he had called 'mother'. The witch who had told him time and again that his soul was twisted, evil . . .

Rachel latched the door behind her and clattered down the steps. She grabbed Simon's sleeve and pulled him through the darkness. Stumbling after her, he scuffed his shins against half a dozen unseen obstacles.

'Someone's been eating more than their RDA of carrots.'

'This was my playground when I was a kid,' Rachel explained. 'I know it like the back of my hand.'

She came to a halt, and Simon blundered against her. The impact made the quiver of arrows on her back ride up until a sharp tip scraped the underside of his jaw.

'Like the back of your hand, huh?'

'Shhh!'

He could hear her shuffling along the wall, slapping the bricks as she sought out the coal chute. Meanwhile, from above came the sound of timbers being spliced and a groan of submission from the rusty hinges of the door. Talons clicked against stone as the creatures made their way across the hall. It wouldn't take them long to find the little opening under the stairs, the rickety steps that led down, the near-blind mortals groping in the dark . . .

The optic muscles behind Simon's eyes pulsed and tightened. Next to the agony of full transformation, the pain was insignificant, but still he had to stifle a scream. It felt as if someone had reached into his skull, cut out those sensitive optic nerves, and was now slowly stretching the exposed muscle to its limits.

'What's happening?' Fear rippled through Rachel's whisper. 'Simon, I can see your eyes. They're *glowing*.'

The pain was too bright for him to answer. He could actually feel his pupils dilate and eat up what little light there was in the cellar. Slowly, Rachel came out of the shadows, grey and hazy at first, like a figure lost in a snowstorm.

'Look.' She fished a compact mirror from her jeans pocket. 'Your eyes.'

There was no dripping muzzle, no questing snout, no razor-sharp teeth, but his eyes *had* changed. As vicious as any predator's, those green, glowing beacons seemed utterly inhuman. He slapped the mirror out of Rachel's hand.

'We'll talk about it later. *If* we're not dead. Now hold this.'

He thrust the painting at the girl and shouldered his

way past her. He had spotted the coal chute. Just as Eddie had said, the dusty metal slide led to a trapdoor beyond the outer wall. Simon climbed over a small mountain of coal and launched himself up the chute. He slammed his shoulder into the wooden doors and the padlock on the other side snapped like a breadstick. Simon shot out of the hole, eyes darting left and right, ears alert for any sign of danger.

He had emerged on the east side of the house. The rain must have stopped while they were in the cellar: he could hear nothing except the drip of water from the gutters, the rustle of wind through the unkempt lawn, the hammer of Rachel's heart echoing out of the hole. Tiny sounds made thunderous by his Cyno-senses. He plunged a hand back down the coal chute.

'Pass me the painting.'

Rachel obeyed without a word. Simon laid the picture face-up on the grass and reached back into the hole. Rachel's hand linked around his wrist and he hauled her into the light. As soon as she was out of the cellar and on firm ground, she pulled away from him and bent to pick up the painting.

'It's too heavy for you. Here, let me carry it.' He hefted the bulky frame onto his shoulder. 'Listen, I reckon we should head for the Witchfinder's tomb.'

He told her what he had noticed on their way to the manor house: out of all the buildings in the Hollow, only Josiah Hobarron's mausoleum had been left untouched. Maybe the Demon Father's minions were afraid to go near the tomb.

'And if you're wrong?'

'We die horribly.'

He managed a rueful grin, and felt his spirits lift as Rachel mirrored his smile.

They sped down the side of the house, keeping to the thick shadow thrown by the wall. When they reached the front, Simon craned his head around and shot a glance at the demolished door. A single intact panel creaked in the breeze.

'Coast's clear.'

The lane leading to the churchyard was hemmed in with blackberry bushes, but the muddy track between the manor house and the lane was open country. Nowhere to shelter, no place to hide.

'We have to move fast,' Rachel said. 'Don't look back until we reach the cover of the bushes. You ready?'

'Aye, aye, Captain,' Simon saluted.

She frowned and stroked the side of his face. His ferocious green eyes had not yet changed back to their usual shape and hue. He could see that it worried her just as much as it worried him. Later, if they survived, he guessed that there would be new questions and fresh concerns, but first they had to get out of here.

They filled their lungs and broke cover. Like a pair of short-distance sprinters, they hurtled down the track, conscious that all their energy must be focused into this brief burst of speed. Their feet pounded the wet earth and sent up sprays of liquid mud. Despite the awkwardness of it balanced on his shoulder, Simon hardly felt the weight of the picture frame. He galloped on, his stride lengthening, his powerful heart pumping blood to where it was needed most. Rachel soon fell behind. He had promised not to look back until they reached the bushes, but he had to know that she was all right.

'Oh God . . . '

It was not the sight of his girlfriend trailing several metres behind that unsettled him—*ARRRK, ARRRK*—it was the things perched on the porch of the manor house.

He slowed to a trot while his mind raced on. He had been the one to give Jake's mental index of myths and monsters a name, and while it was true that his friend possessed far greater knowledge of those things that go bump in the night, Simon's own mental index wasn't too shabby. His knowledge of horror stories and myths was at least sharp enough for him to identify the three bird-like beings on the roof.

Harpies.

They were creatures with the bodies of women and the filthy, oversized wings of vultures. Horribly swollen, their bare, pendulous bellies hung down all the way to their stick-thin ankles. They did not possess arms, and so relied on their snapping mouths and strong talons to take the things they desired. Above ruffs of bloodstained plumage, human heads twitched and jerked with hawkish intensity.

Plucked from Greek and Roman myth, the harpies were agents of torment and destruction. Both scavengers and merciless predators, they were forever hungry. With their black eyes now fixed on Rachel, thick ribbons of drool dribbled over their chins and slipped down their bloated stomachs. The creatures shuffled, stretched out their wings, and launched themselves into the air.

'Rach, look out!'

Rachel wheeled round, her right hand sweeping up and over her head. She snatched an arrow from the quiver on her back and, with her left hand, drew the bow of Nuada. Simon had seen this manoeuvre a hundred times before, but the fluidity and grace of it never failed to take his breath away. He could see the rise and fall of Rachel's shoulders, the slight tremor in her arm as she notched the arrow and pulled back the bowstring. Neither fear nor exhaustion affected her marksmanship. The arrow flew and struck one of the harpies just below its grisly plumage. The bird-monster shrieked, and Simon felt a swell of pride. No one could tell him that it was the magic of the bow that guided Rachel's arrows. It was her own skill and talent.

The wounded harpy hit the ground and stayed there, its feet drawn up to its chest and one giant wing flapping fitfully at the air. Without hands to assist it, the creature burrowed its head into its plumage and snapped at the arrow. If the other harpies felt any compassion for their sister they did not show it. They soared on, making a beeline for what they perceived to be their greatest threat. Rachel had already reloaded her bow, and was preparing to loose an arrow when one of the harpies opened its slavering mouth and spoke—

'No human weapon can kill us, little one.' Despite the thing's hideous appearance its voice was a soothing siren song. 'Soon our sister Aello will recover, then we shall feast on your flesh.'

Surprised by these silky words, Rachel's concentration wavered. Her arrow flew wide, just nicking the speaker's wing. It was a fatal mistake. In a joint attack, the harpies turned into a downward swoop, claws extended, eyes agleam.

The sisters were swift and sure. Simon was swifter still. He let the painting drop to the ground. Then, without missing a single heartbeat, tore the wolfsbane pendant from his neck and stuffed it into his pocket. Adam Harker had told him that the influence of the purple-hooded flower was at its strongest when pressed against his skin. Simon reasoned that, in his pocket, the pendant could still restrict his Cyno-self but might allow some of the creature's abilities to come through, most importantly its strength and speed. It was a desperate gamble. The Cynocephalus could take control and, instead of going for the harpies, might attack Rachel. But what choice did he have?

The moment the pendant was pocketed, Simon felt the lurch of the creature. Like a dog straining at its leash, the Cynocephalus realized its freedom in an instant. Skin stretched, bones broke and reformed, hot blood poured through muscle, toughening the tissue like tempered steel. The transformation came in a single, agonizing burst, but it was not complete. While Simon's mouth had pushed out to form a vulpine muzzle, it was not the murderous jaw of his previous transformation. Likewise, he had not grown the shaggy hair of the Cyno-hybrid and his hands, while claw-like, weren't the formidable paws of old. As he'd hoped, the pendant had kept much of the beast's furious nature in check. All he could do now was pray that the power of this new form would be enough to save Rachel.

Simon's thought process, his pocketing of the pendant, his metamorphosis, all of it had taken less than five seconds.

The harpies were still mid-swoop, unaware of the new danger that threatened them. With pointed tongues lapping their lips, they descended.

'Gedown!' Simon's word came out as a raspy bark.

Rachel twisted round and her mouth dropped open in surprise. Stunned, she nevertheless obeyed his command and threw herself onto the ground.

A savage joy rose up in Simon's heart. It overwhelmed his fear for Rachel—all thoughts of her were pushed to some deeper level of consciousness. He concentrated instead on the two creatures that were falling out of the sky. Soon he would meet them in battle. Soon he would best them. Rough, instinctive calculations ran through his Cyno mind, the kind of formless mathematics that comes naturally to any predator. Mid-run, he shortened his pace, gauged the height of the harpies from the ground, factored in the distance between them and the span of his arms outstretched. Arching onto the balls of his feet, he sprang.

At the last minute, the harpies' attention switched from Rachel to the wolfish form rocketing towards them. They flapped their immense wings and tried to climb out of the swoop, but it was too late. Just before the impact, Simon caught their rancid stench and his nose wrinkled. It was the smell of plague pits and battlefields, of diseased flesh and corpses rotting in the sun. It was the stench of the scavenger.

His arms smashed into the harpies' chests and he heard the satisfying crack of their collarbones. Before either creature could react, he pulled them together into a vice-like headlock, and now they were all falling to earth. They crashed onto the soggy ground, and Simon strengthened his chokehold. Just a little more pressure and the harpies' necks would snap as easily as a sparrow's wing.

'Simon, help!'

At the sound of Rachel's voice, he released the harpies and spun round.

She was a few hundred metres down the dirt track, roughly at the spot where he'd been standing when he transformed. Her bow lay broken in the mud, her arrows scattered. Lying on her front, she was clinging to the bottom left corner of the big oil painting. From inside the picture came the desperate cries of Eddie Rice. Simon's sharp eyes could just make out the boy, his frightened face at the window of the painted cottage.

The claws of the harpy Aello were fastened to the top left corner of the frame. She was airborne, beating her wings and straining upwards, keen to claim the prize. Still, she was less than a metre and a half off the ground, and Simon had already brought down her sisters from a much greater height. As he bounded down the track, he saw Rachel's arrow slip out of Aello's plumage and fall into the mud.

Simon launched himself at the monster, but it seemed that Aello had learned from her sisters' mistakes. At the last moment, she released the frame and swept backwards. It was too late for Simon to correct his trajectory. He sailed past her, his right claw swiping wildly at the air. Even before he had landed, he saw the bird-woman swing back her legs and turn her body into a swoop. Rachel had tugged the painting to the side of the track but there was nowhere to take shelter.

Before Simon could even think about a second attack, Aello had executed her dive.

Her talons pierced the painting and tore a great diagonal shred through the landscape. The sound of splitting canvas was accompanied by a scream so terrible it made the hairs on Simon's neck bristle. There was no mistaking the voice— Eddie cried out in fear and horror. The harpy's claws snagged the frame and wrenched it from Rachel's grasp. In the same instant, a full-sized figure came tumbling out of the canvas.

Mildred Rice collapsed to the ground. While Rachel rushed to her aunt's side, Aello crowed with delight and towed the heavy picture into the air. The beast inside Simon willed him to leap after her but his rational, human mind knew that he could not hope to reach the harpy. Aello's sisters had regained consciousness and joined her in the sky. Battered but jubilant, they spoke with one voice.

'A shame about the woman, but we have at least captured the last child of Hobarron. Our master will be pleased.'

The sisters turned westward, away from the hush of the sea and the ruined village. Before they disappeared over Wykely Woods, Simon strained his ears. It might just have been wind, but he thought he heard the call of a grief-stricken voice.

The call of a child.

'She's dead,' Rachel murmured. 'That thing, it tore her out of the painting . . .'

A thick red gash ran across Mildred Rice's torso. Simon visualized the flapping sections of the canvas and guessed that the harpy's claw must have passed right through the two-dimensional Mildred. Perhaps that was the only way out of an enchanted picture: your painted-self had to die.

While Rachel closed her aunt's eyes, Simon dug in his pocket for the wolfsbane pendant. His long claws made the movement clumsy as he fastened the amulet around his neck. Seconds passed. Minutes. Finally, he lifted his face to the sky and howled like a despairing beast.

Rachel grasped his shoulder.

'Simon, what's wrong?'

'It's not working!'

Tears streamed from his eyes and ran into his muzzle.

'Rach, I'm not changing back . . .'

Chapter 8
A Hero Falls

A vampire raced with leopard-like grace through the crowd. Reaching his leader, he bowed and began to whisper in the Claviger's ear.

Meanwhile, Jake and his friends waited in the half-demolished gymnasium. The situation was bad. Very bad. Roughly two hundred hungry DREAM agents had assembled in the school car park, and hundreds more might be stationed in the forest valley that surrounded Starfall Academy. Jake reckoned that he should either be down on his knees praying to whatever god might listen or thinking up some ingenious escape plan. Instead, his thoughts remained focused on Frija Crowden's message: Eleanor was trapped in the demon world. Right now, she might be walking through that infernal landscape, alone and afraid. Worse, she could already have been discovered and torn apart by some diabolical monster.

And then he remembered what Eleanor had said in the dream void—*I hear his step upon the stair. He is coming. You must hurry, Jake, you must find me* ... What if the dream was not a dream at all? What if that realm of unending darkness was in fact a vision of the demon dimension? If that was the case, then only one mystery remained: the identity of the fearsome 'he' who was holding Eleanor captive.

Pandora brought Jake out of his daydreams.

'Any bright ideas?'

His gaze moved through the forest of dark forms in the car park. Towards the back of the crowd, the orange glare of the security light dazzled across the bodywork of his father's Volkswagen. He shook his head. There was no hope of reaching the car. And then his eye came to rest on the rusting yellow school bus that stood just outside the outer ring of DREAM agents.

'What do you think?' He jutted his chin in the direction of the bus.

Pandora cracked a half-smile. 'If by some miracle we can get through that posse of bloodsuckers I could have it hotwired in five seconds flat.'

'Never thought of you as an expert car thief, Pandora.'

'Got me a disreputable past,' she shrugged. 'Spent most of my teens stealing Model Ts as they rolled off Mr Ford's assembly line. 1909. A good year.'

Jake stole a sideways glance at his friend. 'Just how old are you?'

'You should know better than to ask a lady that question. Now listen up, I've got an idea of my own. Do you think you could work your mojo and get me the wire from that security light?'

Jake could see the rubberized cable sprouting out of the tarmac and running up to a wall-mounted lamp. The wire was a few hundred metres away from the smashed gymnasium window.

'Use your magic to drag it over here, quick as you can. After the first few bursts of electricity the fuse will trip, but all I need is a kick-start.'

'What you two gabbin' about?' Brag grumbled.

The Claviger pulled her head away from the vampire messenger and turned her electric red eyes on Jake.

'An excellent question. Come now, Jacob, won't you share your thoughts with the rest of the class?'

'Rest of the class? Oh, I see! Because we're in a school you said "rest of the class", and that's kinda like a joke. Right. Got it. You should do stand up. No, I'm serious, you're really funny.'

He was playing for time. Before he followed Pandora's instructions, he wanted a little information from this commander of the DREAM agents.

'I've heard about that smart mouth of yours,' the Claviger said, her smile sweetly insincere. 'Such a pity it's not properly connected to your brain. Now take a breath and steady yourself because I want you to really *think*. Are you ready? OK, so tell me: how did the bad guys know where to find you?'

'You picked up Brag's scent.'

'It's true, your pet does have a rather distinctive odour, but even my fine boys couldn't locate the brute by smell alone.

No, Jacob, we knew precisely where you would be. Our spies on Hobarron's Hollow told us.'

Jake remembered that vague sense of something waiting in the deserted village. Something evil. Something hungry.

'Three delightful creatures overheard your little plan,' the Claviger continued. 'First, Simon and Rachel would go in search of the Rices. Well, that suited us just fine. Despite several location spells, the Demon Father has been unable to track down Mildred and Edward. If they were still hiding somewhere in the village perhaps they might answer the call of a friendly voice and reveal themselves.'

'But what's so important about a boy and his mother?'

'Mildred is an Elder; the child is of Hobarron blood. My master leaves nothing to chance.'

'These spies . . . ' Jake had to force the words out. 'Have they hurt my friends?'

The Claviger's smile broadened until her jagged canines flashed in the light.

'All I can tell you is that Mildred Rice is dead and your little friend Edward is now a guest of the Demon Father. But do not fret, he will be put to good service. We will inject my master's blood into his veins and turn him into a Cynocephalus slave.'

Jake fought back his anger. 'So why aren't we dead already? You must have over two hundred vamps here, how come our jugulars are still intact?'

'The Signum, of course. The harpies informed us that you were coming here in search of Josiah Hobarron's talisman. Perhaps the Demon Father does not need to summon

Mr Pinch after all. Perhaps this trinket can be used to create a demon Door. So where is it?'

'Not here.'

'Come now, I can see you've been searching.' She eyed the hole in the gymnasium floor. 'What did you find down there?'

'Be serious,' Jake smirked. 'If I'd really discovered something that powerful do you think I'd be standing here chatting to you? No chance. I'd have blown every stinking bloodsucker to kingdom come.'

'Great idea!' Pandora clutched Jake's arm. 'Quick, bring me the cable.'

Jake summoned his magic.

'And make sure it's still connected,' Pandora instructed.

Caught off guard, the Claviger watched as a blue Oldcraft thread left Jake's fingers and flew over the vampires' heads. The magic reached the wall and wrapped itself around the cable. Jake conducted the spell with his mind, wrenching the wire from its fitting and dragging it towards the broken gymnasium window. Hidden lengths of cable slithered out of the ground and the orange glare of the security lamp flickered and died.

Sparking and fizzing, the raw tip of the wire had just reached the window when Jake felt a sudden resistance. One of the vampires had grasped the end and was holding on as if his afterlife depended on it.

'Take down the troll and the freak!' shouted the Claviger, regaining her senses. 'But do not harm the boy. That is a pleasure reserved for the Demon Father.'

The Last Nightfall

A cry rose up from the vampiric ranks—a ravenous howl that rang through the rain-haunted valley. As one, the DREAM agents surged forward. Locked in a titanic tug-of-war with the stray vampire, Jake managed a sideways glance at the oncoming army. A tide of death, it would soon break through the window and wash away the lives of his friends.

'Take that, bloodsucker!'

The great stone club of Brag Badderson flew through the air and smashed into the vampire's face. There was a nause-ating *kkrruk* as the monster's skull splintered like an over-cooked egg and he dropped to the ground. Jake tried to adjust the force of his spell but wasn't quick enough to compensate for the sudden freedom of the wire. Still straining, he stag-gered backwards as fresh lengths of insulated cable burst out of the tarmac. The live end lashed through the window and landed at Pandora's feet.

'I'll take it from here,' she grinned.

Jake let go of the cable and drew the magic back into his hands. Glancing up, he saw that the vampire horde had reached the shattered window. Crazed with hunger, they had bottlenecked there, desperately fighting to be the first to squeeze their way into the gym. Meanwhile, Pandora had delved into the hidden fold at the back of her dress and drawn one of her ancestral blades from its scabbard. She crouched beside the still-fizzing wire.

'What the hell's she doin'?' Brag said.

Jake was about to ask the same question, when a mem-ory stirred: Pandora at the security fence that surrounded Havlock Grange; Pandora with her knives drawn, slicing through the chain-link; Pandora wreathed in lethal blue light. On that fateful night, she had absorbed raw power and rendered it harmless. Now Jake wondered what else his remarkable friend was capable of.

'You leeches ready for your dinner?' she called. 'Well, come get it!'

Six of the most powerful vampires accepted the invitation and shouldered their way through the window. Pandora reached out and touched the tip of her dagger to the live wire. A burst of electricity crackled along the blade and passed down the length of her arm. It shivered through her hair and sparks shot from her fingertips. Confused, the vampires stopped short of their prey.

'Oh, you bad, bad boys.' Pandora pointed the dagger at the horde. 'Now you're in trouble.'

All I need is a kick-start . . .

'She's a generator!' Jake said. 'A living, breathing generator.'

Pandora's dark brown eyes vanished in a haze of white light. Pulses of electricity skipped down her outstretched arm and seemed to concentrate into the blade. She smiled.

'Ka-boom.'

A lightning bolt blazed out from the dagger and hit one of the vampires square in the chest. The creature burst into flames.

'Dead skin!' Pandora hollered over the screams. 'Nothing burns quite like a bloodsucker!'

The vampire's clothes acted like kindling, stoking the fire. As his pale flesh blackened and peeled from his bones, Jake remembered all those books he had read about these monsters. In some of the stories it was claimed that the only way to kill a vampire was with the purifying touch of fire. Now he witnessed the truth behind the legend. A red and yellow cowl licked around the creature's head and its eyes melted and slipped out of their sockets. From first spark, the living cremation took less than ten seconds.

The five remaining bloodsuckers took one look at the pile of ashes and scrambled for the now empty window. Pandora incinerated four before they reached the sill; the fifth tumbled into the car park, his body ablaze. Like a gunslinger cooling her shooting irons, she blew nonchalantly on the smoking tip of her dagger.

'Ready to catch the bus, boys?'

Brag thundered over to the window. As he passed, he kicked through the dusty remains of the vampires and treated Pandora to a wide grin.

'Some show, Pand.'

'Why didn't you tell us you could do that?' Jake asked.

'I like to see that mouth-gaping, bug-eyed look you do when you're surprised,' Pandora shrugged. 'Reminds me of a pet goldfish I had when I was a kid. Anyway, snap that jaw shut, we need to get out of here.'

They followed Brag to the window.

It had started raining again. Through the grey downpour, Jake could see a sagging portion of fence over which almost two hundred terrified bloodsuckers must have scrambled. The road beyond was empty, but in the forest that hemmed in the south side of the school a few spectral figures haunted the spaces between the trees. In the car park, forty or so of the braver, or perhaps thirstier, vampires remained. There was no sign of the Claviger.

Pandora held out her dagger, and the vampires formed into a narrow avenue, twenty bloodsuckers on either side. Brag stepped over the windowsill and eyed his beloved club. It was lying beside the vampire whose skull it had crushed. That creature was either unconscious or dead, but a line of fully functioning vamps stood between the troll and his weapon. He chanced a sideways step. Teeth bared, three came forward to meet him. Pandora flashed the dagger and they fell back, hissing and snarling.

'For god's sake, Brag, we'll pick it up later!'

'Don't you dare touch it, any of you.' Brag swept a gigantic finger up and down the avenue. 'Not unless you want to end up like mush-head over there.'

Pandora led the way, switching the dagger from hand to hand and thrusting it at any vampire that looked as if it might try its luck. Jake had no doubt that she was bluffing. Her eyes had cleared and that aura of electrical energy had vanished. Like the rage of a lightning bolt, it seemed that Pandora's power was lethal but fleeting.

Jake could almost feel the intensity of the vampires' gaze boring into his throat. For now they were being held back by the memory of their incinerated brothers, but soon enough one of them would give in to its thirst. Jake could probably blast a dozen or so with his magic, and even without his club Brag could handle his fair share, as could Pandora. But the cry would go up and those creatures lurking in the forest would return, hungry for blood and vengeance.

They reached the end of the avenue.

The old yellow bus was now less than two hundred metres away.

'Go get the door,' Pandora instructed.

Fffsss—fffsss—fffsssss

Jake ignored the famished hisses and scurried across the wet tarmac. The vehicle was locked. A quick burst of magic burned a hole through the mechanism and the door swung open with a pneumatic sigh. Meanwhile, Brag and Pandora were backing slowly towards the bus. As the vampires reorganized themselves, this time into a simple perimeter line, Pandora kept her dagger outstretched. Jake was kneeling at the top of the steps by the driver's area, his friends within spitting distance of the door, when the moon rose up and crested the valley. Dark puddles turned into milky pools and the rain fell like liquid silver. One of the vampires peered at Pandora and thrust out a long finger.

'Look at her eyes. The power, it's left her!'

'He's right,' another vampire spoke up. 'Spread the word to our brothers and sisters in the forest. Tell them it's safe to come back.'

'Keep quiet,' the observant bloodsucker muttered. 'There's little enough meat on the boy, and I don't care for troll or freak flesh. Why should we have to share with those cowards?'

'The Claviger told us not to kill the boy.'

'Yeah? Well, the Claviger's not h—'

'Oh, but I am.'

Jake twisted round and looked through the driver's window. He saw the lithe form of the Claviger leap up and over the fence. She had clearly gone to round up her troops, for seventy or more vampires followed her lead into the car park. They assembled by the gate, blocking off the exit.

'You and your funny little friends have put up a valiant fight, Jacob, but now it is time for you to surrender.'

'NEVER!'

Even the Claviger flinched at Brag's bellow. Before she could protest, the troll grabbed hold of Pandora and propelled her into the bus. Then he slammed the door and thrust his huge hands against it until the metal was crumpled and warped. Jake checked that Pandora was all right—a little dazed, she was already getting to her feet—and grabbed the door handle. It wouldn't give.

'What're you doing, Brag? Let us out!'

Brag laid his head against the window. There were tears in his little eyes.

'No, Jake, I won't.'

'Open this door or I'll blast it off its hinges! You listen to me, Brag.'

'No, Jake, I won't.'

And now Pandora was at the door, a blade in her hand.

'Stand back, I'll cut through the metal . . .'

Two vampires landed on Brag's back. They tore at his flesh, vicious teeth ripping and drawing blood. The troll reached back and threw them to the ground with all the carefree force of a child flinging a rag doll across the room. Then he lifted his tear-streaked face again.

'I won't let you do it,' Jake choked. 'There has to be another way.'

'Pandora always said I was stupid—yes you did, Pand, so don't stand there shaking your head at me now—but, Jake, I'm not *that* stupid. In fact, I'm pretty smart.' Brag managed a tight grin. 'Because I thought this plan up all by myself. Now, you get that heap of junk started, Pandora; there's not much time. And, Jake? I want you to tell my dad what I did here. Tell him of my stand . . . I'm going to clear the way.'

For all the days that remained his, Jake knew that he would think often of the words and the deeds of his friend. He would dream of Brag Badderson, forest troll of the north, fearsome and kind-hearted, slow-witted and wise, powerful and vulnerable comrade. And this was the deed he would remember most, and these were the words . . .

Brag stationed himself in front of the bus. He had no club, no weapon of any kind, but his arms were as strong as iron. The vampires had gathered at the gate, a force that numbered more than a hundred. Now, with a roar that scattered at least a dozen bloodsuckers, Brag made his charge.

'NEVER FEAR!'

Inside the bus, Pandora pulled a panel from under the steering column. Her swift fingers located the correct ignition wires, which she stripped back and twisted together. The engine stuttered, the headlights flickered.

'NEVER FAIL!'

Pandora jumped into the driver's seat and pumped the accelerator. Her hand closed around the brake.

'NEVER FLEE!'

'I can use magic.' Jake gripped the back of the driver's

seat. 'Maybe fly him out of there. I flew once, maybe I can use the same power on Brag.'

'There's no time.'

'I could make time!' His voice took on that deep, magisterial tone that seemed so alien and yet somehow so familiar. The voice of the long-dead Witchfinder. 'With my Signums, I could—'

'You don't have the Signums. Don't you see, Jake, this is what Brag is sacrificing himself for: *your* opportunity to go on and find those talismans. A chance to save your world and his. Brag will be the hero today so that you can be the hero tomorrow.'

'NEVER FALL!'

Head down, Brag slammed into the wall of vampires. It was like a wrecking ball smashing against a reinforced concrete barrier—there was resistance there, but not enough for the barrier to remain wholly intact. Hurled into the air, one vampire landed on the iron spikes of the gate, impaled through the leg, stomach, and throat. Another sailed right over the fence and came to a bone-breaking halt against the metal trunk of a street light. Caught by Brag's muscular sideswipe, a third bloodsucker crashed into a telephone wire, the impact powerful enough to tear his head from his shoulders.

Twenty or so were cleared by that first sally, and now Brag was at the heart of the horde. He fought with a ferocity Jake could barely comprehend. It was as if the troll had drawn on all the fury of his race and unleashed it in this single devastating attack. Thick as a ship's rigging, veins stood out on his neck and along his massive arms. Spittle flew from his lips as he punched and pummelled, crushed and cleaved.

'Bless you, Brag.' Pandora released the brake and thrust the gearstick into first. 'He's moving the fight.'

Jake saw what she meant. Inch by painful inch, Brag was manoeuvring the horde away from the gate. Blinded by rage and thirst, the vampires did not realize what was happening; they continued to orbit the troll, biting and clawing at his already torn flesh.

'Just a little further.' Pandora's hands squeaked around the steering wheel. 'Just a metre or so, you poor, brave soul.'

Brag cried out in pain. The sound, low and hopeless, made Pandora gasp and brought fresh tears to Jake's eyes. Six or more wiry bloodsuckers had landed on his back and were ripping great chunks out of the troll. A vampiric claw tore his right ear away, a second gouged his cheek down to the bone. Over the heads of his attackers, a dazed Brag caught sight of Jake and Pandora. He managed to smile and raise his three-fingered hand in salute. Pandora placed her own hand flat against the windscreen.

'Goodbye, my friend.'

With a final roar, Brag Badderson threw himself to the ground, giving Pandora those last, precious metres. The vampires fell on him like wolves on a wounded bear.

'Hold tight!' Pandora cried.

Fumes belched out of the exhaust pipe and the ancient bus jolted forward.

Only one vampire remained blocking the gate. The Claviger's eyes blazed in the headlights, a pair of mocking, ruby-red coals. She wiped a trail of green blood from her chin and smiled down at the unmoving body of Brag Badderson. Pandora swore and smashed her foot against the accelerator.

'Soon they'll be scraping that grin off the asphalt!'

The speedometer had just touched twenty when the lurching, groaning bus reached the gate. Three vampires looked up from their meal and darted into its path. They had misjudged either their strength or the power of the old juggernaut, for they were quickly crushed under its wheels. Jake felt a ridiculous surge of affection for the rusty boneshaker and couldn't help patting the tattered driver's seat. Pandora let loose with a '*Woo-eee!*'—but her jubilation was soon cut short.

Reacting with breathtaking speed, the Claviger sidestepped the bus. She had escaped pulverization by a hair's breadth. Pandora cursed and slammed the steering in frustration. A second later, the bus hit the road and she was wrenching the wheel right and following the moonlit trail out of the valley.

Jake ran down the gangway, leapt onto the back seats, and pressed his face against the rear window. A few vampires were chasing the bus—pale phantoms cutting through the pungent exhaust fumes. Even at forty miles an hour, one or two managed to claw the licence plate before falling back.

In the school car park, Jake could just make out a huge shape lying motionless on the ground. He hurried back down the gangway.

'We have to go back.'

'No, Jake.'

'We have to help him. We have to try. Pandora, listen to me: Brag said "never flee", didn't he? Well, that's just what we're doing, so *turn us round*!'

Pandora reached out and took his hand.

'He's dead, honey.' She burst into tears. 'Brag's dead.'

Chapter 9
Demon in the Safe House

Simon had offered to help, but Jake insisted on bearing the burden alone. Hefting the stone weapon onto his shoulder, he staggered across the school car park. By the time he reached the body, sweat was running down his face and his heart was pounding. As gently as he could, Jake lowered the club into Brag's open hand.

Dawn broke over Starfall valley. Fingers of light spread through the trees and dappled the face of the dead troll. A face that bore the terrible wounds of Brag's final moments, but which seemed peaceful and almost serene now that his pain was over.

'What's happening to us, Simon?' Jake murmured. 'Last night I wanted to kill every one of those bloodsuckers, even before they'd hurt Brag. Kill them, just for choosing the wrong side.' He closed Brag's cold fingers around the club. 'I wouldn't have shown any mercy. I—'

'Why're you telling me this?' No longer entirely his own, Simon's voice came out as a brutish bark. 'For God's sake, Jake, what do you want me to say?'

Like fiery gemstones, Simon's eyes burned in the morning light. Beneath his torn and mud-splattered T-shirt, his barrel chest heaved and his big Cynocephalus muscles flexed and strained.

Several hours had passed since the old yellow bus had trundled into Hobarron's Hollow, and Jake and Pandora had found their friends sheltering in Josiah Hobarron's tomb. They had exchanged their stories in a few short words: the tale of Brag's sacrifice and the news that both Eleanor and the Signums were now trapped in the demon world; the death of Mildred Rice and the horror of Eddie's capture. During the battle with the harpies, Simon had tried to channel the strength of his Cyno-self. He had succeeded, but when he'd replaced the wolfsbane pendant he had not changed back. Now his body was an awkward muddle of human and Cynocephalus.

'I don't know what to tell you, Simon,' Pandora had said, shoving the bus into gear and driving them away from the ghost town. 'You're a human regressed to a Cynocephalus by way of demon blood. I know of remedies to cure lycanthropy and vampirism, but you're a unique case. Short of Adam's necklace, I know of nothing that can reverse what's happened to you.'

Rachel had suggested trying the old control techniques, but Simon had ignored her and stalked off down the bus.

As they turned with the brow of the hill, Jake had glanced

back at Josiah Hobarron's tomb. Shining in the moonlight, this sanctuary was the only place that had been left untouched by evil. Was this because the Witchfinder still resided in the cavern below, his body frozen in that mystical block of ice? Or was there another reason that witches and demons seemed to fear this place? Jake had found his gaze lingering on the painted frescoes that adorned the tomb walls.

The ground trembled, and his thoughts snapped back to the present. A hulking form had passed the school gate and was making its way towards them.

'Where is he?' A rough, broken voice. 'Where's my son?'

Rachel and Pandora had been standing in a solemn huddle by the bus. Olaf Badderson ignored their condolences and marched straight past them. Catching sight of the body, the old troll let out an agonized cry.

'Oh, my boy. My poor, poor boy.' He dropped to his knees and lifted the battered head into his lap. 'There, there, Brag, they can't hurt you any more. No more tears now, you just sleep and your mum and me, we'll sing to you. Always liked a song before lights out, didn't you, son? Songs of the cold north, of frost giants and the Aesir, of Odin and Asgard. Stories of the Old Ones, the demons, the faeries, and the Never Seen . . . '

Jake almost recoiled from these words. His vision turned inwards and again he saw the forbidden room with the light spilling out from under the door. Suddenly the door flew open and beyond the glare he could make out the figure of a woman. Not Eleanor this time, but a fearsome, burning presence. Her voice made his heart tremble.

Here is the Orb and here is . . .

'He trusted you, Jacob Harker, and you betrayed him.'

Jake pulled himself away from the vision.

'Oh, the stories he used to tell about his powerful friend, the great boy conjuror!' Spittle flecked Olaf's beard. ' "You've never seen magic like it, Dad. My pal Jake, he's a real hero." Some *hero*! You left my boy to die.'

'That's not fair, Mr Badderson,' Simon protested. 'Jake wanted to go back.'

'How would you know? From what I hear you were fighting harpies in Hobarron's Hollow while my son died. Well, freak you may be, but at least that shows you've got some gumption in you. Not like this—' Olaf flicked his fingers towards Jake, 'coward.'

Pandora laid a gentle hand on Olaf's shoulder. 'It was Brag's choice to save us. Don't disrespect his sacrifice with these graceless words.'

'Take your hand off me,' Olaf seethed, 'or I'll tear each of your pretty arms out of their sockets.'

Pandora pulled her hand away, as if stung.

'I told Brag that the trolls would go to war, that we'd stand with you in this foolish crusade against the Demon Father.' Olaf shook his head. 'Damn you, Jacob Harker. Damn you and all your kind.'

'Madness!' Pandora cried. 'This is your world, too, Olaf Badderson! The demons will destroy you and everyone you love.'

'The Demon Father has already made contact with the trolls. He's assured us that it's only the humans he's interested in. Come the Demontide, we'll be valuable allies.'

'But that betrays everything Brag stood for!' Rachel shouted. 'He fought with us against the demons.'

'And look where it got him.' Olaf buried his head against his son's chest. 'For the love of Odin, my boy was only ten years old!'

Rachel, Simon, and Pandora looked dumbfounded.

It took Jake several minutes to find his voice.

'Brag was a child? How's that possible?'

'It never occurred to me,' Pandora said quietly. 'Trolls, they live long lives, but they mature very quickly. My gods, Olaf, you knew the risk, why did you let Brag come with us?'

'Because he wanted an adventure. Because I thought that *you*—' he stabbed a gnarled finger at Jake, 'would look after him. Well, now I curse you, boy conjuror. You will receive no aid from me nor any of my kind.'

Eight large shadows loomed across the car park. An honour guard of trolls had assembled to bear Brag's body away.

'Never fear, never fail, never flee, never fall.'

'What?' Olaf stared at Jake through misty eyes. 'What d'you say?'

'It wasn't me who said it. It was your son. He asked me to tell you about his last stand. His last words. He said you should be proud of him. For my part, I'll never forget my friend.'

The derelict sweet factory stood by itself in the middle of an abandoned industrial estate. It was the only structure still in one piece, most of the surrounding factories and warehouses having been demolished or simply left to rot. A few iron girders poked out of the ground like the half-buried bones of some strange metallic giant. In fact, the whole area looked like a graveyard for forgotten buildings. Yet even here, in this north London wilderness, the DREAM agents had been at work. Every freestanding wall bore a fresh poster—

HM Department for the Regulation, Examination and Authorization of Magic

INVITES YOU TO JOIN THE

WAR ON WITCHCRAFT!

Are family members, friends or neighbours behaving suspiciously? If so, it is your duty to report their names and addresses to your local DREAM office or email details to waronwitchcraft.gov.uk

TOGETHER we can defeat the demon threat!

Pandora pulled into what had once been the factory car park. There had been very little conversation during the journey from Starfall: Rachel and Jake had drifted in and out of sleep while Simon stared into space, the collar of his coat turned up so that passing motorists wouldn't catch sight of his half-developed Cyno features. Hungry and exhausted, they all tumbled out of the Volkswagen.

Jake ran his eye over the three-storey ruin. Framed against a cold sky, the factory's black hulk looked as if it was about to come tumbling down at any second. Wind whistled through cracks in the boarded windows and shrieked back out again, like a terrified child fleeing a haunted house. Jake sucked the dusty air through gritted teeth.

'So, Pandora, this is the *safe* house?'

'It's safe enough, as long as you watch where you put your feet.'

She led the way over a carpet of broken glass and rusty nails to a battered metal door. Graffiti decorated every inch of the factory, mottos that included:

WHERE DO THEY TAKE THE TAKEN?

DREAM Agents R Fascists

WHO WATCHES THE WITCH WATCHERS!

Jake took comfort from these messages; they meant that not everyone had been taken in by Prime Minister Croft's propaganda.

He was about to comment on the graffiti when he felt the presence of a strange force. The intensity of the sensation was something like his feel for evil or his ability to see what he now called 'soul-lights', but it was different, too. The force seemed to reach out from behind the factory door. Like some kind of radiation, it baked Jake's skin and throbbed beneath his flesh. It was painful, and yet it felt oddly familiar, even comforting.

'Jake, you all right?'

Simon's strong hands locked onto his shoulders.

'Yeah,' Jake breathed. 'It's just . . . I can feel . . . ' He struggled for the word. Not goodness, that was too blunt a term. 'Protection.'

Pandora kicked open the metal door.

'Right on the money. Protection. Told you it was a safe house.'

Spray-painted onto the damp concrete floor just inside the factory entrance was another bit of graffiti. Only this time it wasn't a message, it was more like a tag. A simple design that sent tremors through Jake. Each time he tried to focus on it, his eyes would slip away, as if to look upon the silver symbol was somehow forbidden:

'Do you recognize this sign, Jake?' Pandora frowned.

'No.' He knew that his next words were literally the truth, and yet they felt like a lie. 'I've never seen it before.'

'Is it a cross, a crucifix maybe?' Simon said.

Rachel shook her head. 'I think we're looking at it the wrong way up. The cross-section is curved, like the guard on a sw—'

Jake flinched. 'Who cares what it looks like? You said it's protection, Pandora, protection against what?'

'Demons. This symbol is very old and very secret. It pre-dates the pentacle, the ankh, the Star of David, the Christian cross, every known religious icon. Scholars have traced it back throughout history, finding it in the hallowed places where the first magical meetings were convened. I won't call it a religious symbol because the teachers and movers of what it represents always maintained that it was never supposed to inspire a religion.'

'Then what is it?'

'It's the Sign of Oldcraft. The symbol of true magic. The earliest example can be seen in Neolithic cave paintings, thirty-two thousand years old, or thereabouts. All we really know is that the symbol repels demons, clouds their minds, scares the bejesus out of them. It should keep us hidden for a while.'

'Hang on,' Simon said. 'If this bit of mojo's been kicking around for so long, how come we haven't used it before? God knows, we've been in loads of situations where it could've come in handy.'

'That might just look like a bit of graffiti,' Pandora pointed at the symbol, 'but a lot of spellcraft goes into creating a protection that powerful. I had to call in every favour I could think of to get this place set up. And now I'm all out of goodwill. From here on in, we're on our own.'

She stepped carefully over the symbol and took them down a narrow corridor and onto the factory floor. This vast central area reached up through all three storeys to the corrugated iron ceiling. Pigeons cooed in the rafters and startled rats scurried for shelter under a mountain of cardboard boxes. A huge sorting machine dominated the floor with a conveyor belt rolling out of it like a long, rusty tongue.

Jake shivered, and not just because the factory was icy cold. He could still feel the power of the symbol reaching out to him, stirring a cauldron of hidden memories.

Pandora ushered them to the back of the factory. Here they found a couple of wooden cabins tucked against the far wall, dirty brass nameplates on each door. They entered an office marked **'Boothby's Bonbons—General Manager'**.

'I'll just check on Dr Holmwood and Joanna.'

Pandora flicked on the lights and went to a connecting door. The office was cramped and musty, the phantom scent of boiled sweets lingering in the air. Mould-spotted posters for chocolate bars Jake had never heard of decorated the walls. A gunmetal-grey filing cabinet had been pushed aside to make space for four comfortless camp beds.

'Still asleep.' Pandora returned from the adjoining room with an armful of itchy blankets, half a dozen bottles of water, and a selection of packaged sandwiches. 'Rations. All I could arrange at short notice. I suggest we eat and get some shut-eye. We'll talk about our next move in a few hours.'

'Our next move?' Simon fell back onto one of the camp beds. 'Aren't we all out of "next moves"? Both Signums are in the demon world and we've no way of getting to them. Olaf Badderson's pulled the plug on the troll army, and we can't launch an attack on the prison camp without that kind of support.'

'And Brag's dead.' Rachel went to Simon and curled up in his big arms. 'Remember when he used his underpant elastic as a slingshot? Those banshees didn't know what'd hit 'em!'

Jake smiled. 'I'll always remember his catchphrase.'

'Catchphrase?' Simon's canine lips drew back into a grin. 'Oh, right! "Bloody Cynocephalus!", "bloody humans!", "bloody vampires!"'

'And that club of his,' Pandora laughed. 'Trolls love their clubs, but that weapon was like his baby. Dear boy, he was—'

'Ten years old,' Jake said, and the laughter ceased. 'Well,

now we fight in his name. In the name of all those we've lost. There *will* be a next move, Simon, and the Demon Father won't see us coming . . . There's something we're missing here, guys. Something staring us right in the fa—'

SKAAARREEEEK! SKAAAREEEEK!

All eyes turned to the closed office door. Something inhuman was screaming on the factory floor, its call reaching up to the ceiling and echoing from rafter to rafter.

'Sounds like some kind of bird.' Jake glanced at Simon and Rachel. 'Harpies?'

'No.' Simon jumped to his feet. 'I'd know that sound anywhere.'

They all spilled out of the wooden cabin. In the dingy light that streaked through holes in the metal roof, a small, dishevelled man stood alone. There was a cage at his feet— a tiny prison inside which a dark form squawked and screeched. As it thrashed about, beetles fell from the creature's dirty plumage.

The demon's master stepped forward.

'Hello, my friends. I am here to help . . .'

Chapter 10
They Swarm

Jake conjured a magical leash and sent it flying. The restraining rope looped around the interloper and locked his arms against his sides. Together, the four friends moved forward, each of them suddenly on high alert. They knew that this witch was one of the least powerful they had encountered, but with the cunning Demon Father as his master it was best to treat even Roland Grype with a degree of caution.

'What're you doing here?' Pandora whipped an ancestral blade from its hiding place. 'Speak quickly or I'll fillet you where you stand.'

'Please, I just want to help!' the librarian yelped.

'Help us?' Simon roared. 'I seem to remember that it was you who kept me prisoner, first in that filthy bookshop and then at Havlock Grange. Month after month, knocking me out with sleeping spells and feeding me scraps, when you remembered. And now you want to do what? Swap sides?'

'Exactly,' Grype nodded.

'But why?' Pandora pressed the tip of her blade against Grype's throbbing throat. 'Has the Demon Father confiscated your books or something?'

'No. He tried to kill me.'

'Really?' Simon laughed. 'Well, it seems the demon ain't all bad.'

'Simon . . . ' Rachel looked from Grype's shivering form to the caged demon-bird at his feet. 'I think he's telling the truth.'

'Come on, Rach! This little git, telling the truth? I wouldn't trust him as far as I could throw him.' A sly grin slipped across Simon's lips. 'Actually, I could probably throw him pretty far.'

'Tell us what happened, Roland,' Rachel said. 'And if we find out you've lied to us, I'll let my boyfriend use you for frisbee practice.'

Grype began his story at a gallop.

'It was while we were still at Havlock Grange: the Master, Tobias Quilp, the universal coven and me. The Master got me to assemble the coven in the great hall, said we were going to work the spell that would summon the demon Door. Quilp came down the stairs and stepped into the nightmare box. Then he caught sight of me, and I saw this strange emotion in his eyes. I think . . . ' Grype frowned. 'I think it was pity. He told me to run. I'd just reached the door when they started to burn. Over a hundred witches sacrificed so that the Master could send Quilp back in time. He lied to them, destroyed them. He would've destroyed me.'

Pity, Jake thought—Tobias Quilp, the monster that had killed his mother and denied his father life, had felt pity for a fellow witch . . .

'As I ran from the hall, I saw the faces of the demons as they watched their witches burn. Gleeful, gloating, merciless faces. The sight inspired one of my visions. I saw a glimpse of the future—the world *after* the advent of the Demontide. Saw those same laughing, demonic faces revelling in their triumph. But it was what I did *not* see that frightened me. In this future-world that witches have strived so long to bring about only the demons ruled. There were *no* witches. Like the rest of humanity, we had been utterly destroyed.' Grype took a deep breath. 'After the inferno, the Master was surprised to find me alive. We never talked of what had happened, but from that moment he kept a careful eye on me. A few days later, we journeyed to London and met up with Cynthia Croft.' Grype stole a glance at Simon. 'Until then, I had no idea about her involvement. From Downing Street, we travelled to Dartmoor and the prison that Croft had set up for her Cynocephali experiments. Every day, DREAM agents would deliver a fresh batch of specimens.'

'People,' Jake corrected. 'Not specimens, people.'

'Yes, of course. I'm sorry.'

The witch's insincerity made Jake bristle. 'Get on with it.'

'I was put to work in what you might call the bookkeeping department. I made a record of every prisoner who was processed and the outcome of every Cyno experiment. There were three columns: Immediate Death; Successful Transformation; and Mutant, TBD.'

'TBD?'

'To Be Destroyed. Any human who didn't transform into an acceptable Cyno-slave was considered a freak and would be incinerated in the prison ovens. And then there were the humans who weren't experimented on. Anyone who exhibited a magical gift was taken straight to the Master. What happened to them after that, I cannot say.'

'But he can't have found a potential witch yet,' Rachel said. 'Otherwise we'd already be knee-deep in demons.'

'Oh, but he *has* found the potential. That's why I'm here. In the excitement of the child's arrival I slipped away and came straight to London. Now, please, Jacob, I have risked everything. You have to save me!'

Jake swatted away the librarian's imploring hands.

'Who is this potential?'

'Your friend, Edward Rice.'

Jake rocked back on his heels. 'Eddie? But the Claviger said he'd be injected with demon blood and changed into a Cyno.'

'That was her natural assumption. But when the harpies brought the enchanted painting to the prison, the Master immediately recognized Edward's potential. The Catechism of the Canvas Man is a most difficult piece of magic. Even Quilp might have struggled with it. Now all the Master has to do is find the complete spell and bring Edward out of the painting. Cynthia Croft is working on it as we speak.'

'Eddie will never agree to summon Pinch,' Rachel said.

'Oh, he'll do it, have no doubt. Our job is to find a way to stop him. Here is what I propose: I'll give you all the information you need to break into the prison. Once inside, you can kill the boy and—'

'We don't kill people, Grype. We'll just have to get to Eddie before the Demon Father can extract him from the painting.'

'Whoa, whoa, whoa.' Simon held up a clawed hand. 'Let's not get ahead of ourselves. Who's to say we can believe a word this snivelling little creep says? Maybe he was sent here to spy on us.'

'A reasonable conclusion, Master Lydgate.'

'How exactly *did* you find us?' Pandora asked. 'The symbol of Oldcraft should've kept us hidden.'

'In almost all respects my magic is poor,' Grype said, 'but I have one special talent. I am a skilled Dark Seer. Although the symbol successfully cloaked this charming factory, I saw your movements from Starfall to London. After that, a little detective work was all that was required to track you down. But you should have no doubts about the power of that symbol—I assure you, my demon screamed heartily enough when we passed over it. Now, Jacob, if you will?'

Somewhat reluctantly, Jake closed his fist and the magical leash disappeared. Grype bent down and picked up the cage.

'I am fully prepared to prove myself worthy of your trust.'

'How?'

'To earn your protection, I will cast my demon aside.'

Mr Hegarty smashed his head against the bars and a spray of beetles scattered across the ground. Then, to everyone's astonishment, the bird spoke—

'Do not do this, Roland. You are my master, I your faithful servant. When the Demontide comes you will sit at the Father's right hand and he will reward all your pains and sacrifices. No one will ever dare laugh at you again.'

Jake could see the struggle in the librarian's face. Grype knew that the monster spoke with a forked tongue, but he had long believed the demon lie. To free himself from that lure took an enormous effort. Trembling head to toe, Grype beckoned the friends to follow him to the factory door.

'Now you will see what Roland Grype is made of.'

Jake felt the power of the Oldcraft symbol reach down the narrow corridor. The force stroked him with burning fingers, a painful and troubling caress. Grype turned his head, as if he could not quite bring himself to look upon the strange emblem. He placed Hegarty's cage on top of the spray-painted pattern and fresh screams burst from the demon-bird's beak. Without thinking, Jake stretched out his hand.

'Back to the incorruptible prison. Back to the formless shadows.' He intoned the words as if reading from scripture or some holy book. 'Back to the darkness. Back to the desolation that was crafted for you.'

The symbol on the floor glowed with the blue light of Oldcraft.

Trapped inside his cage, Hegarty called out—

'How do you know such things, boy conjuror?'

'Because . . . ' It was there, waiting behind the door. 'Because I . . . We . . . '

As ever, the truth eluded him.

Fire erupted from the symbol and set the wooden cage

ablaze. Hegarty's burning beak screeched from between the melting bars.

'Our shadows are no longer formless and the darkness no longer complete. The humans have given our prison shape and light.' Despite the pain of its cremation, the demon cackled. 'And soon, very soon, their magic will release us!'

The blue flame billowed and the demon disintegrated into smoky atoms. A handful of dust swirled and settled, and the magic fell back into the cold concrete floor.

Pandora took Jake's arm.

'Are you OK? Jake, you spoke with that voice again. The voice of the Witchfinder.'

'Did I?' He ran a hand through his cropped hair. 'Maybe I did. He seems to creep up on me these days. Like a ghost.'

'You need to get some rest.' She glanced at each haggard face. 'We all do. Simon, escort our guest back to the office, find some rope and tie him up.'

'What?' Grype gasped. 'But I've proved myself! I sacrificed my demon!'

Pandora cocked her head to one side. 'Hmm. Nope. Sorry, I don't seem to give a damn. Simon: office, rope.'

'Consider it done.'

Simon grabbed Grype and manhandled the witch down the corridor.

'If he's got his powers he could still escape,' Rachel said.

Jake shook his head. 'Grype believes the demon lie. Without his familiar, he doesn't think he can work magic, and with magic belief is half the battle. Course, that doesn't mean he's not a spy. The Demon Father might have convinced him to sacrifice Hegarty in order to persuade us he's on our side.'

'I know this worm of old,' Pandora nodded, 'and I'm not taking any chances.'

Jake woke with a start. He had been dreaming again about the door inside his mind. Three things waited beyond: the formless void, which he was now convinced was a vision of the demon dimension; a frightened Eleanor, holding out the Signums and desperate to escape her unseen captor; and a secret—a brilliant, burning mystery that continued to elude him.

Not wanting to wake the others, he eased himself off the camp bed and crept across the cabin. Rachel, Simon, and Pandora were fast asleep while Grype, trussed up like a Christmas turkey, groaned through his dreams. There had not been enough beds for all of them, and so Simon had deposited Grype on the bare wooden floor, a pillow stuffed roughly under his head. Jake felt a twist of sympathy and covered the little librarian with his own blanket. Then he headed for the door that connected with the adjoining office.

A blast of warm air greeted him as he stepped inside. Before they'd settled down to sleep, Rachel had found a small convector heater in the manager's storeroom. Everyone except Grype had agreed that Dr Holmwood needed the heater most, and as Simon had pointed out, Grype didn't get a vote. As Jake's eyes adjusted to the light, he saw the shadowy form of Joanna Harker sitting next to Dr Holmwood's bed. The old man stared into space while she stroked his thin yellow hand.

'You're back then.' Joanna didn't turn her head. 'What happened?'

He told the story in a few short sentences. When he got to the part about Brag's death, his aunt looked up.

'The troll that brought us here? I'm sorry, he was a kind soul.'

'Yeah, he was.'

Despite the throb of hot air, Jake shivered. He couldn't get warm for the life of him. Perhaps he was in shock— a delayed reaction to his father's death, Brag's murder, the news of Eleanor being trapped in the demon world, Eddie's abduction, all of it. He was sixteen years old, for God's sake, how was he supposed to deal with this stuff? He shoved his hands into his pockets and his icy fingers brushed against a crumpled piece of card. Curious, he plucked it out:

F.C. LOCKSMITH— MARBLE ARCH

Something niggled at the back of Jake's mind. Words spoken by Brag Badderson in answer to the question about how they were going to smash their way into the demon world:

Why don't we ask the lo—The Demon Father's arrival in the square had cut Brag short, but now Jake wondered, had his friend been about to say '*locksmith*'?

'He told Pandora he knew my dad . . . F.C. . . . .'

And now he remembered his father talking about the perils of time travel: ' . . . *the beetle is highly dangerous. I know of only one case in which it's been used successfully. And even then, the man who took the Scarab Path came back changed. Horribly changed.*' Jake looked into the empty face of Gordon Holmwood. Think, think, what had the old doctor told him? Something about that friend of his father's—details, a name . . . '*Fletcher had some minor magical gifts . . .*'

Fletcher. Fletcher Clerval. A man who had crossed dimensional barriers. A man who can make demons disappear. A locksmith.

'Joanna, did you ever know a man called Fletcher Clerval?'

'Of course.' She looked surprised. 'He worked at the Institute for a while. A brilliant scientist—particle physics was his speciality, I think. He was very keen on bringing magic and science together, had crazy ideas about mystic portals.'

Jake slapped his hands together. He could feel excitement bubbling inside.

'And he was friends with my dad, right?'

'He and Adam did seem to hit it off. At that time my brother was working on the Hobarron Weapon Project.' She blinked at Jake. 'Similar areas, I suppose, science and magic working together. But when Dr Holmwood found out what kind of experiments Clerval was doing, he cut his funding and cast him adrift. A good thing, too.'

'Why'd you say that?'

'Because sometimes opening doorways is a dangerous business. You ought to know that better than anyone, Jacob. Unfortunately, Clerval wouldn't be deterred, not even when Adam pleaded with him to stop. He got his hands on a Khepra Beetle and, using some kind of pseudo-scientific contraption, he ventured onto the Scarab Path.'

'He came back changed.'

'More than changed. Fletcher did not have the magical skill to sustain himself on the Path. What came back was barely recognizable as human.'

'But he's still alive.' Jake looked down at the card. 'And he could help us.'

'Help from witches and madmen,' Joanna sighed. 'Dear God, is there so little hope?'

'Maybe we should slow down.' Jake pressed his hands against the dashboard. 'Pandora, we should definitely slow *DOWN*!'

The Volkswagen hurtled out of Edgware Road and joined the big roundabout that fed onto Oxford Street and turned with Park Lane. Pandora chuckled as car horns blared and brakes screamed. She weaved past an articulated lorry, missing the rear end by millimetres. Hugging the roundabout's inside lane, the kamikaze dark creature gave Jake a playful wink.

'Hold tight!'

She slammed the brakes and yanked the steering wheel right. Jake just had time to glimpse the famous landmark— a blur of Corinthian columns, carved figures, and white stone——before the car left the road and rocketed through the monument's central gateway. It wasn't a tight fit——Marble Arch was big enough to have squeezed a bus through——but the speed at which the Volkswagen took the gate convinced Jake that a crash was inevitable. He held his breath and waited for the squeal of metal against stone.

The Volkswagen sailed through without a scratch. Pandora pulled up the handbrake and they came to a screeching halt on the north side of the gateway. Jake took a few deep breaths before staggering out of the car.

Pandora had parked on the wide traffic island in the middle of the Marble Arch roundabout. At the north-west corner stood the arch itself, a two-hundred-year-old block of stone with a soaring middle gateway flanked by two smaller arches. To the south-east, Hyde Park stretched out towards Kensington and Knightsbridge, its bustle of trees like the golden thumbprints of autumn. Tourists, who a moment before had been posing for pictures and admiring the arch, now looked goggle-eyed at Jake and Pandora.

'What were you thinking?' Jake hissed. 'You could've killed someone.'

'With my reflexes?'

One of Pandora's two visible arms (the other six were tucked discreetly inside her duffle coat) shot out and she plucked a white feather from Jake's shoulder.

'I've been driving since Dwight D. Eisenhower was in diapers. I know how to handle a car.'

'That's not the point! We're supposed to be keeping a low profile. The DREAM agents are looking for us, remem——'

'Hey, you two! Yes, YOU!'

A traffic warden stormed down the avenue of international flags that led up to Marble Arch. The woman's fingers were wrapped so tightly around her handheld ticket machine that her knuckles stood out, sharp and white. She pointed at the battered Volkswagen.

'You—you—you,' she blustered, her face growing progressively purple. 'You can't park there!'

The tourists whispered excitedly and took videos with their mobile phones. Two maniac drivers having a bust up with an authority figure under the shadow of one of London's most famous landmarks: this was internet gold. The warden marched straight up to Pandora and eyeballed her with all the ferocity of a sergeant major fazing a new recruit.

'That kid's just a . . . well, kid.' She stabbed a finger at Jake. 'But you? You've gotta be forty if you're a day.'

'Only forty?' Pandora preened. 'My moisturizing routine must really be working.'

'So what do you think you're up to, driving like that?' The warden thrust her face to within a few centimetres of Pandora's. 'Not a good example to be setting, is it?'

'You may not be aware of this,' Pandora said, 'but your breath reeks of tuna fish. Any chance you could take a step back?'

'Right, that's it, I'm making a citizen's arrest. I'm within my powers. Lady, you're in big, big tr—*tra-curgh*.'

A yellow and black object, like a large, dried-up leaf, had dropped out of the sky and fallen straight into the warden's jabbering mouth. Her lips snapped shut—probably not the best move, Jake thought—and her eyes bulged. Hands locked around her throat, she made several guttural, choking noises. There were a few sniggers and exclamations of concern from the tourists.

'Heimlich,' Pandora sighed.

She positioned herself behind the warden and executed a swift abdominal thrust. The woman hunched, doubled over, and spat up the leaf. Half drowned in phlegm, it landed at Jake's feet. The crowd called out in disgust and even Pandora swore with surprise, because the leaf was not a leaf at all.

It was a grasshopper.

The insect picked its way out of the drool pool, lifted its hind legs, and chirruped. As if in answer to the grasshopper's song, a sudden darkness fell across the traffic island. Jake guessed that a cloud must have passed overhead, but looking up he saw that a single shadow, as dense as night, had cloaked Oxford Street and Park Lane. The traffic warden turned her face to the sky, and screamed. As she staggered back down the avenue of flags, more screams broke out. Some of the tourists dropped their phones and fled while others stood openmouthed and continued filming, their focus no longer the maniac motorists but the undulating cloud.

'Qu'est-ce que c'est?' a woman cried, her hand clutching the rosary around her neck.

A Japanese man grabbed his partner's hand and sprinted for the shelter of the shops on Oxford Street.

'Let's get the hell outta here!' shouted an American sporting a Sherlock Holmes deerstalker. He followed the Japanese man's example, ushering his family between honking cars and taxicabs.

Jake stared at the yellow and black mass that had covered the sun. It was like looking at a colossal grainy beach hovering over the city; a buzzing, billowing, brooding mass that blocked out the autumn-blue sky. As more grasshoppers fell, and the shouts and screams of frightened people filled the air, Jake turned to Pandora.

'A swarm of locusts.'

'Pretty biblical.'

'Not biblical. Demontide. It's an Omen. The first of the four.'

'The first Omen of the Demontide's a rain of toads,' Pandora objected.

'But this Demontide isn't in Hobarron's Hollow.'

'You mean . . . ?'

Pandora's gaze swept the streets. Apart from her and Jake, the Marble Arch traffic island had been deserted. People were now crammed into shops or sheltering in the underground station across the road. The roundabout had come to a standstill. There were no blaring horns, no growling engines, radios had been switched off and telephone conversations abandoned. There was an occasional shriek when a grasshopper hit a windscreen or shop window but, on the whole, silence reigned.

Not quite silence.

There was the buzz of the swarm overhead.

'London,' Pandora breathed. 'It's going to start in London.'

Chapter 11
The Walls of Reality

'Omens or not, we better get our butts in gear,' Pandora said. 'Where does this Fletcher Clerval live?'

'F.C.—Locksmith—Marble Arch. That's all that's written on the card.'

'Jake, this *entire* area is known as Marble Arch, from the south end of Edgware Road to the northern part of Park Lane. Hundreds of offices, shops, hotels, apartments.'

Jake took out his phone and checked the internet.

'No Fletcher Clerval listed under any residential or business address.'

'We ought to have brought Rachel with us. That girl's as smart as paint, she'd be able to work it out in ten seconds flat.'

'Hey, we're smart, too.' Jake bowed his head, acknowledging Pandora's wry smile. 'OK, Rach is smarter, but let's just think about this. Marble Arch. F.C. Look around, see if you can see those initials anywhere.'

While they scouted around the island, peering at office names and shop signs, more and more locusts fell from the swarm. Jake was soon having to swat them from his neck and shake them out of his hair. He had no real phobia of insects, but the scrape of those barbed legs against his skin and the scratch of their ceaseless song made him shudder. They fell in a drizzle. Then a shower. Then a deluge. Panicked by the rattle of little bodies above their heads, a few of the drivers started their engines, but with the roads gridlocked and a layer of grasshoppers cloaking their windscreens they were going nowhere. Sightseers and commuters ran through the streets, banged on shop windows and pleaded to be let in. Sometimes doors were opened and they were ushered inside; more often the crowds mouthed 'no room!' and waved them away.

Jake crunched across the crawling carpet that now covered the island. He reached Pandora, who had taken off her jacket and was busy shooing locusts with all eight of her arms.

'Octopus lady swats monster swarm.' She thumbed in the general direction of the roundabout. 'They'll think it was one big hallucination.'

'I should do something,' Jake shouted over the insect drone.

'Like what?'

'Magic? Maybe I could burn them somehow?'

'You think you can direct that kind of spell precisely enough?' Pandora looked dubiously at the cars, the offices, the shops. 'Lots of people behind those windows, Jake. Lots of flammable fuel in those gas tanks.'

'Then what can we—Ow!'

Blood trickled from a tiny wound on Jake's wrist. A lone grasshopper had attached itself to his flesh, its sharp little jaws gnawing beneath the skin. A thousand times brighter than a paper cut, the pain reminded him of another wound and an older agony. As it reached along his arm and clawed behind his eyes, he remembered *bufo bufo*, the poisonous toad that had bitten him in Hobarron's Hollow. As if to confirm his suspicions, three spots of green goo oozed out of the bite. While his Oldcraft began to heal the wound and leech the poison, he recalled what had happened in the Hollow when his powers hadn't been this strong: then it had taken the special skills of Alice Splane, a magical infections expert, to save his life.

Jake stared at the teeming millions already on the ground, then at the multitude hovering overhead.

'These things are going to kill thousands of people.'

Blue orbs of magical fire ignited in his palms. The locusts seemed to shy away from the light.

'I'll just have to risk it.' He pulled his right hand back over his shoulder, preparing to send a blast into Oxford Street. 'I can't just stand here and watch while people are devou—'

He felt, rather than saw, the wave of energy that pulsed out from the island. It spread into the streets and the swarm's song changed in an instant. The pitch of the chirrup went higher, and Jake had to cover his ears. It sounded as if the locusts were screaming. Then a second wave hit and the scream was silenced. Silenced because the swarm had vanished.

Sunlight broke over London, rays that seemed fiercer

after the darkness. People came blinking out of the shops and stumbling out of their cars. They took small, baby steps, their cautious eyes lifted to the sky. Strangers held each other, laughing and crying.

'It was magic!' a voice shouted. 'A spell of some kind.'

'Call the DREAM agents!' an old woman shrieked. 'There's a witch and demon around here somewhere.'

Shaking fingers jabbed at mobile phones. Then one finger pointed at Pandora.

'That woman by the arch. Look at her arms!'

'Oh my God, he's right. Eight arms. She—she's a—'

'Demon. And the boy must be her master.'

'I've got an agent on the line. They're sending a response team.'

Jake took one of Pandora's offending arms. 'Time to go.'

They were hurrying towards the car when Jake froze. Pandora tugged at his hand while he gaped and gestured towards the great marble monument.

'Not the best time to be practising your mime act, Jake. Baying mob at five, six, seven—hell, baying mob at every o'clock on the dial.'

'Stupid.' Jake smacked his forehead. 'Marble Arch!'

'Come again?'

Sirens split the air. Blue light arced across the shopfronts of Oxford Street.

'"Marble Arch" doesn't mean the general area.' He held up Fletcher Clerval's card. 'It literally means *Marble Arch*. The monument itself. That was where the energy wave came from, that's where Fletcher lives.'

He raced to the monument and stood beneath the central gateway.

'There must be something here, a clue of some kind, otherwise why give us the card? He wanted us to find him.'

'Three riot vans approximately two minutes away. We have to get out of here.'

'Pandora, just tell me what you see!'

'Big white marble landmark,' Pandora said, exasperated. 'One large central archway, two smaller gates either side. Eight Corinthian columns. Panels with carved reliefs showing, I think, the figures of Justice, Peace, and Plenty. Winged Victories on the spandrels and a beardy guy on the keystone. Two bronze gates with lions, royal insignia, and St George slaying the dragon. More carved figures representing—'

'The dragon!' Jake dropped to his knees and examined the bronze carving on the right-hand gate. 'What was it Fletcher said to you? That he was a "monster in the crowd". Look at every other figure on the arch: all of them noble and beautiful, except the dragon. This figure is the one that Fletcher would identify with—the monster in the crowd.'

Jake pressed his hand against the dragon. Nothing happened.

The riot vans reached the gridlocked traffic at the roundabout and screeched to a halt. Masked DREAM agents spilled out and raced between the cars. A loud hailer blared:

'*The suspects will stay where they are. You're now under arrest for the crime of witchcraft.*'

'Not again,' Jake groaned, and lunged for the dragon on the left-hand gate.

The Walls of Reality

A flash of light. A blast of arctic air. A thunderous clatter, like the sound of a train hurtling through a tunnel.

'My advice, Jacob,' a small voice echoed all around, 'in matters supernatural you should always try the left side first. The "sinister" side, you might say.'

The glare fell back, and Jake found that he was still kneeling under the big central archway. He jumped to his feet. The riot vans, the DREAM agents, the crowd, the roundabout, the shops, the people, the sun, the sky, all of it had vanished. Beyond the arch there was just a curtain of darkness, like a bleak and starless nightscape. Framed against this emptiness, Pandora stared over Jake's shoulder.

'What is this place?'

'My home,' came the voice. 'Well, don't just stand there gaping, come on in.'

They stepped out from under Marble Arch and into a cavernous corner of the impossible. Instead of the wide traffic island, Jake and Pandora now found themselves inside a warehouse roughly the size of a jumbo jet aircraft hangar. At least four times the height of the arch, shining metallic walls soared upwards and met a rectangle of utter darkness. Bright, clinical light with no obvious source gleamed against the long stainless steel workbenches that ran along the walls. Collected on these tables were Bunsen burners and dreamcatchers, centrifuges and voodoo dolls, microscopes and scrying mirrors, spectrometers and spell books. Towards the far end of the warehouse objects of varying size were hidden under tarpaulin sheets.

Jake took a couple of steps into the space and turned

back. It was odd, seeing Marble Arch built into the metal wall—something old and something modern colliding head on. Like science and magic, he thought.

On a nearby table stood a familiar object. From each upright finger of the Hand of Glory wires ran back to a Petri dish filled with a layer of black oil. A single dead locust floated in the gloop.

'A rushed job, but effective enough.'

A figure in a trench coat and sackcloth mask hobbled towards them. He seemed to have appeared out of nowhere. Jake almost winced at the man's rolling, jarring movements—a walk that spoke only of pain. And yet, reaching the workbench, he disconnected the wires with swift and nimble fingers. Fletcher Clerval threw the Hand of Glory into a cardboard box filled with similar grisly talismans and turned to face his guests.

'Soon as the screaming started, I popped out and picked up a specimen,' Fletcher explained. 'Then I configured the Hand to focus its energy on the specific genetic signature of the locust. A slight adaptation of the old incantation and, hey presto!'

'But where'd they go?' Pandora asked.

'If my calculations are correct, one of the dark regions on Ganymede. Jupiter's seventh moon. They shouldn't get up to much trouble out there. In fact, they should all be dead. By the way, I heard through the Arch what you said about the locust swarm: the reason this Omen is different from the toads in Hobarron's Hollow isn't just because this Demontide will take place in London. It's because a different dark soul is on the brink of conjuring it. The Hobarron's Hollow Demontide was the work of Marcus Crowden—its Omens were uniquely tied to him. We stand now in the shadow of an apocalypse worked by the Demon Father himself. His Omens will be his own, and no doubt will be significantly more terrible. Only the last will remain the same. The Lament of Nature is the cry of the Earth itself; it has nothing to do with the darkness of demons and witches.'

'Well, I guess we should thank you, Mr Clerval,' Pandora breathed. 'This is the second time you've saved our skins. But I gotta say, you could've helped us out with the address. Marble Arch? And then your dragon doorbell?'

'It wouldn't be wise for a man like me to advertise his whereabouts,' Fletcher shrugged. 'My skills could be very valuable to certain individuals. The Demon Father, for instance. Or you, Jacob Harker.'

Jake came straight to the point. 'I need you to get me into the demon dimension.'

A long pause followed. And then Fletcher Clerval burst out laughing.

'Bold and brave and stark raving mad!' He slapped his gloved hands together. 'You remind me very much of your father. So, the demon world, eh? That's quite a challenge.'

'We heard you were an expert in trans-dimensional travel.'

'I *am* an expert.' Fletcher's strange little voice quivered and he touched the corner of his mask. 'I was once taught a hard lesson about those forces that strive to keep reality in check. The universe does not like it when jumped up primates like us try to bend its laws. There is only one way to defy the universe and stay safe. You must never flinch.'

'So you can help us?'

'Might as well. Just being here, in my laboratory, you are already defying reality.' Fletcher gestured towards the monument. 'Tell me, where do you think you are?'

'You opened a portal, transported us away from London.' Jake looked again at the cosmically dark ceiling and thought about locusts and Ganymede. 'Are we in space?'

'Please don't be dense. I can do many things but breathing in the void of space is not one of them. No. Where we are is where you were. I haven't transported you anywhere. You, me, this gracious lady, my laboratory, we're all standing on the traffic island to the south of Marble Arch.'

'But how?'

'Magic and science. I have fused two realities together so that the lab and the island can exist simultaneously at exactly the same moment in space-time. This is possible because of the unique psychic properties of the Marble Arch location. The monument stands on the axis of two ancient Roman roads, a place of meetings and partings. It's also close to the location of the Tyburn Tree.'

'The old London gallows,' Jake said.

'Precisely. For over half a millennia, people were executed at Tyburn, their souls wrung slowly out of their bodies. That creates a kind of psychic thumbprint, a weakening of the walls of reality. The perfect place for me to create my secret lab. Plus, it's very handy for the shops. The only downside is perpetual night—I just can't seem to get the sun to rise in this reality. And therein lies the danger.'

'What do you mean?'

'I know more about trans-dimensional travel than any man alive, but I cannot perfect my ceiling. Jacob, you are asking me to send you to the demon world. A prison that was never supposed to be opened, either from inside or out. I want you to be aware that making such a journey will be very dangerous.'

'I've got to risk it.'

'Very well. Then you will need to get something for me. The Bone of Ullr.'

Pandora laughed. 'That's impossible. They'd never part with it.'

'The Bone of Ullr.' The pages of Jake's dark catalogue stirred. 'How will that help?'

'I have everything here to power transportation through dimensions, but breaching the demon prison? That will require a little more juice than usual. The Bone may be able to provide that extra burst of psychic energy.'

'OK, so where can we find it?'

'The talisman is in the possession of the Unseelie Court.' The magical scientist's voice lost its playful edge. 'The dark faeries will not give it up easily.'

Jake thought of the impish voice in the tunnel beneath the borderland desert.

'We'll give them whatever they want.'

'Don't say things like that out loud.' Pandora looked uncomfortable. 'They may have eyes even in this strange place.'

Fletcher did not contradict her. 'The dark faeries are cunning and spiteful, even when it is in their own interests not to be. They will demand a heavy price for the Bone.'

He moved over to a computer terminal mounted on the wall beside the arch. As he staggered across the warehouse, Jake could see oddly placed bones pushing against the scientist's clothes. What looked like knee and elbow joints rose and fell out of his spine. Fletcher Clerval *came back changed* . . . What exactly did that mean? Jake wondered. Then he thought of the little mouth Simon had seen resting just above Fletcher's collarbone, and connected it to his own experience on the Scarab Path. The magical force of the path had almost pulled him apart.

Fletcher was pulled apart, Jake thought. *And then he used all his skill and knowledge to put himself back together . . . as best he could.*

Fletcher's dexterous fingers moved over the keyboard.

'I've reset the coordinates. You should now come out somewhere near London Bridge.'

He punched the 'Enter' key and the central gateway flashed with white light.

'Go now, quick as you can.'

Pandora thanked the scientist and stepped into the light. Before Jake joined her, he held out his hand to Fletcher. The scientist took it, his grip like iron.

'You haven't asked why I'm going to the demon world.'

'Demontide's coming,' Fletcher mused. 'Three days to go if that swarm was any indication. I trust you have your reasons. In any case, I see *him* in you. Your father was the best and wisest man I have ever known, and although you are not his blood, you were raised by him. The son of Adam Harker wouldn't ask for such a thing lightly.'

Fletcher turned Jake to the bright white gateway.

'I'll get you there, Jacob. Even if I have to tear down the walls of reality, brick by brick.'

Chapter 12
For Fear of Little Men

Jake, Rachel, and Simon stood once more under the purple hue of the borderlands' twin moons. Pandora had thought it best if she stayed behind at the factory.

'The dark faeries and I don't get on,' she'd muttered. Pushed for an explanation, she said, 'You've heard of changelings, right? Faeries steal human babies and replace them with one of their own. Malevolent little critters that more often than not end up eating their human mothers.'

'What happens to the human baby?' Rachel had asked.

'Spirited away to the Unseelie Court, where they're usually dipped in hot caramel and served up as dessert. Faeries have a sweet tooth. Anyway, 1932, New Orleans, I'm living in the French Quarter and my landlord and his wife come to see me. A Creole couple, good people, scared people. They know I "know things". The wife tells me her baby isn't her baby, that its skin has this green tinge to it. So I work a bit of hoodoo and the fairy child bursts into flames. Soon as its ashes are dusted out the door, the human baby reappears in its cradle. Ever since then I've been off the Unseelie's Christmas card list . . . '

Rachel took the Bow of Nuada from her back and examined the upper limb. Jake had used magic to mend the place where it had been snapped in two by the harpy's claw.

'Feels different.' She tensed the string. 'The balance is off.'

'You'll adjust.' Jake glanced at Simon. 'OK, mate?'

Still trapped mid-transformation, Simon held the wolfsbane pendant tight in his fist. His piercing green eyes gazed across the empty square, all the way to the door of the Grimoire Club. The door once guarded by Razor.

'Let's get moving,' he barked.

They assembled around the hole that Jake had blasted through the flagstones. Below, the silvery marble of the spiral staircase twisted away into shadows. Jake summoned a ball of magic to light their way, and was about to step into the hole when another flash of silver caught his eye. Half buried in a heap of rubble, the tarnished bowl of the old fountain glinted in the moonlight.

Jake felt the colour drain from his face. Again, the door, the light, the words—*Here is the orb and here is the* . . . He could see it, gleaming in front of him, but his mind would not, could not make the connection. Because once the word was uttered there was no going back. It would be fire and fury and death, and the time was not right. So he did his best to close it off. For now.

'Jake, what is it?' Rachel asked.

'I don't know.'

Simon's laugh was hard and empty.

'Same old story, eh, Jake? What exactly *do* you know?'

He spat out the words and jumped into the hole. They could hear the echo of his footfalls racing down the stairs.

'He's changing,' Rachel whispered. 'So slowly we can't see it. He's angry, Jake, bitter. He's beginning to frighten me.'

'We'll bring him back,' Jake promised. 'When this is over, we'll find a way.'

'By then it could be too late.'

Together, they hurried down the steps and into the tunnel beneath the desert. When they reached the bottom of the staircase there was no sign of Simon.

'So, this bone, what do you know about it?' Rachel asked.

Jake pushed the magical light forward and the darkness retreated.

'The Bone of Ullr. Most of the stories about Ullr himself seem to have been lost. He was somehow connected with the Norse sagas and might once have ruled Asgard in Odin's stead. But the legend we're interested in concerns Ullr the wizard, a cunning man from the twelfth century who carved dreadful spells into a large bone. He could then ride the bone across the seas, seeking out new worlds.'

'New worlds,' Rachel echoed.

'New dimensions, maybe? If so, the bone might still have that power. I guess that's Fletcher's idea.'

Their feet scraped through a scattering of sand, and Jake looked up at the arched ceiling.

'I think this is where I fell through.'

Simon's voice, faint and gruff, echoed out of the shadows. 'I've found something!'

Jake and Rachel ran down the tunnel. Bit by bit, the sheen of the silver-white walls grew duller, the once gleaming marble now marred and mottled with mould. Overhead, the spider webs thickened until they had to duck to avoid the heavy swags. They stumbled over the floor, which rose and fell at crazy angles like the treacherous walkway in a funhouse.

Finally, Jake's flame picked out Simon. He was standing inside a doorway at the end of the tunnel, his hands resting on the high lintel. In the chamber behind him, a warm yellow light flickered across rough stone walls.

'Did Pandora say anything about faeries eating people?' he asked.

'She said changelings ate their human mothers,' Rachel panted. 'And the Unseelie ate the taken babies.'

'Yeah.' Simon clicked his tongue against the roof of his mouth. 'I think I might've found the leftovers.'

They stepped into a small rotunda, its circular floor covered with crisp autumn leaves. Candles housed in iron cages hung from the dank walls and cast fitful shadows on the floor. The place reminded Jake of his seventeenth century prison cell in Rake's keep: it had that same doom-laden atmosphere, an impression that was only enhanced by the heap of human skeletons piled against the walls. The candlelight danced in and out of eyeless sockets and scurried up and down the ladder of fleshless ribs. Jake killed the magical light and, crouching down, ran his finger over a stripped femur.

'I don't think these people were eaten. There're no teeth marks, no signs of butchery. Except . . . ' He looked closer. 'There *are* cuts, hundreds of them. Tiny nicks sliced deep into the bone.'

Simon toed away some of the dead leaves.

'These people bled. A lot.'

Dark red marks stained the stone floor.

'Jake, look at this.'

Rachel directed his attention to a second door opposite the rotunda entrance. Hewn from granite, it stood about a metre high and had no handle. Above it, a series of runic symbols had been carved into the stonework. As Jake looked down at the inscription the runes blurred and reconfigured into different shapes:

Dusty air billowed against their backs and a dry *boom* echoed around the rotunda. The candles flickered and went out. Jake reignited his magic. In the wavering blue light, Rachel clutched his arm.

'Where's the door?'

Simon crossed the chamber in a single bound and started hammering on the solid wall: the place where, only a moment before, the doorway to the tunnel had been. Jake pushed against the bricks, hoping that one might slide back and engage a mechanism that would reopen the door. Suddenly, this place seemed even more like his old prison cell.

'Can't you use magic?' Simon snarled. 'Blast a hole in the wall or something?'

'A blast of magic in a confined space? Do you want us to burn to death?'

Simon's hands tightened into fists.

'Don't talk to me like I'm some sort of ignorant animal!'

A second flame sparked in Jake's free hand. Magic with a dark, red heart.

'Then don't behave like one.'

'What's that supposed to mean?'

'You know what it means. We're fighting a war here, Simon, and we don't have time to stroke your head and say "there, there". You've got issues, so either deal or shut them away until this is over.'

'Issues?' A long stride brought Simon to within striking distance of his friend. 'Look at me, Jake! What am I supposed to do with *this*? How can I shut *this* away?'

Jake had no easy answer, no reassuring words. Would Simon still be Simon in a few days' time, or would the leash finally snap and something darker emerge? Something that could no longer be trusted. He opened his mouth to speak— he had no idea what he was going to say—when Rachel's cry rang out. Forgetting their quarrel, Jake and Simon ran to her side. She was kneeling at the little granite door, a trembling hand pressed to her cheek.

'Let me see,' Simon said.

A fine laceration ran from the side of her nose to the corner of her cheekbone. Rachel's eyes darted around the room.

'I thought it was an insect, a fly buzzing around my head. And then I saw a glint of metal. It was so fast, I—'

'*G'ah!*'

Jake turned in time to see a blur of green light sweep across Simon's face. He heard the buzz of nimble wings and saw the flash of a minuscule blade. A cut had opened up down the length of Simon's muzzle, exposing his great, jagged teeth. Simon tried to swat his attacker, but his clawed hand was too slow and clumsy. The light spiralled into the domed roof of the rotunda before swooping down to its next target. The blade cut a thick slice out of Jake's scalp and blood fell like hot rain down his forehead.

'You can't use your magic, Rachel hasn't a hope of shooting the bloody thing,' Simon shouted. 'So whadda we do?'

'I don't know, but we better think of something fast, otherwise we'll end up like them.' Jake looked down at the corpses. 'Sliced and diced.'

'Sorry to be the bearer of bad news,' Rachel broke in. 'But this could be about to get a whole lot worse. Look at the walls.'

Tiny green lights burned like fireflies between the bricks. Hundreds of little slicers and dicers were pushing their way through gaps in the stonework. Simon dug a nail into the mortar and pulled out a creature the size of a housefly. The fairy's green glow brightened as it waved its little sword.

'*Speak the words and live,*' the creature fizzed, '*or hold your tongues and die.*'

'What words?' Simon grunted. 'What does it mean?'

'The runes,' Rachel said. 'But that's impossible. How can we read runic symbols?'

Jake scrambled over to the stumpy door, pressed his hands against the granite, willed his magic to open the lock. Nothing happened.

Meanwhile, an army of green swordsmen had gathered in the ceiling. Six bright lights broke away from the rest. In less than a second they had fallen on the friends and opened fresh wounds. Jake pressed his hand to the deep gash on his forearm and heard a trill of malevolent laughter. Bleeding from her face and hands, Rachel pulled Jake away from the door. She knelt in his place, her gaze sweeping back and forth over the runes.

'When we came into the room, the symbols changed. Why did they do that?'

'Who—*Arggh*!' Another fairy had dive-bombed Simon and ripped into his skin. 'Who knows? They're probably just playing with us.'

'Exactly. This is a game, and they may be mischievous—'

'Damn it!' Jake wiped fresh blood from his cheeks. ' "Mischievous" is putting it lightly.'

'But I think they play fair. We just have to work out how to win the game.' Rachel ran blood-wet fingers over the inscription. 'The secret must be here.'

'OK, but how can you even begin to translate—?'

'I don't know!'

Simon tore the leather coat from his back and threw it over her.

'Get busy. We'll give the little gits something to play with. Jake, spark up your magic, maybe it'll draw them in.'

'Like moths to a flame,' Jake nodded.

The plan was rough and ready but it seemed to work. With Jake and Simon on one side of the rotunda, Rachel went to work on the runes.

'Talk to me, Rach,' Simon called. 'Give us some hope over here.'

'I don't know, I don't know!'

'More hope than that would be nice!' Jake shouted.

Simon's long jaw hitched into something that resembled the crooked grin of old, and Jake felt a smile lift the corners of his own lips. Under that ferocious mask, his friend was still there. The boy who'd looked out for him, who'd taught him how to build a fire, snare rabbits and catch fish. The older brother he loved and looked up to.

Dozen of faeries descended from the dome. They whirled around the two friends, a murderous cyclone that spilled blood onto the walls. Then, as if wanting to admire their handiwork, the creatures fell back. Jake and Simon collapsed against the brickwork, gasping with pain and shock. Strips of skin hung from their faces like lengths of peeling wallpaper.

'Are you guys OK?'

'Don't look,' Simon ordered. 'Just hurry.'

The buzz deepened. Became denser, darker . . .

'Wait a minute. No . . . But it can't be that simple!' They

heard the slap of Rachel's palm against the little door. 'Substitution code!'

'Substi-what-now?' Jake called.

'I don't think it's an ancient language at all.' Rachel used her bloodied finger to mark out dashes on the wall, one to correspond with each rune symbol. 'It's just a code, substituting a symbol for a letter. The most frequently used letter in English is "E"—the most common symbol here is "ℵ", so that gives us —'

$$\_\_\,E \quad \_\_\_\,EE\_\_E \quad \_\_\_\_\_$$
$$E\_\_E\_$$
$$\_\_\_\_\_ \quad \_E\_E\_ \quad \_\_\_\_$$

'The next most common letter is "T" but that doesn't seem right, because who or what are we visiting here? *The Unseelie Court.* Look at that arrangement of E's in the second word. Must be "Unseelie", and the word "court" fits too. So that gives us "T", "H", "U", "N", "S" "L", "I", "C", "O", and "R". So we know the third word is "Enter".'

'Hurry it up, Rach,' Simon growled.

Rachel rattled off her workings. 'The Unseelie Court—Enter—Blank-blank-C-O-blank. Sixth word: N-E-blank-E-R. Probably "Never". Seventh word: Blank-O-R-N. "The Unseelie Court, Enter . . . " '

Suddenly, it clicked. The name that he had been called by both the Oracle of the Pit and the Demon Father. Jake grabbed hold of Simon just as the full ferocious flock descended. Using all his strength, he thrust his friends at the little door.

'Enter, Jacob Never Born!'

The runes glowed fiery white, then flashed with an intensity that bleached the walls of the rotunda, transforming the drab chamber into a cell fit for an angel. No longer buzzing and laughing, the swordsmen screamed. Jake and his friends also cried out against the glare.

They were within a whisker of the door when its seldom-used hinges groaned and the granite slab swung open. Simon and Rachel fell headlong onto a bed of cold, damp earth; Jake landed in a sprawl beside them. Ignoring the pain from his wounds, he managed to scramble to his knees and peer back into the chamber. He saw a shower of red lights falling to earth. Burning and dying, the swordsmen settled on the dead leaves and faded into lifeless motes. The door closed and shut out the last of their screams.

Jake could feel the stir of Oldcraft inside. The healing process had begun, knitting skin and sinew back together. At his side, Rachel still sported the deep gash in her cheek while Simon's face was a grisly patchwork. Jake had once used his powers to heal Eleanor; now that same instinct to heal began to direct his magic. He was about to lay hands on his friends' wounds when a laughing voice called out—

'Allow me, Master Harker.'

Another flash, this time a little less blinding. When Jake recovered his sight he saw that Rachel's and Simon's flesh had been regenerated and the tracks of blood on their hands and faces magically cleansed. His own injuries had healed long before his Oldcraft had a chance to complete the job.

'A well-played game, Miss Saxby,' the voice tittered. 'Now, follow my words and we shall find each other. Shall I sing to you? *Up the airy mountain—Down the rushy glen—We daren't go a-hunting—For fear of little men . . .*'

Helping Rachel to her feet, Jake whispered, 'Still got the arrow?'

She checked her quiver and nodded.

'Then it's time to hunt some little men.'

The granite door through which they had tumbled was set into the side of a boulder. This stone sat by itself in the clearing of a forest and was much too small to have housed the rotunda chamber, let alone the underground tunnel. The doorway to the Unseelie Court was clearly some kind of dimensional portal.

Silver trees the size of four-storey buildings bordered the glade. Between their branches garlands of Spanish moss hung like shawls draped over long, withered arms. As they followed the fairy's voice, Jake could not shake the feeling that this was a dead place. Where was the birdsong, the buzz of insects, the scuttle of forest creatures? Come to that, where was the life-giving sunlight? The only illumination in the wood seemed to come from a few limpid puddles that gave off a spectral glow.

Through the branches, Jake could see what looked like a dome of earth rising overhead. He recalled one of the myths he had read long ago: the courts of the little people were once thought to have existed in ancient burial mounds hidden under hillsides . . .

Somewhere up ahead the fairy moved from song to song, rhyme to rhyme.

'*Come away, O human child!—To the waters and the*

The Last Nightfall

wild—With a faery hand in hand—For the world's more full of weeping than you can understand.'

It took them a few minutes to reach the edge of the forest and the lake beyond. A wide expanse of deep green water lapped at an empty, shingled shore. Close to the earthen horizon, a beautiful glass boat was ploughing a path towards them.

Chapter 13
Hurtling Into Hell

'Welcome!' the musical voice called. 'Welcome to my court!'

Three hooded figures occupied the boat: a pilot at the stern; an oarsman bent to his task; and the singer standing at the prow, his hands held out in greeting.

'At my signal,' Jake whispered.

Glass screeched against the stony shore. While his servants remained in the boat, the singer hopped on to dry land and approached Jake, arms outstretched. He was still a fair distance away when his body suddenly became a blur. Wind whipped in the slipstream around the little figure and threw Rachel's hair into her eyes. A second later, the singer was standing in front of them, an arrow clasped in his fist.

'Iron-tipped? Really, Jacob, you shouldn't believe everything you read.'

The creature tore off its robe. A tiny, wasted form was

unveiled, its skin as grey and lifeless as dead tree bark. Tattered wings flapped at its back like the weak flutterings of a suffocated moth. Coupled with a pair of green, bulging eyes, these wings gave the fairy an insect-like appearance.

'Not the pretty little nymph you were expecting?' The creature gave a toothless grin. 'If you wanted beauty you ought to have visited our simpering cousins at the Seelie Court. But here you are, so let old Norebo provide some entertainment.'

The fairy opened its mouth and slowly, slowly, pushed the arrow down its throat until the projectile was swallowed, feathers and all.

'Despite the legends, iron has no effect on my kind.' He winked at Jake. 'I suppose you thought to use the weapon against me. Such behaviour warrants your immediate execution, but would I dare kill one such as you?'

'Why not?'

'"Jacob Never Born".' The fairy lifted a beetling brow. 'Do you not wonder why we higher life forms—faeries, demons—call you that?'

'Because I was cloned.' Jake shook his head, as if disagreeing with his own explanation. 'Because I was made from the cells of Josiah Hobarron.'

Norebo laughed. 'Human science has no significance in the dominions of the Old Ones. It is in a mystical sense that we say "Never Born".'

Jake made a sudden leap—a connection which he couldn't altogether understand. His forefinger blazed with magic and he used it to draw a symbol in the air. The Sign of Oldcraft held for a few seconds before drifting apart.

'You're old,' he said. 'So tell me, have you seen this symbol before?'

'Of course.'

There was something in Norebo's eyes: mischief, but perhaps also a desire for Jake to grasp the truth.

'What does it mean?'

'It is the sign of the Falling Night.'

'And what does that *mean*?'

'It means the oldest of the Old Ones.'

In Jake's mind, light began to spill out from under the forbidden door.

'It means the Three.'

Light burning brighter than ever.

'It means this . . .' Norebo started to sing again, but this time his tone was solemn and respectful.

'Graceless mortals, be not afraid
If night falls fast, you may survive.
No gods will come to thy aid
The chronicler must burn alive
Hell will fall and he will cry
He sees the truth behind the lie . . .

'Remember, Jacob, there have only ever been Three. Three to fight in the far off days. Three to fight and lay the trap. Three to fight on a dead man's walls. For an age, there have been Two, but the third will return, soon, very soon, to the Rising Sun and the Dying Day. Look to the *Third*, Jacob, and you will find the answers you seek.'

Jake shivered. 'Chronicler . . .'

'Do you keep a journal?' the fairy asked. 'Your previous

incarnation kept a diary in which he recorded all his works.'

'I used to write stories,' Jake said. 'Horror stories. Just fiction, nothing real.'

'But woven into the tapestry of fiction is always a thread or two of truth. Stories can be diaries, too, and when does a man write his diary?'

Norebo left the question hanging. A mystery to ponder at Jake's leisure.

'So tell me, how did you like my little runic riddle?'

'You killed them,' Rachel said. 'Your own kind.'

'One of you had to die, otherwise what kind of game would it have been?'

'And the people?' Jake pictured the corpses on the rotunda floor. 'How many have come looking for you over the years, only to be cut down by those fairy lights?'

'What do *people* matter to me?' Again, that strange look entered Norebo's eyes. 'What do they matter to you? You are special, Jacob. A worker of Oldcraft, at least that. So why do these—' he gestured to Simon and Rachel, 'infants matter?'

'Because I saw . . .'

Pain rippled along Jake's spine and spread out across his back and shoulders. He gritted his teeth against it, tried to focus.

'Really, there's no need to strain yourself,' Norebo laughed. 'I'm sure that all will be revealed in good time. At least, I hope so, for their sakes. Now, tell me, what is it that you want of the Unseelie Court?'

'We need to get into the demon world,' Simon said.

Norebo could barely hide his disgust. 'Ah yes, we've heard of you, Master Lydgate. I should say, I'm not very fond of cross-breeds polluting the air of my Otherworld.'

'Really? Well, just let me tear your throat out and that shouldn't be a problem.'

'I'd like to see you try.'

'Stop it, Simon,' Jake ordered. 'And you, fairy, speak to my friend that way again and I'll bring this "Otherworld" crashing down around your ears.'

A flicker of fear crossed Norebo's features.

'You *could* do it. You could. Just not yet . . .'

'Enough with the riddles,' Rachel said. 'We need something from you. Will you help us?'

'Perhaps. For a price.'

'Maybe you should understand why we're going to the demon world,' Jake said. 'We need to get hold of two supernatural objects. Signums. They'll help us send the Demon Father back to his prison and defeat the Demontide.'

'And that's the *only* reason? Come, Jacob, I know the stink of human love when I smell it. It's not just about the Signums. The girl's there, too, isn't she?'

'What do you know about it?'

'Only what your eyes tell me. And as noble and courageous as all this sounds, I still say there is a price for my help.'

'But don't you understand?' Rachel said. 'The demons won't just stop with our world. They'll use it as a base to invade all other dimensions and realities. Even your Otherworld won't be safe. By helping us you'll help yourself.'

Clever, Rachel, Jake thought. But the stony face of Norebo turned his hopes to dust.

'Humans cannot understand the ways of the Old Ones. Now I say for the third and final time, there *will* be a price. Tell me what it is you want.'

'The Bone of Ullr,' Jake sighed.

'That old thing? Well, why didn't you just say so.'

Norebo picked up his rumpled grey cloak and reached into its folds. With the flourish of a stage magician, he produced a gigantic bone almost as tall as himself. The size and shape of a shark's rib, it was covered in strange talismanic engravings: symbols and numerals, signs and ciphers. Jake started to reach for the bone when the fairy snatched it back.

'Ah, ah! No touching until payment has been made.'

'But it doesn't even sound like you value it that much,' Rachel objected.

'Ullr was a poor excuse for a deity. He could never decide who his worshippers ought to be——Germanic peasants, Viking warriors, off-piste skiers, he tried them all. But there was something at which he did excel——wizardry. So although I have nothing but contempt for him as a god, I do value his enchantments.'

'All right,' Jake said, 'what do you want for it?'

'Oh, to haggle with one such as you, Jacob! I must take my time. I must think.' The bug-eyes glinted. 'What mischief can I cause you and your friends.'

Holding the bone as if it weighed no more than a toothpick, the little fairy hopped from foot to foot. The dance might have appeared ridiculous except for the look of joyful malevolence on Norebo's face.

'I have it!' he cried. 'Oh, this is going to be fun!'

'Just tell us,' Simon said.

'How very apt that you have spoken, Master Lydgate, for it is you who must pay the piper.'

'Pay with what?'

'Oh, just a bauble, a trinket, a nothing really.'

Norebo skipped over to Simon. All the playfulness drained from his face and suddenly he looked every inch the ancient being he claimed to be. Older than the weather-beaten cliffs of Hobarron Bay; older than the fragile pages of the *Codex Tempus*; older even than the demon Door of Crowden's Sorrow. In fact, Jake had experienced only one thing that struck him as more ancient than the fairy: the call of the second Signum.

'I want your pendant.'

'NO!'

Rachel pushed, and the little fairy tripped over his heels and fell to the ground. A gasp rose up from the servants in the glass boat.

'You dare touch me!' the fairy shrieked. 'I'll flay you alive! I'll tear the pretty flesh from your bones and eat it in front of you. I'll—'

Simon snapped the pendant from his neck. Shivering, he held it out to Norebo.

'Take the bloody thing.'

'Simon, you can't.'

Rachel tried to grab the amulet but Simon held her back.

'Anything else,' Jake pleaded, 'we'll give you whatever you want, just don't take this from him.'

'But it's what I desire. I want to see what will happen to the boy now that the Cynocephalus is unchained. Can he withstand it? Or will the beast become the master?' Norebo clapped his hands together. 'What larks!'

The fairy snatched the pendant and placed it in the folds of his cloak.

'*Aarrgghhhh!*'

Simon doubled over, his face in his hands. While the faeries in the boat and the fairy on land fell into fits of laughter, the transformation progressed. Coarse black hair pushed through Simon's fingers and his T-shirt ripped along its seams. They heard his jaw break and remould itself into a new and more terrible shape. At last, he pulled his hands away. The face revealed was certainly more feral, more wolf-like, but it was still not the full Cynocephalus form. Some steely part of Simon was holding the beast at bay.

'Simon?' Rachel whispered. 'Are you—?'

'It's still me.' The voice was gruff with pain. 'Just.'

Recovering himself, Norebo clicked his fingers and the Bone of Ullr flew into Jake's hand.

'A pleasure doing business with you, Jacob Never Born.'

'One day I'll come back to this place.' Jake's deep, magisterial tone had returned. He spoke again with the voice of Josiah Hobarron, the Witchfinder—a voice that had invaded his conscious mind many times before. 'Then we will settle accounts . . . *Oberon.*'

'You knew it was me?' Fear rang through the fairy's question.

'Wordplay was always your game, fairy king. Now, send us back to the desert.'

Fletcher Clerval snatched the bone from Jake and scurried away to the far end of his laboratory. Pandora put aside the crystal ball she'd been examining and came over.

'I couldn't stand one more minute of Grype's whining— *the ropes are too tight, my pillow needs plumping, I need the toilet, stop hitting me with that fly swat.* So I left him under Joanna's watchful gaze. OK, so tell me, how did you get the——?' She caught sight of Simon. 'What? You gave them your pendant!'

'Don't look at me like that, I'm not the only freak in this room.' Simon jutted his long chin towards Fletcher, who was too far away to hear the insult. Then those blazing eyes focused on Pandora herself. 'Not by a long shot.'

Rachel threw Pandora an apologetic glance and chased after her boyfriend.

'Mischief,' Pandora sighed. 'I should've gone with you.'

'I don't think it would have turned out any different,' Jake said. 'It was almost as if Simon wanted to get rid of the pendant. Like the attraction of the Cyno was becoming too much. He's holding it back now, but I reckon it's only gonna take one more temptation, one more prompt.'

'Rachel's in danger.' Pandora nodded. 'But, you know, there's not a damn thing we can do about it.'

'Why?'

'Because she's in love, and love doesn't care about danger.' Pandora smiled. 'Does it, Jake?'

A warm blush reddened Jake's cheeks.

'What do you know about the oldest of the Old Ones?' He wanted to change the subject, but it was not an idle question. 'I showed one of the faeries the protection symbol from the factory. He didn't call it the Sign of Oldcraft. He called it the Sign of the Falling Night—said that it meant the oldest of the Old Ones. The Three.'

He recited Norebo's poem as if he had learned it by heart.

'Sounds like some kind of legend attached to the Never Seen.'

Jake winced at her words. 'My dad mentioned them once, but what are they?'

'A whisper, a scrap of a myth, that's what my mother says. It's what all the dark creatures say. Unlike faeries and demons, no one has ever seen them, hence the name. If they ever existed they died out long ago.'

'Then what *were* they?'

'Who knows? Some say heroes, others that they were creatures without mercy, worse than any demon. If they do exist in some far off plane of reality then it's as if . . .'

'Yes?'

'They don't want to be found.'

Jake shook his head. It was time to forget about vague fairytales.

'What time is it?'

Pandora checked one of her watches. 'Eleven p.m.'

'Night of the first day. If the pattern's the same, there'll be three more omens before the Demontide. Three days left to rescue Eddie. Three days to find Eleanor and the Signums.'

A clawed hand came to rest on Jake's shoulder.

'You can't do all that on your own. There's not enough time.' Simon looked at Pandora and bowed his head. 'I'm sorry for what I said.'

'Don't sweat it, wolf boy. And you're right, there isn't enough time. It might take days to locate Eleanor and the Signums.'

'Then what do you suggest?' Jake asked.

'We split up,' Rachel said. 'You and Pandora take the demon world, me and Simon get the prison break.'

'No, it's too dangerous.'

'But surely we've got the easy gig!' Rachel said.

'He means leaving you alone with me,' Simon said. 'And maybe you've got a point, Jake, but I don't see what else we can do. We're against the clock here.'

'I trust him,' Rachel said simply.

'Mate, listen to me.' Simon's big arm latched around Jake's shoulder. 'If I think for even a second that I'm gonna lose control, I'll run. Rachel won't see me for dust, I promise.'

Jake pulled Simon into a hug. Then he went to Rachel and put his arms around her.

'The trolls won't help you, but you've got Grype.'

'Terrific,' Simon grunted.

'He sacrificed his demon for us,' Jake shrugged. 'Plus he knows the prison like the back of his hand. Maybe he really is on our side.'

'Grype's on no one's side except his own,' Pandora said. 'You watch him like a hawk.'

Something exploded at the far end of the lab. Before they could call his name, Fletcher Clerval came staggering out of the smoke.

'I've done it!' He swept his gloved hands through the air like a maestro conducting an orchestra. 'It's ready.'

'Gods help us,' Pandora muttered, and led the way.

Passing through the smoke, they came to the heart of Fletcher's scientific sanctuary. Banks of computer equipment occupied one wall while the workbenches were strewn with a variety of interconnected test tubes and cylinders. Half-built inventions littered the floor, a Frankenstein assortment of cutting-edge technology grafted onto odds and ends of mystic bric-a-brac. A printer hooked up to a Ouija board spilled out page after page of dire predictions. Floating in an immense tank of electrified fluid, the mummified remains of what appeared to be a merman gave Pandora a baleful glare.

Fletcher hobbled around to a large object covered by a tarpaulin sheet. The tarp flapped like a leathery wing as the scientist unveiled his work.

'Here she is.'

Motes of spiralling dust settled on the bonnet of Adam Harker's Volkswagen people carrier. A couple of dead locusts were trapped under the windscreen wiper and a yellow 'DREAM Agents Aware' sticker was taped to the passenger window.

'I towed it through the arch,' Fletcher explained. 'It's got a good, solid framework, should hold up to inter-dimensional tempest. Probably.'

Jake was hardly listening. He couldn't drag his eyes away from the Volkswagen's grisly new bonnet ornament. The Hand of Glory had been fixed to the front of the car.

'I've hooked the Hand up to the engine to give the magic an extra boost,' Fletcher said. 'Of course, that old talisman can open doorways too, but the primary power source is here.'

He opened the driver's door. Attached via electrical tape to the dashboard, the Bone of Ullr took up most of the width of the car. Its arcane symbols looked even stranger in the humdrum interior of the Volkswagen. One side of the bone was attached to a wire that led back to the Hand.

'Had to shave a bit off to fit it inside,' Fletcher shrugged, 'but I'm sure we've kept the most important inscriptions. Probably.'

'That's your second "probably" in under a minute,' Pandora pointed out. 'Not filling me with confidence here, Fletcher.'

'The co-ordinates might be a bit awry, that's all. So you could end up a hundred metres or so off course. But that's why I've been careful to choose an uncluttered part of the demon world as your landing strip.'

He took a folded square of parchment from his pocket. Opening the fragile page with the methodical care of a steady-handed surgeon, he placed the parchment on one of the few uncluttered work surfaces. Jake and his friends gathered around. While the others asked questions and mar-velled at the terrible beauty of the map, Jake felt his soul quake. He knew this place, this dimension, this realm, this prison. Knew it as a dark and shapeless void. Knew it because *she* had crafted it from the heart of nothingness. Knew it because he——Jacob Harker, Josiah Hobarron (three names . . . *Three*)——had made a record of it in his journal, his diary, his stories.

'So what exactly are we looking at, Fletcher?' Rachel asked.

'A chart of the infernal realm. Legend has it that it was drawn by William Reclusus.'

'The guy who wrote the *Codex Tempus*?'

'That's the monk.' Fletcher's sackcloth mask bobbed up and down. 'If you remember the story, a demon came to William and offered to show him all of Time and Space. Well, before he was walled up by his brethren, William had a vision of the hellscape from which the demon had spoken to him. He saw the dimension as it was in his time, but of course things changed over the years. The demon world developed.'

'It what?'

Fletcher waved a hand over the map. 'No one knows the full story of how this prison came into being, but we do know that it is constantly shifting and reforming. It is believed to have started as a void . . .'

Jake's breath caught in his throat.

'A world of nothingness, the demons themselves relegated to things of shadow. Then the demons made contact with the human race. They convinced us that it was only through them that we could work magic. When the first demon came through its witch gave it a form, a face, substance. It took this psychic solidity back to the demon realm, and from that day every demon familiar has returned home with more psychic energy clinging to it.'

'Do you mean ectoplasm?' Rachel asked.

'Something like that perhaps. Anyway, the demons have used this substance to build a solid world out of the airy shadows. This—' he laid a careful finger on the map, '—is that world. Since William's time, trusted Seers have added to the changing geography of the chart. This is how the demon world stands in the twenty-first century.'

'It's an island,' Rachel said.

'Something like an island,' Fletcher agreed. 'The Sea of Shadows surrounding the landmass is just that—a swirling ocean of nothingness that stretches out into the old void. Only the demon's island holds firm.'

'The land part looks a bit like a goat's head,' Simon observed.

'That's probably how medieval psychics saw it in visions,' Fletcher nodded. 'Then the legends became confused and everyone thought the Devil himself possessed the horned head of a goat. And it's not just the shape of the island that's influenced human ideas about an underworld. Look at the rivers cutting through it—they each have demonic names that were then used for the five rivers of Hades. And look at the volcanoes at the top of the island and the frozen lake in the middle—all classical hellscape features. And there are bound to be other things on the island; terrible things that have never found a place in human art and mythology.'

'These symbols dotted around the northern half of the island, what do they mean?' Pandora asked. 'That looks like a hieroglyph, that one's a castle, classical pillars, something that looks like a covered wagon . . .'

'No one knows. You must understand that humans have only ever seen the demon world in dreams. But we do know that the Shadow Palace is the capital of this realm. The stronghold. My guess is that Pinch and the witch ball will be there, waiting to be summoned.'

'So you drop us just outside, we storm the Palace and grab the ball. Easy.'

'Not quite. As I said, I cannot accurately pinpoint where you're going to end up. I don't want to land you slap-bang in a nest of demons, and so I've chosen the north of the island as a landing site. It's believed that the Burning Badlands are more or less uninhabited, the demons preferring to congregate around the Shadow Palace.'

'There's no scale to this map,' Simon pointed out. 'The Badlands are in the north near the volcanoes; the Shadow Palace is on the southern tip of the island. How long will it take Jake and Pandora to cover that distance?'

'A couple of days should do it.'

'A couple of days are all we have,' Jake said.

He leaned over the map, examining every detail. Somewhere on that island Eleanor was waiting for him.

Fletcher popped the boot of the car.

'I've prepared backpacks for you. Water, food, clothes for all terrains and conditions, and these . . . '

He ferreted inside one of the side zips and brought out two ordinary-looking wristwatches. His nimble fingers strapped one of the watches onto Jake's arm.

'Wind-ups—inter-dimensional travel would fritz a battery-powered watch. These are set to London time, so should

Hurtling Into Hell

give an idea how long you have left until doomsday.'

'A Demontide Timer.' Pandora exchanged one of her watches for Fletcher's timepiece. 'Nice work.'

'And so, if you're ready?'

Fletcher held open the driver's door for Pandora.

'Mad scientist and a gentleman, what a combination,' she smiled. 'Seriously, thank you.'

'I'd do anything for Adam Harker's son,' Fletcher said, 'and I see you would, too. He helped you, didn't he? Showed you what kind of person you could be. He did the same for me.'

Pandora touched Fletcher's gloved hand, then slipped into the driver's seat. Before joining her, Jake said his good-byes to Simon and Rachel.

'Good luck at the prison. I'll see you soon.'

A rough hug from Simon; a soft kiss from Rachel. Fearful odds were stacked against them—on this side of reality, the Demon Father, the dark alchemist Cynthia Croft, the vampiric DREAM agents; on the other, the full force of the demon world. They knew that this could be their final goodbye.

Jake got into the passenger seat and Fletcher poked his head through the window. This close, Jake could see the strange, bony protrusions that rubbed up against Fletcher's cloth mask. Not for the first time, he wondered what kind of face the scientist had been left with after his journey on the Scarab Path.

'Start her up.'

Pandora twisted the ignition key. The engine growled and the headlights glared against the laboratory's back wall.

'Jake, I want you to picture the map of the demon world. Specifically, you need to focus on the Burning Badlands to the north. I've already spent a couple of hours imprinting my own mental image of that place into the fabric of the bone, so we should be doubly sure of the location. Now, summon your magic and place your hands here.'

Jake's palms tingled with Oldcraft light. He gripped the bone. The carved inscriptions burned blue and the entire car started to shake. Fletcher hurried around to the front of the Volkswagen. He spoke spellcraft over the Hand of Glory and the tips of those five upright fingers burst into flame. Although Pandora hadn't touched the accelerator, the engine roared and the car lurched forward. Quick as a flash, Simon swept Fletcher out of the Volkswagen's path.

Inside the car, the Bone of Ullr burned with the intensity of an iron drawn from a furnace. Jake snatched his hands away. A second later, flames flickered out from the carved symbols: letters, numerals, devices and pictograms, all blazing like an infernal alphabet.

'Buckle up,' Pandora cried, 'it's happening!'

The wires connecting the Bone of Ullr to the Hand of Glory sizzled as psychic energy passed through the engine. With an ear-splitting clang, the bonnet lifted off the car and smashed into the wall. Fire burst from the screaming motor, the heat strong enough to punch out the windscreen. Particles of glass scratched Jake's face, but neither shock nor roaring flames were enough to obscure his view as reality morphed around him.

A beam of green light shot out from the palm of the

Hand. It hit the laboratory's back wall and burned a hole right through the brickwork. Instead of being blasted to dust, the bricks just seemed to melt, as if they had never existed in the first place. The hole widened, solid matter dissolving into nothingness, until it was twice the width and height of the Volkswagen. Beyond the hole: space as dark and empty as the void from Jake's dreams.

And then light broke through. It was dusky red. Not like a sunset, more like a blade of light escaping a burning building. And with the light came the force.

EVIL.

Evil beyond anything Jake had yet experienced.

The first evil, ageless and unending.

The evil of the demon race.

Jake and Pandora exchanged a fatalistic glance. Then she gripped the steering wheel and he released the handbrake.

The Volkswagen leapt forward.

Hurtled through the hole in the wall.

Hurtled straight into hell.

Chapter 14
The Burning Badlands

'WHAT THE H—!'

A shriek of magical energy, a gut-juddering jolt, and the Volkswagen materialized in the demon world. Scratch that. Materialized in mid-air at least six thousand metres *above* the demon world.

Jake's surprised cry was cut down by the rush of hot air that blasted through the broken windscreen. G-force pinned him to the passenger seat, pulled his lips over his teeth and stretched the skin tight around his skull. He couldn't breathe. Couldn't blink. It felt as if a pair of invisible thumbs were pushing down on his eyeballs and that, any minute now, they'd pop the orbs back into his head and straight through his brain.

The Volkswagen plummeted through a sulphurous cloud. All that Jake could see of Pandora were two hands wrapped tightly around the wheel, almost as if she thought she could steer them away from the inevitable. *No chance,* Jake thought, and returned his gaze to the fast-approaching landscape.

He could see the entire island. Shaped in a ragged triangle, it did indeed have the appearance of a horned goat's head. Cosmic oceans of red mist swirled around its shores and crept across its headlands. To the north, volcanoes crowned the goat's brow and spewed yet more red shadows into the air. Shadows that rolled down into gullies and canyons and spread wispy fingers across the long, featureless tracts of the Burning Badlands. Further south, Jake could see light reflected off stone and glass: buildings clustered together, communities, towns perhaps, scattered across the middle of the island. *Communities of demons?* His gaze moved on to the southern shore. There, half-shrouded in crimson smoke, a gigantic silver structure reached into the sky; a bright, shimmering needle driven into the tip of the demonic island. The sight reminded him of something . . .

The Hand of Glory came loose, shot past the windscreen and fluttered out a fond farewell to Jake and Pandora. Then the electrical tape snapped and the Bone of Ullr flew off the dashboard. Wielded by gravity, the heavy talisman missed Jake's head by inches and ricocheted down the length of the car, finally smashing through the back window.

Jake's eyes widened.

The rocky ground of the Burning Badlands was coming up fast. Those words of Fletcher Clerval's tripped through his head like a cruel joke: *The co-ordinates might be a bit awry . . . you could end up a hundred metres or so off course.*

The Last Nightfall

Had it ever occurred to that half-crazed scientist that they'd wind up *vertically* off course?

There was only one thing for it. He had never attempted magic like this—it would certainly take more control than a simple blast spell—but if they were going to die anyway, what was there to lose? He lifted his right arm, forced it through the hurricane, and pushed his fingers towards the demon terrain.

Now only the top half of the island filled the windscreen.

Now just the volcanic brow.

Now the Burning Badlands.

Now a scrap of earth.

Fifty metres to go.

Light burst from his hand . . .

'Reports of fatalities from yesterday's disaster are still coming in. The death toll for what is being described as the "Locust Plague of London" currently stands at two hundred and sixty-three. Thousands more are in a critical condition suffering from locust bites which will not respond to conventional medicine.

'This morning, Prime Minister Cynthia Croft held an emergency press conference. Miss Croft claimed that the phenomenon was the result of magic and laid the blame squarely at the door of a fugitive witch named Jacob Harker. A warrant for Mr Harker's arrest has been issued by the Department for the Regulation, Examination and Authorization of Magic. Miss Croft responded to questions from journalists . . .'

Simon turned up the radio.

'Let's hear what mother's got to say.'

A weary-sounding reporter asked the first question:

'Miss Croft, can you explain how this inexplicable swarm was exterminated so quickly?'

'Marcus Crowden and his team have been working on certain weapons to combat dark hexes and the like.'

Rachel sensed Simon stiffen at the sound of that prim, impatient voice.

'In this case, I believe they used a pulse of magical energy sent out from a transmitter near Marble Arch to neutralize the threat.'

'I hope Fletcher's listening to this,' Simon grunted.

Another journalist posed a question. 'Prime Minister, how do you respond to criticism from organizations like Amnesty International who say that you have suspended democracy in this country? Who even claim that you are acting like the head of a police state, rounding up innocent people without charge.'

'We're facing a national emergency here,' the Prime Minister insisted. 'Anti-witchcraft laws need to be implemented quickly, not debated over till the cows come home. As you are well aware, there has been some needless panic following my announcement about the witch-threat. People rioting, hoarding food, building bomb shelters in their gardens, paying out huge sums for "magical protection trinkets" from every kind of confidence trickster. Well, I am here to reassure the public that the government has everything under control. The people of Britain should remain calm and continue to go about their daily business. As long as no one interferes with their work, the DREAM agents will keep this country safe.'

'But even your fellow world leaders are questioning Britain's actions. Just yesterday the President of the United States joined calls for us to close the detention camp on Dartmoor.'

A third journalist jumped in. 'What exactly are you doing to the detainees there, Miss Croft? We have reports of experiments being conducted on prisoners. And Marcus Crowden, leader of the DREAM agents, when is he going to answer allegations about agent brutality? We even have reports of his agents *biting* people!'

Uproar in the Downing Street pressroom. The first journalist made himself heard over the clamour—

'Is it not time to admit that you have overreacted to the reality of witches and demons? This claim in your latest dossier suggesting that dark witches could launch a "Demontide" in forty-five minutes seems rather implausible.'

'Enough!' Cynthia Croft's order silenced the press pack. 'I will not stand here and justify my actions to a bunch of snivelling hacks. My duty is to keep the men, women and children of this country safe. Good morning.'

Simon switched off the radio. His huge hand gripped the gearstick and he thrust the car into fourth and toed the accelerator. Rachel gave her boyfriend a sidelong glance. Although his head was covered by a tracksuit hood, the tip of Simon's dog-like nose could be seen poking out. As if giving voice to Rachel's thoughts, Roland Grype piped up from the back seat.

'I've said this before and I'll say it again: a Cynocephalus driving a car is bound to attract attention.'

'Do you want me to gag you?' Simon glared at the witch in the rearview mirror.

'I was going to suggest that I could drive, that's all.'

'You, drive this beauty? I don't think so.'

'But it's not even your car!' Grype looked around the plush upholstery of the BMW 5 series, as if the cup holders and sunblinds might suddenly speak up in his defence. 'You stole it.'

It was true. A stone's throw from the factory safe house, Rachel had kept watch while Simon jemmied open the driver's door and hotwired the beemer's engine. Jumping into the saloon, her boyfriend had treated her to a wolfish grin. She'd been unable to meet his gaze, and the smile had fallen from his lips. He'd slammed the car into gear and they'd roared back to the factory to pick up Grype. After a quick goodbye to Joanna Harker, they hit the road and the early-morning traffic.

Since leaving London, Roland Grype had cowered on the back seat. When a black van of any description passed by, he would scream 'DREAM AGENTS!' and dive into the footwell. If the little librarian really was luring them into a trap, then he was a pretty good actor, Rachel thought. Out of the fifty or more suggestions Grype had made to avoid agent detection, the only one they'd followed was to steer clear of motorways and stick to the B roads. They were now driving through South Oxfordshire, approaching the town of Henley-on-Thames.

'I don't even know why we're rushing to Dartmoor,' Grype grumbled. 'I told you, the only way we'll be able to get into the prison undetected is during processing, and fresh prisoners aren't scheduled to arrive until tomorrow.'

'And *I* told you, we want to recce the whole area,' Simon said. 'Make sure we've got an escape route worked out.'

'Waste. Of. Time. I've the plan all mapped out. First, we make our way to the ambush point, then we intercept the prison van transporting the new detainees. We take care of the guards, steal their uniforms, and then we head to the pris—'

'Will you please SHUT UP!' Simon exploded.

Silence in the car, except for the squeak of Grype's finger as he drew pictures on the steamed window. Pictures of demonic birds. After a while, Rachel stirred.

'Do you think they got through OK?'

'Jesus, Rach!'

'What?'

'Must be the twentieth time you've asked that question since we left Fletcher's lab.'

'I'm just worried.'

'And I'm not, I suppose?' He turned to her, his Cyno face shadowed by the hood. 'You don't have to remind me to care.'

A titter from Grype. 'This is what you call "love", is it? What a delightfully destructive emotion. Now I see why people say it's stronger than magic.'

'Shut your weasel mouth,' Simon roared, 'or I'll reach back there and—'

'Oh God! Simon, *STOP*!'

The BMW had been sweeping over the little bridge towards Henley when a flash of yellow and red light erupted out of the river. Simon reacted like lightning. He stamped on the accelerator and sent the car hurtling onto the west bank. Rachel freed her seatbelt and was out of the BMW before it had fully stopped.

'Don't move.' Simon flung the order at Grype before following Rachel along the riverbank. 'Rach, wait!'

She could not wait. Not with the screams ringing in her ears.

Flames as tall as houses rose up from the Thames. It was as if the river had been transformed into a gigantic spill of petrol and that some cruel or foolhardy soul had set a match to it. The wind whipped the fire and all along the bank yellow hands lashed out and trees burst into flame. Pedestrians and sightseers staggered out of the black smoke that now covered the bridge, family, friends, and strangers cradled in their arms. Singed skin and hair was the worst of their injuries. Those on the river—the punters and rowers, the people on scenic cruises and mucking about in motorboats—had been less fortunate. Already blackened bodies were drifting out of the flames and bumping against the banks.

Simon wrapped his arms around Rachel.

'Come away, there's nothing we can do.'

Smoke funnelled into the cold October sky. Over screaming and crying, they heard Grype call out from the car.

'They're talking about it on the radio. It's everywhere! The Thames in London, the Severn, the Trent, the Clyde, the Tyne. Every major river in the country's gone up in flames!'

There was a kind of excitement in the librarian's voice. Rachel turned away in disgust.

'Rivers of fire. It's the second Omen, isn't it? Only two days to go . . .'

Jake woke with stars in his eyes.

It took a moment for him to realize what was wrong. The heavens—could he use that word here?—were darkly red, a bruised and brooding colour that he had never seen in an earthly sky. Stitched into this bloody blanket, stars shone down as bright and black as fire-polished jet. Black stars in a demon-red sky.

'Close it up, sister,' he murmured. 'Close up their prison . . .'

When he woke again, the sky was still sunless but the red was of a lighter hue. The black stars had vanished, and he guessed that this was what passed for morning in the demon world. Tentatively, he stretched his arms and legs. Nothing appeared to be broken or, if it had been, Oldcraft had healed him while he slept. He sat up and placed his palms flat against the ground.

'Jeeze!'

The rocky terrain was hot to the touch, and now Jake realized that his back and shoulders were badly blistered. Not that it mattered much, his magic was already at work, soothing and healing the burns.

Jake jumped to his feet, his thoughts suddenly full of Pandora. Shielding his eyes, he looked around.

Twenty kilometres to his right a razorback sierra of mountains and volcanoes stretched away with the horizon. Streams of molten lava ran down their slopes and slumped into great burbling pits that lapped against the mountain-side. Red smoke rose from each volcanic throat, and Jake wondered if it was this poison that gave the demon realm its artificial atmosphere. He felt sure that somewhere beyond the smoke was the void from his dreams; the demon prison as it had been before human imagination had given it form and substance.

Close it up.

A half-remembered dream . . . Jake shook his head. He had to concentrate on finding Pandora. He turned on the spot, carefully scanning the badlands and trying to ignore the heat that had worked its way through the soles of his trainers and was now slow-cooking his feet. The sulphurous air stung his eyes and made his lungs burn. Nothing to be seen except miles of red ground interrupted here and there by deep, dark canyons that ran like scars across a frontiers-man's face. Where the hell was she?

Then he saw it. A little way off to his left the ground had splintered, as if a heavy object had impacted there. He was running towards the crack when something brought him up short—a wing mirror glinting in the ruby glare. He picked it up, turned it over in his hands, just to check it was real and not a heat-induced hallucination. Suddenly, a dreadful thirst clawed at his throat and he retched, bringing up lungfuls of stale air. There was water in the backpacks, he remembered. Water in the boot of the car. He reeled forward and almost fell face-first into the dust.

Tyre marks in the dirt—and a third trail dragging behind, perhaps made by a broken exhaust pipe. There were footprints too—a pair of three-toed creatures with feet a little larger than a man's. Between them, they must have dragged the car away with Pandora still inside, but then why had they bothered to take Jake out of the Volkswagen? Unless . . . He looked back. The ground dipped, and from this vantage he could not see the spot where he had woken. What if his magic had only cushioned the fall a little? The impact might have thrown him clear of the car.

'Pandora . . .'

He swiped the sweat from his brow and struck out.

The map of the demon world was with the water and the backpacks in the boot of the car, and so he had little idea in which direction he was going. He knew that he must be heading south because the volcanoes were at his back. For the hundred and thirtieth time he checked his watch. He'd been walking for almost five hours (it was just after 3 p.m. London time—had the second omen arrived yet, he wondered?), but looking over his shoulder he saw the sierra loom as large as ever. Perhaps it was a trick of the light. He couldn't *still* be in the Burning Badlands, could he?

Exhausted, Jake let his chin drop to his chest.

'No.' The word creaked through his lips. 'No!'

The tyre tracks had disappeared. He spun round. No tracks behind him. Then what had he been following for the past five hours? A mirage? No, they'd been real . . . Hadn't they? Yes. Yes, he was sure of it. Tyre tracks and demon footprints. For some reason, those two images made him want to break out in hysterical laughter. He opened his mouth, ready to laugh or scream or swear, when he heard the sound of voices. A strange language that unlocked a hidden mechanism in his brain.

'High Demon Tongue,' he said to himself, and the question came back at him: what's High Demon Tongue? No idea.

The voices came from some distance away, but were raised in argument so each word rang out (as High Demon Tongue is wont to do when spoken in anger, he thought). Wiping sweat from his eyes, Jake saw the beginnings of a rough road up ahead. Wide and rutted, it was bordered on both sides by large red boulders. The demons' voices seemed to come from behind these rocks.

'You know the rules, Serpine: anything like this ought to be reported to the Hunter.'

'My days of serving humankind are over, Murkridge. The Demontide's coming.'

'But it's not here yet.'

'Yeah, yeah. Listen, I say we take her to the cave and have ourselves a private banquet. Long as you keep your big mouth shut no one need know she was ever here.'

'We have to tell him. She's a living creature, Serpine. How'd she get here? What does she want?'

'Who cares? Just keep your thoughts on the Demontide and the feast that'll be waiting when we break through the Door. In the meantime, a little snack will sharpen our appetites.'

'I suppose you're right. Anyway, I don't like going to that castle of his. For one of his kind, he's a creepy bleeder.'

Their quarrel forgotten, the demons laughed and started to move away.

'I hope you're ready for some juicy dark creature flesh, old friend,' the monster called Serpine hooted. 'By my reckoning we've got a leg and four arms apiece.'

Chapter 15
Monster Hunt

Jake crept onto the demon highway. He gritted his teeth as the stony ground crunched underfoot, a sound that seemed deafening in the stillness. Shinning his way up one of the boulders, he peeked over the top. The terrain beyond was almost as barren as the badlands, except in the near distance there was a patch of ground marked out with what appeared to be dozens of white sticks; and beyond, a rocky mound rising out of the earth. Jake could see a cleft in the face of the mound, like the entrance to a cave. The battered shell of the old Volkswagen stood just outside this natural doorway.

There was no sign of the demons.

Jake eased his way over the boulder. Magic tingled at his fingertips, but for now he kept the blue light contained. No point alerting the demon horde to his abilities just yet. He felt horribly exposed, crossing the open ground, but there was nowhere to hide until he reached that strange collection of white sticks. Coming closer, he saw that they were in fact fossilized trees, and that a forest must once have covered this entire corner of the badlands. Why on earth had the demons planted trees in their wilderness world?

He darted between the trunks and came gradually to the cave. A fleeting glance at the Volkswagen showed that the front end had been crushed into a rumpled snout, the doors wrenched off and the roof torn clean away. It was clear that the car could never make the return journey to the human world, and that all hope now rested with the Signums. The magic that those talismans might inspire in Jake was the only way out of this dark realm.

Jake wondered why the demons had bothered to drag the wreck all the way out here, and guessed that the monster called Murkridge might originally have wanted to show their find to the mysterious 'Hunter'.

'Hold her steady, Serpine. I'll get my knives.'

Jake followed the voice into the cave.

The light from the demon sky faded as he hurried along a winding tunnel. Soon it was so dark that he was forced to spark a tiny magical flame. He kept the glow shielded with his free hand and moved deeper into the rugged folds of the cavern. The air here was as dry as the baking badlands, but the temperature had dropped and the coldness raked at his throat. He wanted desperately to cough.

A light shone up ahead, and Jake killed his Oldcraft flame. He craned his head around a screen of rock and saw that the demons had dragged Pandora into an inner chamber. She didn't flinch as they dropped her onto the ground.

One look told Jake why. The injuries Pandora had sustained from the crash were severe and she had lost consciousness.

The demons towered over their dinner. As tall as Brag Badderson, they possessed lean, almost skeletal bodies covered by gleaming plates, like the hard outer shell of an insect. Their arms and legs also had the segmented appearance of insect limbs, but they were not completely bug-like. Their three-toed feet and three-fingered hands were covered in plump, pink flesh and their heads were—Jake thought he was going to puke—their heads were *human*. Not just human: those were the soft, round faces of little children.

'I'm going to start with the legs,' Serpine slurped. 'Work my way up.'

'Then I'll begin with the skull.' Murkridge nodded his horribly cute head. 'Meet you around the stomach. Don't worry, I'll save you some brain.'

In his right hand, Serpine held a torch which he played over Pandora's bare feet.

'Now, which leg first?'

Jake's body tensed. To hear these monsters talk about his friend as if she were a piece of meat to be divided up and devoured was too much. Magic sprang out of his palms.

'Take your filthy hands off her.'

Startled faces looked back at him. Serpine's cupid's bow lips curled into a smile.

'Another one. Definitely human this time.'

Murkridge blinked. 'How did you come here, boy? How did you . . . By the Father! Look at his hands, Serpine!'

The demons sprang away from Pandora and retreated

to the cavern's back wall. For creatures so monstrous it was strange to see the look of bafflement and fear on their faces.

'Oldcraft, but no demon in sight,' Serpine hissed. 'He must have seen through the lie.'

'It's more than that. There's something familiar about him, but I can't quite put my finger on it.'

Serpine soon recovered his nerve. 'Oldcraft or no, he's in our world now, and I want my dinner!'

The demon held out its arms, wrists bent back like a criminal waiting to be handcuffed. Six bone-white spines emerged from hidden pockets along its forearms and shot out like darts. The first two buried themselves in the rock a centimetre from Jake's head. The third and fourth ripped through his T-shirt and right trouser leg, one grazing his bicep, the second puncturing his thigh. He was prepared for the remaining darts. Numbers five and six were swatted aside by blasts of Oldcraft. While Jake tore the bloody spine from his leg, his magic was already at work, leeching the poison from the wound and repairing his skin.

'This isn't any ordinary witch!' Serpine cried.

Murkridge shrank back against the wall.

'I remember that power . . .'

'What're you talking about?'

'It's him! It's the C—'

A voice, at once familiar and strange, rang out from that mysterious room inside Jake's mind. A woman's voice— *Cannot know. Not yet. You must stop him. NOW!* Oldcraft surged into Jake's hand. He looked down at the furious blue-red orb dispassionately, thinking to himself: *Such power. Such power . . .*

Murkridge was still speaking when Jake launched the magic. It struck the monster in the chest and incinerated him on impact. Serpine looked on aghast as his friend blazed and burned. Within seconds, the demon had been reduced to a pile of flaming bones.

The light from the fire licked up the cavern walls and illuminated the paintings that had been etched onto the stone. Jake was groping his way back from the shadows of his mind, part of him still wondering about the female voice and the power it had prompted, when he saw the ancient artwork. Cave paintings of Neolithic hunters chasing a herd of bison—and outside the cave, the remains of a petrified forest. What was going on here?

Serpine looked from the smoking remnants of his friend to the magic in Jake's hand. Jake had never seen such terror in a child's face; but this thing was *not* a child. It was a monster. A monster that, if allowed to escape, would run through the demon world repeating the story of Murkridge's demise. Within hours, Jake's and Pandora's presence in the infernal realm would be known, and hunting parties would be sent out. Serpine seemed to read the purpose in Jake's eyes.

'I won't tell anyone you're here,' the demon promised. 'If you let me go, I'll—'

'Shut up.'

This was cold-blooded murder. A calculated, ruthless killing. His father's spirit told him so, but another voice, the mysterious woman's, was somehow stronger.

You must do this, it whispered. *That thing is just a demon, don't waste your pity on it. If the tables were turned, it would destroy you without a second thought. Kill it. Kill it. KILL IT!*

Then his father's words came to him like a soft echo: *You've learned to be better than this, Jake. You've lived a human life and learned the compassion of a fragile being. Make the lessons count . . .*

'I'm sorry,' Jake said.

Was he apologizing to the demon, his father, or the unknown woman? Perhaps he spoke to all three.

He aimed his fingers at Serpine and sent a magical charge racing. It hit the demon's right flank and burned into its exoskeleton: a serious wound, but not immediately fatal. The demon howled and collapsed to the ground.

'J-ake?'

Pandora blinked through swollen eyes. Jake summoned the warm glow of healing Oldcraft and laid his hands against her wounds. The magic passed like starlight into her body, a brilliant blue sparkle that anaesthetized pain, reset bones and stitched skin back together. All the dark glory he had felt when conjuring destructive magic paled in comparison to the joyful peace of this sorcery. Something inside—a memory, an instinct—told him that *this* was the true purpose of Oldcraft. To help, to heal, to bring comfort and solace. It was the reason magic had been given to humanity.

'Why're you crying?' Pandora whispered. 'Are you hurt?'

'No.' Pain lanced across his shoulders, but he barely felt it. 'I'm happy.'

Pandora's terrible injuries had almost healed when

Serpine made his move. Swift as a scorpion, he snatched a flaming bone from the ashen pile that had once been his demon brother. The weapon came crashing down on Jake's skull and sparks flew into the air. Through stars, Jake watched the creature's flight from the cave. He thought of how quickly Murkridge and Serpine must have crossed the badlands, dragging the Volkswagen behind them. These creatures were strong and, although he was clearly hurt, the wound wasn't going to slow Serpine down too much.

'We have to stop him,' Jake groaned. 'Properly this time.'

'You know a bit about the mythology of this world,' Jake said. 'Have you ever heard of a human being living here? Someone called "the Hunter"?'

'Humans in the demon realm?' Pandora frowned. 'I've never come across any stories or legends. Why'd you ask?'

'Murkridge wanted to take you to the Hunter's castle. Said it was the law.'

'Sorry.' Pandora shrugged.

Jake's thoughts kept returning to Eleanor in the dream void and to the words she had spoken: *I hear his step upon the stair. He is coming. You must hurry, Jake, you must find me. Find me before he . . .*

He.

It had been four hours since they had left the cave and followed the blood trail over the boulders and onto the demon highway. Since then, splatters of green had appeared every few hundred metres, but they had seen no other sign of Serpine. Neither had they encountered any more demons, and so were at least confident that the creature had not told his tale. By 8 p.m. London time, the red sky had darkened. Nicotine coloured clouds formed like blotches of infection on a weeping wound.

'There's something else bothering me.' Jake explained about the petrified trees and the cave art. 'What do you think it means?'

Another shrug. 'Not being very helpful today, am I? Falling from twenty thousand feet can rattle your brains a bit, I guess. Gotta say, Jake, that wasn't much of a landing.'

'Yeah, well a tailspinning Volkswagen people carrier isn't the easiest thing to pilot, you know.' Jake rolled his aching shoulders and peered down the shadow-thick road. 'So, any idea where in *hell* we are?'

Pandora retrieved the infernal map from her backpack and spread it across the belly of a boulder. Meanwhile, Jake took the opportunity to give his feet an airing. Although the walking boots Fletcher had packed for them were better suited to the rocky terrain than his trainers, the heat of the volcanic earth still throbbed through the thick rubber soles.

'Gods, what's happening to me?' Pandora groaned. 'I'm out of my depth here, Jake. I don't know where we are.'

She was about to repack the map when Jake took it from her. He laid it back on the boulder and tapped a finger against the fragile parchment.

'That's one of the images from the cave wall. The bison. And there's the castle you pointed out, Pandora. The Hunter's fortress . . .'

Pandora looked over his shoulder.

'We're not even halfway there. Jake, we'll have to rest soon.'

'But she could be there. At the Hunter's castle. Eleanor . . . '

'These other symbols,' Pandora bit her lower lip, 'do you think they could be——?'

A rattle of falling stones made Jake look up. Crouching on a boulder a long way down the road, Serpine blinked back at them. Realizing that he had been spotted, the demon leapt down from the rock and scuttled along the highway.

'It's weakening.' Jake thrust the map into Pandora's hands and dragged on his boots. 'Come on!'

They raced after the figure—a black stickman that jerked like a primitive animation on a simple scarlet back-ground. Green splatters appeared in the dust more regularly, thicker and deeper pools. Jake pulled ahead of Pandora. His heart bumped against his ribs and sweat washed down his face. Blue and red magic sparked in his hands as he tasted the thrill of the chase.

He'd never been much of a runner at school—generally too nerdy for sports—but now he tore up the demon high-way like a sprinter. Like something possessed. He worked his arms, pounded the dirt, while inside the mysterious woman spoke to him—*You were always too forgiving. Too softhearted. That failing, that flaw, was what made you think your little pets were like us. Well, I'm sorry, my dear, but now you must be hard.* He nodded as he ran, agreeing with the phantom voice.

Serpine ducked around a turn in the road. As he did so, he brushed against a boulder and left a green marker for Jake to follow, almost as if he were the hare in a game of paper chase. Seconds later, Jake skidded around the turn. He glanced up, his legs braced, and he came to a dead stop.

Pandora cannoned straight into him. She was halfway through a mumbled apology when she saw what had brought him to such a sudden halt. Dumbstruck, they stared in wonder as Serpine limped out of sight.

'Pinch me,' Pandora whispered. 'This has to be a dream.'

'Then we're both dreaming, because I see it too. And now I think I know what those symbols mean . . .'

He shuddered, his gaze roaming over the dark miracle before them.

'Oh, they've been clever, Pandora. What was it the Claviger said to you at Cynthia Croft's cottage? "The Demon Father's played the long game"? Well, this proves it. His preparations for the Demontide stretch back centuries, millennia. He needed to know his enemy: how they thought, how they lived, their weak points, their fortifications and defences, where they would hide and shelter, and so . . .'

Jake spread his hands. The span of his arms just about took in the sweep of the great wall.

'The long game.'

'You think there'll be others?'

'If it's as I suspect, there'll be hundreds. Because, you see . . .'

A cry of pain. It was Serpine, out of sight but still close by.

'Save the theories,' Pandora said. 'We have a demon to catch.'

They left the road and raced across the hard ground, making for the ancient gateway.

The entrance to the Roman city.

Chapter 16
The Hill that overlooked Forever

Shortly after his mother's murder, Jake and his dad had gone on something of a world tour. They'd taken in some amazing sights: the pyramids of Giza, the falls of Niagara, the rose red city of Petra, half as old as time. Three weeks of the six month holiday had been spent in Italy where they'd pounded the tourist trail from Rome to Herculaneum and the lost city of Pompeii. Desperate to escape the grief of his mother's death, Jake had thrown himself into the wonders of the ancient world, devouring guidebooks and dragging his father on endless sightseeing tours.

Now, stepping into the demons' version of a Roman city, all those half-remembered experiences came back to him. The replica was a walled settlement, built in the regular shape preferred by the methodical Roman mind. Jake and

Pandora passed under a defensive gateway and onto a wide, cobbled street.

As they followed the blood splatters along the street, Jake pointed out the fine detail of this recreated town: the stepping stones that ran from pavement to pavement, designed to keep togas dry when the drains flooded; the open shops stacked with clay amphorae for holding wine and oil.

They passed warehouses ranged along the bank of a dried-up river. Long, rectangular structures with flat roofs and barrel vaults in which Roman merchants might have haggled over the price of Chinese silk and Egyptian porphyry. Every building they saw, from grand townhouse to toppling tenement, from lowly bakery to serene temple stared back at them with empty eyes. Whatever its original purpose, this settlement was long deserted.

At last, the street brought them to the centre of the town.

'The forum,' Jake panted. 'The marketplace. Most important part of any Roman town.'

A large paved area open to the sky, the forum was surrounded by dozens of freestanding columns. Jake turned on the spot and took in the grand buildings that bordered the marketplace: the colonnaded law court, the Senate house, the Capitol.

'Stonework, decoration, architecture—every detail's absolutely accurate.'

Pandora touched his arm. 'Not every detail.'

She pointed at the statues that stood on plinths around the forum. Jake knew that the statuary of Rome almost always depicted gods and goddesses, military generals and steely-eyed emperors. But this was one area in which the infernal architects that had designed the city had departed from the Roman model. Instead of gods and emperors, the plinths supported an array of demonic forms. Jake recognized some of the characters: the ravenous Mr Pinch, little pebbles of drool dripping from his jaws; the spider-like Miss Creekley with her eight long legs and her beautiful human face.

'Jake.' Pandora drew a sharp breath. 'That statue on the other side of the square, that's not a demon, is it?'

He followed the direction of Pandora's finger, and felt the skin shrink around his bones. The shadow of the stone man seemed to stretch out to greet him. Beneath the shade of a marble hat, a pair of sightless eyes returned his gaze. Jake remembered those eyes from long ago. Eyes that had danced with joy as the Cravenmouth witch was led to the gallows.

'No . . . How can *he* be here?'

'It *is* him, then?'

'The Hunter,' Jake nodded. 'Matthew Hopkins. He's here, in hell. And he's got Eleanor.'

'How can that be?'

'I don't know, but right now we have to—'

Serpine's agonized cry rang out across the hollow city.

'Maybe the monster'll be able to tell us.'

They sped out of the forum.

Bigger blotches of blood now. Great green puddles lying in the spaces between the cobbles. They followed the screams for another three blocks before the trail led to the open door of a two-storey townhouse.

Jake had seen many such residences in Pompeii and Herculaneum: thousand-year-old homes that had been perfectly preserved under layers of ash after the eruption of Mount Vesuvius in AD 79. Except, in this case, the townhouse had never been buried; probably never even occupied. This demon city had only one purpose that Jake could think of, and now he was going get Serpine to confirm his theory.

Beyond the door a long line of corridors ran the length of the building, giving Jake and Pandora an almost uninterrupted view of the entire premises. They followed the blood trail into the atrium, an oblong room with its roof open to the sky. Dominating this space was a shallow pool filled with dirty, rust-red water.

The faded figures of demons decorated the atrium's crumbling walls. As Jake's eye ran over the classical paintings, he saw that they depicted a battle scene not unlike the one daubed onto the walls of Josiah Hobarron's tomb. Armies of demons faced off against a trio of warriors; a lone band of fighters whose faces were hidden behind tongues of painted fire.

'The battle,' Jake whispered. 'The battle before the Great Deceit . . . '

'You speak with knowledge, boy. Knowledge no man should possess.'

Serpine crawled out of one of the little cells that branched off from the atrium. The demon's armoured shell scraped over the mosaic floor and weak trickles of blood pumped from his side. He hauled himself to the edge of the pool and took a long, deep drink.

'Show mercy,' he murmured. 'Kill me.'

'First I have some questions.'

'I can't! It hurts too much. Please, just end my suffering.'

'No.'

'But you're human. You feel the pain of poor creatures, don't you?'

'Some people would say I'm *not* human. Not completely.' Jake squatted down beside the demon. 'I was made, you see? Put together from the scraps of a dead man's skin. And in the last few days, I've started to wonder . . . ' He placed his lips to the creature's ear. 'Who was that man: the Witchfinder, Josiah Hobarron? What secrets did he keep . . . ? But that doesn't really matter, because you're not interested in *me* are you, Serpine? You just want an end to your pain. Well, I *could* do that.' Blue light tinged with red flamed in Jake's hand. 'Or I *could* keep it going. For hours. Days. Weeks. It all depends on your answers.'

He saw Pandora stiffen, but she didn't say anything. The truth was, they needed this demon to talk.

'What do you want to know?'

'The cave, this city, you built them for your war games.'

'Yes.'

Jake placed his hand against Serpine's wound and the flesh hissed. 'I'm sorry?'

'YES! J-just follow the road out of the city. Go to the temple on the hill. You'll find your answers there.'

'All right. Now I want to know about this man your friend Murkridge was so spooked by. This hunter.'

'The Human Hunter.' Serpine spat the name through his

baby teeth. 'That's his title, conferred by the Demon Father himself.'

'What does he do?' Pandora asked.

'Isn't it obvious?'

'But this is the demon prison, there are no humans here.'

Serpine managed a bitter chuckle. 'Of course there are humans here. This is hell.'

'Hell's just a myth,' Pandora said. 'Throughout history, seers have caught glimpses of this place and thought it a realm of punishment. They were mistaken.'

'Then where do you think human souls go after they die? The good, the bad, the majority who are a bit of both?'

'The Veil,' Jake said, a part of him already knowing that this answer was wrong.

'They pass *through* the Veil. After that journey a few wind up here.'

'Why?'

'Because, deep down, it is where they believe they deserve to be, and they expect us to punish them for their sins. Of course, some of us jump at the chance! A little payback for all the indignities we suffer during our time as familiars. But more and more of them started popping up in our world; there weren't enough demons to round them all up and dole out the torture . . . But then a very special man came to us. A man who'd devoted his short life to hunting down and torturing "innocent souls". The Demon Father took him into the Shadow Palace, and soon enough we had our Human Hunter. Someone to organize hell on our behalf.'

'Matthew Hopkins believed in God,' Jake objected. 'He might've been evil, but he would never serve demonkind.'

'Ah, but the Demon Father warped Matthew's fragile little mind. Convinced him that he was still on his godly crusade. For the glory of heaven, he would now become a rat-catcher in hell.'

It was a cruel trick, to take an avowed enemy of demons and make him their plaything. If it had been any man other than Matthew Hopkins, Jake might have felt pity.

'So when human spirits arrive here the old Witchfinder goes out and tracks them down. Then what?'

'He takes them to his fortress. The Castle of the Tortured Souls lies beyond the Shore of Damnation. A thousand agonies await them there.'

'Is this it?' Pandora thrust the map under Serpine's nose. She pointed at the castle symbol, and the demon nodded.

'Do you ever go there?' Jake asked. 'Have you ever seen a girl at the castle? She has blue eyes, blonde hair.'

'I never see the prisoners. Only a few demons work for the Hunter now—Murkridge was one of them. Pity you slaughtered him, eh? He might've been able to answer your questions.'

'How far?' Pandora tapped the map.

'I could run it in a day and a half. For you? A three, maybe four day journey.'

'How can we get there quicker?'

'Damn you,' Serpine cried, 'just kill me!'

Jake pushed a healing hand against the demon's flank.

'I'll keep mending, just enough so that you don't die.

You'll feel the same pain over and over again, unless you tell us what we need to know.'

'Look in the stables behind the next townhouse,' Serpine groaned.

'Tell us about the castle defences.'

'I don't know. The Hunter's a wily old lunatic, he keeps changing them. It's been ages since I was in his domain, I swear!'

Pandora touched Jake's shoulder. 'This is cruel. Let him die now.'

It knows more than it's telling, Jake thought. A little more agony and the thing would spill its guts. Literally. But . . . *I'm Jacob Harker, Adam Harker's son.*

He looked down on the shivering demon. The baby-faced insect drew its long, spindly legs up to its chest and closed its big eyes.

Magic burst from Jake's fingers.

Between them, Jake and Pandora led the skeleton horses into the street. Hooves clomped on cobbles and bones creaked and rattled against each other. The sight of these fleshless steeds shining in the gloom of the stables had sparked a memory. Jake found himself thinking of that brief riding lesson with Eleanor in the lane outside Starfall church. He remembered how she'd rolled her eyes and clucked her tongue as she instructed her inept pupil on the basics of trotting fifty paces without falling off. In the end, she had been unable to hold her laughter down. Warm, generous laughter that now haunted Jake's ears and made his heart ache.

The Hill that Overlooked Forever

Jake laid his hands against the long, hard faces of the undead animals. He could sense no evil—just the mindless motions of creatures that could not die. Maybe they'd had a purpose once, when the demons built the city, but they'd been left in the stables for hundreds of years, abandoned and forgotten. He stroked a smooth nose and a phantom whinny rolled through the horse's teeth. Pandora fitted saddles and reins.

'The ectoplasm holding these nags together is pretty weak,' she said. 'We better keep to a gentle canter.'

'You kidding?' Jake threw himself onto his mount. 'These poor boneshakers haven't had a decent run in a thousand years. Catch us if you can!'

He dug his knees against the horse's shoulder bone and the creature broke into a gallop. They rattled around the little avenues, rejoined the main street, and streaked towards the gate that led out of the city. A hard demon wind blew against Jake's face. The air was growing cooler as night set in and they moved further south, away from the badlands and the island's volcanic crown. There was no setting sun but, to the north, those black stars had reappeared like specks of pepper in a smoky-red stew.

Nightfall in the demon world.

Jake rolled his neck. There was that pain again, spreading hot fingers through his spine and shoulders. Pandora pulled alongside.

'We have to rest.'

'Can't. Got to get to the castle.'

'We will. Maybe tomorrow night.'

'But he's got her, Pandora. That monster. He—'

'You can't fight if you're half-dead. Food. A few hours rest. Then we go on.'

Jake was about to argue further when he saw the temple on the hill. The temple the demon had told them to go to if they wanted answers. It stood alone on a grassless mound, an ancient ruin set against an alien sky. They left the horses at the bottom of the slope and began the short climb. It took less than a minute to reach the summit.

It was not the temple that made them reach for each other's hands. That building was just an ordinary replica decorated with the usual statues and ionic columns. No, what filled them with wonder and horror was the view.

'They never knew when the Demontide was going to come,' Jake said. 'So every time humanity moved on, progressed, evolved, the demons would build. It started with caves, then fortified towns; castles, then modern cities.'

'Sneaky little architects travelling through dimensions,' Pandora murmured. 'And because human belief and imagination had given the demon world substance, they could start recreating what they'd seen on Earth.'

'They built themselves model worlds. Worlds in which to play their war games and test themselves before the real slaughter began.'

Jake and Pandora looked out across the middle-ground of the demon realm. To north, to south, to east, to west, stretching further than the eye could see: hundreds, maybe thousands, of cities and settlements, towns and hamlets, boroughs and metropolises, colonies and encampments. Some of the cities sprawled out for miles while other communities huddled in tight, medieval-sized pockets. Some were lit by electric light, most skulked in darkness. There seemed to be no logical historical progression in the design. An ancient Sumerian city rubbed shoulders with a Georgian sea fort; a classical Greek town stood cheek-by-jowl with what appeared to be a perfect model of modern-day Berlin. A haphazard scattering of human history. A view of forever.

In one thing only were the settlements the same: not a single one was inhabited. They had been used to train troops, to perfect tactics, and then they had been abandoned. Demons moving with the march of progress, dogging humanity's footsteps, licking at our heels.

'Thousands of years of preparation, all for this one moment.' Jake turned to his friend. 'They're ready, Pandora. Ready to destroy our world.'

Chapter 17
Road Rage

Chu-huh-huh—Chu-huh-huh—Ch—

Jake's eyes snapped open. He had been lying on the floor inside the deep porch of the temple, his body blanketed by shadows. Something had woken him—a low, breathy whisper—but, as he eased himself to his feet, the sound distanced and vanished. Perhaps it was just the breeze sighing around the hilltop. Careful not to wake Pandora, he went to stand in one of the spaces between the temple columns. The horses tethered at the foot of the slope turned their creaky heads and looked up at him, but Jake only had eyes for the view.

Again, he found himself lost in the terrible wonder of the thing. The sheer determination that had gone into reconstructing all those towns and cities rocked him to the core. It showed that the demons were not just mindless murderers. They were studious, patient; they—

Chu-huh-huh—Chu-huh-huh—

Turning to the roof, Jake saw yellow claws scramble across the triangular pediment that sat on top of the columns. He backed down the hill and tried to get a better view of the thing moving about on the temple tiles.

Pandora appeared on the porch, and Jake waved her back. He didn't want her stepping out from under the shelter only for a demon to descend and take her unawares. Oldcraft bristled at his fingertips. He could send up a magical flare, light up the roof like a Christmas tree, but then the demon horde would know something was amiss. On the other hand, this new creature posed a threat similar to that of Serpine: if it escaped, it could spread the news of Jake and Pandora throughout the infernal realm. Only one thing to do, then. They had to capture it.

He stole back up the hill and whispered instructions to Pandora. While she took the front of the temple, he'd scale the rear. Pandora's arms were strong, her fingers agile; before Jake had even made it to the back wall she had climbed a column and was reaching for the pediment. The temple's walls were sheer, but Jake was prepared for that. He rubbed his palms together and laid his hands flat against the stone. He didn't know if he could work the spell correctly, or even if such magic existed, but it was worth a try.

Stick, he thought, *climb*. Syrupy light pulsed from his palms and fixed him to the wall. Hand over hand, he began to move up the side of the temple. It didn't feel like a conscious thing—Oldcraft did the work while he just hung there, wrists aching, legs dangling. Puppet of the spell, he was soon hauled up and over the roof.

Pandora was already there, standing astride the pediment. Behind her, a sky of deepest red picked out with black stars; in front—nothing. No sign of the creature anywhere.

'It's here,' Pandora said. 'You just have to look *very* carefully.'

'*Chu-huh-huh—Chu-huh-huh.*'

And then Jake saw it. Or, to be more precise, *didn't* see it, because the demon was almost invisible. Encased in a smoky shadow, the little creature appeared to have taken on the humble shape of a squirrel. Jake could just make out a pair of black eyes hovering inside a small, feral face. Strips of scarred flesh held together its diseased body while a prickly tail reached up and twitched behind its head. A twig-like finger suddenly became visible and wagged at Jake.

'We'll play our chase game later, human,' the demon crooned. 'First, I must tell my brothers and sisters what I have found.'

With a final *Chu-huh-huh—Chu-huh-huh*, the creature dissolved into its rippling shadow.

'Do I want to know?' Jake asked.

'That,' Pandora said, 'was a rabicus. And now we're really in trouble.'

To the west, pale red streamers yawned over the empty cities.

It was a new day in hell.

They had spent a cold, comfortless night on the hillside. Snuggled into the entrance of a disused tin mine, the BMW had been rocked by breezes that whistled relentlessly up and down the old shaft. The mine's location had been chosen by Grype, and Rachel had to admit that it was a perfect observation point. Situated halfway up the hill, the low-slung doorway provided an uninterrupted view of the road as it wound through the bleak and beautiful moorland.

Five miles to the west stood Princetown Prison, the Demon Father's detention camp. Between here and there, a high tor screened off the road from the prison's surveillance cameras and the sharp eyes of the DREAM agents stationed there.

While Simon and Grype slept, Rachel scanned the landscape. On the heathery plain opposite the hill, a circle of prehistoric standing stones stood black against the dawn. The morning sun smouldered on the horizon, and Rachel shivered. Her thoughts kept returning to the Omen that only yesterday had ravaged Britain's rivers and thrown burning bodies onto its banks. She tried her best to shake off the horror of what she had seen—there was work to be done, lives to be saved—but she couldn't stop the silent tears coursing down her face.

She knew there was hope, but it seemed so small, so fragile. Dr Harker was dead, Dr Holmwood broken, the Hobarron Institute destroyed, the Elders finished; the trolls had retreated and the dark creatures didn't want to know. Ranged against them: the power and resources of Cynthia Croft's government, the full might of demonkind, and, despite odd voices of protest, the eyes and ears of the British public. So what hope was there? Just Jake, Pandora, Simon, and herself, four little souls standing in the shadow of annihilation.

She felt suffocated by despair. The walls and ceiling of the mineshaft seemed to press down, the impossible weight of stone threatening to smother her. She fumbled with the door handle and staggered out of the car, finally making it into the sharp, moorland air.

Further down the hill, a family of wild ponies blinked at the dawn. The sight reminded Rachel of her father. Malcolm Saxby had enjoyed giving his daughter presents and, for her tenth birthday, had bought Rachel a pony and taught her to ride. It was a happy memory, but the past was the past. Rachel knew that she would never trust her father again, that part of her had even come to hate him.

A black dot was making its way down the road. Rachel checked her watch and ran back to the mine. She banged on the bonnet of the car, jerking Simon and Grype out of their slumbers.

'Wharisit?'

She pointed down the hill. The dot had defined itself into a prison van. Simon leaned onto the back seat and cut the rope that bound Grype's wrists.

'Betray us and I'll kill you.'

'There's no time for threats!' Rachel called.

The van was growing larger by the second. Simon popped the boot and retrieved Rachel's bow and quiver. Then he shuffled his way out of the mine, pushing Grype ahead of him.

'We've got about two minutes to get into position.' He shoved the little librarian down the hill. 'Time to get into character, Grype. You're roadkill and I'm the distressed hitchhiker who's found your grubby little corpse.'

'Better put up your hood, then,' Grype snapped. 'We wouldn't want that great slavering dog-face of yours to put them on their guard.'

Simon swore and covered his head. Free of his captor's grasp, Grype reached into his raincoat and brought out a small green bottle. Before Simon or Rachel could react, he had uncorked the potion and thrown it into their faces. The watery mixture had a smell that Rachel couldn't quite identify: a putrid, pestilent stink that made her think of squirming maggots and open catacombs. *He's double-crossed us*, she thought, *just like Simon said he would* . . . And then she saw Grype splash the mixture onto his own face.

'*Parfum du* graveyard,' he said, licking the foul stuff from his lips. 'The natural aroma of the undead. It should help to mask the smell of our blood.'

Simon wiped his dripping muzzle. 'You could've warned us.'

'And miss the look of terror on that ugly mug? No fear.'

Simon shoved Grype the last couple of metres to the roadside. While the witch arranged himself on the tarmac, Rachel stood on tiptoes and kissed Simon's cheek.

'Good luck.'

'You too.' He took her hand. 'I love you. You do know that, Rach.'

'I love you, too.'

For now, said a little voice at the back of her mind. *But if he changes much more, if the darkness takes him completely, will you love him then? Or will you just love a memory? Look at him, little girl. What big eyes he has, what big claws, what big teeth . . .*

It was like her own inner fairy talking to her. Her own dark imp making mischief. She pushed away from Simon and ran across the road, heading for the shelter of the pre-historic henge. She took cover behind the first upright stone and notched a silver-tipped arrow. Wet tyres sloshed along the road, coming closer, closer. With her back pressed against the stone, Rachel looked to the horizon. The sun rolled over the craggy tors, a puncture wound in the pale flesh of the sky. Her hand slipped up and down the bowstring.

Closer. Closer.

The blare of a horn scattered the birds nesting on the henge. Rachel licked her lips. Her fingers shook. It was the first time she had used her bow since Jake repaired it. Now she prayed that its magic had held, that her skills wouldn't desert her.

'We need help!' Simon shouted. 'This man's hurt. Please, you have to stop!'

It was probably just her imagination, but his voice, hard and barking, didn't sound human. Would the sharp ears of the vampires be able to tell?

The whirr of an electric window. A muffled voice called out—

'Drag the corpse out of the road. We're DREAM agents on official business, we don't have time for this.'

'But he could still be alive.'

'I said, get rid of it.'

'You can't order me about.'

Rachel heard the touch of aggression. *Don't lose it. Just get them out of the van.*

'Subsection 12A of the new Witchcraft Act gives any DREAM agent the power to command a citizen to do his will. So, yes, I can order you about. Now, for the last time, get that cadaver moved!'

'Say "please".'

A door squeaked open. Boots slapped the ground.

A second cold voice called out: 'Mortimer, wait. You know what the PM said after that press conference yesterday—no more bloodshed until the Demontide.'

'Oh, but this won't take long,' Mortimer said, his voice as hollow as an empty grave. 'I just have to teach our friend here a little lesson in the art of obedience. He has to learn that when a DREAM agent gives a comma—*argh*!'

'Mortimer! What the hell?'

The squeak of another door. The rush of heavy boots.

'Rach!'

Her fear vanished. Her hands steadied. The cool, calm detachment of the trained marksman settled over Rachel. She took a measured breath, stepped away from the stone, pulled back the bowstring, sighted her target, and fired. As the arrow whipped across her thumb, she realized for the first time that she no longer needed the magic of Nuada. It was her own skill that worked the weapon. She wasn't sure if she should be proud or ashamed of such a talent.

The scene on the road: Grype lay motionless on the ground, playing his role of corpse to perfection. Standing beside him, Simon grappled with the DREAM agent Mortimer. His hood had fallen back and his wolfish mouth snapped at the vampire. A second agent, the van driver, had just left the prison transport and was hurrying to assist his vampire brother when Rachel's arrow struck home. Both agents were wearing the uniform of their office and, as it was now dawn, the gasmask-style helmets.

The arrow slammed into the back of the driver's head. A millisecond later, the tip shattered the helmet's left eye-hole and the vampire collapsed on top of Grype. Fine white smoke fizzled out of the broken lens as the undead became the dead once more.

Meanwhile, Simon raged against Mortimer. The creature didn't dare remove its mask—not with the sun blazing the horizon—but even without its teeth, it remained a deadly opponent. Its gloved hands locked around Simon's neck and squeezed. Despite layers of thick muscle protecting his windpipe, Simon's long tongue rolled around in his mouth and his eyes bulged. He smashed his fists against the vampire's sides, and Rachel was sure she heard the dull crack of the creature's ribs, but still it went on crushing.

Rachel notched another silver-headed arrow. She glanced down the shaft, following the fight, but couldn't get a lock on Mortimer. And then she noticed that Simon was flailing his right arm, as if reaching for something. Was it possible? Could his Cyno reactions really be that quick?

'I know you, don't I?' Mortimer grunted. 'You're the mutant friend of Jake Harker. Recognize you from the Grimoire.

You know, I was one of those who killed your troll friend. He died screaming.'

Rachel aimed a little to Simon's right and released the bowstring. It seemed no more than a silver blur, a whisper of wood travelling at ninety metres-per-second, but Simon stretched out his hand and plucked the arrow out of the air.

The DREAM agent released his grip. He looked at the arrow clasped in the big fist, then at the smiling, wolf-like face. Round gasmask eyes seemed to mirror Mortimer's horrified cry.

'For Brag.'

The arrow punctured the vampire's throat. There was no blood, just that fizzing vapour. Simon threw the agent to the roadside and rubbed his bruised neck.

'That was unbelievable,' Rachel said.

'Yeah. Just a shame you didn't cotton on a bit quicker. That thing nearly crushed the life out of me.'

'I'm sorry, I—'

'We don't have time for a lover's tiff,' Grype said. He had crawled out from under the driver and was now busy removing the creature's jacket and helmet. 'You two need to get into these uniforms. We'll throw the bodies into the mine, then you drive straight to the prison. When you get to the gate, speak as little as possible, and for God's sake don't remove your helmets.'

'Whoa, whoa! What about you?'

'I'll meet you inside.'

Simon strode over to the witch and prodded a clawed finger into his chest.

'I *knew* it. This is a set-up, isn't it? Well, no way. You're coming with us.'

'I can't! Look, I thought there'd be three agents in the transport, not two. In that case, I would've put on a uniform and accompanied you.'

'Why don't we just chuck you in the back? Pretend you're a detainee?'

'Because I'd be recognized. Listen, all anyone knows is that I've been away for a few days. There might be some awkward questions, but I should still be allowed access to the camp. Now, do you remember the plan I sketched out? Good. I'll meet you in the Elders' wing as soon as I can.'

'If you're lying, Grype, I swear—'

'Why would I lie? I've no hope of surviving the Demontide, let alone being rewarded for my efforts. I've sacrificed my demon. There's nothing more I can do to prove myself.'

'What do you think, Rach?' Simon looked over his shoulder. 'Rach?'

Sitting in the front seat of the van, Rachel had barely heard the to and fro of the argument. Simon paced around to the driver's door and followed her gaze into the back of the transport. Thirty drugged and blindfolded prisoners had been squeezed onto two narrow benches. Their feet were shackled to the floor, their hands bound with plastic strips.

'We can't do this,' Rachel said. 'We can't take these people to be tortured.'

Grype shuffled in behind Simon. 'You have to. If you want to get into the prison, if you want to save your father and your friend, this is the only way.'

Simon took her hand. 'We have to get inside. We've gotta free Eddie or they'll use him to summon Pinch and the witch ball.'

'Can't we at least release the children?'

'The prisoner manifest will be checked and rechecked,' Grype said. 'If there's any discrepancy you'll be summoned to the Demon Father's office. He will want to speak to you *face* to *face*. No masks.'

'We can't do this,' Rachel insisted. 'These are innocent people.'

Simon pulled his hand away. When she looked up, Rachel saw a cold, dead light in his eyes.

'This is war. Innocent people suffer . . . for the greater good. Now, help me with the bodies.'

Chapter 18
The Redemption of Prisoner 35712

The transport pulled up at the prison gate, and Simon sounded the horn.

'Uniforms pinch,' he grumbled.

The helmet's eyeholes obscured her peripheral vision, so Rachel had to turn her head to look at him. It was true, the DREAM agent's clothes were ill-fitting: Simon's muscles bulged against the leather tunic and the gloves didn't quite contain his clawed fingers. She felt the need to say something, an off-the-cuff remark about her own uniform—too loose, too baggy—but found herself suddenly afraid. Those things he had said at the roadside might easily have come from her father or Dr Holmwood. *Innocent people suffer for the greater good.* Words that had no place on the *real* Simon's lips.

She held the list of names to her chest and tried to ignore the heavy breathing of the drugged prisoners behind her.

Princetown was a Victorian prison of sombre granite and grey slate. It rose like a perfectly rectangular tor out of the Dartmoor countryside and dominated the land all around. Heavy metal doors had been set into its imposing gateway and on the high walls security cameras blinked down between garlands of barbed wire. An ordinary-sized door beside the main gate opened, and two DREAM agents stepped out.

'You do the talking,' Simon said. 'Make your voice sound dead, hollow.'

You'd be better at that than me, Rachel thought, and hated herself for thinking it.

Leather-clad knuckles tapped her window. She wound it down and handed over the paperwork.

'These all from Lincolnshire?' the agent asked. 'Seems to be a bad county for witches.'

'And Cyno-slave wannabes,' his colleague said. 'Did you have any trouble on the road? No? That's good. We keep hearing about protesters blocking the transports as they leave the cities. Ah well, the Demontide will roll in tomorrow, and then we can tear them all to shreds.'

The first agent leaned through Rachel's window. She could hear his whispered count.

'Fourteen adult males, eleven adult females, three female children, two male. They'll check names and D.O.Bs during processing, but I could swear . . . ' He sniffed. 'Smells like more than thirty.'

Rachel could feel the sweat rolling down her face, diluting Grype's potion. The second agent sniffed and shook his head.

'All this daylight's addling your senses, Seamus.'

'Maybe.' The masked head twitched. 'Why are you two so quiet?'

'Hungry.'

The second agent dragged Seamus back from the window. 'Come on, let them clock off and get to the canteen. They were bleeding the youngsters yesterday, so the blood's as thick and as red as you could want it.'

The agents strode back to the gate. Before he entered the doorway, Seamus turned and looked back at the prison van. Rachel held her breath. Counted the seconds. The agent ducked under the door and she felt her heart beat again.

' "Bleeding the youngsters",' she echoed. 'You still think this was for *the greater good*, Simon?'

'Rach, you have to understand—'

The gate swung open.

'Just drive.'

The van rumbled over the cobbles, a judder that seemed to rattle Rachel's already shaken spirit.

Following Grype's instructions, Simon brought the van to a halt in the big open courtyard. So far, the librarian's information was proving accurate: this was the entry point to the soulless sprawl of bricks and bars, concrete and cages that made up Princetown Prison. Four towering walls with tiny windows faced the courtyard: the wings of the original prison building. In recent years, new blocks had been built onto this shell, but Grype had told them that the Demon Father's detention camp was focused entirely in the old jailhouse.

Each original wing was accessed by a reinforced metal door that faced the courtyard. Dr Saxby and the Elders were being held in the north wing, which was where Simon and Rachel had agreed to rendezvous with Grype. Eddie Rice's enchanted painting was kept under lock and key in the old hospital block where the Cynocephali experiments were also conducted.

Rachel looked again at the prisoners in the back of the transport. Some of the adults were stirring.

'W-where am I?' a woman asked. 'What's happening?'

'Why's it so dark?' a man shouted. 'Oh God, they've taken us, haven't they? Listen, is there a DREAM agent here? I'm a wealthy man, I can pay you whatever you want. Keep the rest, I won't tell anyone, but just let *me* go!'

And now they were all stirring. Stirring and writhing, wrenching and screaming, crying out for mercy, for themselves and for others. *I'm sorry*—the words had only just formed in Rachel's head when Simon pulled her out of the van. She staggered on the rain-slick cobbles, almost fell. He righted her and stepped away.

'Pull yourself together. They're watching.'

A dozen agents had poured out of the west wing—the 'Processing Block', Grype had called it—and were marching over to the van. Rachel didn't think that Seamus was among them, but the identical uniforms made it difficult to be sure. One of the agents opened the back door and began pulling prisoners out of the transport. Frightened questions and requests were answered with a punch or a slap.

'We've got this covered,' the agent said. 'You two get some R & R.'

'Thanks.' Rachel found it hard to keep the disgust out of her voice.

They headed over to the north wing and sheltered in the shadows under the door. A huge iron-armed clock on the south wall ground out the passing minutes. Agents passed back and forth, moved the van back through the gate and pushed half-starved prisoners from one block to another. After twenty minutes, Simon smashed his fist against the wall.

'He should be here by now.'

'Grype said there might be awkward questions,' Rachel said. 'Maybe they're more suspicious than he thought.'

'No, he's been lying all along. We should never have——'

Bolts screeched and the door behind them swung open.

'You two agents, what are you doing lurking in doorways?'

A woman stood silhouetted against the glare of a fluorescent strip light. Her small, compact figure was pressed into a business suit so formal that it looked something like a military uniform. With the light shadowing her face, Rachel could only pick out a few features—a beaky nose, a jutting chin, prominent cheekbones and thin lips. Her voice was deep and commanding, but seemed naturally shrill at its top-end, as if she'd had elocution lessons that had never quite stuck.

'Well?' She stepped forward and the shadows fell away. 'Cat got your tongue?'

Rachel saw the striking green eyes and felt her soul shrink.

'That's the problem with vampires, no conversation. Come on, out of my way!'

Prime Minister Cynthia Croft flapped her hands and Simon and Rachel fell back. She barged past them, her ginger tomcat Chequers trailing in her wake. Like its mistress, the cat was a sharp-featured creature with little grace or patience.

'And get some fresh uniforms,' the PM called over her shoulder. 'Those ones were poorly tailored. I must have my agents looking the part.'

They watched Simon's mother unlock the door of the hospital wing and disappear inside.

'Are you OK?'

'Jesus, Rachel, don't ask stupid questions.'

Simon covered his face with his hands. For a moment, she feared that he might tear off his mask and scream at the sky. Instead, he grasped the handle of the security door and pulled. The multiple-lock mechanism snapped, and Rachel found herself being bundled into a long grey corridor.

While Simon marched ahead, Rachel looked through the little window in every door they passed. Nothing but cobwebbed storerooms full of broken mops, old detergent boxes and obsolete computer equipment.

'Grype's diagram showed the Elder cells on the fifth floor,' Simon said.

True to the librarian's plan, at the end of the corridor they found an old-fashioned lift cage. Simon clattered back the grille door and they stepped into the wood-panelled compartment. Instead of buttons the lift had a crank handle that Simon thrust forward. Rachel watched through the grille as dreary corridors, identical to the one they had just left, rolled by. On the fourth floor, the gleaming boots, lean torso, and maskless face of an agent came into view.

'Stop the lift,' the vampire requested.

'Sorry, no room.' Simon pushed the crank to its limit.

The fifth floor was quite unlike the others. With its dank, moss-coated walls, it conformed more to Rachel's idea of a dungeon than the cluttered storerooms below. To her right, a series of cramped cells ran away into the gloom. She took the standard-issue torch from the belt of her DREAM agent uniform and clicked the switch. Her light flashed through the bars of the first cell and laid yellow stripes across a dozen sleeping faces. She recognized the inmates: friends and neighbours from Hobarron's Hollow.

Rachel hurried down the corridor. They would release as many Elders as they could, but first she had to find her father. Reaching the last cell but one, she skidded to a stop.

Beyond the bars, six powerful creatures blinked their way into wakefulness. They had once been Elders of Hobarron, but inside the hospital wing of Princetown Prison, Cynthia Croft had worked her alchemy and transformed them into Cynocephali slaves. The black-and-brown-striped Cyno nearest the cell door fixed its eyes on Rachel and smacked its lips. The creature's sensitive nose must have detected human blood through the mask of Grype's potion.

Rachel approached the cell and played her light over each

formidable form. In the depths of their eyes, in the twists of their features, in the subtle differences between them, she tried to find clues that might lead her back to the people they had once been.

Suddenly, the black-and-brown Cyno threw itself at the bars. Hairy hands reached out and the monster's immense jaw snapped an inch shy of Rachel's face. Simon pulled her away with such force that she slammed into the opposite wall. Breathless, she watched as he tore the helmet from his head and smashed his spade-like palms against the bars. A snarl rippled his upper lip, and the imprisoned Cyno whimpered and fell back.

Like a wolf obeying the command of its pack leader, Rachel thought.

'You all right? Talk to me, Rach.'

'It's like they know you.'

'What?'

'Maybe they sense that you were the first. Simon, do you realize what this—?'

'Rachel?' A weak voice trickled out from the last cell.

'Dad?'

Her father appeared, framed by the bars. Malcolm Saxby was only forty, and yet his haggard face looked as if it belonged to a seventy year old. Even the few days since Rachel had seen him in the borderlands desert seemed to have added lines and whitened hair. Drawn and bearded, he was dressed in filthy prison clothes, the number 35712 marked in felt tip on the breast of his tunic.

'Why have you come here?'

Rachel pulled off the mask. 'To save you.'

'No! You have to get out. Run while you still can.'

Her father's eyes were wide and staring, and Rachel thought she could see the glimmer of insanity dancing there.

'Rach.' Simon stood against the wall, his ear pressed to the brickwork. 'Movement on the ground floor. A dozen, maybe more . . . ' His jaw clenched. 'She's with them.'

At the end of the corridor, the lift rattled and the grille snapped shut. The light inside flickered twice before the compartment began to trundle downwards.

Simon's hand shot past Rachel and grabbed one of the bars of Dr Saxby's cell. Grunting, he tore it free and sent the iron rod skidding down the corridor. Again, Rachel found herself amazed by his superhuman reflexes. The bar slipped smoothly through a gap in the grille and jammed the elevator ceiling against the floor of the corridor. Cables shrieked and the compartment leapt a couple of inches, but the bar held. From downstairs came a burble of confused voices.

'We have to go,' Simon said.

'My dad . . . '

Simon cursed and wrenched open the cell door.

Malcolm Saxby staggered into his daughter's arms. 'It's no good. I'll just slow you down. You should leave me here.'

'He's right.' Simon looked down the hall to the door marked **'FIRE EXIT'**. 'I can hear their boots on the stairs.'

'We're not leaving him!' Rachel's voice cracked with anger.

'Fine. Then we've no time to get to Eddie. If they know they've got intruders, this place will go into lockdown. We might just be able to get into the hospital block and out again, but we can't do it while carrying *him*. Make up your mind, Rach, they're on the third floor.'

She didn't hesitate. 'We're taking him.'

Simon scooped up Malcolm Saxby. His smile was the coldest Rachel had ever known.

'This man lives and the world dies,' Simon said. 'You should remember this moment, Rachel. Fix it in your mind. This was *your* choice and I . . . I went along with it.'

He bounded down the corridor, her father secure in his arms. For a split second, Rachel could only stare after the retreating figures and feel the doom of the Demontide smother her heart. Simon was right: her choice had condemned Eddie to dark witchcraft and the world to demon rule . . .

Simon pulled open the fire exit door. 'Come on, Rachel! Move it!'

Reaching the stairwell, she found Simon halfway up a ladder, her father slung like a scarecrow over his shoulder. One floor below, a rabble of DREAM agents sprinted to intercept them. Simon slammed his fist against a hatch in the ceiling and a square of heavy-weathered sky opened up. He hefted Malcolm through the hole and reached down for Rachel. His hand encircled her wrist and she flew into the air.

Rain chattered across the flat roof of the prison block. Immediately to Rachel's left was the long drop down to the courtyard; to her right, the wire-topped outer wall and the rolling moors beyond.

'I can make the jump,' Simon said, eyeing the courtyard,

'but I don't know if I can carry you and your father.'

'Take him.'

'No, Rachel. I won't let you sacrifice yourself for this—'

' "This" what? He's my dad, Simon.'

Agents began to pour through the hatch. Simon set Malcolm Saxby down and they all backed up to the edge of the roof.

'He's right, Rachel,' Malcolm gasped. 'I was willing to let you die once before, I can't let that happen again. You're my daughter, my little girl.'

'Plain and pitiful words, Dr Saxby. Or should I say Prisoner 35712 . . . ?'

The dark witch floated up into the light. Cynthia Croft looked at each of them in turn—her son, the prisoner, and the girl. Then she turned to the agents.

'Restrain my . . . ' A cruel smirk twisted her pale-pink lips. 'Restrain the Cynocephalus.'

Simon stepped away from Rachel and her father, thereby saving them from the vampiric swarm. It took sixteen agents to subdue him.

'Indeed they *were* pitiful words, Dr Saxby,' Miss Croft continued. 'And, unfortunately, they'll be the last your darling daughter will ever hear.'

A bolt of magic screamed out from the witch's hand. It streaked towards Rachel and filled her eyes with red light. She heard Simon's struggle to free himself, heard his cry, half-frightened, half-grieving. In the midst of terror, a smile threatened to break out across her lips: he was still there. Her Simon . . .

The bolt struck with just as much devastating power as she had expected.

But it did not strike her.

Malcolm Saxby had thrown himself into the path of the hex. Rachel's father clutched the ragged hole in his chest as if it were something precious and dear to him, and tottered back to the very edge of the roof. That was where Rachel caught him. She looked down once, saw the dark red shimmer of internal organs, then lifted her eyes again.

'I'm so sorry, Rachel. Sorry I didn't save you. Sorry I . . .'

Trickles of blood ran out from the corner of his mouth.

'I forgive you,' Rachel said. 'And I love you, Dad . . . Dad?'

The rush of blood had stopped. A final, almost contented sigh passed through Malcolm Saxby's lips. Rachel laid her father's body gently on the ground. As she did so, those words of the borderlands' Oracle came back to her: *You must learn the grace of forgiveness, child* . . . Well, she had learnt it, and the lesson now made her grief more bearable.

'Rachel!' Simon called out to her. 'Are you hurt? Talk to me!'

She heard the smart click of the Prime Minister's heels on the wet rooftop. Closing her father's eyes, Rachel turned to find Cynthia Croft standing over Simon. There was a curious look on her face, somewhere between puzzlement and disgust. The agents had to tighten their grip as Cynthia ran her beautifully manicured fingers through his hair.

'You really care for her, don't you? You always were a silly, sentimental boy, but this time your weakness *may* prove useful.' She gestured to the DREAM agents. 'I have decided not to kill the girl . . . yet.'

The bloodsuckers grappled Simon to his feet.

'Take them both to my laboratory.'

Chapter 19
Rabicus on the Road

They had been riding since dawn, lone travellers in the impossible hellscape. Passing from city to city, they had met no other life forms, just the odd demon-faced statue that, from a distance, made them wary. After a while, Jake came to the conclusion that Fletcher Clerval was right: most demon activity must be centred around the Shadow Palace in the south. Perhaps the hordes only ventured north to build fresh settlements and play their games of conquest.

As night began to close in they found themselves passing through a perfect recreation of war-torn London: blitzed buildings and barrage balloons, blackout blinds and sandbagged bomb shelters. Vintage cars and military trucks lined some of the roads. By this time it was obvious that the skeleton horses could not plod on much further, and so Pandora dropped down from her mount and started going vehicle to vehicle. She tried her luck under the bonnets of Bedford trucks and classic Bentleys, none of which would start.

'Maybe the demons never learned about the combustion engine,' Jake suggested.

'But they got every other detail right?' Pandora looked up from the innards of a Triumph motorcycle. 'I don't buy it. These babies have been tampered with.'

'How?'

'Starter motors ripped out, spark plugs missing. As to who did it . . . ' She got back onto her horse. 'Three guesses.'

'Right, so run me through this rabicus thing again.'

They had now reached the city's East End: street after street of buildings and warehouses that looked as if they had been bombed by German aircraft.

'OK,' Pandora sighed, 'but then we stop for rest and food. Deal?'

Jake wanted to press on. Somewhere out there Eleanor was waiting, trapped in the Human Hunter's castle. But Pandora was right—they had to rest.

'Food and then an hour of sleep, that's all.'

'You know something, Jake? You're turning into a real hard-ass.'

'Coming from you, I take that as a compliment. So, rabicus?'

' "Rabicus" in the singular, "rabici" the plural. They're a subspecies of demon.'

'Demons have subspecies now?'

Pandora nodded. 'Like all demons, the original rabicus was given his form by the first witch that summoned him. When that creature returned to the demon world, others saw his shape and coveted it. I guess you could say he started a trend. Rabici are fiercely loyal to their clan and tend to shun other demons, so when the one we saw last night said he'd tell his "brothers and sisters" about us, he only meant his fellow rabici.'

'That's good, I guess.'

'Hold that sigh of relief. The rabici are a brutal, blood-thirsty race. They're more animalistic than most demons, but that doesn't mean they're any less cunning.'

'So what are we dealing with here?'

'You caught a glimpse of the rabicus on the temple roof?'

'I saw a shadow. Black eyes. Scarred flesh. It looked a bit like . . . You'll laugh.'

'I won't.'

'A squirrel.'

Pandora smirked.

'Hey!'

'Sorry, you're right, it does look a bit like a squirrel, but this creature is actually more like a piranha. It can strip your flesh in five minutes flat. The only real defence against a rabicus is its fear of the earth, the ground.' Pandora cast Jake a sidelong glance. 'We're going to have our work cut out.'

Up ahead, the bombed-out buildings fell away and the London street broke up into the rocky terrain of the demon world. In the far distance, Jake could just make out another ghost town waiting to be discovered.

They tied their horses to the hitching post and stepped

up onto the raised wooden sidewalk. The saloon's batwing doors creaked in the breeze and the dirty lace curtains at the windows fluttered out like languid ghosts. Before entering the bar, Jake glanced up and down the dirt strip that sliced through the town.

He assumed that the buildings and features here were just as accurate as those in the Roman city, war-torn London, and all the other places he and Pandora had traipsed through. Parked on the strip were a couple of buckboard wagons and a stagecoach with travelling trunks lashed to its roof. Most of the buildings were wooden: the 'Great Western Hotel', the feed store, the dry goods store, the blacksmith's shop, the bathhouse, the church, the land office. Only the bank and the jailhouse were made of brick. Right down to the bullet holes in the saloon doors, this was every inch a Wild West town.

Pandora pushed through into the bar.

'All clear, pardner.'

Circular tables with stools stood in front of a long bar. Jake imagined Clint Eastwood or John Wayne propping up one end while an aproned bartender sent slugs of whisky sliding down the counter.

Pandora unpacked provisions from her backpack. She handed Jake a bottle of water and a slab of Kendal Mint Cake. While he dropped onto a stool and rolled his aching shoulders, she busied herself finding matches and a paraffin lamp—even these details were not too small for the demons' attentions.

'Will you take the first watch?' Pandora looked at him as if from the bottom of a well. 'I'm real tired.'

'Sure. You get some rest.'

Jake pushed through the batwing doors. Out on the raised sidewalk the yellow mist made his eyes water. He could just see the ghostly gleam of the horses at the hitching post. Across the strip, the black-eyed windows of the jail-house stared back at him. He noticed these things in passing. Despite his tiredness, the urge to move on, to find Eleanor, to rescue her from the clutches of the old Witchfinder General, was hard to resist.

Mist streamed over the sidewalk and a single white feather trembled at Jake's feet.

'*Chu-huh-huh—Chu-huh-huh.*'

Magic sparked in his hands. He stepped off the sidewalk and waded into the yellow river that rippled down the road. The mist was up to his chest, the lights in his fists little more than bluish smears in the dimness. There was no sign of rabici on any of the roofs. Exhausted from a day in the saddle and anxious to reach Eleanor, perhaps he was beginning to see and hear things that weren't there. Hallucinating in hell? Not a good sign.

He was about to head back to the saloon when he saw the tiny figure. As he watched, a dozen more rabici appeared on the tiles. Then more and more, until the entire roof was covered. Their throaty chirrup filled the air and Jake spun round. Rabici had materialized on the top of every building. On the balcony of the Great Western Hotel, at the first-floor windows of the jail, on the tin roof of the bathhouse smoky bodies quivered like a thousand dying candles.

One of the rabici atop the saloon stepped forward.

'Hello again, child. Are you ready to play the chase game?'

Chapter 20
Feeling Time

'Down!'

Pandora bellowed the command, and Jake dropped. He watched through the haze of mist as she threw herself from the raised sidewalk and scrabbled over to him on knees and elbows.

'How many?'

'A thousand, easy.'

'Enough to strip us to the bone in the blink of an eye. OK. Any bright ideas?'

'You said they don't like being on the ground, which I guess is why we've got our faces in the dirt.' Jake eyed the horses still nuzzling at the hitching post. 'Reckon you could create a diversion?'

'What are you thinking?'

'I can deal with a lot of these things with magic, but there are too many for me to take on alone. You need a way to fight.'

'My blades.'

'That's close quarters combat. By the time you've hacked down thirty, a hundred could be on your back. We need a way to take them out from a distance.'

'So you blast them with magic, what can I do?'

'What does every one of these replica towns and cities have in common?' Jake asked.

'They're ghost towns. Empty.'

'And they're perfect, right down to the tiniest nut and bolt. Right now we're in the middle of a nineteenth century Wild West town, so what does that tell you?'

Pandora followed his gaze to the jailhouse.

'Guns.'

Jake sketched out the roughest of rough plans.

'Certifiably insane,' Pandora nodded. 'I like it.'

While she set off back towards the saloon, Jake made a writhing path across the dirt strip. He had reached the jail-house steps when he heard a change in the rabici's chunter. The voice of the temple demon rang out—

'See, she rises!'

Jake looked back. Standing beside one of the horses, Pandora had a hand looped around the rein and her foot in the stirrup. She threw herself into the saddle, and horse and rider took off down the strip. Before the rooster-tails of dust had a chance to settle, the rabici were on the move. They vanished from one rooftop only to reappear on another further down the road—a legion of demons streaming after its prey. In their hurry, they seemed to have forgotten about Jake. He scrambled up the steps and pushed at the jailhouse door. Locked.

A surprised cry drew his attention back to Pandora. One of the rabici had materialized on the bony rump of the horse and had locked its twig-like fingers around her throat. Jake saw a flash of silver, and the monster's black eyes went round with shock. The tip of an ancestral blade poked through its chest and the squirming, screaming creature was lifted into the air. With a grunt, Pandora threw her attacker to the ground.

'The earth!' the temple demon shrieked. 'She's thrown him onto the earth! See, it burns him!'

The felled rabicus shrieked as if it were on fire.

Meanwhile, Pandora turned her horse and thundered past the jail.

'Hurry up, Jake!'

He pushed the tip of his index finger into the keyhole and ordered the door to *open*. A tiny blue light crackled into the lock, the mechanism clicked, and Jake stumbled inside. With the light in his hand, he saw that the jailhouse was one big room, the sheriff's desk facing the door and a wood-burning stove in the corner. The cells were towards the rear, cages with narrow beds and slop buckets. On the wall next to the desk hung the gun cabinet.

He raced across the room, pulled open the cabinet, and an arsenal of weaponry tumbled onto the floor. He scooped up a pair of rifles, two pistols, two revolvers, a bandoleer and a leather holster, its pouches stuffed with bullets. Then he moved to the window and rubbed a spy hole in the grime. Pandora caught sight of him and galloped back towards the jail.

She was almost at the steps when Jake kicked open the door. Reining in the horse, she reached out six free hands. He threw weapons in quick succession. Then he stepped out onto the strip, conjured magic, and blasted any demon that looked as if it might be about to pounce. Meanwhile, Pandora worked like lightning. She looped the bandoleer over her shoulder, opened loading gates, rotated cylinders, and slugged bullets into chambers. Jake could hear the click of each firearm being readied.

'That's what I'm talking about!' she cried. 'Double-barrel coach gun, Colt Peacemakers, a Winchester '92.'

Jake had taken out a dozen demons but hundreds more were clustering.

'We need to get out of here. Jake, take the reins.'

Pandora flipped round so that she was facing the rear. Her topmost hands brandished the rifles while the four below held pistols and revolvers. The lower pair reached behind and held fast to the saddle. Jake gave the jailhouse roof a final blast and jumped onto the skeletal steed. He kicked the horse's flank and they rocketed away down the strip. At his back, he could feel the jolt as Pandora fired off round after round, juggled her guns, and reloaded. It seemed to be doing the trick—none of the rabici had dared to materialize on the horse again. In fact, when he glanced over his shoulder, he saw that they were falling back.

'Looks good,' he shouted over the clatter of hooves. 'But are they just gonna materialize again when we stop?'

'They have to visualize a place down to the last detail before they can appear there,' Pandora called. 'That's why a hundred of them didn't just manifest on the horse. It was in motion, difficult for them to study. Only the most experienced could do it.'

'OK, but—WHOA!'

Jake seized the reins and brought the horse to a screaming halt.

'What is it?' Pandora tried to crane her neck round. 'Jake, talk to me.'

But Jake couldn't talk.

The horror of what he saw stretching out before him had robbed him of speech. With a sickening jolt, he realized that everything before this had been just a prelude to terror . . .

Now he could see and hear the darkness of demonkind.

Now he had reached the Shore of Damnation.

Now he had truly entered Hell.

'He betrayed us. I told you he would, but you—*you* wouldn't listen!'

Rachel tried to shut out Simon's ranting, increasingly hysterical voice.

'That little piece of scum. If I get my hands on him, I'll rip his throat out. I'll—'

'Shut up!' she cried. 'You don't know that Grype betrayed us. The vampire at the gate, the one who wanted us to stop the lift, they were both suspicious.'

'Still sticking up for him, eh? Gullible, Rach, gullible.'

'Better to be gullible than a—' She caught herself just in time.

'Than a what?' Simon hissed through clenched teeth.

Rachel didn't trust herself to answer.

It had been twelve hours since her father's death. Taken from the rooftop, they had been dragged across the courtyard and into the old hospital block. Between a confusion of shoving hands, Rachel had caught glimpses of Simon. His eyes had burned and she had heard the wet crack of his nose as it pushed out further from his face. His claws and teeth had lengthened and fresh hair had sprouted along his jaw. Alert to the danger, another pack of agents had come forward to restrain him.

She looked at him now, his huge body squeezed into the cage next to hers. He kept grasping the bars, only for jolts of electricity to sear through his hands and send him whimpering to the back of the cell. It was as if he were a dumb animal that couldn't learn from its mistakes. Or perhaps the fury, focused in those blazing green eyes, wouldn't allow him to give up.

The hospital block was the oldest part of the prison. A warren of musty-smelling corridors with mildewed walls and mouldy windows. They had been taken to a long, rectangular room which might once have been a ward but which now served as Cynthia Croft's laboratory. The chamber in which her Cynocephali experiments were conducted. It appeared to be the only part of the prison that had received any attention. The walls had been freshly painted, the floorboards scrubbed until they gleamed. A few pieces of scientific equipment—Bunsen burners, bell jars, Petri dishes, crucibles, and retorts—were arranged on stainless steel tables. It was a basic set-up; nothing compared to the high-tech wonders of Fletcher Clerval's lab.

One end of the room was occupied by Simon's and Rachel's electrified cages. At the other end stood a wall of glass. Rachel could see no light in the space beyond, but once or twice during their long hours of imprisonment she had noticed shapes moving behind the glass—slow, sluggish shadows. She had asked Simon what they might be: more Cynocephali, perhaps?

'No,' he'd answered. 'They're something . . . else . . .'

The swing doors burst open and Cynthia Croft marched into the lab.

'Sorry to have kept you waiting. I trust you've been made comfortable in my absence?'

A pair of DREAM agents wheeled in a flat screen TV and set it up in front of the cages. With a wave of her hand, Miss Croft dismissed the vampires.

'Now, children, I have a little entertainment for you.'

She clicked a remote control and an image appeared onscreen. Rachel recognized the playground of Masterson High, the school she and Jake had attended. There was nothing particularly unusual about the sight—it was just a space of empty tarmac with a hopscotch course marked out in faded paint—but Rachel was nonetheless surprised to be confronted with this reminder of her old life. That popular girl that had once swanned around the corridors of Masterson High now seemed a distant memory.

Cynthia clicked the play button.

Screams. A thunder of feet. Suddenly, a stream of

children raced across the screen. A few looked back over their shoulders with expressions that made Rachel's blood run cold. Friends stopped to help wounded classmates while teachers herded the children on as best they could.

The camera shook and the image blurred. When the static cleared, the children had vanished. A moment of stillness. And then an immense hand reached up and pulled the camera down. It hit the ground and the lens cracked. Before the screen blipped to black, Rachel caught a glimpse of a blank face with grey, pitted skin and a simple carved line for a mouth.

'What is it?'

'That, my dear, was an Omen,' Cynthia said matter-of-factly. 'The third and penultimate sign. It came at 3:17 p.m. exactly and took the shape of living stone. All across the country, gargoyles and statues, figures and carvings came to life. An hour of rampage and murder.'

'At the school?'

'Twenty-three fatalities.' She waved her hand, as if to dismiss the triviality of these deaths. 'But now we have a pattern, do we not? It seems that these new Omens are not so different from those of Hobarron's Hollow: locusts instead of toads, fire instead of mist, manmade statues instead of stalactite golems. The only difference is the scale of the "disasters"—these Omens are not restricted to a tiny, backwater village, but are nationwide. What does that tell you?'

Rachel and Simon exchanged glances.

'It indicates the certainty of the Demontide.' She spoke as if to dimwitted toddlers. 'The final Omen is at hand. Tomorrow, my master's long wait will be over.'

The swing doors opened a crack and Cynthia Croft's ginger tomcat sidled into the room. It padded over to its mistress, and Simon's nose wrinkled.

'You remember Chequers, don't you?' Cynthia said.

'Course I do. It was the only thing in our house you ever had a kind word for. Never liked me much, though. Always spitting and hissing whenever it saw me. But I can smell it now—that isn't any ordinary cat.'

'Your senses are sharpening by the minute. Soon you'll be ready for what lies ahead . . . But, of course, you are right.' She picked up the cat and rubbed its cheek against hers. 'This is my demon.'

Rachel shook her head in disbelief. 'We were told the Demon Father was your familiar.'

'So he is.'

'I don't understand.'

'Then I'll explain it to you slowly.' Cynthia placed her familiar on a laboratory bench and scratched behind its ears. 'All my life I have heard the call of demonkind. From the moment I was born, *he* spoke to me, and by the age of eight, I had managed to summon him into our world. He knew that I was powerful beyond any of my peers; stronger even than the famed coven master Marcus Crowden. But the Demon Father is as wise as he is terrible. He could not come to Earth and leave his realm without a ruler. And so he split his spirit, leaving half in the demon world and giving over half to this familiar.'

'Just looks like an ordinary cat,' Rachel pointed out. 'Other demons have deformities, weird traits.'

'The Demon Father likes to hide in plain sight. When the Demontide breaks the dark spirit split between Marcus Crowden's body and that part which resides in this creature will be joined again. Then you shall see the wonder of the Demon Father's true form.'

'You injected me with its blood,' Simon seethed. 'Your own son.'

'Don't you understand, Simon?' Her voice was soft, almost kind. 'You are *nothing* to me. You never were. In my eyes, you are a speck of dust floating through the cosmos, an insect to be trampled without a second thought.'

She came to Simon's cage, stared him straight in the eye.

'But you *could* be so much more. Beneath that frail human form a radiant creature is waiting to be set free. A general that can lead my army into battle. Become the beast, my son, and I promise that I *will* love you.'

Rachel shuddered. So Cynthia Croft had worked it out, too: of all the Cynocephalus hybrids, Simon was the alpha male. The leader that they would follow. How much easier it would be to control the slave race if she had Simon on her side.

Cynthia clicked her fingers and the door to his cage swung open.

'Listen to your mother and accept what you are. You feel the lure of the darkness, don't you? Then give in to it. Stop this futile fight and embrace the glory and the power. I will be so *proud* of you, my son.'

Simon screamed as his bones snapped and reformed. Jagged teeth slid from his gums and coarse hair grew out and covered every inch of his skin. The Cynocephalus burst from its cell, circled round its creator, threw back its great head and howled.

The creature was almost twice the size of its previous incarnations. At the sound of its call, the shapes behind the glass wall let loose their own gargled shrieks. In some small part of her mind, Rachel noticed that these echoes were different from any Cyno call she had yet heard. She saw out of the corner of her eye the awkward shapes bustle up against the glass.

Standing on all fours, Simon's head was level with his mother's shoulder. A contented growl rumbled in his throat as she stroked the fur at the nape of his neck.

'You have kept the monster caged too long,' Cynthia soothed. 'His thirst rages and his hunger is as deep as the ocean. He must be fed.'

Another click of those manicured fingers, and Rachel's cell opened, the electrical current cutting off in the same instant.

'Go now. Show me that you have truly changed . . . '

Bright green eyes bored into Rachel. She could find no trace of Simon.

'Kill her.'

Chapter 21
Forest of the Damned

'The skin is easily ripped away. The meat beneath is warm and tasty, the blood hot and wholesome. Does that not sound delicious, my child?'

Cables of drool slipped from Simon's lips. He slapped his massive jaws and padded towards Rachel's cage. Behind him, Cynthia Croft watched with the detached interest of a scientist observing an experiment.

The Cynocephalus's shadow stretched out before him and draped darkness over Rachel. Unable to stand in the cramped cell, she scurried back on her feet and hands. Her back hit the bars and the tears swimming in her eyes were jolted onto her cheeks.

'Please, Simon, if you can hear me—'

'He can't,' Cynthia said. 'Dr Harker's amulet is gone and the beast is so very strong.'

Simon, or the thing that had been Simon, bowed its head

to clear the cage door. The Cynocephalus crept forward, and Rachel felt its hot, raw breath against her face. She kept her gaze level with its elliptical pupils, slits so black they looked like a tear in the fabric of space. A teardrop doorway into the soul.

Are you there? She projected the thought. *Do you see me?*

'Observe my creation.' Cynthia lifted the cat-demon into her arms. 'Watch now, my master, as it fulfils its purpose.'

Those big green eyes rolled back in Simon's head. His mouth yawned wide.

Rachel reached out and touched the murderous muzzle.

'Remember Pandora. Remember Brag Badderson and Adam Harker . . . '

A slight hesitation. Then a hungry growl that seemed to come from the very pit of the creature. It edged forward again.

'Remember Jake, your best friend. Two lonely boys who found each other on the canal bank. They loved comic books and stories. They loved each other and became brothers.'

The Cyno's long tongue lashed around its teeth. Rachel leaned forward so that her face was within an inch of that terrible jaw.

'Remember *me*. Remember what I told you just before our first kiss. I don't believe in this stupid monster your so-called mother created. It's an illusion, it's not real. It has no power to hurt you . . . or me.'

'Ridiculous!' Cynthia laughed.

Simon half-turned his head towards his mother.

Rachel pulled him back to face her.

'A transformation spell put together from a bit of old demon blood?' She laughed through her fear. 'Does she really think that something so feeble could change—*really* change—my brave, beautiful Simon? He's better than her and her magic, stronger than any spell or enchantment, and he doesn't need an amulet to tell him who he is. He *knows*.'

She rested her head against his. Felt the mighty thud of his heart beat against her.

'Deep down, he's always known.'

Two immense hands gripped the bars on either side of Rachel's head. A cry burst from its lips and the Cyno strained, spine arching, muscles rippling as it pressed its back against the roof of the cage. Rachel looked up into a pair of moist eyes. The beast was crying. *Simon* was crying.

'I—love—you.'

The words were hard and rough, but they were his. Somehow, he had won the fight. He had come back to her.

Simon gritted his teeth and thrust his broad shoulders against the cage. The iron bars groaned and began to bend against his fearsome bulk. Suddenly, the bolts holding the cage to the floor snapped and the entire cell was lifted into the air. Rachel crawled out from under the frame, rose shakily to her feet, and stumbled towards the swing doors.

Cynthia Croft glared at her son.

'What do you think you're doing?'

At her words, Simon seemed to falter. The bars slipped through his fingers and he struggled to regain his grip. Again, Rachel heard the horrible snap and rattle of his transforming skeleton. For a moment, he appeared to shimmer in the cold, hard light of the lab. The coat of coarse hair that covered his body began to withdraw into his skin. In a series of violent jerks, the Cyno's canine snout pushed back into his face. Before the regression to his human form was complete, Simon stared his mother down.

'Why?'

A simple, pleading question that broke Rachel's heart.

Cynthia looked at her son with an expression of utter contempt.

'No child of mine should ever ask such a question.' She clicked her fingers and a red flame sparked into life. 'I've had my fill of games. If you will not embrace your nature then you must be punished. Say goodbye to your little girlfriend.'

Simon latched his hands around the bottom of the cage. With a final burst of supernatural strength, he hefted the frame onto his shoulders and launched it across the laboratory. Cynthia Croft threw herself to the ground, and the dark magic in her hand spluttered and died. As the cage soared overhead, the witch smiled, clearly thinking that Simon's makeshift weapon had missed its target. A split second later, she realized her mistake and cried out in horror.

Rachel stood transfixed as the cage hurtled towards the glass wall. Reflected there, she saw herself, pale and frightened; Cynthia Croft, wide-eyed and screaming; Simon, his hairless body shaking and his smooth, regular features streaked with tears. And then the scene disintegrated into a million falling fragments.

Beyond the shattered wall, strange shadows moved. Rachel caught sight of crooked teeth stuffed into disfigured mouths and bodies horribly twisted. Blood-filled eyes blinked out from faces half-human, half-animal.

Simon grabbed Rachel's hand and pulled her towards the swing doors.

'What's happening? What are they?'

Before she could think of questioning him further, Simon had pushed her into the corridor and the doors swung to. A terrible scream rang out from inside the lab. Red light flashed in the gap under the doors—a few frantic bursts of dark magic—and then another bloodcurdling shriek. And another. And another. Rachel could hear the scrabble of animal feet on the wooden floor and the crack of splitting bone. Simon pressed the heels of his hands against his ears.

She went to him, made him look at her.

'What are they?'

'Mutants,' he whispered. 'Experiment subjects where the demon blood didn't take. That room behind the glass must've been some kind of holding cell. I . . . '

A final scream, this time accompanied by a victorious howl.

'I could've stopped them.' He buried his head against Rachel's shoulder. 'They weren't fully Cyno, but they could sense me. If I'd told them to stop, they would have obeyed. But I was so scared, Rach. Scared she'd hurt you, and so I let them . . . '

'She gave you no choice,' Rachel said.

Footsteps echoed along the corridor and a cold shadow fell over Simon and Rachel. They looked up to find themselves reflected in the dark moons of the Demon Father's glasses. He treated them to a wintry smile, a movement that made the corners of his lips break apart and bleed. The last time they had seen the demon, his skin had been dry and crumbling. Now it looked truly diseased.

'My poor mistress, she really was the best of her kind.'

There was no emotion in the demon's voice as he watched a pool of blood seep out from under the door. He clicked his fingers and a red leash lashed through the handles, locking the mutants inside.

'Better to be safe than sorry. Now, my dears, perhaps you would like to see your little friend Edward Rice?'

'*Oh gods . . .*'

Pandora shuddered, but, unlike Jake, quickly mastered her horror.

'Come on, we've got to keep moving!'

She pulled his hands out of the reins and dragged him down from the saddle.

'The horse can't run on ice, we'll have to continue on foot. Jake!' She clicked her fingers an inch from his face. 'Snap out of it or we'll die here. The rabici are only afraid of the earth, ice won't bother them.'

'But, Pandora . . . '

'What?'

She had tugged on her backpack and was eyeing the roof-tops. It was a long leap from the last of the old west build-ings to the shore, but one or two of the more daring demons seemed to be on the point of risking the jump.

Meanwhile, Jake remained spellbound by the sight that spread out before him. As far as the eye could see, a vast frozen lake glinted under the demon sky. All along the lakeside, the outskirts of other replica cities and towns dwindled down to the shore. These were the last empty war zones before the true horror of the demon world was revealed.

At first, Jake had thought that the distant shapes on the lake were trees. That some strange, stunted forest had broken through the ice. When he saw the branches begin to move, he'd just assumed that a breeze was blowing across the icy wilderness. Then he'd realized that there was no breeze. That the branches were not branches. That the trees were not trees.

'Pandora, are those things . . . ' He could hardly bring himself to say it. '*People?*'

Pandora thrust his backpack into his arms and pushed him onto the lake. Together, they started to scrabble across the shimmering stretches. Fletcher Clerval's walking boots kept them more or less upright, but the going was treacherous. If they made it across the frozen waste without a broken arm or a shattered leg, Jake would consider it a miracle.

Occasionally, Pandora twisted round and fired off a shell at any rabicus that had dared to make the leap. Demons exploded in mid-air: a greenish flurry of bones and brains that fell wetly onto the road. But the rabici were undeterred. Greater numbers began to mass on the rooftops, ready to make the jump.

Despite the dangers of snapped limbs and ravenous demons, Jake's focus remained on the twisting human forest in front of them. From shore to shore, hundreds of thousands, perhaps even *millions* of people had been planted waist-high in the ice. Whoever had designed this freezing torture garden had been an expert in the art of agony. Locked into the lake, the people reached for each other, desperate for the comfort of human contact, but they had been arranged at precisely measured intervals, so no matter how they stretched and strained a few cruel millimetres would for ever separate them.

The first human forms came gradually into view. Ice crystals coated their naked, shivering bodies. They were horribly thin—little more than stick figures with dark blue flesh dripping from their bones. Most had clearly been here a long time, and they must have known that to touch each other, to even brush fingertips was impossible, yet still they reached. With each movement their frozen bodies creaked and a low, hopeless moan rattled in their chests.

Jake heard the empty click of Pandora's rifle. The last bullet was gone. She tore the bandoleer from her shoulder and threw the weapons aside. No sooner had the rifles and revolvers skidded out of sight than the first demons landed on the lake. The rabici chuntered and set off in pursuit of their supper.

The demon's clawed feet were not well-suited to the ice, and if it had been a straight race then Jake and Pandora might easily have outpaced them. As soon as they reached the first humans, however, all bets were off. Hungry for the warmth of living creatures, these lost souls snatched at Jake's clothes and grabbed at his legs. He leapt over a reaching arm only to fall against the torso of another frozen spirit. In life this thing had been a man, in death it looked more like a worm-eaten scarecrow. Like a parent cradling a beloved child, the soul locked its arms around Jake and drew him close.

'*I'm sorry,*' the dead man whispered. '*Please tell my wife I'm sorry. I was so cruel . . .*'

Jake pressed a glowing palm against his captor's chest and the tortured soul burst into flames. Its ectoplasmic body disintegrated like dry parchment and blew away in motes on the night air. Jake wondered: was this a soul freed or destroyed, a life finally exhausted or a spirit that had moved on to another plane of existence? He did not know the answer to this question. Even in the time before flesh, he had not known.

The time before flesh . . .

Pandora pulled him to his feet and they hurried on. Dead hands continued to reach for them and dead voices confessed their sins, some trivial, some terrible. Panting for breath, Jake glanced up and saw a blanket of yellow cloud sweep in and blot out the sky. The stars vanished and the lake transformed into an inky nothingness. It was suddenly like running across the black reaches of space.

Pandora bellowed with pain and fell to her knees. Jake was on the point of summoning a blast spell when he heard a demonic howl. The next moment, Pandora was at his side and they were running again. She wiped a smear of green blood from her ancestral blade.

'You OK?'

'Flesh wound. But take my advice: don't turn round.'

As soon he looked back, Jake wished he'd listened to Pandora. Thousands of seething, snarling monsters were rampaging through the human forest, breaking off stray arms and heads as they went. They did not stop to feed on the spirits, for the rabici knew that there was no pleasure to be derived from flavourless ectoplasm. What they desired most was the fresh meat and hot blood of living creatures.

Jake and Pandora broke through the last ranks of humans just as a wave of rabici landed on their backs. Jake hit the ice with a dull thud. He could feel a hundred little fingers scrabbling at his skin and twenty stinking mouths breathing in his ear.

'You led us quite a chase, but we have you now,' a rabicus chirruped. Its fingers squeezed his flesh. 'We shall share you out, pound by pou—'

'GET BACK!' another rabicus screamed. 'Brothers, sisters, we must withdraw! The chase game has led us into *his* domain! Fall back!'

Jake and Pandora jumped to their feet and, exchanging puzzled looks, turned to follow the rabici's retreat. One by one the smoky shadows vanished into the darkness.

'What's going on?'

'No idea.' Pandora wiped crystallized ice from her coat. 'Something seems to have spooked them pretty bad.'

'They said "*his* domain". Do you think—?'

A scream like no scream Jake had ever heard pierced the demon night. All across the frozen lake, the human forest bowed down as if each soul was cringing against the cry. As the scream died away, a chink appeared between the clouds and a shaft of red light streamed down. It touched the turrets of the castle that stood at the centre of the lake.

'What was that?' Pandora whispered.

'Him.'

Jake started running.

'Matthew Hopkins.'

Chapter 22
The Witchfinder's Revenge

Light spread over the ramparts of the castle: an arc of illumination so bright and brilliant it could shame the dawn.

'Do you see that?' Jake whispered.

Pandora squinted at the patch of sky where his finger pointed.

'I don't see anything except a bunch of poisonous clouds. What am I supposed to be looking at?'

'Nothing.'

Jake hurried on. Of course Pandora could not see the aura hovering over the castle, for only he could perceive those shimmers he had called 'soul-lights'. Like magic, he had once thought that this ability was his genetic inheritance from Josiah Hobarron, but somehow that idea now seemed wrong. These gifts that stirred within him felt much more ancient than the mere four hundred years that separated him from Josiah.

With his gaze fixed on the light, Jake's thoughts flew back to his time on the Cravenmouth gallows. He remembered how, in his last moments, twilight had descended and he had accepted his death and the journey he was about to take. The journey *home* . . . And then he had seen the light coming towards him. The same light that now hung over the battlements. Eleanor had rescued him from the clutches of Matthew Hopkins. Now the roles were reversed, and she was the one who needed saving.

They had almost reached the castle gate when Jake stopped in his tracks. He lit a magical orb and swept the flame over the outer wall and turret watchtowers. He didn't know why he was so surprised: they had passed through dozens of replica towns and cities, and what was a castle except a fortified town in miniature? Nevertheless, the sight of this particular recreation stirred up painful memories.

'Rake's keep, the place where Hopkins tortured me. It's an exact copy.'

'Maybe not exact,' Pandora said. 'Look at this.'

Unlike Rake's keep, the castle did not stand on a mound. Its thick walls broke through the ice and soared upwards, as if the mighty fortress had grown organically out of the lake. Pandora led the way to the outer gate. Taking Jake's wrist, she guided his light so that it shone on the castle's sealed-up entrance. Jake could hardly believe his eyes. In the place normally occupied by a portcullis, a stranger barrier had been erected.

'Is that what I think it is?'

Before Pandora could respond, they heard footsteps on

the battlements. A voice speaking in High Demon Tongue called out—

'Hear that, Spewter? I think there's someone down there.'

'It's just your imagination, Withernake. What're you so frightened about, anyway? A few stray souls wandering the lake? Let 'em wander.'

'But we're the night watch. We see any lost souls then we have to bring them straight to the Hunter.' The fear in the demon's voice was unmistakable. 'You know what happens if we miss even one.'

'I know what *used* to happen,' Spewter snorted, 'but our days of serving that lunatic are almost over. You can feel it as strongly as I, Withernake: tomorrow the Demontide will dawn. When that hour comes, we'll leave this wasteland and flood through the great Door. Humanity's rich, lush world will be ours.'

'And what'll happen to *him*, I wonder. When he came here the Demon Father said it was our duty to serve him.'

'He'll be left behind,' Spewter laughed. 'Him and all those pathetic spirits. Hell will be closed for business!'

Jake and Pandora listened to the watchmen's retreating footsteps before turning back to the gateway and the gruesome barrier.

'Looks a bit like skin,' Pandora said.

Dotted here and there with an assortment of spots and pimples, warts and moles, the barrier did indeed resemble a huge sheet of rubbery, pale-pink flesh. The screen was far too large to have come from any living creature and was clearly some kind of artificial material made to look like human skin. Great hooks fastened the barrier to the walls and the arched ceiling of the gateway—there was no obvious way through.

Pandora drew her blades from their scabbards. She was about to cut an opening when Jake noticed the spear. A wooden-handled weapon, it rested in a bracket attached to the wall.

'Wait,' he said. 'Look at the mouth.'

He pointed to the centre of the screen where a pair of withered grey lips sighed in the breeze.

'That's the only mouth I can see.' He lifted the spear out of the bracket. 'And do you know what this looks like? An oversized bodkin. The weapon of a witchfinder.'

'So?'

'Preacher Hobarron told Eleanor that I had to suffer at Matthew Hopkins's hands. Only then would I be prepared for the journey I had to take into the land of shadows and torment. This barrier was designed by Hopkins, crafted by his twisted logic. Warts. Blemishes. A mouth.' He held up the spear. 'And a bodkin.'

'It's a test.'

'One of those used to uncover witches,' Jake nodded. 'Witchfinders used bodkins to stab any blemish they could find on a suspect's body. If they discovered one that didn't bleed, and which didn't cause the suspect to scream when it was pricked, then that was deemed a devil mark: proof of witchcraft. My guess is, we have to stab the right mark and then we'll be allowed through.'

'And if we get the wrong mark?'

'The mouth screams, alerting the demons we're here.'

'Great. So how do we choose?'

Jake remembered the random way in which Hopkins and his helpers had driven the bodkin into his flesh. After hours of searching, they claimed to have discovered two places insensible to pain around Jake's shoulder blades. It had been a haphazard search.

'There must be a clue—something that sets one of the marks apart, otherwise how would the demons get in and out without setting off the "alarm"?'

'Maybe they memorized the spot.'

'That's possible, but I don't have any better ideas, do you?'

Pandora admitted that she didn't. The castle walls were sheer and there didn't appear to be any other point of entry. Jake bent down and peered through the mouth. He could see no sign of life in the courtyard beyond. For the next ten minutes, the two friends examined every inch of the skin barrier. Each wart and mole, boil and bump, blackhead and beauty spot was checked and double-checked.

'I don't even know what I'm looking for,' Pandora said. 'I mean, how can we be sure that any of them are devil marks? Did the witchfinders *ever* discover a real one?'

'Of course! Pandora, you're a genius. None of them are devil marks because devil marks don't exist.'

'Come again?'

'The witchfinders only ever pretended to discover them. They used trick bodkins: when they touched the tip against the suspect's skin they'd press a hidden button and the blade would slide up into the handle. It looked like the bodkin was

sinking deep into the witch's body, but there was no blood
and no cry of pain.'

'They falsified evidence.'

'Yeah, and if I'm right . . . ' Jake felt along the wooden
handle of the spear. 'We don't need to find a "real" witch
mark either.'

He chose a dark brown mole covered with hair. Before
putting spear to blemish, he clicked the hidden button on the
shaft. The metal tip slid neatly up into the handle, leaving
the mole without so much as a scratch.

The leathery lips creaked open. They spread wider and
wider until they had swallowed up a large area of the skin
barrier, eventually forming a hole big enough for Jake to step
through. Pandora followed his lead into the courtyard, her
blades at the ready in case of an ambush.

The courtyard, or outer bailey as it was more properly
known, was empty. Jake guessed that the watchmen didn't
take the guarding part of their duties very seriously. After
all, who would be foolish enough to sneak into a castle run
by a crazed witchfinder? Jake and Pandora crept towards the
inner gateway. Like the outer, this entrance was blocked,
except there was no gruesome barrier, it had simply been
bricked up.

'Eleanor's in the keep on the other side,' Jake said, looking up at the soul-light that hovered over the castle's central
compound. 'There must be a way through.'

'Maybe the brickwork's an illusion.'

Pandora took a step forward.

'Stop!'

'What's the matter? Jake, it's just a . . .'

Puddle. A puddle of water so deep and black that they could not see the cobbles beneath. Roughly three metres in circumference, the murky mini-lake lapped against the bricked-up gateway. Jake bent down and prised a stone out of the ground. He dropped it into the puddle and watched as it sank out of sight.

'I want you to follow my lead,' he said. 'No matter what happens, you have to stay under.'

With that, he dived headfirst into the puddle. The freezing water took his breath away and ice crystals crackled through his hair. Jake immediately realized his mistake. He had plunged into the frozen lake beneath the castle. He tried to turn, to kick his way back to the surface, but his limbs felt like dead weights. Dimly, he heard the splash as Pandora followed him into the glacial graveyard.

Down he sank. Down, down, down into smothering grey-green shadows. A current rose up from the depths, latched a phantom hand around his leg and dragged him deeper and deeper. As he tumbled, he saw Pandora falling behind him. He had been so sure of himself, so arrogant. He . . .

Broke the surface. Coughing up what felt like a gallon of lake water, Jake grasped the cobbles and hauled himself onto dry land. Before he could catch a second breath he was on his knees and reaching back into the puddle.

'Come on!'

Fingertips brushed against his. He grasped one of Pandora's flailing hands and heaved. She emerged from the pool and collapsed onto the cobbles beside him.

'What kind of crazy ass plan was that?' she panted.

'The Swimming Test.' Jake rubbed warmth into his frosted joints. 'Like the first gate, it's a twisted take on one of the Witchfinder's old trials. With the Swimming Test, you had to stay under water to prove you were innocent. We had to stay under to show we were worthy of entering Hopkins's lair.'

'But we've resurfaced in the same place. Same damn courtyard, same damn puddle, same damn bricked-up door.'

'Same medieval keep?'

Jake pointed to the imposing fortress that dominated the castle's inner bailey. Bolstered by four immense towers, this was the Human Hunter's stronghold.

'We came up on the other side.' Pandora blinked.

Again, there was no sign of any demonic watchmen. Jake clicked his damp fingers, lit a magical orb, and moved swiftly across the bailey. A flight of age-worn steps ran up the side of the keep. He took them three at a time and reached the iron-studded door that served as the stronghold's only entrance.

'Feels like a trap,' Pandora said.

'I don't think so.' Jake switched the orb from hand to hand. 'Why would they ever expect an attack? I think those tests were to stop souls escaping rather than to keep invaders out.'

'Let's hope you're right.'

The door opened onto one of the towers and led directly to a spiral staircase. Jake started to climb. There were brackets on the winding walls but no torches; if it hadn't been for his Oldcraft flame they'd have been groping their way through utter darkness. They soon reached the second level and, passing through a stone arch, came to a long, narrow room with an altar and a simple stained-glass window.

'A chapel,' Pandora frowned. 'A chapel in hell.'

Unlike the rest of the crumbling castle, this room had been well-maintained. The stained glass sparkled and the altar gleamed. Clearly, this little corner of worship was important to the master of the keep.

Pandora motioned for Jake to join her at a second archway. In the space beyond, faint flickers of candlelight fought against the gloom. Jake felt a shudder run the length of his spine. If the castle was truly a reflection of Rake's keep then this chamber must be the banqueting hall: a replica of the room in which he had been tortured.

'Welcome, my friends . . .'

A bearded, blood-smeared face loomed out of the darkness. A young face, though cruelty and pain had aged it beyond its twenty-six years. Matthew Hopkins stepped forward. As the shadows fell away, Jake could see that the Witchfinder was dressed in a raggedy version of his old uniform: high-crowned hat, bucket boots, three-quarter-length jacket. Hopkins was almost at the archway when his lips twitched and he stopped dead.

'You are not lost souls. You are . . . *alive*.' Then his brow smoothed out and he placed his hands together, as if in prayer. 'You have come in search of the girl. Well, well, this is a wonder! I have been serving my God in this infernal place for hundreds of years, and in all that time have seen nothing but demons and the dead. Now three living, breathing creatures turn up in as many days? That can hardly be a coincidence.'

'Eleanor's here?'

'A child from my own time.' The Witchfinder's bloody lips stretched into a smile. 'I think she's been waiting for you.'

A hopeful voice came out of the shadows: 'Jacob? Is that you?'

Jake ran headlong into the banqueting hall. He had thought that he would never see her again, never speak to her, never hear her voice or touch her hand, but Jacob Josiah Harker had found his soulmate again. Perhaps it would never matter how they were parted—by gods or men, by continents or oceans of time—they would always find each other. In the light and in the darkness.

Jake poured power into his hand and held up a flaming ball. Standing in a dark corner, Eleanor blinked back at him. Her golden hair fanned out like a halo and her cornflower blue eyes mirrored his tears. Three white scars ran down the side of her face—the marks left by Mr Pinch's attack—yet, for Jake, they did nothing to mar her beauty.

A saddlebag was slung over her shoulder and in her trembling hand she held out a small leather pouch. Immediately, he felt the power emanating from inside the bag.

Here is the orb and here is . . . the second Signum.

'Eleanor.'

He had almost reached her when Pandora cried out. Jake turned in time to see a huge demonic shape loom out of the chapel. Its rough hands caught Pandora around the throat and lifted her into the air. Jake was on the point of transforming the light in his fist into a hex when Matthew Hopkins's shrill voice addressed him.

'Did you really think I'd forgotten you, old friend?' The Witchfinder coughed and a spray of blood flecked his beard. 'I have been in Hell for almost four hundred years, but my memory is as sharp as ever. You are the Cravenmouth witch that escaped the gallows. When your lovely friend arrived here a few days ago, I knew that you would come to rescue her, as she once rescued you . . . '

Jake eyed the demon in the doorway. The creature was like a slab of poorly moulded clay, its flabby, dark-brown body immensely strong. The faceless thing was using Pandora as a shield. If Jake flung a hex he risked hitting his friend.

'God has delivered you unto me, Josiah Hobarron. Now, in my little corner of Hell, you will pay for your life of witchcraft. But first . . . '

The Witchfinder General reached into his pocket and took out a bodkin.

'You have to die.'

Chapter 23
Three Years in the Nightmare Box

Under the watch of at least three hundred DREAM agents, Simon and Rachel had been taken to the prison courtyard and tied back to back against an iron stake. Simon feared that the Demon Father meant to burn them alive, perhaps re-enacting an execution method that had once been used for convicted witches, but no kindling had been built around their feet.

Hours passed. At first, Simon had talked to Rachel, reassuring her as best he could. Exhausted, she soon lapsed into a kind of daze or waking sleep. Perhaps it was delayed shock from her father's death. Reaching out with his now subdued Cyno-senses, Simon had listened to the steady beat of her heart. Physically, at least, she was still strong.

He glanced behind him at the human hands bound to

the stake: those were *his* clawless fingers. All physical traits of the Cynocephalus were gone. In the end, he had not needed the help of amulets and control techniques; his love for Rachel, and her insistence that he was stronger than the beast, had helped him to reclaim his soul. Even so, he knew that the creature would never leave him. That it would remain a lurking presence at the back of his mind, a constant reminder of his potential for evil. But in that potential he now realized that he was not unique. Every human being had, at some time, to come to terms with their own inner monster.

Clicking away on the south wall, the prison clock registered five past midnight. By the time those iron arms came full circle the Age of Man might well be over. How ironic that Simon's mother, who had fought so long for the Demontide, had not lived to see it.

'Matricide!'

The Demon Father's voice echoed around the prison, and every DREAM agent jumped to attention. The demon came out of the hospital block and marched up to the stake.

'The murder of one's own mother is a terrible crime.' He pushed his decaying face into Simon's. 'Do you not agree?'

'I didn't kill her.'

'But I heard you with my own ears. You could easily have stopped the mutants, instead you let them devour her. What's the matter, Master Lydgate? No bullish denial? No self-righteous justification? You certainly strike a less heroic figure than your friend Jacob . . . but perhaps that's only to be expected. He is of a much nobler breed.'

'What do you mean?'

The Demon Father ignored the question and posed one of his own.

'Where is he, Simon . . . ? You won't tell me. I suppose trying to torture it out of you would do no good? Ah well, whatever he is planning, he will be too late. By midday, I will have taken possession of the witch ball and opened the Door. Without his precious Signums, the enemy cannot hope to stand against me.' The demon turned to one of the agents. 'Bring out the painting.'

The vampire saluted and disappeared into the hospital block. Seconds later, he re-emerged carrying the picture that had once hung above the door of Holmwood Manor. Simon's sharp eyes picked out the painted cottage and the image of Eddie frozen in the window.

'Help! Someone, please help me. Simon? Ra—?'

The Demon Father clicked his fingers and Eddie was immediately silenced. Meanwhile, the vampire laid the picture face-up on the ground. It was positioned in such a way that Simon could still make out the whitewashed cottage and the face of the horrified child. The demon took a scrap of paper from the pocket of his immaculate suit.

Simon knew he had to stall. Play for time.

'Did you have any feelings for her? My mother. She served you all those years, believed in your cause. Now it's the eve of your victory and she's dead.'

Red light danced behind those dark glasses.

'Feelings? I'm sorry, but you misunderstand the nature of demonkind. We do not grieve, we do not empathize, we do not love. Indeed, from the very beginning we saw human emotion for precisely what it is: a weakness to be exploited.'

As he spoke, flakes of skin fell from the demon's jaw and wafted away across the courtyard. Beneath, the flesh was raw and weeping.

'As for Cynthia, she understood our arrangement perfectly. In her short life, all she ever wanted was power, and she would sacrifice anything to get it. That quality was what drew me to her. So, no, I do not mourn your mother. She served her purpose to the end.' He flourished the paper. 'Without her I might never have found this.'

'What is it?'

'The full text of the Catechism of the Canvas Man. Tell me, do you enjoy magic tricks?'

Simon looked down at the painted boy.

'What are you going to do to him?'

'Rescue him from his folly.'

'That's all?'

'Well, I *may* have another trick up my sleeve.'

The demon waved a hand, and from out of the darkness a tall, black box emerged. A magician's cabinet. A repository of nightmares.

'Don't do this,' Simon pleaded. 'He's just a little kid.'

'Do what?' Eddie's panicked voice called out from the painting. 'What's happening?'

'It's gonna be OK, Ed.' Simon glared at the Demon Father, and in the depths of his soul he felt a shadow stir. He breathed deeply. Steadied himself. 'I'll do anything you want. I'll bring the Cyno back, lead your army, just leave the kid alone.'

Simon remembered the story that Sidney Tinsmouth had once told him and Jake. How Marcus Crowden, desperate to exploit a small boy's potential for magic, had forced him into the nightmare box. How this bizarre demonic entity had twisted and reformed Sidney's soul, drawing out every scrap of darkness.

'Don't put him in that thing.'

'Yet again you mistake me for a creature of pity.' The Demon Father shrugged.

Pleading hadn't worked, and so Simon switched tack. A growl rumbled in his throat, just enough to suggest the power of the monster still inside.

'If you do this, then I swear to God—'

'God doesn't exist, Master Lydgate, and you are too afraid of the beast to let it out again. Don't waste my time with idle threats. Not when I have wonders to perform.'

The nightmare box rotated silently behind its master. Passing a gloved hand over the painting, the Demon Father began to read from the paper. The words of the catechism echoed around the courtyard, an incantation made sweeter by his lyrical voice. He reached the final rhyming couplets and a red light pulsed in his palm.

'*Locked in the canvas, what shall I see? Your pursuers confounded by this mystery. And when they have left empty-handed, what then? On these vital words your freedom depends* . . . RELEASE ME NOW, HEAR MY PLEA; RELEASE ME FROM PAINTED MISERY!'

Simon squinted as the light brightened. It left the demon's hand as four crackling streaks that latched on to the corners of the golden frame and lifted the painting high into the air. Eddie Rice cried out in terror.

'It's going to be all right, Ed, I promise.'

Simon winced at the lie, and turned his head to look at Rachel. She still seemed to be lost in her waking sleep. For the time being, he was glad—he didn't want her to see what was about to happen to her cousin. Simon continued to struggle against the ropes that bound his hands and feet. If he could break free from the stake, then he might be able to throw himself in front of the magical streams. He just needed a little more time . . .

But there was no more time.

Not for Simon. Not for Eddie.

A fifth stream leapt from the Demon Father's palm and plunged into the heart of the painting. Simon could see the tip of it strike the window of the cottage.

'Stay perfectly still and let the spell do its work,' the demon instructed. 'If you wriggle about you might emerge in a two-dimensional form, your brain and organs compressed to a hair's breadth. It would be a very *messy* way to die.'

The four magical streaks held on to the corners and kept the frame floating in mid-air. The fifth, meanwhile, drew back into the Demon Father's hand, dragging the painting with it. The canvas bulged out from the frame to such an extent that Simon expected it to tear. Instead, the material stretched with amazing elasticity. The painted lines of the cottage blurred and Eddie's face elongated until it looked like a distorted reflection in the bowl of a spoon.

A full-sized, three-dimensional head popped out of the painting. Simon gasped in amazement as Eddie blinked, twisted his neck, and cried out in fear. The fifth magical streak released the canvas and latched around the boy's neck. It tugged, and with a creak like the bows of an old ship, Eddie's shoulders and torso emerged. Now that his arms were free, the kid grasped the frame and did his best to help the spell. Finally, his legs appeared and he came tumbling out of the picture.

'Ed, are you OK?'

The boy rose shakily to his feet. He looked at the Demon Father and the hundreds of DREAM agents stationed around the courtyard, then glanced back at the tattered picture still hanging in the air. With a wave of his hand, the demon dismissed the magic and the painting fell to the ground, its frame splintering on impact.

'Simon.' Eddie stumbled towards the stake. 'Rachel . . . '

Simon caught the sudden movement behind Eddie's back. Breaking through the rope that bound his right hand, he reached for the kid.

'WATCH OUT!'

The warning came too late. The nightmare box flew at the boy, its doors swinging wide. Eddie looked fearfully over his shoulder. He saw something in the depths of the cabinet, a nameless horror waiting to greet him. From his position lashed to the stake, Simon could see only a faint red glow emanating from the shadows of the box. Nevertheless, he could sense the evil heart of the wooden demon—a heart that loved nothing better than the corruption of an innocent soul.

The box swallowed Eddie whole.

Before its doors slammed shut, Simon caught a final glimpse of the terrified child.

'Ed, hold on . . .'

He used his free hand to tear the ropes from his wrist and ankles. Leaving Rachel at the stake, he made a rush for the nightmare cabinet. If he could somehow open those demonic doors maybe there was still a chance of dragging Eddie out. He had reached the box, and was scrabbling at the handles, when a DREAM agent locked its arm around his throat and dragged him back to the stake.

The Demon Father muttered ancient words and passed his hands over the doors. From inside came the muffled screams of a spirit tearing itself apart.

'What's happening to him?' Simon cried.

The demon came to the end of his incantation.

'Again, I have your mother to thank. While researching the catechism, Cynthia came across another arcane spell she thought might be of use. She knew that, once we'd released Eddie from the painting, we would have only a limited amount of time to transform him into a dark witch. Such a process usually takes weeks, months. With the spell you just witnessed such time can be compressed into seconds.'

The screams ceased and the cabinet whirled noiselessly above the ground.

'How long has he been in there?'

The demon laughed.

'How *long*?'

'Three years.'

'What?'

'Minutes have passed for us. For him, twelve seasons of pain . . .'

Three hollow knocks sounded from inside the box.

'And now I think Master Edward is ready to face the world again.'

The doors creaked open.

'Eddie?'

Black smoke spilled out from the base of the box and curled across the ground.

'Ed—?'

'Eddie Rice. Yes, that *was* my name. You may now call me Edward.'

A pale fingerprint of a face pushed out from the shadows. In the three years that had passed since he entered the box, Eddie's boyish features had been sculpted into those of a young man. Dark hollows ringed his eyes and sharp cheekbones tented his face. Tall, lanky, painfully thin, Edward stepped out of the cabinet. He was dressed in the tattered remains of his old clothes: the tight trousers of a twelve year old which stopped just above his calves and shirtsleeves that rode up almost to his elbows. The sight might have been funny if it wasn't for the expression on his face.

'I remember you. I asked you to help me. *Begged* you.'

Simon could feel the hatred radiating out from Edward. In those coal-dark eyes, in that stony face and curling lip, he could find no trace of the child he had known.

'I'm sorry.'

'Sorry?' Edward nodded. A gentle, careful motion of the head. 'Yes, you *will* be sorry, Simon. All of my good friends will be very, very sorry for abandoning me.'

Edward turned to the monster that stood behind him.

'Now give me my demon.'

Chapter 24
Face Your God

'You will not cheat God a second time, Master Witch.'

The rope of a hangman dropped down from the shadowy ceiling and swayed at a point just level with Jake's head.

'Put the noose around your neck.'

'And if I don't?'

'As a child, did you ever pull the legs off a spider?'

'No, but I bet you did.'

Hopkins gestured to the colossal clay demon that held Pandora.

'This dull-witted creature obeys my commands to the letter. If you do not follow my instructions, it will rip the arms from your arachnoid friend, one by one. So be a good boy and slip your head into the noose.'

Jake wondered why Hopkins had ambushed him in this way. The Witchfinder couldn't have known that Jake would have a companion that he could threaten. Why hadn't he simply used Eleanor as a hostage? And why hadn't Hopkins searched Eleanor and taken the Signum from her? Jake's gaze turned to the girl. Although tired and frightened, she had clearly not been harmed in any way. Something had kept her safe.

His eyes fell on the leather pouch in her outstretched hand. The phenomenal Oldcraft emanating from the second Signum inside the saddlebag had blinded him to the lesser magic coming from the pouch, but now he felt the power of this protective charm. He also noticed the terrible strain in Eleanor's eyes: she had been awake for days, holding out the enchantment, warding off the Witchfinder until help could arrive.

'I am waiting. Shall I instruct my servant to remove the first limb?'

'Don't do it,' Pandora said. 'He'll kill us anyway.'

Hopkins went to the corner of the banqueting chamber and unlocked a wooden trunk. He returned, a threadbare Bible in his hand.

'I swear on the Testament that I will kill no one, *if* the witch accepts his just and godly punishment.'

'He's a liar.'

'No, Pandora,' Jake said. 'He wouldn't dare betray his God, would you, Matthew?'

An idea. A chance. Jake took hold of the rope.

'My life has been devoted to His service.' Hopkins nodded.

'And your death. You serve him here in Hell, his noble Human Hunter.'

'That's true.'

The Witchfinder coughed and a spray of blood stained his beard.

Jake leaned forward and hitched the noose around his neck. The feel of the tarred rope brought back memories of the Cravenmouth gallows. He recalled the crackle and pop of his stretching spine, the flutter of his lungs, the thud of death in his ears. For a moment, he had seen a light waiting for him. The light of *home* . . .

'Human Hunter,' Jake murmured. 'Who gave you that title?'

'My Lord, of course.'

'When you arrived in Hell?'

'Yes.' Hopkins's eyes took on a lost, dreamy look. 'I had been ill for so many years. By the end, the consumption had eaten away most of my lungs. I was in constant pain, could not eat or sleep, and every time I opened my mouth the blood would issue forth. Death came as a sweet release.'

'But you didn't go to heaven. Why not?'

'It is not our place to question the wisdom of God!'

'You were his most tireless servant,' Jake persisted. 'You found and executed over two hundred men, women, and children. You stretched their necks in His name and sent them screaming into Hell. So when the blessed Witchfinder breathed his last why did his god abandon him?'

'He didn't! I closed my eyes and, when I opened them again, I beheld his terrible glory. He was waiting for me in his celestial Shadow Palace. He spoke to me. In life, I had rounded up the devilish and the damned and now, in death, it was my task to harvest their souls. To punish them for their misdeeds.'

'And what was *your* reward? This empty castle? The company of demons? Your merciful god didn't even take away the illness that had killed you. Do you know why? Because he probably found the idea of your constant suffering funny.'

Matthew Hopkins ran fingers across his blood-smeared lips.

'Listen to me, Matthew: you *know* the truth. That's why you scream, isn't it? We heard you as we crossed the lake. The screams of a man who's glimpsed the truth but can't face it. All these centuries you've hunted down lost souls, but do you know why they end up here?'

Hopkins coughed, and a throatful of blood splashed across the floor. He clamped his hands over his ears and cried out in fear.

It's because they believe that this *is where they belong...*

Jake had not spoken out loud. Like his old friend Leonard Lanyon, he was now communicating with the whispers of Oldcraft. Magic that allowed him to project his thoughts into Hopkins's mind...

All your life, you mutilated and murdered innocent people. You sent them to their deaths in the name of God and lined your pockets with blood money. You lied to yourself, but the lie didn't reach your soul. It knows that you never truly believed in your mission. That you did it all for greed and glory.

Blood dripped from Hopkins's mouth and into his cupped hands.

You choke on the blood of your victims and your hands run red. You are a vicious killer, and you've been used by the demons to police their realm. But why am I telling you all this, Matthew? You know it, don't you? Your god is the Father of Demons, and you ...

Jake took his head out of the noose and went to stand in front of his old enemy, now a sad, pathetic figure. A spark of human sympathy flared in his heart, but an ancient wind seemed to rise up and snuff out the flame.

You are worse than any demon, Matthew Hopkins ...

The Witchfinder's pale blue eyes found Jake's.

'Worse, because you have a soul. Now, *face your god*!'

The Human Hunter screamed. A hopeless, piercing shriek that made the walls rumble and the stone floor quake. The clay demon in the archway dropped his prisoner and stumbled back into the chapel. While Pandora ran to Jake's side, the demon tottered, hit the ground, and shattered into a thousand pieces.

Eleanor came out of her corner. Jake took her small, strong hand in his and together they watched the Witchfinder's psychic disintegration. Cracks appeared across Matthew Hopkins's face and, in the spaces between, a sickly grey light shone through. Jake knew that this was the diseased soul-light of the man—a spirit corrupted by greed and malice. Layer by layer, his paper-thin face began to peel away, crumbling and burning on the air. There was no sinew, muscle or skeleton beneath, nothing but that cold, grey light.

Hopkins's body dissolved. His hat, jacket, boots, breeches, shirt and gloves flopped to the ground. Hovering in the

air, the last few puzzle pieces of his face gradually mouldered and burned. Finally, just an eye and the still-screaming
mouth remained.

'What will happen to me now?' he cried.

'I don't know.' Jake's voice found that deep, magisterial
tone. 'Even the Old Ones do not know if life persists beyond
the physical destruction of the soul. We think . . . '

The door in his mind creaked open, the light beyond
burning brighter than ever. Memories waiting to be discovered. He struggled to turn away from the light . . .

'We think *not*.'

The Witchfinder's eye disintegrated. Only the mouth
remained—

'I see you now. You are no witch. You are darkness and
light. You are justice and fury. You are the ancient benefactor
and the burden is yours.' Flames caught at the lips . . . 'You
are Night—' . . . and burned the mouth to a cinder.

Jake stood silently for a moment while the last motes of
Matthew Hopkins's soul died around him.

Then he turned to the girl, brushed back her golden hair,
and kissed her.

'Eleanor. I've missed you.'

Edward Rice pushed fingers through his long, filthy hair.

'I want my demon.'

'The impatience of youth,' the Demon Father smiled.
'You shall have your demon soon enough, but first we need
to take a little trip.'

'No.' The boy stood toe to toe with the monster. 'I want it NOW!'

'Do not test me.'

'Or you'll do what exactly?' Edward sneered. 'You need me, don't you?'

Fascinated by this upstart child, every DREAM agent was focused on the exchange. Simon tried to take advantage of the distraction. He wriggled his wrists, attempting once more to free himself from the stake. He quickly realized that the struggle was in vain. It was as if the knots had been tied by some kind of vampiric boy scout—the more he struggled, the tighter they became.

'You *shall* bend to my will, Edward,' the demon circled the boy, 'or you will suffer.'

'I've suffered for three years.' Edward laughed. 'There's nothing you can do to me that hasn't been done already.'

The Demon Father stroked his chin and the last shreds of skin fell away, revealing the jutting bone beneath.

'The boy has courage.'

Three hundred DREAM agents laughed in unison.

'Unfortunately, courage is often a prelude to pain.'

The demon made a sweeping motion with his hand, and Edward was lifted from the ground and propelled across the courtyard. His thin body smashed into the old prison clock, shattering the glass face. The Demon Father snapped his fingers and a bloodied Edward dropped to the ground.

'You will do as you're told, Master Rice. If not, I will ensure that no demon *ever* serves as your familiar. Do you understand?'

'Ye-esss.'

'Speak up.'

'Yes!'

'Excellent. Now, you two.' He called a pair of agents from the ranks. 'Help the boy to my car. Then I want you to load up all the Cyno-slaves.'

The vampires spoke in unison. 'Yes, sir.'

'You know the co-ordinates of our rendezvous?'

'103—1F.'

'Good. How long will it take to complete the necessary arrangements?'

'A few hours.'

'No later than noon, then.' The Demon Father turned on the spot. 'Rejoice, my vampire brethren, for soon you will feast on the blood of thousands!'

A cheer rose up from the guards, and with that, they began to disappear through steel-clad doors. Moments later, the cries and howls of Cyno-hybrids echoed out of the prison blocks.

'What about those two?' An agent gestured towards Simon and Rachel.

'Oh, I've finished with them,' the demon said. 'I just wanted them to see the futility of all their grand schemes. You may eat them, of course.'

'And the other prisoners? The ones Miss Croft didn't have time to turn?'

The Demon Father clapped a hand on the vampire's shoulder.

'*Bon appétit.*'

Chapter 25
Army at the Gates

It took over an hour for the vampires to load all the Cyno-slaves into the prison transports. Tied to the stake, Simon watched the parade of drugged and manacled creatures being led out. He was amazed to see the variations between them: some had shaggy hair, others short, wiry coats; there were wolfish muzzles and stunted snouts; a few walked upright while most crawled on all fours.

As they were kicked and dragged into the waiting vans, every Cyno head turned and looked in his direction. Simon read despair in their eyes. Soon these manmade monsters would be set loose. They would do the job they had been created for: slaughter the population and lay it out like a buffet for demons and vampires to devour. But right now, as they stared at him, their hidden humanity stirred. They called out—

Please, don't let us do this thing . . .

The Last Nightfall

Simon lowered his head. *I can't help you. I'm not your leader.*

The vampires left Simon and Rachel untouched until the final transports had trundled away into the night. Twelve agents had stayed behind to tidy up loose ends. Loose ends that consisted of Simon, Rachel, and forty-three human beings that Cynthia Croft had not got round to transforming. Simon recognized the prisoners from the transport that he and Rachel had brought into Princetown. He remembered those dark words he had spoken—*Innocent people suffer for the greater good*, and cringed. He'd been willing to sacrifice these people, and for what? To rescue Rachel's father, to stop his mother, to save Eddie Rice. Well, the price had been paid, and the results were like ashes in his hands.

'Doesn't the freak look sad?' one of the vampires said. 'What's the matter, boy? Missing your mummy?'

'Never tasted a Cyno before,' said another agent. 'Bet it's all gristle and sinew.'

A hook-nosed bloodsucker strode up to the stake and locked eyes with Simon.

'But he's not a Cyno any more. This boy is prime human meat. And the girl? Well, she looks as tender as can be.'

Rachel didn't react as the vampire took her face in its hands.

'Leave her alone,' Simon growled.

'Or you'll do what?' Hook Nose cracked a grin. 'Release the hound? To save this zombie girlfriend of yours, you'd do that, wouldn't you? But here's the thing: let's just say you turned Cyno and wiped out the big, bad vampires.' He

304

pointed at the huddle of frightened humans corralled into the corner of the courtyard. 'What's to say you wouldn't turn on them? What's to say you wouldn't turn on *her*?'

'I didn't.' Simon took an unsteady breath. 'I stopped myself. I saved her.'

'And you think you could do it again? Bet your life? Bet hers?'

'You're gonna kill her anyway.'

The agent's laughter was cold and hollow. He turned to his comrades and the laughter became infectious.

'Of course we're going to kill her! But what's worse? The bad guys killing her or *you*?' The agent snapped his fingers. 'Why don't we make this interesting? I'll give you thirty seconds to decide. You can stay human and let the nasty vampires take all the blame or turn Cyno and try your luck. It's up to you. Will you take the risk?'

Suddenly, one of the women prisoners tried to make a run for it. Faster than the eye could see, a vampire intercepted her by the gate. He punctured her neck and started drinking.

'Put her down, Varney. I say when the killing starts.'

Varney dropped the dying woman. 'My apologies.'

Hook Nose turned back to Simon. 'Ten seconds left, Mr Lydgate.'

'You know something?' Simon smiled.

'What?'

'You're funny. Really, really funny.'

Hook Nose frowned. 'I think your time's up.'

Simon glanced at the roof of the north wing, and his smile broadened.

'OK, one question before we all die hideous, painful deaths. Vampires have amazing hearing, right?'

'Correct.'

'Right, but you vamps are all about the blood. Put twelve hungry *'suckers* in an enclosed space with forty-five humans and they're gonna be a little distracted. Super hearing? *Pffft.* Goes out the window.'

'Your point?'

'My point is that you are about to have your butt well and truly kicked.'

More laughter, sharp and full of ridicule. Simon burst out laughing too, until Hook Nose's hand clamped around his throat.

'You and whose army?'

Simon pointed at the rooftops. 'That one.'

Silhouetted against the moon, a huge figure looked down into the courtyard. He held his club aloft and his voice rumbled like thunder—

'Never Fear! Never Fail! Never Flee!'

Simon grabbed Hook Nose's hand. He dragged strength from his other self, just enough to snap the vampire's wrist and throw the creature to the ground. Then he buried the darkness again, and echoed Olaf Badderson's battle cry—

'NEVER FALL!'

Six colossal trolls, none of them under nine feet, dropped down from the roof. They hit the ground, and the human prisoners fled screaming back into the jail. Distracted by the newcomers, the vampires let them go.

Silver-coated clubs rose into the air and half a dozen

bloodsuckers went flying. The agents hit the walls of the east and west wings and crumpled into bony, bloodied heaps. Meanwhile, Olaf strode over to where Hook Nose writhed on the ground. His meaty fingers latched under the vampire's jaw and he pulled with all his might. Simon looked away just before the vampire's head was torn from its shoulders.

While Olaf stood panting over Hook Nose's corpse, his fellow trolls dealt with the remaining bloodsuckers. There was much wrenching of limbs, splitting of skulls, and ripping out of hearts. The savage joy the trolls took in their work stirred the instincts of Simon's sleeping monster. He could feel it keening at the door of his consciousness, like a dog begging to be let in. Then he saw something that diverted his thoughts.

Towards the back of the fight, two resilient vamps had taken on one of the trolls. This sandy-haired soldier sported the fluffy beginnings of his first beard and seemed to hold his club with less assurance than the rest. Indeed, he looked even younger than Brag Badderson, who had been only ten years old at the time of his death. Simon suppressed a shiver: how old was this young warrior? Seven? Eight?

The troll stood his ground. He did not call for help, Simon realized, because to do so might be seen as cowardice. The vampires circled, darting in and slashing his flesh with their razor-sharp claws. After only a few seconds, the boy had lost a lot of blood. He stumbled to one knee, his outstretched club trembling. The vampires' eyes gleamed. If they were going to die, then they would take at least one stinking troll with them.

Simon was about to shout a warning to Olaf when a small figure whispered over the wall. Simon's eyes were still sharp, but even he had trouble focusing on the flitting form. Little more than a blur, it weaved around the vampires with all the frantic grace of a hummingbird's wing. Within five seconds, the bloodsuckers had been cut to ribbons, their bodies folding to the ground in grisly chunks. Its work done, the young troll's mysterious saviour jolted to a stop.

'Norebo?'

The dark fairy winked a bulging green eye, stepped over the felled vampires, and came forward to meet Simon. Norebo's wings folded behind him and he slipped a short, bloodstained sword into his belt.

'Master Lydgate, what a pleasure!'

Norebo wagged a finger and the ropes securing Simon and Rachel to the stake disappeared. Olaf came forward to catch Rachel before she fell.

'Is the girl all right?' he grunted. 'My son was very fond of her.'

'She's in shock.' Simon took her from Olaf and drew his girlfriend gently to the ground. Rachel's eyes were still wide and staring, her expression blank. 'Her father was murdered. She—'

'She's not in shock,' Norebo sniffed.

'What?'

'This girl's a fighter. She has a tender heart but a spirit of iron.' The dark fairy laid his withered hand against Rachel's cheek. 'You think she needs your protection? She's worth ten of you, my friend.'

'I know that,' Simon said.

'So what's wrong with her?' From his expression, Simon could see that Olaf Badderson disliked the fairy almost as much as he did.

'She's in a psychic trance. Dreaming of things beyond human sight.'

'What things?'

'The past? The future?' The fairy shrugged.

'But she's never had visions before.'

'She is a descendant of Josiah Hobarron.' Norebo rolled his eyes. 'However diluted, magic is in her blood. And we are now standing on the threshold of the Demontide. In all the long history of demonkind's struggle for freedom, they have never been this close to succeeding. The Oldcraft hidden inside Rachel is responding to this threat—magic stirs in her veins. If you'll allow me, I can bring her out of the trance.'

'I don't think so,' Simon bristled. 'When we met in your "Otherworld" you didn't want to help us, so what's changed?'

The smile vanished from Norebo's lips.

'You want to know the truth? I'm afraid.'

'*You*, afraid? Of what?'

'Of your friend. The one some have called "Never Born".'

'I don't understand.'

'Why should you? You belong to a young species, born in darkness. You rise like worms through the layers of the universe, blinking stupidly at every fresh glimmer. You do not see the wonder that walks beside you. And, constrained by his adopted flesh, even *he* cannot comprehend the fearful glory that awaits him. But *I* know his power. When you came to my Otherworld, I played games with you, thinking myself funny and clever. I realize now that it was a terrible mistake.'

'Why?'

'Because one day he will return "to settle accounts". I must make amends while I can. That is why I came tonight. That is why I'll help the girl.'

'Jake would never hurt you,' Simon said. 'He couldn't hurt anyone.'

'Is that so?' Norebo nodded. 'But Jacob Harker is fading. Soon he will be but a memory. Then the mercy of his mortal life will be forgotten.'

'What are you saying?' Simon wasn't entirely sure he wanted to hear Norebo's answer.

The dark fairy took Rachel's hand and lowered his great green eyes.

'The Third is returning . . .'

Simon tried to question him further, but Norebo would say no more. Reluctantly, he allowed the fairy to do what he could. While Norebo closed his eyes and tried to reach Rachel, Simon and Olaf walked to the far side of the courtyard. The other trolls had congregated by the gateway and were busy teasing the sandy-haired soldier.

'Never seen a troll rescued by a fairy!' bellowed a brawny, warty-faced warrior. 'Wait till I tell yer mother!'

The trolls' laughter shook the walls until Olaf told them to lay off the lad.

'Don't let Günter here lecture you about bravery, boy,' he said. 'When we was young 'uns fighting in the Boggart

Wars, I remember him finding a baby wyvern in his kit bag. Screamed like a girl and damn near wet himself into the bargain. After that, we called him Günter the Yellow, and not just because he was a scaredy-cat.'

The young troll grinned, and Günter's mouth clamped shut.

Turning back to Simon, Olaf held out his huge hand.

'Can you forgive an old fool?' Tears welled in the troll's eyes. 'Those things I said after Brag died, I didn't mean any of 'em.'

'It's all right, Olaf, you were grieving.'

'It's not all right! I dishonoured the memory of my son and cheapened his sacrifice. He would've wanted me to stand with you, to fight for the things he believed in. And you know what he believed in most of all? His friends. He believed in *you*, Simon.'

'Thanks . . . ' Simon found himself deeply moved by Olaf's words. 'But listen, how did you know where to find us?'

Before Olaf could answer, they heard a knock at the prison door. One of the trolls pulled it open, and a small, stooped figure stepped through.

'Grype!'

Olaf sensed the danger and made a grab for Simon. His big hand closed around thin air.

As he raced to the gate, Simon could feel white-hot rage spilling out of his mind and surging through his body. Here was the witch who'd played them for fools and sent them stumbling into a trap. If it wasn't for him, then Rachel's father might still be alive. He grabbed Grype by the throat and slammed him against the wall.

'Give me one good reason why I shouldn't snap your neck.'

A hand came to rest on Simon's shoulder.

'Because Roland saved your life. Yours and Rachel's.'

'Fletcher?'

'Let him go,' Fletcher Clerval said gently. 'You owe him your thanks, not your wrath.'

Simon stepped away from Grype, allowing the librarian to sink to the ground.

'Is this my fate?' Grype wheezed. 'Hexed by the Demon Father or choked to death by a Cynocephalus. Seems whichever side I choose, someone'll end up killing me.'

'Pull yourself together,' Fletcher laughed, and helped Grype to his feet.

'What's going on?' Simon said.

'Allow me to explain.' The witch massaged his bruised throat. 'Despite what you may think, I fully intended to join you here. After you drove off, I started the long trudge up to the prison. I'd been walking for about five minutes when my sight clouded. It was the beginning of a vision! I was overjoyed! It proved that Jake was right: magic is *not* the gift of demons—'

'Get on with it,' Olaf grumbled.

'I saw myself in the Demon Father's office. He was interrogating me. He wanted to know where I'd been, with whom I'd spoken. I knew then that I had no chance of helping you.'

Fletcher took up the tale. 'Grype returned to London and

sought me out. I tried several different methods to open a portal into the prison, but Cynthia Croft had left nothing to chance. The place was protected against all forms of transportation magic. Then I remembered that Jake had history with the trolls.'

'I knew Fletcher from the days of the Great Scandinavian Purge,' Olaf put in. 'When he turned up in our forests with the story of your capture, I assembled a few friends and we set out right away. Truth to tell, I'd been waiting for an opportunity to find you again. To tell you how sorry I was.'

'And the fairy?' Simon asked.

'The Unseelie Court have eyes and ears in every woodland,' Olaf grumbled. 'We were about to set out when he appears out of nowhere, promising to help us out.'

'For all his bravado, he looked truly scared,' Fletcher said. 'I've never seen a dark fairy frightened before.'

'It has something to do with Jake.' Simon nodded.

'That boy has always been special.' Fletcher's small voice quivered. 'And I don't just mean because he's a clone of Josiah Hobarron. There's something more to him. Something . . . *old*. I think Adam must have sensed it, too.'

'Well, it's no good us standing here speculatin',' Olaf muttered. 'Jake's in the demon world and we can't do a damn thing to help him. It's up to us to concentrate on our side of things. So what's the next move?'

'We do what we can to disrupt the Demon Father's plans. He's got about a thousand vampires working for him and, on top of that, roughly five hundred Cyno-hybrids under DREAM command. He's also in control of what's left of the

British government. The Prime Minister . . . ' Simon took a deep breath. 'Cynthia Croft is dead, but as head of DREAM, the demon can still mobilize the police and the army.'

'That's a lot of manpower,' Fletcher said. 'My guess is he'll use it to set up a security cordon around himself. He'll want somewhere relatively safe to bring Pinch and the witch ball through. Question is, where's he planning to start the Demontide?'

'He spoke to one of the vamps before he left. They were to assemble at a rendezvous. He gave coordinates: 103—1F.'

'Does that mean anything to you, Grype?'

'Nothing.'

'He must be going to a highly populated area,' Simon said, 'or else why would he need such a huge security force? Given the time the vamp said it would take to get things ready, my bet is he's gone back to London.'

'103—1F. Those coordinates don't accord with Ordnance survey or latitude and longitude.' Fletcher let out an exasperated cry. 'What does it mean?'

'It means a soft point.'

They all turned and looked at Norebo.

'The Demontide originally threatened the town of Hobarron's Hollow because it stood at a weak point between worlds. The Demon Father must have identified another soft spot. He has taken his newborn witch to that location.'

'Rachel, is she OK?' Simon asked.

'She's back with us.' Norebo made an airy gesture. 'And she has news.'

They all hurried across the courtyard. As they ran, Simon turned to Grype.

'Sorry I doubted you.'

'Apology accepted.' The witch smiled.

They found Rachel sitting on the steps of the hospital wing. She reached for Simon, who dropped down beside her.

'I've seen them. Jake, Pandora, and the girl. Eleanor. She . . . She looks just like me.' Rachel's gaze passed from human to troll to witch to fairy. 'The moment he found her, connected with her, the vision came to me. Jake's on the last leg of his journey. The boatman is waiting to take him to the citadel.'

'What do you mean, Rach?'

'I mean that we haven't much time. If Jake can reach the citadel before the Demon Father summons Pinch, then we still have a chance, but it's a long journey. We have to find the Demon Father and delay him for as long as possible.'

She stared up at the waning moon.

'Time's running out.'

Chapter 26
The Passengers of Charon

You are the ancient benefactor and the burden is yours . . .

Part of Jake's mind lingered on the Witchfinder's dying
words. Another tantalizing clue that stoked the light behind
the door. In a corner of his consciousness, a series of sounds
and images spilled out: a glittering fountain; the name 'Jacob
Never Born'; the 'time before flesh'; the cries of battle; the
painted walls of Josiah's tomb; the writing of stories—
chronicles—in his youth. Not the youth of Jacob Harker or
Josiah Hobarron, but a third and very distant childhood.

Third.

He was close now. So close . . . Again, it took a titanic effort for Jake to turn away from the door and the light within.
Deep down, he knew that he had to close his eyes against the
light, to avoid it until the time was right. If he did not then
the consequences could be disastrous.

'Jake?'

The Passengers of Charon

Eleanor stood before him, her beautiful face a picture of concern. Jake leaned forward and kissed her again. As he did so, he felt the pull of the second Signum. She saw his gaze wander to the saddlebag and took a step back.

'It's all right,' he said. 'I know I can't claim it yet. It's like Preacher Hobarron said: only when all hope is lost . . . '

He glanced at Pandora. 'We need to talk. All of us. I think I'm beginning to understand—'

'First things first,' Pandora said. 'We have to get out of here. The watchmen could come looking for Hopkins at any time.'

'And we need to keep moving.' Jake looked at his watch. 'If the Omens have arrived as regularly as before, then the Demontide's on its way. We have to get to the Shadow Palace. We have to reach Pinch and the witch ball.'

Pandora pulled out Fletcher's map. It was soggy with lake water, and some of the ancient ink had run, but the main features of the island were still recognizable. Her finger hovered over the southern tip of the landmass.

'Could still be a day's walk.'

'Not if we take the river. By the way, we haven't been introduced, I'm Eleanor.'

'Glad to meet you.' Pandora shook her hand. 'Now, what do you mean, "take the river"?'

Eleanor led them to the corner from which she had defended herself against the Witchfinder. Jake asked about the leather pouch, and she explained that it had been a parting gift from Frija Crowden. A charm to keep her safe.

From an arrow-slit window, she pointed over the ramparts

of the castle. There was no sun in the demonic heavens but, to the south, the sky was brightening by the second. The black stars faded and a glowering dawn spread across the hellscape. Unlike the northern half of the island, there were no replica cities to break up the view; for mile after mile, all that Jake could see was a stark wilderness cloaked in mist. On the horizon, a silvery speck glittered like a lodestar, and Jake remembered the gigantic steel and glass structure he had seen during the fall into the badlands. By far the largest building on the island, this had to be the Shadow Palace.

A winding trail shone through the red mist. Like some meandering road, it threaded across the landscape, linking the faraway Shadow Palace to the Human Hunter's castle. Except it wasn't a road. It was a river. As his gaze returned to the frozen lake, Jake saw a wooden jetty at the back of the castle compound. The ice below had been broken up to form a narrow channel that fed into the river.

'Hopkins used to talk to me,' Eleanor said. 'He'd gabble on about his life in the demon world, the burden of his duties. Every fifty years, he'd have to leave the castle and journey to the great city in the south. To the palace of his god, where he'd make his report: how many souls he'd hunted down and what punishments they'd received. He'd travel by way of the ferryman.'

She pointed to the large gondola moored at the jetty, and to the pilot waiting silently at the stern.

'Hopkins was an ally of the demons.' Pandora frowned. 'How are we going to convince this ferryman to take *us*?'

'I don't know,' Jake said, 'but we must, and we have to do

it quickly. Pinch could be summoned at any moment.'

Taking Eleanor's hand, he led the way out of the banqueting hall and down the staircase. All the while, he could sense the energy of the second Signum calling out to him. It was all he could do not to make a grab for the saddlebag.

At the keep door, he waited. Listened. There was no sign of the watchmen. He guided Eleanor down the steps and to the blocked-off gateway. He was partway through explaining the rules of the puddle when she held up a brass ring crowded with keys.

'I saw them sticking out of the Witchfinder's clothes.'

Pandora looked at the gate. 'Keys won't help us here.'

'Maybe not.' Jake's eye had been drawn to a caged drain at the base of the south wall. 'But why don't we try the back door?'

They hurried across the bailey. As he'd hoped, Jake found a keyhole in the cage. It took seconds to locate the correct key and open the grille, and they soon found themselves squeezing through the drain. It was a tight fit, especially for Pandora with her many arms, but in no time they had tumbled into the outer courtyard. A channel for rainwater ran from the first drain to an identical cage in the outer wall. Jake had dropped to his knees, and was busy searching through the keys, when the cry went up.

'Sound the alert! *Mortals* have breached the castle!'

Jake heard the disbelief in that word—*mortals*.

Pandora grabbed the keys from him.

'No point hiding any more. It's time to break out the big guns.'

She was right. These demons weren't isolated scavengers like Serpine and Murkridge, or selfish pack-hunters like the rabici. They were creatures of duty. Even if Jake and his friends escaped, the news of their presence would spread like wildfire.

Inspired by the power emanating from Eleanor's saddle-bag, Jake conjured an Oldcraft orb. It burned with breath-taking intensity and, in passing, he noticed the scarlet flickers at the heart of the spell. He caught Eleanor's wary gaze, but she said nothing.

'Got it!' Pandora cried, and the lock of the second cage clicked.

Jake scanned the windows and battlements facing the bailey.

'You two go ahead. I'll be right behind you.'

He felt Eleanor's hand squeeze his arm. 'Be careful.'

Jake stood guard over the drain while they shouldered their way through. Eleanor's ankles were still poking out of the hole when the guards marched into the courtyard.

Clad in mismatched armour and wielding a variety of weapons, they were a ragtag bunch, twenty or so in number. Some wore helmets while others went bareheaded. A few sported ill-fitting chain mail, breastplates, gauntlets and flak jackets. Swords and shields, crossbows and halberds, knives and revolvers were among their weaponry. Unlike the rabici, each demon was different in appearance. Jake saw wolf heads and bird bodies, scorpion tails and lobster pincers, human heads and octopus limbs. A demon with the face of a vampire bat and the body of a man pointed at Jake.

'It summons Oldcraft!'

Another monster whose flesh dripped like a tallow candle burbled: 'What manner of creature is it?'

Jake gave a thin smile. 'That's just what I'd like to know.'

His magic smashed into the demonic ranks and scattered them across the courtyard. Bodies flew through the air, broke against the castle walls and burst into flame. Jake looked down at his hand. All he had done was summon a simple spell, yet the magic had taken on a life of its own.

'What's happening?' Eleanor's voice echoed from the other side of the wall.

Jake surveyed the carnage. Not a single guard had been left alive.

It's no more than they deserve, he said to himself, getting to his knees and crawling into the drain hole. *All demon scum must burn, as should any creature that aids them.* In answer to these thoughts, the voice of the mysterious woman that he had heard once or twice before spoke to him: *That's right, my brother, we cannot show pity or evil will win.* In the darkness under the castle wall, a cold smile twisted Jake's lips. And then he heard another voice. His father, Adam Harker: *Remember the lessons of your mortal life, son. Pity, compassion, forgiveness—these are the things that make us human . . .*

Jake emerged into the light. He put his arms around Eleanor and held her close.

'Jake, what's happened?'

A dull ache throbbed in his shoulders and made him wince.

'It's what's *going* to happen that frightens me. I'm hearing

329

things, seeing things. I can't hold it back much longer. I . . . '

He released Eleanor and stalked off across the frozen lake. Reflected in the ice, his downturned face looked as pale and expressionless as a waxwork. The wind whispered in his ear and a white feather danced around his feet.

He joined Pandora on the jetty. The rotting wooden planks creaked underfoot and the whole structure swayed in the breeze. In the channel between the broken ice, a thick, tar-like river frothed and bubbled. The gondola that they had seen from the castle window bobbed gently up and down. There were faces painted on the bodywork of the boat—human faces that dipped in and out of the black water.

'He won't speak to me,' Pandora said.

The ferryman looked as old as time. His yellow-grey beard snaked all the way down to his sandalled feet and twisted between his long, filthy toes. He was dressed in a foul-smelling cloak, the hem of which dropped over the side of the boat and trailed in the river. His glassy eyes stayed fixed on the horizon while his lips drew back over toothless gums. So far so eerie, but what really marked the ferryman out were the leathery, bat-like wings that sprouted from his back.

The pages of Jake's dark catalogue began to whisper to him.

'You remember what Fletcher told us about psychics seeing glimpses of the demon world and reinterpreting them into the legends of hell? Well, I think *this* is the original Charon. The ferryman from Greek myth who carried the souls of the dead across the rivers of Hades.'

'Great. So how do we get him to take us to the Shadow Palace?'

'We pay the fare.'

While Jake searched his pockets, Eleanor joined them on the jetty. Passing from the borderlands desert to the seventeenth century and back again, it had been a long time since Jake had needed to use money. Now he dug among the pocket fluff, hoping to find a few stray coins.

'What's happening?'

'If Jake can find the correct change, we're going on a boat ride. Isn't that right, grandad?'

Charon continued to stare dead ahead.

'Hmm, I don't think we should expect too much from the in-flight entertainment.'

Jake handed Eleanor and Pandora a coin, keeping one back for himself.

'Five pence?' Pandora frowned. 'Wow, big spender.'

'In the legends, you had to pay Charon a silver coin to transport you across the river. That's why people used to put coins on the eyes of the dead—the ferryman's fare.' Jake's voice fell to a whisper. 'Modern coins aren't made of real silver, but I'm hoping Captain Creepy won't notice.'

Jake stepped to the edge of the jetty. The heavy gondola swayed and bumped, the painted faces sinking and resurfacing. Coin in hand, he leaned out as far as he could.

'For passage down the river.'

Eyes still fixed on the horizon, Charon opened his mouth. Runners of yellow drool stretched between his shrunken gums. What did it mean? And then Jake remembered that in some of the legends a coin had been placed not on the corpse's eyes but in its mouth. Grimacing, he dropped the five pence piece onto Charon's black tongue.

The boatman swallowed, and turned his ancient head.

'Come aboard,' he said, his voice gurgling like the tide.

Jake stepped into the boat. Aged timbers groaned beneath his feet and a little of the black river water squeezed between the planks. He took a seat at the prow, as far away as possible from the stinking oarsman. Eleanor and Pandora got their payments over and done with. No sooner had they stepped into the gondola than Charon unhooked the rope that moored them to the jetty and ploughed his pole into the river.

Jake had expected a gentle start. In fact, looking at the feeble old man, he'd wondered if it might not have been quicker to have walked to the Shadow Palace. He was surprised, therefore, when the boat jolted forward and started cutting through the water with the speed and grace of a Great White.

'Impressive,' Pandora conceded, 'but what's to say he won't turn the boat over and drown us?'

'He won't.' A flicker of magic sparked in Jake's hand. 'If he knows what's good for him . . . '

Eleanor gave him a hard stare. 'Back at the castle you said you were beginning to "understand". What did you mean?'

Black foam splashed over the prow and doused their faces. The water was icy cold and the chill reached into their bones. It had only been a few seconds since their departure, but they had already left the frozen lake behind. Now the river widened and they passed through fields dotted here and there with patches of black grass. The mist that they had seen through the arrow window lapped over the sides of the boat and coiled around their feet.

Jake turned to Eleanor.

'Did the Preacher ever say anything to you about Josiah's birth? Was it unusual in any way?'

Eleanor seemed reluctant to talk.

'If you know something, honey—' Pandora began.

'I do, but the Preacher insisted that Jake cannot know until the time is right.'

'I'm not talking about *who* I am,' Jake said, 'I'm talking about *what* I am. I think there's an important difference. Eleanor, you have to trust me . . .'

'All right.' When she turned to him, her cheeks were wet with tears. 'Preacher Hobarron told me that Josiah was *not* his son. That the baby was brought to Starfall, and that the one who brought him swore the Preacher to secrecy.'

Images, feelings, sights and sounds flashed into Jake's mind: a conversation—*It is your duty to stop this for you were their benefactor*; a commitment, words and offerings—*Here is the Orb and here is . . .* ; burning; falling; hyacinths growing from the altar steps; a young Josiah Hobarron and his father contemplating the storm-blighted church—*Five years ago the church was hit by . . . lightning, as you say . . . It was a blessing, my child.*

'Not *his*.' Jake's voice echoed through the mist. 'Josiah Hobarron wasn't a human child. He was one of the Ancients. He was . . . Never Seen.'

Chapter 27
The Time Before Flesh

'Never Seen?' Pandora echoed. 'I told you, Jake, the Never Seen are just a myth, a story.'

'But we're willing to believe in demons and faeries? My dad told me there were three old races: the demons, the faeries, and the Never Seen.'

'All right.' Pandora threw up her hands. 'Let's say they do exist—these things are supernatural entities. How can one turn up in the seventeenth century as a mortal child?'

'I don't know, but remember what the Demon Father said when he was torturing me? He'd show me a "glimpse of the time before flesh". A time before I was human.'

'But why? For what purpose would a Never Seen become mortal?'

'To fight demonkind? To stop the Demontide? All I know is that, every time I hear those words—Never Seen—it's like

326

something in my brain wants to shut down. Like it's forbidden knowledge.'

'Are you buying this, Eleanor?'

'Something always struck me as strange,' Eleanor said. 'Where did the Signums come from? I remember the day Josiah's father gave him the witch ball. The Preacher said that he'd found it at a county fair and that it contained protective magic. Josiah never believed that story. He felt a kind of kinship with the ball, as if it had *always* belonged to him. He said that it was as if he had—'

'Wielded it against a terrible enemy.' Jake nodded. 'I've felt the same.'

Pandora held up her hand. 'So let me get this straight: you're a medical miracle, a powerful practitioner of Oldcraft, and you share a soul with Josiah Hobarron, who, before he became human, was one of the Ancients? A Never Seen. Jake, are you sure these aren't delusions of grandeur?'

'Maybe. But everything inside tells me I'm right. I'm not just a clone of Josiah, I'm a clone of something else. Something old.'

'Then I have one question for you: what exactly *are* the Never Seen?'

Jake summoned a brilliant blue flame and used it to trace a symbol in the mist:

'Norebo said that there were *Three*: The Rising Sun, The Dying Day, The Falling Night. They are the oldest of the Old Ones. And I . . . '

The magic faltered. The Symbol of Oldcraft, the Sign of the Falling Night, fractured and wafted away into the fog.

'I am . . . '

Benefactor

Jake screamed. The door inside his mind burst open and the light within almost blinded him (*just as it had once blinded the Preacher*). *Have to turn away. Can't look. Can't know. Not yet, not yet.* Pain roared along his spine and he toppled into the bottom of the boat. He could feel blood weeping out of his back. It bloomed in the black water that sloshed around him.

'Turn him over. Quickly!'

Jake screamed again as they lifted him. The pain had worked its way from his shoulders into his brain. Synapses fired and his thoughts burned like magma. Such thoughts that could not be contained by a human mind. His vision dimmed and he felt himself drifting into a merciful sleep. Before the darkness took him, he was turned again.

He saw Charon ploughing on with his pole, indifferent to the drama that was playing out in his boat. He saw Pandora and the fearful amazement in her eyes. He saw Eleanor looking down at him as if he were a ghost . . . or worse.

'What does it mean?' Pandora whispered. 'My gods, those *things* . . . '

'I think we know what it means.' Eleanor's tears fell and spotted his face. 'It means the end of everything.'

Rachel jolted forward in her seat. Before she knew it, Simon's arms were pressed around her.

'It's Jake,' she gasped. 'I saw him, just for a few seconds. He was lying in shallow water—black water streaked with red. Pandora and the girl were there. They love him so much, but I think . . . God, I think they're frightened of him.' Her eyes found Simon's. 'I think they know who Jake really is.'

Fletcher leaned over the passenger seat headrest.

'Who?'

'I don't know. But Eleanor, she said it meant the end. The end of everything.'

Roland Grype had been so absorbed by the conversation that he didn't see the cat in the road. At the last minute, he yanked the wheel left and mounted the pavement. Simon, Rachel, and Fletcher called out in protest as the witch steered them back onto the road.

'For pity's sake, Grype, let me drive,' Fletcher fumed.

'I'm perfectly capable,' the little librarian flustered. 'It's just I was so interested in what Miss Saxby was saying.'

'It's all right, Grype.' Simon leaned forward and slapped his shoulder. 'You're doing fine.'

They had been driving since 3 a.m. Simon had hotwired the first car they found in the prison car park—a rusty Ford Fiesta—and Grype had insisted on getting behind the wheel. Olaf Badderson had taken his leave, promising to meet them in London with as many trolls as he could muster. Word of their location would come through Norebo, who had assured Simon that he would know exactly where to find them. All Simon had to do was whistle.

Dawn was breaking over London as they hit the commuter rush. Despite locust swarms and fiery rivers, stone monsters and dark witches, life in the city seemed to be going on pretty much as normal. Simon felt a twist of pity for those human beings that seemed to take comfort from their daily routine, as if the humdrum cycles of their lives could protect them from the horror that was about to descend.

While Grype negotiated road works and traffic lights, Fletcher asked Rachel about her vision.

'All I know is that Jake was in a real state. I don't know how they can hope to reach the witch ball now.'

'If Eleanor's with them then at least they have the second Signum,' Fletcher sighed. 'That's something, I suppose.'

'Small comfort if Eddie manages to summon Pinch and the witch ball,' Simon grunted. 'Then it's Armageddon for sure. We have to buy Jake as much time as we can. If only we knew where the Demon Father had taken Eddie.'

'The weak point between worlds.' Fletcher nodded.

The sunlight that had been pouring through the windows flickered and vanished. Simon was about to make a throwaway comment about the last day on Earth being overcast when Grype slammed on the brakes.

'That does it!' Fletcher exploded. 'I'm driving!'

'It's not my fault,' Grype grumbled. 'The driver in front just stopped dead. Why don't you go and shout at him?'

Simon stared through the windscreen. 'Guys, cool it. Something's happening.'

They all followed him out of the car. The Fiesta had come to a halt on a hill in an outer suburb of London that Simon did not recognize. A trail of traffic wound all the way down the hill where it met a gridlocked three-lane roundabout. People had simply stopped their cars and walked open-mouthed into the road. One by one, blaring horns fell silent as a quiet terror took hold.

'The final Omen,' Rachel said. 'The lament of Nature for the world of Man.'

From the wooded park by the roundabout came the unmistakable rustling, creaking, sighing song that Simon had once heard in Wykely Woods. Its melancholy tugged at his heart, but it was not the only strange thing to have caught the attention of the crowd.

People shuffled out of shops and houses. There was no screaming, no fleeing; after plagues of locusts, fiery rivers, and rampaging statues, Simon wondered if the world was getting used to supernatural horrors.

One or two voices rose above the stillness:

'Where are the DREAM agents? Why don't they do something?'

'Where's Cynthia Croft, more like. Nobody's seen her for days.'

'Talk sense! You can't trust Croft or the DREAM agents!'

'Spoken like a true witch!'

'Who you accusing of——?'

'Stop it, all of you! Just look at the sky. Something bad's

going to happen. Something unimaginable. Please God, won't someone help us? We need a miracle . . . '

Simon couldn't help agreeing with the last speaker. When a clear autumn sky suddenly transforms into a cauldron of stewing, scarlet clouds then what was called for was definitely a miracle. Spiralling high overhead, a stormy vortex flashed and crackled.

'It's the sky of hell,' Rachel murmured.

'A taster of the Demontide,' Simon said.

Everyone was so spellbound by the clouds that no one remarked on the man in the sackcloth mask.

'It's a strange day indeed when I can walk around unnoticed,' Fletcher said.

A fork of blood-red lightning cracked through the whirlpool. In the tiny spaces between the clouds, Simon thought he could see a scattering of coal-black stars.

'We have to do something.' He smashed his fist against the bonnet of the Fiesta. 'Find the Demon Father. Kick his crumbly ass. Something!'

When the handbell started ringing, they all turned to the pavement. An elderly man dressed in a black cassock was making his way up the hill. He had already gathered a following of over forty people. There was a placard around his neck with various quotes from the Bible scrawled across it. Taking pride of place was the slogan 'THE END IS NIGH!'. The preacher locked eyes with Simon and his voice rose up—

' "I am the Beginning and the Ending," He has said. "The First and the Last". *Alpha and Omega.*'

The preacher blinked as if coming out of a trance. Then he moved on, followers shivering in his wake.

'He got that passage the wrong way round,' Fletcher observed.

'Alpha and Omega,' Simon said slowly. '*Alpha and Omega!* Of course!'

He raced across the road, squeezing through the crowds and making for the little bookshop on the corner. A bearded man with a shiny bald head stood in the doorway, his eyes fixed on the sky. He was wearing a name badge that identified him as 'Larry'. Simon skidded to a stop and waved a hand in front of the shopkeeper's face.

'Maps?'

'Huh?'

'Maps.'

'Oh. Yeah. Back of the shop, right-hand shelf. Um, you do see this big scary storm thing, right?'

'Yup.'

'But you wanna browse in my shop?'

'It may be the end of the world, Larry, but there's still time to support your local independent bookshop.'

Simon pushed through the door, followed by Rachel, Grype, and Fletcher. He soon found what he was looking for and laid out the book on Larry's counter.

'Alpha and Omega,' he explained, riffling through the pages. 'In other words, A to Z. Or, to be more precise, the London A–Z. Coordinates 103—1F. Page 103, square 1F, which takes us to . . .'

He jabbed his finger against the page.

'But why there?' Grype asked.

'Symbolically it's significant,' Fletcher said. 'A nexus point. A crossing place. Obvious, when you think about it.'

Simon closed the book and looked out onto the storm. Then he put two fingers between his lips and whistled. Norebo arrived in a whirlwind of autumnal leaves.

'Yes, my liege?' the fairy asked in a mocking voice.

'Contact Olaf. Tell him to gather his trolls and meet us in an hour.'

'And where shall I say this council of war is to be held?'

'South-east London,' Simon said. 'Tower Bridge.'

I see great potential in them. I see artistry and intelligence. I see the beginnings of wisdom and the compassion of sensitive spirits.

Compassion? His sister threw the word back at him. *Did you learn nothing from the war? Compassion is a luxury no species can afford.*

They are apes, his brother mused. *Come now, they can barely walk upright, and you wish to show them the glory of our kind?*

They could be a great life form, he insisted, *and our magic could help them to rise further still.*

Or it could send them hurtling into oblivion. I have the gift, brother... His sister paused. *My eye sees far. There are grave dangers in what you are suggesting.*

If you mean our dark cousins—

What else could I mean? The little ones? They are the

youngest of us, and though touched with magic, they remain a foolish species . . . Remember the horror of the war, brother. Remember what we sacrificed in order to deceive the dark ones. However remote, we cannot allow the possibility that they might exploit your generosity. If these pets of yours were ever contacted—

Impossible, he objected. *The trap was foolproof. There are no weak points.*

None . . . of which we know. But we are not all powerful. Whatever your pets may think, we are not gods.

I never claimed we were. I just want to help them. They could be like us, I know it. Aren't you lonely, brother? Sister . . . ? His thoughts sighed. *You won't help me, will you? Then I'll do it myself.*

Very well, but know this: they are now your responsibility. A father cannot bestow a gift and then watch as his children use it to destroy themselves. There may come a day of reckoning when you will be called upon to account for your actions. And remember, my brother, even we are not immortal.

He bowed his head in acceptance of the responsibility.

Will you visit them soon? his brother asked.

Yes, although my time among them is brief. Their reality is wondrous, but it cannot sustain our forms. I must give the gift and leave. I will return to watch over them when I can.

You may have to do more than that . . . his sister warned. *But come, I want to hear stories. Make us a chronicle of the lives of these mountain and river dwellers. Tell me again what they call you.*

Sister, you forget: I too have the gift. My name will change many, many times. For now, they call me . . .

'Ayyuk.'

Jake blinked at the forks of crimson lightning that flashed across the sky. He could feel it in the air: this was the tipping point—the dawn of the Demontide.

And it's my responsibility to stop it.

His thoughts scurried back to the dream. It floated before him, cracking and breaking apart, forbidden knowledge slipping back under the door. Except, this time, fragments remained and the door stayed slightly ajar. A sister. A brother. The lonely Never Seen. For the fatherless, motherless Jacob Harker the thought of a family warmed his heart but, like all families, there had been disagreements. They had tried to prevent him from bestowing 'the gift' on the people of the mountain and the river.

Jake suddenly remembered something that he'd said to his friend Leonard Lanyon in the cellar of the Shire Hall—

Sometimes I think I know where it comes from. Oldcraft. Magic . . . Who placed it in the Earth. Who allowed humans to feel its touch . . .

'Me,' he whispered, incredulous.

A hand stroked his hair. Eleanor smiled down at him. He had always been able to read her like a book. Now, in the fine lines around her eyes, in the twist of her perfect mouth and the tremor of her jaw, he read the opening chapters of heartbreak.

'Stop thinking about it,' she pleaded.

'Why?'

'Because I'm afraid that, any minute now, you're going to remember that last, little detail. And if that happens . . . '

Jake knew the consquences. Deep down, he knew, but again he strove to push the thought away. He also managed to ignore the grinding pains in his back and shoulders, for they too spoke a truth that he could not face. Not yet.

'I think I'm going to lose you,' Eleanor said. 'For good this time.'

'You won't ever lose me. Not again.'

'How can you make that promise? Jake, I *know* what you are.'

He sat up and took her hands. Placed them against his young, human heart.

'I swear, I'll *never* leave you. That's my most sacred promise.'

They sat in silence, heads bent together. For a while, all they could hear was the steady slosh of Charon's pole and the ripple of the river.

Then Pandora touched their shoulders.

'We're here.'

Chapter 28
Citadel of the Demons

'A group of escaped prisoners from Princetown Prison have re-leased a statement describing how they were saved from certain death by what appear to have been huge, troll-like beings. They have also made serious allegations of torture and human genetic experimentation against Prime Minister Cynthia Croft...

'In related news, large numbers of DREAM agents have been spotted in the area around Tower Hill. Traffic is being diverted and tourists and pedestrians have been denied access to Tower Bridge. Confined to the west side of the bridge, a march against the government's "War on Witchcraft" has taken the opportunity to assemble at the famous landmark. Hundreds of thousands of protestors...'

Simon turned off the car radio.

'They're playing right into the Demon Father's hands. The more people in the streets, the more victims for the Cynos to round up.'

'And the bigger the meal for the demons when they come through,' Rachel said. 'The news coverage will draw larger and larger crowds. This is going to be carnage.'

'Yeah, and there's nothing we can do about it.'

'I wouldn't say that.'

Simon, Rachel, and Grype turned to Fletcher Clerval.

'Remember how I got rid of the locusts? Well, one swarm is very much like another. All I would have to do is program a Hand of Glory so that it focuses on the genetic signature of human beings, and then concentrate the blast on the area around Tower Bridge. It won't eliminate the entire crowd, but a good many could be saved.'

'When you say "blast" and "eliminate".' Rachel raised an eyebrow. 'Didn't the locusts end up in space?'

'My dear girl, of course I'd *aim* to transport the pro-testors somewhere with a relatively benign atmosphere. Lincolnshire, maybe.'

Rachel nodded. 'If we do nothing then they're as good as dead anyway. OK, Fletcher, what do you need?'

'A few things from my lab.'

'Then we better make it quick.' Simon checked his watch. 'We're supposed to be meeting Olaf at St Katherine's Docks in half an hour.'

Grype toed the accelerator and swept the car onto Holland Park Avenue. As luck would have it, they were not far from Fletcher's Marble Arch hideaway.

Simon looked up at the tempestuous sky. It was 11:16 a.m., but it could well have been the middle of the night. With the brooding red clouds darkening by the minute, it seemed as if

The Last Nightfall

an early nightfall had settled over London. Not just London, he corrected himself, the entire world.

Reports had been coming in on the radio all morning. The same darkness had gathered over New York, Tokyo, Paris, Berlin, Madrid, Sydney, Cairo, Beijing; every major city, every town, village, field and forest, river and mountain on the surface of the planet was now capped with swirling, volcanic clouds. While scientists and priests, politicians and journalists argued over the cause of the global storm, the people of Earth tended to agree on one thing.

Something very bad was about to happen to their world.

Charon moored his ferry in a corner of the colossal harbour. Another faultless recreation, this time of a twenty-first century port. Loading cranes towered over the jetties and there were even replica ships on display. Jake could see passenger ferries and merchant vessels, military boats and cruise liners. Beyond the harbour gate, the jagged silhouette of a modern city clawed at a troubled sky. They had reached the southern tip of the island and the citadel of the demons.

The boat rocked as Jake got to his feet. He helped Pandora and Eleanor onto the quayside, then took a final look at the ferryman. Charon seemed to stare right through him, out of the harbour and back into the river. Charon was a demon, and yet he had brought the enemies of his kind to the gates of the citadel. Jake wondered why. The answer came to him from that deep store of knowledge that, for the time being, he was trying his best to ignore.

Demons, faeries, the Never Seen: the Old Ones were not immortals fixed in time. They were as affected by the slow tread of eternity as any creature. Like Matthew Hopkins, Charon had been given a job by the Demon Father. A dull, monotonous task that, over the course of centuries, had eaten away at his mind and left him a hollow shell. Jake wondered whether, one day, *he* might end up like that. A mindless ghost walking through the ages . . .

As Pandora and Eleanor hauled him onto the quay, Jake felt two bright stabs of pain drive into his shoulders. He staggered onto his hands and knees, screaming against the agony. Blood pulsed out of his back and dripped down his arms. He held up his hands—fingers splayed, they looked like two scarlet wings.

'You know, don't you?' he groaned. 'No. Don't say it out loud. I'm holding the words back, but only just.'

He rose to his feet and wiped his palms against his sides.

'I'm Jacob Harker. Son of Adam and Claire. I'm me.' He took a deep breath. 'Still me.'

When he tried to walk his legs trembled, and so Eleanor and Pandora took an arm each and supported him to the harbour gate. It felt to Jake that his body was weakening. That bone and muscle were losing cohesion, that organs and sinew were failing. He thought of that phrase—*the time before flesh*—and shuddered.

The harbour's chain-link fence stood open. Jake and his friends passed through and walked out onto a wide city street uncluttered by traffic or litter. As far as the eye could see, skyscrapers reached into the stormy heavens. This long canyon of steel and glass reminded Jake of a typical New York street, beautiful in its empty, eerie way.

The clouds rumbled and red lightning strobed the sky. When it flashed against the windows of the buildings, an army of dark forms was revealed. Thousands, perhaps millions of watchful demons. The doors of the skyscrapers swung open and the monsters filed onto the street. They formed into an avenue that stretched the entire city block.

'This is *not* good,' Pandora muttered.

'Understatement of the millennium,' Jake said.

'What are we going to do?'

'Nothing else we can do . . . '

Jake marched forward.

All demon life was here. Every conceivable mutilation and deformity, every combination of animal, bird, fish, insect and man. Every horror that had ever haunted a wardrobe or lurked under a child's bed. Spider-forms with raven heads; giant millipedes with razor feet; dogs with the gnashing jaws of moray eels sprouting from their stomachs; creatures that looked like circus clowns until they opened their eyes and you saw the maggots feasting inside their skulls. Zombie demons whose flesh mouldered. Pyro demons whose bodies burned. Shadow demons who you could not see, but whose anger and hatred slashed at you like iron hooks.

A few months ago, Jake would have closed his eyes in terror.

Now he looked at each face, his gaze sure and steady.

Pandora reached for her knives and Rachel held out the charm given to her by Frija Crowden.

'Don't bother,' Jake said. 'The entire demon horde is here. If they wanted, they could tear us apart in seconds.'

'Then why don't they?'

'Because they want me to see their victory.' Jake spoke in those magisterial tones he had once associated with Josiah Hobarron. Now he wasn't sure *whose* voice it was, nor did he fully understand the words: 'I was there when the trap was sprung and they were consigned to the shadows. I stand witness now to their resurrection.'

A high, sing-song voice rang down the street—

'I can hear you, boy conjuror!' The unseen speaker laughed. 'Come, we shall not hurt you or your friends . . . That is a pleasure reserved for our Father. Hurry now, time is running short. You can feel it, can't you? The march of the Demontide. The inevitable darkness drawing in. We all of us wait to be summoned.'

Though pain still pressed against him (*ignore it, deny it, push the truth away*), Jake dredged up a hidden reserve of strength and strode on. He no longer looked at the avenue of demons, for in the distance he could see the end of his long journey.

'That's it!' the voice called. 'Come to the Shadow Palace and you shall witness the final act in this great drama. The fall of your beloved humans and demonkind's return to the universe!'

As Jake marched on his long, barren shadow was thrown before him. A shadow that stretched a mile or more down the road until it reached the foot of a gleaming tower. The mocking voices of the demons on either side dried up. A simple shadow, and suddenly they were less sure of themselves. They whispered nervously and some even stumbled back into the safety of the skyscrapers.

You might well be nervous, Eleanor thought.

He had promised that they would be together, that he would never leave her again. But she had seen what was slowly growing out of his back, and she doubted that Jake could keep his promise.

He stopped at the glass doors of the tower. The tallest of the skyscrapers, it shone like a new pin.

'It's a replica of Hobarron Tower,' he said. 'The head-quarters of the Elders remade by demons.'

'But this is their Shadow Palace,' Pandora objected. 'Their ancient citadel.'

'And like everything else here, the palace changes as the centuries pass. Once it might have been a castle of airy shadows, now they've re-imagined it to look like this.'

'Why would they do that?'

'To mock their enemies. Arrogance was always a weakness of theirs.'

He opened the skyscraper doors and they stepped inside. The reception area was another spotless recreation, complete with panpipe muzak drifting through concealed speakers. They made their way to the lifts and Jake punched the call button. The carriage arrived with a cheery *ping*.

'Which floor?' Pandora asked.

'All the way to the top, I think.'

Pandora pressed '67' and they started their assent.

'So, what's the plan?'

'We take the witch ball from Pinch. Then, somehow, I use the Signums to transport us back to Earth. I'll deal with the Demon Father when we get there.'

'Wait a minute: how do we know Pinch is even here?'

'That was his voice we heard in the street.'

'But we've never heard Pinch's voice before, have we?'

'You haven't,' Jake agreed. 'More important than Pinch, though, I can feel the witch ball.'

His gaze wandered to the bulge in Eleanor's saddlebag.

'It's waiting for me.'

'Well, this all sounds very promising.' Pandora took the blades of her ancestors from their hiding place. 'Gods help us, that's all I can say.'

Another ping. The digital display above the button panel flashed '67'.

Jake stepped forward.

A supernatural wind, furious and fiery, blasted through the gap between the doors. Jake licked his lips, tasted the ionized air.

'It's a portal.'

He conjured his magic.

'Pinch is being summoned . . . '

Chapter 29
The Bridge Between Worlds

They had been forced to abandon the Ford Fiesta under a dingy arch in a little side street called Savage Gardens. The name had struck Simon as strangely appropriate: if the Demontide came to pass then the entire world would become a savage garden. A paradise for monsters.

It had been impossible to drive any closer to their rendez-vous at St Katherine's Docks on the east side of Tower Bridge. All routes through were blocked to traffic by DREAM agent barriers. In any case, the streets were so choked with anti-War on Witchcraft protestors that there had been no hope of driving anywhere.

Rachel voiced the question that had been rattling around in all their heads.

'Agents are stationed at the junction of every road. We have to assume they've got our descriptions—'

'And my appearance always attracts attention,' Fletcher

said, self-consciously touching the hem of his sackcloth mask.

'So how are we going to get through?'

Fletcher fished in the seemingly bottomless pockets of his trench coat. He pulled out the Hand of Glory that they'd collected from his laboratory.

'I could use this.'

'What was it you said about transporting the protestors?' Grype squeaked. 'A forty mile margin of error? We could end up in the North Sea!'

'Entirely possible,' Fletcher conceded.

'So what are we going to do?'

They had reached the end of the street when Norebo appeared in his usual whirlwind of dying leaves.

'Olaf sent me to seek you out.' The fairy rustled his insectile wings. 'I found him and his men lurking around the fashionable cafés and bistros of St Katherine's. Fortunately, the sky looks like the very pits of hell, and DREAM agents were scaring the living daylights out of everyone, so the trolls didn't attract too much attention.'

'There are agents around the docks?' Simon groaned. 'The security cordon was supposed to be concentrated on the west side of the bridge.'

'Vampires,' Norebo shrugged. 'A law unto themselves.'

'But surely they spotted Olaf?'

'They certainly *would* have. Now, boys and girls, I'm really going out of my way to help you, so I hope that, when you speak to your friend Jacob, you'll tell him what a sport Uncle Norebo was. Then he might forget about "settling accounts".'

'Get on with it,' Simon grunted.

'First, a present for the young lady.'

Norebo waved his fingers through the air. There was a fizzle of energy and Rachel's bow and quiver appeared in her hands.

'The Bow of Nuada returned to its rightful owner. I found it in the boot of a car stuck down an old mineshaft.'

'Thank you!' Rachel slung the bow over her back.

'And for my favourite half-breed . . . '

Another flourish and fizzle. Norebo held out Simon's wolfsbane amulet.

'It was just a little mischief,' the fairy piped. 'A joke, really. You *will* tell him that I gave it back?'

Simon stared at the purple-hooded flower encased in its amber resin.

'Keep it.' He took Rachel's hand. 'I don't need it any more.'

'Very well.' Norebo blinked. 'Now, Mr Grype, do you still have that foul-smelling potion of yours? The aroma of the undead?'

'How'd you know about that?'

'Doesn't matter, do you have it?'

Grype ferreted in his pocket and brought out the little bottle.

'Good. Splash it on your companions . . . No, none for me, I smell sweet enough already . . . Excellent. Now, I have a little concoction of my own. A good dollop on your tongue should do the trick. Open wide, Miss Saxby.'

Norebo produced a potion bottle. Made of cut glass crystal with a sapphire stone stopper, it was a little grander than Grype's plain green phial. Simon voiced his doubts about trusting the fairy's magical brew until Rachel pointed out that they didn't have much choice. Uncorking the bottle, Norebo poured a measure of yellow gloop onto her tongue.

'Urgh!' she screwed up her face. 'What's in that stuff?'

'The ground skin of a Cape Dwarf Chameleon, the ink of a Mimic Octopus, and venom from the stinger of the Cloaked Carnivorous Chaffey. That last one's a dark creature, in case you were wondering.'

'Great, so what does it do?'

By now they had each choked back a mouthful of potion.

'Take a look at yourselves,' Norebo instructed. 'Then tell me I'm a genius.'

Simon stretched out his hand: fingers with chewed nails, cuts and scratches from his encounters with the DREAM agents, slightly hairy wrists. Nothing unusual . . .

The colour and texture of his skin started to change. The pale pink of his hand transformed to match the yellow pebbledash on the walls of the pub across the street. Startled, he squatted down and pressed his palm against the pavement. The pebbledash texture rustled away to be replaced by a mottled grey that mimicked the paving slabs perfectly.

Glancing at Rachel and the others he saw a similar chameleon effect. Rachel's body seemed to sink into the text and pictures of the colourful advertising board behind her. Grype had taken on the appearance of a red-brick wall and part of Fletcher's body now resembled a street lamp.

'It's like one of those annoying magic eye pictures,'

Norebo said. 'Once you've deciphered it, you'll see through the illusion every time.'

'But it's not just our skin, it's our clothes.'

'The potion acts fast. It's already worked its way through your sweat pores and seeped into your clothing. Combined with Grype's *parfum de la mort*, you should now be able to pass by the DREAM agents unnoticed. I've already given Olaf and his troops a dose. He's waiting for you at the bridge.'

Simon nodded his thanks, and was about to set off when Norebo grabbed his arm.

'A word of warning. If one draws attention to himself then the spell will be broken for all. That includes your troll friends—they drank from the same bottle and are subjects of the same spell. You break cover, they'll be seen, and vice versa. My advice: whatever you're planning, choose your timing wisely.'

And with that, the fairy disappeared with his customary flurry.

Simon waved a rippling hand and the others followed him out of Savage Gardens and onto Pepys Street. As they ran, their bodies constantly adapted to match their background, incorporating grey brickwork and black railings, parking meters and passing taxicabs. Turning onto Cooper's Row, Simon spotted the Tower of London up ahead. The old palace was a stone's throw from the bridge that shared its name.

They dashed along a pedestrian walkway, dodging a few tourists and anti-war protestors. So far, they had seen only small pockets of the two hundred thousand strong march. At the four-lane carriageway that curved around the Tower, they ran straight into the main body of demonstrators—a surging, seething, simmering press of people. Placards bearing slogans like '*Stop the War on Witchcraft!*', '*Who R The DREAM Agents?*', '*CROFT & CROWDEN: War Criminals*', and '*Witches Are People Too!*' were waved through the air. Chants and songs called on the government to respect human rights and disband DREAM.

Simon pushed his way through the throng. Over their heads, he could see the stern majesty of the Tower of London. This stronghold of the kings and queens of England was almost a thousand years old. It had witnessed the murder of royal princes, the beheading of traitors, grisly interrogations and inhuman torture. Even so, the medieval prison-palace might soon bear witness to death and carnage on a new scale.

It took a long time for Simon and the others to jostle their way around the Tower and reach the bridge. Despite the risk of lightning strike, DREAM helicopters hovered in the stormy sky and swooped over the protestors. A couple of agents had been dotted in the crowd but most of their forces were concentrated at either end of the bridge—no one was allowed onto Tower Bridge itself.

The last few metres were hard going: the protestors were packed tighter than a clenched fist. Anxious not to lose her in the chaos, Simon grabbed Rachel's hand. They had almost reached the vampire's barricade at the northern end of the bridge when they were forced to stop. Behind a line of riot shields, agents stared down the demonstrators. In a way it was funny, Simon thought. When the word was given, these creatures would need neither shields nor batons to defend themselves. They would simply surge forward and, with the help of the Cyno-slaves, massacre every human in sight.

A few reporters had made it to the barrier and were shouting questions at a figure standing on the bridge. Dressed head to toe in DREAM uniform, the only difference between this agent and the rest was the fact that she didn't wear gloves. Simon's eyes came to rest on those long, steely fingers, and his pulse quickened.

'Miss, do you know what's going on here? Is Cynthia Croft going to make an appearance, and if so why has she chosen to come to Tower Bridge?'

Another reporter called out: 'Has Marcus Crowden taken control of the government? The people deserve answers.'

The woman walked up to the barricade. She loomed behind the riot shields, and the journalists and some of the protestors shrank back. In the black eyeholes of her gasmask, two red pinpricks shone like dying stars.

'Your questions will be answered soon enough. You are all in for a big, BIG surprise . . . '

Simon and Rachel whispered the name together: 'Claviger.'

The gasmask head twitched in their direction. After three long minutes, the Claviger turned and marched back onto the bridge.

Simon had only ever seen Tower Bridge in pictures and news reports. He vaguely remembered from some documentary he'd seen at school that, although its grey-white bricks made it look as ancient as the Tower of London, the bridge was in fact only about a hundred years old.

From north to south bank, Tower Bridge yawned across

the wind-whipped waters of the Thames. The central span was divided into two arms which could be raised whenever large ships needed to pass down the river. Four huge suspension chains painted blue and white anchored the bridge's twin towers to the shore. With their turrets and mullioned windows, these gothic structures looked like the kind of fairy-tale fortress in which an ogre might imprison a sleeping princess. Linking the towers, a pair of high-level walkways overlooked the great city.

The Claviger made her way to the north tower and a flight of steps that led to a small door. She knocked once and the door opened. Simon's Cyno senses hadn't completely abandoned him and, above the cries of the crowd and the rumble of the sky, he heard her words—

'It is time, Master. The sheep are penned in—' The gas-mask helmet turned to the crowd, '—and the transports are here. Shall I give the signal?'

A terrible face shone in the gloom, its eyes hidden behind dark glasses. The Demon Father nodded, and the Claviger spoke into a walkie-talkie. Seconds later, thirty or more prison vans screeched across the bridge and into the surrounding streets. Simon felt the hairs on the nape of his neck stand to attention.

'The Cynos. They're here. Better start working your magic, Fletcher.'

Simon's eyes had now fully adjusted to Norebo's spell. He saw Fletcher dip into his pocket and take out the Hand of Glory. With Grype's help, the scientist placed five electrodes into a Petri dish filled with black oil, then attached the ends to the upright fingers of the Hand.

'Hold the dish steady,' Fletcher whispered.

'Easier said than done,' Grype said, as elbows jostled and shoulders barged.

Fletcher reached out and plucked a hair from the head of the girl standing in front of him. This provoked a mystified '*What the hell?*', but the rest of the crowd were too absorbed by the sight of the vans to pay her much attention. Fletcher dropped the hair into the oil, took out a lighter, and touched a flame to each finger.

'What now?' Simon asked.

'It'll take a few seconds for the Hand to lock on to the DNA signature and start transporting. It won't be possible to clear the entire crowd, a thousand or so will be left behind.'

'Wait a minute, what if it transports us too?' Rachel asked.

'That's a risk we'll have to take. Working at this intense level, the Hand will not be able to send out a stable pulse. It'll be more like random bolts of magic striking at the crowd. We may remain here or vanish with them.'

During this conversation, a few of the protestors had begun to panic, thinking that DREAM reinforcements had been called in to make arrests and haul them away. Others relished the prospect of a fight and banged their fists against the van doors. Answered by ravenous howls and the sound of scraping claws, they soon drew back.

Meanwhile, the little door had been thrown wide and the Demon Father stepped out of the tower. The marchers erupted.

'War criminal!'

'Monster!'

'What happened to the prisoners at Princetown, Mr Crowden?'

'You owe us answers! You owe us the TRUTH!'

The Demon Father smiled as he came down the steps. Approaching the barricade, he held up his hands for silence. Surprisingly, most of the protestors obeyed. Was it due to the demon's natural authority, Simon wondered, or because the people had noticed his face? Whispers spread as more and more of them saw the changes in the once beautiful leader of the DREAM agents.

'You ask for truth, humanity? Very well, the truth is this: it is time for your miserable species to crawl into the darkness of myth and legend. The Age of Man is over. The Time of Demons is at hand.'

Silence, but for the wind and the thunderclap of the heavens.

Then one of the braver protestors spoke up.

'He's not human. He . . . He's a demon!'

His smile broadened and the last scraps of the Demon Father's handsome features crumbled away. Skin disintegrated into dust and blew over the parapet of the bridge and out across the river. His scalp slid from his skull and flopped onto the ground, taking all of his hair with it. Screams erupted as the demon's teeth dropped out of his bleeding gums and his nose was eaten back to its skull snub. Soon only a few strands of flesh remained, dangling from his chin and cheekbones. When he spoke again, exposed strips of tendon worked his jaw.

'Reveal yourselves, my brothers.'

The vampires removed their masks. With the sun blotted out, they no longer feared the day. More screams split the air as the protestors saw the agents' savage fangs.

'Bring out the Cynocephali,' the Demon Father instructed.

The vampires unlocked the van doors. Panic took hold and people started to push and surge, trampling others underfoot in a desperate bid to escape whatever was about to be unleashed.

'Fletcher!' Simon shouted.

'Just a few more seconds!'

Green flames blazed from the fingertips as Fletcher held the Hand of Glory aloft.

Meanwhile, dog-headed creatures pushed the van doors wide. Their hungry howls rang across London.

'Flet—'

Blasts of green light struck out from the Hand. They crackled across the crowd, cut short their screams and filled their eyes. Thousands of people began to phase in and out of reality. Before the Cynocephali could make it out of the transports, most of the protestors had already vanished. Simon only hoped that Fletcher's calculations had been accurate, and that they would all end up in safe locations.

He had turned to congratulate the scientist when he saw Roland Grype disappear into the ether.

'Guess it's just the three of us . . . ' Simon began.

Fletcher dropped the Hand of Glory. He looked as if he was about to speak—to tell them something—when he phased for the last time and vanished.

Simon looked around. The scientist's spell had been more successful than he had predicted. Only a few hundred humans remained in the streets around Tower Bridge. On the approach to the bridge itself, twenty or so stood screaming and trembling.

'What's happened?' the Demon Father demanded.

Now unmasked, the Claviger stood by his side and stared at the almost empty streets. Her metallic voice betrayed a trace of fear.

'I do not know, my Master. Some kind of spell. Powerful magic, but—'

'My children will *not* go hungry, Claviger. Your agents will take the Cynocephali and round up all the humans you can find. In the meantime, harvest those already here.'

The Claviger bowed. 'The order has been given—kill the humans! Bring their corpses to the north tower! A feast for the demons!'

A voice rose up from under the bridge.

'NOW!'

Led by Olaf Badderson, a troop of eighty or more trolls swarmed over the parapet and spread out in front of the vampire barricade. *Trolls under the bridge,* Simon thought, *figures.* The moment the army revealed itself, Norebo's spell was broken and Simon and Rachel lost their magical camouflage. The Demon Father spotted them at once.

'I can delay no longer,' he barked. 'Claviger, take care of these . . . intruders.'

He stalked back to the north tower. Climbing the steps to the little door, he thrust a hand into the darkness and dragged out a pale-faced boy. Edward Rice followed the demon to the centre of the bridge.

'Is it time?' His voice was shrill with excitement.

'Yes, child. Now, you must follow my instructions very carefully . . . '

They had moved too far away for even Simon to hear what passed between them. In any case, he and Rachel had more immediate worries. The vampires had broken ranks. Flinging their shields to the ground, they had engaged the trolls. Olaf was in the middle of the scrum, swinging his great club and scything down vampires left and right. Bloodsuckers dropped in pulpy heaps, but the trolls weren't having it all their own way. They were vastly outnumbered, and on one side of the battle, twenty or so vampires had overwhelmed a trio of fighters.

Rachel slid the bow from her back and notched a silver-tipped arrow. She shot, reloaded, shot again. Within a few seconds, she had taken down fifteen vampires and given the trolls a fighting chance.

Meanwhile, all five hundred Cynocephali had left the vans and were prowling the streets. Like dog handlers, the vampires guided the monsters to their prey. Screams of pain and terror drew Simon's attention to the riverside walkway below the bridge. DREAM agents and Cynocephali had cornered a group of protestors. While Rachel kept the vampires at bay with her bow, Simon jumped onto the parapet.

'What are you doing?' she hissed.

'I've no idea.'

He could feel the frantic stirrings of his other self; the

beast responding to the presence of the Cynocephali. Simon could almost taste its desire to dominate. To allow the creature any freedom at all was risky, but he couldn't just watch as innocent people were slaughtered. Thrusting out his chest, he roared the command—

'STOP!'

The Cynos immediately obeyed their alpha male. Every blazing eye turned to him, every hairy head bowed in submission. The vampire handlers looked at each other with mystified expressions. An idea occurred to Simon, and he felt his Cyno-self purr in agreement. There was no need for words—the order came in a psychic burst that no Cynocephalus could ignore.

Destroy them.

The creatures howled with delight, and Simon wondered whether a little of their human selves took joy in this new task. After all, it had been the DREAM agents that had captured these poor souls and taken them to Cynthia Croft's hellish laboratory. Now they would have their revenge. The Cynos turned their dripping jaws away from the terrified protestors and fixed the vampires with murderous stares. Spines arched and hind legs tensed. The vampires braced themselves, hissing and throwing their arms wide . . .

The Cynos pounced. Simon saw vampire heads ripped from shoulders and heard the cries of wounded bloodsuckers. Still perched on the parapet, he was about to turn back to the bridge when a familiar voice addressed him.

'Call off your dogs or I'll snap her neck.'

He looked down at Rachel and the Claviger. The creature

had her powerful arm locked around Rachel's throat. If he made any move, then the girl he loved would die instantly. A quick glance to the left told him that he could expect no help from Olaf and his army. After the Cynos switched sides, many of the vampires had quickly retreated to the barricade. Hundreds of them now held back the trolls, protecting their demonic master who stood with his pupil in the middle of Tower Bridge.

'Do you hear me?' The Claviger stroked Rachel's hair. 'Call them off or I'll drain her dry. Hurry up, little boy, my patience is running thin.'

Simon had opened his mouth, hoping that a plan would form on his lips, when the air behind the Claviger shimmered. Suddenly, a bright red bonfire burst into life. Simon heard Edward Rice's distant and delighted cry, and out of the corner of his eye saw a similar bonfire burning on the bridge.

'My demon! He's coming!'

The Claviger was turning her head towards her master when her eyes went round with shock. She opened her mouth to speak but produced only a wet, gargling sound. Her grip loosened, and Rachel was able to twist free. Simon jumped down from the parapet. Together they watched as the tip of an ancestral blade pierced the Claviger's throat.

Simon shook his head in amazement.

'*Pandora?*'

Chapter 30
Behold The Horror

The lift doors opened.

For a moment, all that Jake could see was the inferno that burned in the centre of the room. Beyond the floor-to-ceiling windows, the demon sky raged with an intensity that seemed to echo the fury of the fire. Jake pushed against the heat and stepped onto the Shadow Palace's sixty-seventh floor.

'It's still here,' he shouted over the blaze. 'The witch ball—I can feel it!'

Both Signums in the same place. Not just objects that contained and inspired magic but puzzle pieces that, when joined, would reveal a secret long hidden. A secret that yearned to be set free.

Pain like he had never felt before shrieked into Jake's shoulders. Bones ground against each other, new muscle and sinew growing over fresh limbs. He fell to his knees, gasping and weeping. The door inside his mind was smashed off its hinges as the truth tried to overwhelm him. Frescoes on

The Last Nightfall

the tomb. A silver fountain. The words of the Witchfinder General: *I discovered two places insensible to pain just below his shoulders.* Names, names, names: Josiah Hobarron, Jacob Harker, Jacob Never Born, The Ancient Benefactor, Ayyuk. And his first *real* name, still hidden . . .

Jake forced the last scraps of truth back into the room and turned away from the door.

Eleanor and Pandora helped him to his feet. They were looking at each other, worry and grief etched into their faces. It was all that Jake could do not to reach back and trace a path along his spine up to his shoulders; to feel that strange, dragging heaviness that now sat upon his back.

'I won't look,' he gasped. 'I won't see. I . . . *Arrgghhh!*'

Pandora stopped him from falling. Again, he felt the grind of bones, the agony of flesh and muscle lacing around spiny stems. He blinked against the pain—saw Eleanor framed against the inferno—saw red lightning flash behind the windows. Brighter than both the fire and the storm, a silvery light was penetrating the saddlebag slung over her shoulder. Jake's human eyes were not designed to behold such luminescence. It was like staring directly into the heart of the sun.

A stray thought winged through his mind. The image of Preacher Hobarron, his eyes like empty caverns, the lids soldered together. *Such things are not meant to be seen by mortal men . . .*

'Eleanor, Pandora close your eyes!'

With his own eyes tight shut, Jake reached out and felt the primal power of the Signum in the saddlebag burn his fingertips.

'Mine.' The word sizzled between his teeth. He moved as if to snatch the bag. 'My Orb, my C—NO!'

Jake drew his hand away. He could not claim the Signums. Not yet . . .

He sensed another light, equally bright, ignite on the far side of the room. Turning round, he rolled his heavy shoulders, took several uncertain steps, and lifted his hands. When it came, his voice was as deep as the ocean and as old as time.

'You have my Signum, demon . . .'

Trusting his instincts, he opened his eyes. His corneas burned and fire licked along his optic stalks, frazzling timid human tissue and scorching every scrap of flesh right the way back to his brain. It didn't matter. As soon as the damage was done, his Oldcraft began to heal him, building stronger, better eyes.

Jake waved his hand, and the light of the Signums dimmed a little.

'I can see you, Old One,' he said. 'Return my Signum and I might let you live.'

Eleanor came forward. While she spoke, Jake kept his gaze on the shadowy presence that lurked by the windows. Mr Pinch cradled the first Signum in his talons.

'Jake, what's happened to your eyes?'

'I . . .' He caught his reflection in the glass. 'I don't know.'

His new eyes blazed: without pupil or iris or white, the left was a silver oval, almost as brilliant as the light spilling out of Eleanor's saddlebag; the right glowed green, mirroring the glare of the witch ball.

Mr Pinch made a bolt for the fire.

'I am summoned,' the demon shrieked. 'I go to my Master.'

Jake threw out a magical lasso. The spell left his nimble fingers faster than any magic ever had, but Pinch managed to outrun it. Pandora threw three of her ancestral blades, but again the demon was too swift. Holding the witch ball aloft, he skipped into the flames of the summoning fire.

'After him!' Jake ordered.

'Is that even possible?' Pandora gasped. 'The portal was created to summon a single demon. We might be scattered across time and space, torn to pieces like Fletcher Clerval.'

'It's a risk we'll have to take. Pandora, there's no time to argue. Look.'

Jake crossed to the window. Far below, the dark sea of demonkind churned in the streets. Every diabolical face was lifted to the sky where the ghostly outline of a Door was slowly taking shape.

'The summoning fire is collapsing.'

Pandora nodded. 'Then what are we waiting for?'

The ball of flame hovered a metre off the ground and was growing smaller by the second. Even so, the heat that radiated from it was enough to singe hair and skin. Jake's strange eyes pierced the flames. Through the dimensional chasm that divided Earth from the demon domain, he could see a familiar silhouette waver against a scarlet sky. In anticipation of the Demontide, the unearthly clouds of the hellscape appeared to have gathered over London.

Pandora stared at the silhouette.

'Is that what I think it is?'

'Yes.' Jake joined Pandora's hand with Rachel's. 'Tower Bridge.'

And with that, he pushed them into the fire.

The Claviger's fingers scrabbled at the tip of the knife that projected from her throat. Just as suddenly as it had appeared, the blade was withdrawn and the vampire dropped to her knees. Simon could hardly believe his eyes. Stepping out of the bonfire that had materialized behind the Claviger, Pandora wiped the agent's blood from her blade.

'That was for Brag Badderson,' she said.

Like electric lights deprived of their current, the Claviger's eyes flickered and dimmed. The creature swayed for a moment before hitting the tarmac with a metallic thud.

Simon and Rachel rushed to their friend.

'How the hell did you kill it?' Simon asked. 'I thought that thing was virtually indestructible.'

'No such thing.'

Pandora used the tip of her boot to turn the Claviger over. She pointed to the keyhole in the back of the vampire's neck. Simon remembered that time in his mother's cottage when Pandora had slotted a key into the hole and the keeper of secrets had been forced to reveal what she knew about Simon's past. Now that neat little hole was a gruesome wound.

'Grim,' Simon said.

'Effective,' Pandora smiled.

'But how did you get here?' Rachel asked.

Pandora gave a brief summary of their adventures in the

365

demon dimension, culminating in Jake pushing her through the summoning portal.

'Lucky for us you ended up here,' Simon said.

'Luck had nothing to do with it. My guess is that a temporal genetic bond drew us here.'

'And in English?'

Simon and Rachel had been so stunned by the Claviger's death and the reappearance of their friend that neither had noticed the small figure standing outside their circle. Now Pandora ushered the girl forward. As she did so, the summoning fire evaporated.

Simon stared at the newcomer. The hair and eye colour were different, but this girl could be Rachel's twin.

'Miss Saxby,' Pandora bowed, 'may I introduce your great-great-great-great-great—probably a few more greats in there—grandmother. This is Eleanor.'

Too stunned to speak, the girls just stared at each other. At last, Eleanor broke the silence.

'Whatever the reason for our arriving here, we've now been separated from Jake. Have you seen him?'

The similarity was more than skin-deep, Simon realized. In the face of wonders and horrors, Rachel and Eleanor shared the same fierce practicality. Chitchat could wait, there was work to be done.

'We haven't seen him,' Rachel said.

'But there was a second fire on the bridge,' Simon put in. 'I'm assuming that's where Pinch came through. Maybe Jake wound up there.'

'Makes sense.'

Pandora caught sight of Olaf Badderson. The warrior was at the barricade, mowing down vampires with his club. With the Cynos on the attack, most of the DREAM agents had retreated to the bridge and were busy defending the Demon Father's position. They still outnumbered the trolls and Cynocephali almost two to one.

'The old swine came round I see,' Pandora laughed. 'Olaf! Any sign of Jake?'

The troll turned his head and blinked at Pandora.

'Ya what?'

'Can you believe it? Even deafer than Brag. I said, ANY SIGN OF JAKE?!'

Two younger trolls came forward to relieve their leader. Olaf stood on his tiptoes and peered over the heads of the bloodsuckers.

'All I can see is that mouldy old corpse of a Demon Father, the human child, and a runty little monster.'

'Pinch?'

'Looks like. The demon's got something in his hand. A glass ball. By Odin, there's some strange green light pouring out of it. Powerful magic, I reckon. But no, Jake's nowhere to be . . . Wait a minute! What's that up on the walkway? Looks like a man, except . . . Well, there's something wrong with his back.'

Simon followed Olaf's gaze. There, clinging to the edge of one of the high-level footpaths strung between the towers, the figure of a boy. Jake dangled fifty metres above the thrashing, iron-grey waters of the Thames. He kicked and scrabbled, desperately trying to haul himself onto the walkway roof.

'How'd he get up there?' Rachel gasped.

'Travelling through portals is never an exact science,' Pandora said. All eight of her hands tightened into fists. 'Come on, Jake—*climb*.'

For his part, Simon couldn't take his eyes off the strange shape swelling out of his friend's back. A shape that bulged, split and spread against Jake's raggedy T-shirt.

'What the hell?' he murmured. 'Is that—?'

'Don't say it.' Eleanor looked at him with tears in her eyes. 'Please, don't.'

'Why?'

'Because when he knows—knows without any sliver of doubt—that's when we've lost him.'

Pandora turned to the girl.

'Sweetheart, we've already lost him.' She reached for the saddlebag. 'It's time.'

Eleanor pushed her hands away. 'No!'

'To save us, he has to know. The last clue is hidden in the Signums. It's time they were joined.'

They all watched as Jake finally managed to drag himself onto the walkway roof. As his feet disappeared over the edge, the sky exploded with lightning. The clouds burst and dark red rain fell like bloody teardrops over London. Silhouetted against the storm, Tower Bridge cast a bleak shadow.

Eleanor looked down at the saddlebag.

'The key to his identity and the destruction of demon-kind . . . I'll take it to him.'

Pandora took the girl in her arms and held her close. Then she looked up at the distant walkway.

'Only one problem: how the hell are we supposed to get up there?'

Simon cast a glance into the streets surrounding the bridge.

'I may have an idea . . . '

Bruised and breathless, Jake rolled onto his side. With the summoning portal collapsing around him, he had barely made it back to the human world. Indeed, as the portal began to lose cohesion, he'd found himself materializing high above the river and the bridge. Plummeting to earth, he had felt those strange limbs growing out of his back begin to twitch. Then he had hit the side of the walkway, and every thought except the urge to survive had been pushed out of his head. He'd grabbed the guttering that ran the length of the suspended footpath and, after much straining, had managed to drag himself onto the pitched roof. Less than four strides in width, it was a narrow haven.

While his shoulders screamed, Jake managed to rise to his feet. He found that he had landed on the bridge's western walkway. At either end stood the roofs of the towers, their gilded crosses shining dully under the demonic sky. He wondered where Eleanor and Pandora had ended up, and prayed that they were safe.

Much of London was laid out for Jake to see. To the north-west, the dome of St Paul's cathedral rose above office blocks and industrial cranes; and there, just to the north of the bridge, the swollen glass bauble known as the Gherkin building. To the east, Jake could see the steady flash of the beacons on top of the Canary Wharf skyscrapers, but these were not the only illuminations.

Everywhere he looked, soul-lights blazed. Hundreds of thousands of fragile flames hovering over houses and factories, offices and shops, pubs and stations. He closed his new eyes and saw the lights repeated. They doubled, trebled— millions of lights, and then billions as his inner vision widened to take in the entire planet. Not long now until the lights would fail. Not long until each soul was terminated and the world descended into darkness. A darkness of *his* making . . .

'I see that you are becoming like your old self again.'

The Demon Father levitated into the sky. Lifting his gloved hands, he swept a dark-haired boy and a hideous demon in his wake. These he deposited on the roof of the eastern walkway, a stone's throw from where Jake stood. Mr Pinch pointed and snorted with laughter. Beside the demon, Eddie Rice watched from under hooded eyes.

'Ed, what's he done to you?' Jake said.

'My Master has promised me power.' Edward grinned. 'I will be a prince among demons. He has sworn—'

'He lied. Look at him, would a creature like that really keep his promise?'

Would a creature like you? Jake asked himself. He'd sworn to stay with Eleanor, and yet he knew it was a pledge he could not keep.

'Look at *me*?' the Demon Father echoed. 'Are we so different, Jacob? Both of us have hidden our true selves under a guise of human flesh. The only real difference is that I embrace my identity. Watch now as I tear away the last shreds of this mask.'

Hovering in the air just above Jake, the demon put his hands to his face. Except *face* wasn't the right word. With only a few scraps of skin still adhering to his skull, the Demon Father was now little more than a skeleton. Smiling with what was left of his lips, he pinched the bridge of his dark glasses between his fingers and unveiled his eyes. A fire, deeper and darker than the molten sky, boiled inside the gaping sockets.

'I know you,' Jake said. 'I remember . . . '

All at once, Marcus Crowden's body disintegrated, and the dark soul that had been in possession of it was set free. Jake watched the Demon Father's smart black suit flutter down into the river. Then, lifting his gaze, he beheld the true horror of the demon.

Chapter 31
Song of the Signums

It was a shapeless thing—a mist, a fog, a free-floating form that billowed out to the size of the bridge and then contracted to a shadow smaller than a man. It did not possess the wicked teeth of Mr Pinch or the grotesque body of Miss Creekley. It did not have the uncanny presence of the nightmare box nor the soulless stare of Charon the ferryman. Yet the Demon Father was more terrible than anything Jake had encountered.

It was a thing of hopelessness. A night-black void, a swirling chasm of despair. It seemed to draw out every good thought and feeling, every happy dream and scrap of joy. It made Jake want to run to the edge of the walkway and cast himself into the river. Reaching into the sea of his soul, the demon pulled all his fears and doubts to the surface. Told him that his life was worthless, that his friends would die, that the world was already lost.

Other demons could tear you to pieces and feast on your flesh. When he was finished with you, the Demon Father might do the same, but first he would consume your spirit and make you long for death.

The demon began to take on a form: a sleek, humanoid body with two twisting, smoking horns crowning its head. Talons spouted from its hands and a rough slash opened up to form a mouth. It was a crude, almost featureless shape, twice the size of any man. A pair of infernal eyes heavy with blood pressed out from the face.

'Do you feel it, old friend? The tug of despair? The feeling that, no matter what you sacrifice, there is no way you can defeat me. Such thoughts are entirely your own—my only power is to draw them out of you.'

The Demon Father floated towards the bridge.

'Before you die, Jacob Never Born, I am going repay the pain and indignity your kind visited on my children. You shall know something of our long and ceaseless suffering. Then, as you breathe your last, you will see this world you love so much become the domain of demons.'

The old enemy plunged its hands into its chest. In the shadowy depths of its body, a green light glimmered. Slowly, slowly, the Demon Father pulled the witch ball out of himself.

Here is the orb.

Jake reached for it.

'Mine . . .'

Demonic laughter rolled across the city.

'No. *Mine.*'

A dark hex hit Jake in the back. His legs buckled and he fell. Twisting onto his stomach, he latched his fingers around the apex of the roof and looked across to the eastern walkway. Edward Rice smiled back at him and swirled the black magic in his palm.

'It really is your own fault, Jacob,' the Demon Father laughed. 'You were the one who trusted them with Oldcraft, and now humanity has betrayed you.'

The wind picked up. A flurry of grit, smoke, and white feathers swept past Jake and tumbled down into the river. From his position, he could just make out what was happening on the bridge. The storm had drowned out the sounds of battle, but now he watched as an army of vampires faced off against a troop of trolls and what looked like a hundred or more Cynocephali. Were his friends down there? he wondered. Fighting for him . . .

'You're wrong.' He staggered to his feet. 'They're worthy of magic.'

He was about to summon a fistful of Oldcraft when the Demon Father made his move. Wielding the witch ball, he sent out a burst of magic. Green light transformed into a scarlet streak and the hex struck Jake, returning him to his knees and locking his hands behind his back.

'First a little pain,' the demon gloated. 'Then, before I tear the human life out of you, I will show you the depths of your folly. Were it not for your faith in these ignorant apes would I be free to do this?'

Another burst of green-to-red light. Jake sparked Oldcraft in the space between his tethered hands, but the power

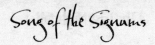

binding him was too strong.. The demon's hex slammed into his stomach and he felt the crack of his ribs.

'Could I do this?' the demon shrieked.

Scarlet magic slashed Jake's face, carving a dozen intersecting lines.

'And this?'

A final burst. Before he felt the pain, Jake saw the blood. It bubbled out of his chest and cascaded down his body. Three gaping lacerations ran from his left shoulder to his right hip, the shredded skin as ragged as the remnants of his T-shirt. It looked as if he had been swiped by a tiger's claw. He breathed in and felt the terrible depth of the wounds: arteries had been severed, vital organs damaged beyond repair.

He tried to stir his healing Oldcraft but the magic did not respond. Injuries inflicted by a Signum were not easily healed.

The Demon Father loomed before him.

'Don't worry, Jacob. I won't allow you to die just yet. First, you must witness the summoning of the Door.'

Red drool ran over Jake's unmoving lips. He could hear the slow, blunt thud of his heart. The light of the world was failing. Darkening. Dying. Home—*home*—was closer than ever . . .

The Demon Father lifted the witch ball high above his horned head.

'Build me a Door, Signum of the Never Seen. Obey my will and form it here, in the hell-blighted heavens of this world. Fashion it from the very heart and soul of this shivering metropolis. Make the labours of humanity contribute to their downfall!'

The witch ball burned like a newborn star. While the sky whirled and the lightning crashed, the Signum sent shafts of magic hurtling across the city. Jake could only watch. Tucked up with pain, he barely felt the presence of Oldcraft in his slow-dying cells. His mind screamed: *You must stop him. They are* your *responsibility. DO SOMETHING!*

Glancing over his shoulder, he saw the boy and the demon.

'Eddie . . . ' He swayed on his knees. 'Please . . . Help me . . . '

A shadow of doubt passed across Edward's face. And then his empty smile returned and he shook his head.

Meanwhile, a dozen scarlet arms had reached out from the witch ball. All across the city, Jake could hear the thundercrack of stone being torn from stone, of timeworn structures crumbling under the insistent hand of magic. From every corner, the cries of frightened Londoners rose up. Their mean and miserable, mighty and majestic city was ripping itself apart.

Cracks appeared in the dome of St Paul's cathedral. A cloud of centuries-old dust shivered into the air as the circle of pillars beneath started to break apart. With a sound like the splitting of a mountain, the entire dome was lifted into the sky. The lantern section with its golden crucifix separated and came crashing down into the streets of Ludgate Hill. Jake heard more horrified screams, and over that area of London saw several soul-lights extinguished.

Supported by one of the witch ball's magical arms, the

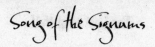

dome was reeled in. Trailing dust, it flew across the jumbled rooftops and out over the river until it reached Tower Bridge. Christopher Wren's magnificent dome hovered over Jake like some strange alien saucer.

Another ear-splitting crack. This time the three-hundred-year-old Monument to the Great Fire of London had been uprooted. The huge column soared through the air and smashed into the dome. Stunned, Jake watched as the Monument shattered and reformed around the cathedral crown. Before he could understand what was happening, more and more of the city's ancient stonework began to collide overhead.

The earth shook and the windows in the towers of the bridge shattered. Scattering debris and stray bricks, the old keep from the Tower of London had levitated into the sky. Like the Monument, the White Tower smashed into the confusion of hovering brickwork and reconfigured on impact. From the bank of the Thames came Cleopatra's Needle; from Trafalgar Square, Nelson's Column; white stone from Marble Arch; pillars from Covent Garden; grand mausoleums plucked out of Highgate Cemetery; the smoke-stacks of Battersea Power Station; the dome of the Old Bailey; chunks of Buckingham Palace, Southwark Cathedral, Somerset House, King's Cross Station, even segments of Tower Bridge itself were stolen by the Oldcraft spell. Finally, the most recognizable part of the Houses of Parliament flew into view. Big Ben spiralled towards Tower Bridge, its broken clock faces flashing as it turned.

As this last component was pulverized and reformed, Jake

beheld the terrible wonder of the demon Door. Thousands of tonnes of stone had been forced together to form a monolithic block a mile in width and three miles high. Hundreds of times larger than the original Door at Hobarron's Hollow, this colossal patchwork floated silently over the city.

At the centre sat the dome of St Paul's.

A fiery symbol imprinted itself onto the dome, and the Door was complete.

Jake weakened. He dropped onto his right side, his face smacking against the walkway roof. He had lost the feeling in his legs and was finding it difficult to focus.

The Demon Father floated down.

'*I* decide when you die, old friend. First you must see the breaking of the seal.'

The demon no longer considered this half-dead boy a threat. He waved his hand and the leash around Jake's wrists disappeared. Despite his sudden freedom, Jake did not have the energy to stand or even rise to his knees. Head resting on the cold lead, he lifted his eyes to the Door.

The Demon Father thrust the witch ball at the dome. The trident symbol glowed a deep and boiling red. Cracks snaked across the stonework, and in those fissures molten lava started to sizzle.

'It begins!'

From the other walkway, Jake heard the squeal of Mr Pinch and Edward Rice's delighted laughter.

The shrill voices of demons echoed through the fissures. Larger cracks formed as great chunks of masonry began to tumble from the Door and plunge into the Thames. The demons called out to their Father, asking questions and seeking reassurances that their long imprisonment was at an end.

'Yes, my children, soon you shall lay waste to the world of Man,' the black shape promised. 'Come now, your feast awaits.'

Eyes blinked in the gaps. Long tongues flickered out and tasted the London air. Tasted the freedom of their new dominion.

The blood-heavy eyes of the Demon Father found him again.

'So near to death.' The cruellest smile in creation. 'And yet what is death to you? All it means is that you cannot come back here. Can never deny us this reality or the destruction of its people. We demons can live in this world—you, your brother, your sister cannot . . . Time to say goodbye to Jacob Harker.'

The demon made a claw of its smoky hand.

A vicious weapon that it thrust deep into Jake's chest.

A gasp. A shudder. Tears streaked from the corners of

Jake's eyes. He could feel the hand dive into his flesh and lock around his heart. A heart that trembled like an injured bird caught in a brutal fist. His body bucked, and the good, strong heart of Jacob Harker was dragged out of him and held up to the weeping sky.

The Demon Father looked down at his ancient enemy—

'Now you may die.'

—and threw the heart into the river.

There was no inner beat to measure out the final minute of Jake's life. He would simply slip away in silence. Chest gaping, he turned his head and took a final look at the world that, for sixteen years, he had called home. Dimly, he could hear the screams of those he had sworn to protect. The frightened tribes of the city trapped under the inescapable shadow of the Door.

The Demontide had come at last . . .

As his vision darkened, Jake caught sight of something moving over the roof of the north tower. A huge, wolfish form rising above the golden pinnacle. It climbed with the stealth of a leopard, its claws grinding out niches in the brickwork. With his knees locked around the Cyno's massive shoulders, Simon Lydgate leaned forward and whispered into the beast's ear. Behind him, Eleanor held on for dear life.

They caught sight of Jake, and Eleanor's hand went to her mouth. Stony-faced, Simon directed the Cyno to crawl down to the walkway. Eleanor slipped off the creature's back and started running towards Jake.

The Demon Father had his back to the bridge, and so did not see the newcomers, but there were two witnesses who could give the game away. Jake's eyes rolled to the eastern walkway and the figures of Edward Rice and Mr Pinch. Their attention was fixed on the Door—on the talons that reached through the cracks, on the faces that peered into this world.

Eleanor was almost at Jake's side when Pinch noticed her. He pointed a claw, and was about to grab Edward's shirt when an arrow fizzed through the air and struck him between the eyes. The little demon teetered backwards. Too late, Edward realized what had happened and tried to save his familiar. The monster's claws slipped through his hands and Pinch tumbled off the bridge and into the waiting water.

Edward's mouth opened, a warning on his lips, when he saw the archer. A second Cyno carrying Rachel and Pandora crawled down to Jake's walkway. Her bow trained on the boy, Rachel shook her head.

Eleanor dropped down beside Jake. Her beauty filled his eyes and the darkness all around retreated. He felt her warm, strong hand in his. Seconds remained. There was no time for a proper goodbye.

'Br-eaking my pr-omise.'

'I know.' She kissed him. 'I forgive you.'

And then a smile. A smile of hope untainted by grief.

'I always have.'

She reached into the saddlebag.

The ghost of Jake's heart throbbed in time to the sweet Oldcraft song. Eleanor pulled the Signum from the bag and placed it in his left hand.

Here is the Orb and here is . . .

The Last Nightfall

The Cup.

A plain silver cup that shone with the light of a falling star.

A chalice that looked something like the fountain from the borderlands.

Dr Holmwood's words echoed in his head: *In some of the old stories and legends of the Witchfinder* this *was the source of Josiah's powers. Other tales tell of different objects—chalices and . . .*

'Swords.'

His eyes found Eleanor.

'Step away from me, child.'

Pandora, Rachel, and Simon had joined Eleanor on the walkway. Each of Jacob Harker's friends managed a final smile, tears of goodbye spilling from their eyes. Somehow, they knew that this was the end. They would never see their friend again. Broken under the weight of her sorrow, Eleanor allowed them to guide her back to the north tower.

Jake rose. The primal power of the Signum radiated through his dead-alive body. He could feel the desperate yearning of the Cup. It longed to be reunited with its brother. Longed to speak the Truth. Jake thrust out his right hand. Still fixated on the Door, the Demon Father cried out in surprise as the witch ball flew from his fingers. He turned, and his blood-heavy eyes narrowed with rage.

'NO! THIS IS MY VICTORY!'

The Orb landed in Jake's palm.

The twin sources of humanity's magic sang in unison.

When he spoke, Jake's voice was no longer his own. It

rumbled with the majesty of Ages—with the heat of burning stars and the chill of the unending cosmos. A voice to be loved and feared.

'*Your kind will never know victory.*'

He took the Orb and placed it in the Cup. A blinding flash of green and silver. A surge of unfettered power. Parted for over four hundred years, the Signums gloried in their unity. Jake felt the stem of the Cup thicken into a silver handle; the Orb transform into a brilliant green blade.

A sword of unimaginable light.

'*It is the Sign of Oldcraft,*' he murmured. '*The symbol of True Magic.*'

And with those words, he entered the forbidden room inside his mind, and the Truth was revealed to him.

I AM NIGHTFALL.

Chapter 32
Nightfall

Time seemed to stop as the Truth unwound.

The first thing that came to Nightfall was Norebo's poem. The dark fairy had always been fond of word games.

'Look to the *Third*, Jacob, and you will find the answers you seek . . . '

GrAceless mortals, be not afraid

When the universe was still young, two life forms existed that were aware of each other. Like all living things that were to follow, these creatures had no knowledge of their origins or how reality had been formed. Gods had no meaning for them, and they knew no power higher than themselves.

Collectively they are called the Old Ones. In their jumble-headed way, humans and dark creatures have extended that name to include the faeries, and, although those beings are very ancient, the demons and the Never Seen are older by far. Oldest of the Old Ones, the Never Seen came first and are the most powerful. They are the keepers and wielders of magic and their individual names as old as the stars—

Dawn, the Judge.

Twilight, the Lawmaker.

Nightfall, the Chronicler. The scribe. The storyteller.

The demons possessed no magic, but they were legion. Thousands of dark-hearted tyrants arrayed against the trio of Never Seen. Both species knew that a time might come when other life forms would emerge and creation might have to be shared. The lonely Never Seen looked forward to this epoch while the demons wished only to dominate and enslave. Something had to be done.

The first battle of the war raged from planet to planet, cosmos to cosmos. It was fought on the lip of event horizons and in the bleakest reaches of space. It blazed across millennia, and each second was recorded in the chronicles of Nightfall. Nightfall, whose commitment to wiping out demonkind made him a merciless warrior. He wrote in his great book—*No evil should ever go unpunished. The price of cruelty is death.*

The Never Seen had the magic but the demons had the numbers. They could not be defeated, and so clever Dawn devised the Great Deceit. She offered the demons a deal: if they promised not to use the power for evil then the Never Seen would grant them the secret of Oldcraft. Of course, the dark ones were suspicious, but Dawn pretended to demand large areas of territory in order to put them off the scent. For creatures that hungered for magic, the bait was irresistible.

The truce and the giving was to take place in the shadow of a dying star. All demons wishing to possess Oldcraft must attend. It had taken the Never Seen years to construct the shadow prison—an inescapable fragment of the universe sealed with mystic locks. Dawn, Twilight, and Nightfall had poured so much of their power into the building of it that afterwards their Oldcraft was never quite the same. Power had been lost.

The time came. Led by their Father, the demons congregated in the orbit of the neutron star. Finding themselves alone, they called out, demanding that the Never Seen honour their promise and hand over the secret. Light years away, Dawn and her brothers channelled the power of their Signums through the heart of the collapsing star. The trap was sprung. The demons were stripped of their forms and the shadowy reality of their new home closed around them.

Their long imprisonment had begun.

If Night falls fast, you may survive

Millennia passed, and the Three kept a lonely vigil over creation.

And then, during his wanderings in a distant corner of the universe, Nightfall discovered a life form not unlike his own. Admittedly, they were a primitive species, in cosmic terms no more than newborns, and yet he immediately saw their potential. They had the rudiments of language, of art, of song. More than that, their soul-lights shone with compassion and tenderness. They had no magic, but during his brief visits to their world, he observed their potential to use Oldcraft for good.

He had found the tribe living in a lush valley beside a great river. At first, they had been frightened of him, with his green and silver eyes, his cup of light and his orb as brilliant as the rising sun. On that first visit, Nightfall had been unable to reassure them. The atmosphere of their planet burned his body and he found that he could stay on the surface for only brief periods. Time enough to talk, but only if they would listen.

Eventually he won the trust of a young girl and, over the course of several years, discovered that his first impressions had been correct. These people were worthy of magic. Given time, they could become a great and wise species. Returning to his brother and sister, he had sought permission to make a gift of their Oldcraft. Dawn and Twilight had not welcomed the idea. Indeed, Dawn had foreseen the possibility of the demons somehow using these people to escape the shadow prison. She had told Nightfall that, if he became the humans' benefactor, then he must also be responsible for them . . .

No Gods will come to thy aid

She was soon proved right. Although it took the demons many centuries to convince all humans that magic had been *their* gift, the first demonic appearance on the planet happened only three generations after Nightfall had poured his Oldcraft into the earth. At first, he was furious. He had wanted to return and wipe out every human whose bitterness and hatred had succeeded in breaching the demon prison. But Dawn would not have it. If the humans wished to use the gift to destroy themselves that was their business. The Never Seen had interfered too much already. In any case, the demons coming through were weak servants—shadows of their former selves. They posed no threat.

And so the years passed, and Nightfall began to forget about Earth and its people.

ThE chronicler must burn alive

In the human era of 1625, Dawn was woken from celestial sleep by a vision.

She had seen a man with a face of breathtaking beauty and a soul as ugly as any demon's. He was a sorcerer, a witch. Together with his familiar, he would summon a Door to the demon prison. Believing that all demonkind would serve him, he planned to release the horde.

The time had come for Nightfall to honour his promise. He said:

'I will go to Earth and destroy this man.'

'We do not murder people because they might one day do evil,' Twilight snapped.

'In any case, my vision is of things twenty years hence,' Dawn said. 'You know what visions are like, my brother. I cannot be sure when or where this nightmare will take place. And none of us can stay on that planet for longer than a few minutes.'

'Then what can we do?'

'I saw this possibility many years ago. One day you would have to take on the veil of their flesh. That day has come.'

'No!'

'They are your responsibility, *Ayyuk*.' She stressed the name that the valley tribe had bestowed upon him—Great Giver.

'I have to live as one of them? But that's impossible! If I remember who I am, even for one instant, I'll burn up. I'll—'

'We will hide your identity. Conceal it deep in your mind and within the hearts of your Signums. When the two meet, your old powers will return and give you the strength to destroy this demon Door.'

'Madness! If I can't remember who I am how will I know what my mission is?'

'I have given this much thought.' Dawn swirled a hand through the air. Inside a screen of cloud, she conjured an image of a middle-aged man standing beside a handsome church. 'We will provide you with a family, a father. This man will be your guide. He will know some of the truth and I will entrust him with your Signums. When you have reached an age, he will give you the Orb to inspire your magic, but will keep the Cup hidden. Only when he senses the time is right will he hand over the second Signum.'

'And how will he know that?'

'I will give him the gift of Second Sight. To prepare you for the fight against the witch, I will tell this preacher man to send you out into the world. You will fight whatever evil you find, honing your skills as you go. Many dark creatures now stalk your once-beloved Earth.'

'I must live a human life.'

'You saw great potential in these people, Nightfall. Perhaps it is time you experienced that potential for yourself. Are you ready?'

He had no arguments left. It had been his mistake to give the humans magic, and now he must pay for it. He held out a Signum to his sister.

'Here is the Orb . . . '

And one to his brother.

' . . . and here is the Cup.'

HeLl will fall and he will cry

The last memories of his Never Seen life—

The fall to earth. The impact that shattered the windows of the church and trembled its walls askew. Together, Nightfall and his sister had smashed through the roof and landed in a storm of light. They had not expected to find the old preacher praying before the altar.

His sight was blasted, his eyes burned out of their sockets. Dawn laid her bundle below the altar and approached the screaming man. She placed her hands against his temples and her magic relieved the pain. Through the whispers of Oldcraft, she communicated with him. Told him of the Old Ones and the great war; of demonkind's imprisonment and the folly of her softhearted brother. Told him of her vision and the trust she hoped he would accept. In return for his help, the Never

Seen granted him sight unbound by time and space.

Trembling, the old man asked if she had been sent by God. Dawn denied knowledge of any creator.

'I hold my faith dear,' he said, 'and I sense much that is good in you. Though you do not know Him, perhaps God works through you.'

'Perhaps,' Dawn conceded.

'Lead me to the child.'

The little fleshy body felt strange, the tiny mind too small to contain Nightfall's sprawling consciousness. In the celestial halls of the Never Seen he had been transformed, his majesty reduced to the form of a human child. Magic stirred in these new veins but it was not the powerful Oldcraft he had known.

He felt himself being lifted and placed into the Preacher's arms. A kindly, wrinkled face smiled down at him. To his surprise, Nightfall found himself smiling back.

'Hyacinths.'

Dawn frowned.

'Hyacinths,' the Preacher repeated. 'Somehow, inside my mind, I see them.'

'There are white flowers growing here.' She touched the buds that flowered around the slab on which Nightfall had been placed.

'They are the flower of rebirth.'

'The Never Seen had nothing to do with this.'

'Then perhaps there *are* powers of which you know nothing.'

Nightfall's sister found herself troubled by this thought.

'What will you call him?' she asked.

'I will name him after my father. He will be called Josiah.'

'Strange names, you humans have.' She touched her fingers to Nightfall's temples. 'Josiah Hobarron is your name, this man your father. Your were born here, in the village of Starfall. Your real name will be hidden in a chamber buried deep inside your mind. You may only know the secret of this room when the Signums are joined again.'

She climbed the steps and placed the chalice and the orb on the altar. The light of both Signums had died.

'Should Nightf—Should *Josiah* fail to stop this Demontide, should he die in this human body, he will return to us. He will be weakened and unable to come back to Earth, at least for a time. If this happens then either my brother or I will come to your planet and do what we can to destroy the Door. Of course, by that time it may already be too late. Josiah— your son—is humanity's best hope.'

She cast one last look at the preacher and the child.

'Farewell, brother.'

In the end, there had been no need for Twilight or Dawn to come to Earth. Josiah had managed to freeze the demon Door and, through his daughter Katherine, his descendants had kept it sealed with their blood. Later, by the miracle of human ingenuity, Josiah had been resurrected in the body of Jacob Harker . . .

He Sees the truth behind the lie

Jacob Harker was Josiah Hobarron.

Nightfall

Josiah Hobarron was Nightfall.

Nightfall was one of the Three.

Merciless destroyer of demons.

Chronicler.

Angel . . .

Chapter 33
Parting of the Ways

The memories of the forbidden room came to him in a single rush.

Within seconds, his ancient mind had recalled and understood everything . . .

The flaming sword of his Signums combined; his green and silver eyes: all that remained was the final transformation. The stripping away of this frail human body and the reclaiming of his Never Seen self. Now that he had full access to his magic, the transition from one entity to another was over in the blink of an eye.

An explosion of light swept out from the bridge. Light that cut through the demonic clouds and allowed the sun's rays to shine through. The storm eased to a gentle rumble, the wind died, and an uncertain stillness settled over London. When Jacob Harker's friends regained their sight, they beheld Nightfall's true form.

A pair of beautiful, white-feathered wings stretched out from his shoulders. The pain that had accompanied these slow-growing limbs had vanished. In fact, all human pain had left him. He lifted his three-fingered hand to the side of his head, and smiled. The ear blown away by Sergeant Monks's bullet had regrown, although the lobe was gone. He looked down at his arms; green and silver scales shimmered in the sunlight. Despite their wings, their eyes, their skin, the Never Seen were humanoid in appearance, and Nightfall was still recognizably Jacob Harker.

But I am Never Seen, he told himself. *The Chronicler and the enemy of darkness.*

The ageless warrior's skin began to tingle. Already, he could feel the effects of the planet's atmosphere. He must act quickly.

The Demon Father had retreated to the Door, his arms thrown wide as if to protect it. Nightfall cast a stray glance at beings gathered on the bridge. These people had been dear to Jacob Harker, and now they looked at *him* with such wonder and sadness that memories from his human life came back to him. There had been a noble troll called Brag Badderson, and a mother who had sacrificed herself for him . . . for Jake. There had been two fathers, both wise, both loving, one called John and the other . . .

'Adam,' he whispered.

His eyes came to rest on the girl. A fragile thing with cornflower blue eyes and hair like the dawn. The Never Seen did not possess hearts, and yet he felt something miss a beat.

395

No time, no time, he repeated, and turned away from his friends.

Jacob's friends.

The Door was on the point of opening. The gaps between the fractured stone were so wide now that some demons had managed to squeeze partway through. Arms thrashing, mouths screaming, they reached for their new dominion. Hanging upside-down from the gigantic monolith, their forms were reflected in the rippling river below. The sight reminded Nightfall of the humans trapped in hell's frozen lake. Another memory from a spent life.

While bricks and lava continued to rain down over London, the Demon Father hovered in the shadow of the Door. Nightfall spread his wings, and the demon flew to the dome of St Paul's. The creature placed his hand against the fiery symbol at the centre and intoned an arcane spell. Although he had rid himself of the body of Marcus Crowden, some of that powerful Coven Master's magic had remained with him. Nightfall looked on as the demon plucked a volcanic trident out of the dome. No longer just a symbol, the weapon spewed molten magic.

'This time we fight to the death, *angel*,' the demon sneered.

'That is humanity's word for me.' Nightfall raised his sword. 'In their mythology, angels tend to show mercy. Expect none from me.'

Nightfall launched himself into the sky. He flew with grace and speed, hurtling towards the old enemy. Trident in his fist, the shadowy monster waited to meet him. Nightfall's eyes narrowed. In the time of the great war, the Never Seen had been unable to destroy demonkind because of their strength and numbers, but this was a more evenly matched fight. Although the Demon Father was powerful, at present he fought alone. There was a chance Nightfall could defeat him.

Sword met trident with an earth-shattering explosion of magic and brute force. Up close, Nightfall could feel the infernal despair that came from the core of the creature. In Jacob Harker's skin, he had almost succumbed to that draw of hopelessness; now he was able to withstand it. He pulled his sword back and swept it at the demon's head. Another deafening clash of mystic weapons. With the smallest of grunts, the Demon Father thrust his trident against Nightfall's blade and sent the angel plummeting towards the river.

Nightfall managed to turn his body into a swoop. His feet grazed the Thames and he arched his spine, manoeuvring his wings to catch the breeze. Then he was climbing again, streaking back towards demon and Door. Thousands of dark forms were close to breaking free. From a distance, they looked like insects burrowing their way between the cracks in a paving slab. A shower of stone rained down, and Nightfall used blasts of Oldcraft to clear his path to the enemy.

The Demon Father conjured his own magic. The first hexes missed their target, but the closer Nightfall came to the Door, the more accurate the demon's aim. A missile grazed his shoulder and a second tore through his wing.

Unbalanced, he tumbled towards the Door. As he spun head over heels, he caught glimpses of the people on the bridge. Simon, Rachel, Eleanor, and Pandora looked back, fists clenched, jaws set. Through the whispers of Oldcraft, he could hear their thoughts. If they had been willing him to succeed simply so that their world would be saved, he might have understood their prayers. But this was not the message he heard. They wanted Nightfall to beat the demon and return to them. They wanted him safe. They loved him. The Never Seen was almost as shaken by this thought as he was by his injuries.

The Demon Father caught him around the throat and an arm as strong as a tornado slammed him into the Door. More hands reached out from the demon's smoky body and fastened his limbs to the monolith. With his sword arm locked to the stone, Nightfall could not use his weapon. Nevertheless, he would not let go of the Signums, no matter how hard the demon's hands squeezed.

Sprouting from the stonework, thousands of demonic heads turned to him. They shrieked with laughter, glorying in the downfall of their old foe.

'I will break you.' Those sagging, blood-filled eyes swam before him. 'You know my strength of old, and now I have you under my fist. No magic can aid you, no wisdom, no tricks. I will grind the life out of you. I will reduce you to powder and ash.'

The iron bones in Nightfall's neck creaked under the pressure of the demon's fingers. Eons had passed since the war, and he had forgotten just how strong these creatures could be.

'I will taste your celestial blood. But before you die, I want you to know this . . . '

Nightfall looked into the sky. The storm had returned, knitting the scarlet clouds back together. Lightning strobed and the stink of sulphur filled the air. He suddenly remembered how much he loved this world: its creatures, its people, its evolving complexity and beauty. For time untold he had explored the cosmos and had found no better, brighter place than this. A word swam through his head . . .

Home

'You have failed,' the demon declared.

Nightfall closed his eyes . . . *Home*.

His brother and sister, Dawn and Twilight.

His mother and father, Margaret and John Hobarron.

His mum and dad, Claire and Adam Harker.

He found that he loved each, and that each meant *home* . . .

A cry of pain. Nightfall felt the grip around his sword arm slacken and his eyes snapped open.

The Demon Father was staring down at the smoking hand that, a moment ago, had been fastened around Nightfall's wrist. Seven silver-tipped arrows and eight curved blades stuck out of his swirling flesh. In order to fight his enemy, the demon had given himself substance, and so not only did the weapons strike, they *hurt*. Admittedly, it was a small amount of pain for such a creature, but it was enough to distract him. Enough to give Nightfall his chance.

Free to direct his magic, the Never Seen expelled a blast of liquid fire. Oldcraft struck, and smashed the left side of the demonic face to atoms. Half a mouth screamed, and the demon's remaining eye blazed with pain and fury. All across the Door, his dark children cried out as they shared their father's agony.

Nightfall used the element of surprise to his advantage. He sent out wave after wave of Oldcraft until the half-blind demon was forced to release him. Compensating for his damaged wing, he kicked away from the Door and flew in a tight semi-circle around the north tower of the bridge. He hovered for a moment. Sighted his target.

The Demon Father floated at the centre of the Door. Still clutching his devastated face, he writhed and roared. All around him, hundreds of thousands of demons reached for freedom. *They* would return to their prison to serve out their sentence, Nightfall decided. For the Demon Father, there was only one penalty left. He poured fresh Oldcraft into his sword, crafting a complex spell of banishment and destruction.

'We tried to be kind,' he said. 'My sister, my brother and I might have destroyed your shadow domain from outside, but we let you live. We showed mercy . . . '

The demon lifted his single-horned head.

'Mercy is weakness. Strike.'

Blue flames engulfed his blade as Nightfall charged the demon. The monster's final roar rang across the city, damnation dripping from every ragged note.

Nightfall's sword plunged through an unloving heart and pierced the dome of St Paul. Pinned to the Door, the Demon Father gargled his last words:

'You believe you ha-have won? But I am cunning, and e-even you cannot see all things. We shall meet again. And again. A-and again. Unto the ending of Time.'

Nightfall retrieved his sword.

The demon's half-demolished head sank into his shoulders and his arms and legs dissolved into shapeless darkness. The thing had returned to its shadow-cloud form, and now it billowed into a swirling vortex, an empty whirlwind, an inescapable black hole whose remorseless gravity could not be resisted. Stone by stone, the Door succumbed. Slabs of masonry were torn from the monolith and swallowed whole. Pulled out of the brickwork, the demons tasted a moment of freedom before being wrenched into the void and propelled back to their prison. Dozens of fragmented landmarks disappeared with them—the clock faces of Big Ben, blocks from the Tower of London, the gates of Marble Arch, the statue of Admiral Nelson. After twenty seconds, all that remained was the dome of St Paul's hovering in the wake of the vortex.

The storm broke up, the scarlet clouds crumbled, the sun shone through. Finally, the dome collapsed. Pulled inside out, it tumbled into the void, which in turn folded in on itself and contracted to the size of a pinhole. There was a tiny burst of red light, a minuscule flicker, and then . . . nothing.

The demons were gone.

Their Father's life force was spent.

But there was still evil here . . .

Nightfall wheeled his sword overhead and plunged towards the bridge's eastern walkway. He could feel the hatred and cruelty coming off the boy in waves. If left unchecked, this child could become a dark sorcerer of tremendous power. He had to be stopped.

The Last Nightfall

Edward Rice was too stunned to summon his magic. Awed by the angel, he fell onto his back and screwed up his eyes. He held up trembling arms, pitiful human limbs that could not stop a man, let alone a Never Seen. Nightfall landed on the walkway. Feet planted either side of the child, he raised his sword.

Whispers of Oldcraft reached out to him—

Jake—Jake—Jake—Jake...

A silent gallery, Jacob Harker's friends watched him from the western footpath. Nightfall looked at each of them in turn, studied their faces, listened to their stories.

Rachel Saxby, who had found the grace to forgive her father, showing the infinite possibilities of a human heart.

Simon Lydgate, who had faced down the monster inside, showing that humans could overcome their inner darkness.

Eleanor of the May, who had taught Jacob Harker the folly of revenge, and whose own willingness to see the good in people had shown him the way.

Pandora Galeglass, whose kindness fell like summer rain on the hearts of all who knew her . . .

A stranger called Adam Harker.

Nightfall remembered the words of Jacob's father. *His* father:

You've learned to be better than this. You've lived a human life and learned the compassion of a fragile being. Make the lessons count, son . . .

Mercy stirred in a merciless soul. The angel lowered his sword.

'Jake,' Eleanor whispered.

Nightfall smiled.

'I am him. He is me. A soul shaped and reshaped by its experiences. I have learned much . . . '

He soared over the chasm between the walkways. Standing before his friends, he said:

'Jacob Harker lives.'

Eleanor approached. Her cornflower blue eyes held his as she reached for him, held him, kissed him. In the complex structures of his Never Seen body, Nightfall felt the final breath of Jacob Harker begin to leave him. He had not realized until then that he had been holding on to it, keeping it safe until the last possible moment. Now, as their lips parted, he released the breath into the cold autumn air.

There came a sound like the dying gasp of a star. The ground trembled and the old bridge quaked to its foundations. The sky went dark. The scarlet storm had returned and a sulphur mist materialized in the streets of London. The water in the Thames vanished, leaving behind a bone-dry valley that cleaved the city in two. Scattered all along the bottom of this trench was mile after mile of human bones—a highway of death stretching east and west. Most of the buildings of the great metropolis had been razed to the ground. In their place, the misty ruins were overrun with rats and other small monsters.

'My gods,' Pandora murmured. 'Demons everywhere!'

'What's happening?' Rachel asked. 'I thought you'd stopped the Demontide.'

'I did. I—'

'RACHEL!' Simon cried. 'Jake, what's happening to her?'

Rachel had begun to phase in and out of existence. One second she was there, large as life, the next she simply ceased to be.

Nightfall soon deciphered the mystery.

'Realities are colliding. One timeline is overlapping another and destroying the sequence of history that we have lived through. Rachel is the first casualty because she is a direct heir of Josiah Hobarron, but one by one we shall all succumb to the dominance of this alternative world. We shall die. All except Eleanor, of course.'

'In English!' Pandora snapped. 'Quickly as you can, angel boy.'

'History has it that, in 1645, Josiah Hobarron fought Marcus Crowden and sealed the Door. That has still happened. But what came next?'

'Eleanor and Josiah's descendants!' Simon said, his eyes riveted on Rachel's phasing form. 'Hobarron blood kept the Door sealed for three hundred years.'

'Exactly. Except, as it stands, there *were no* descendants. Eleanor's daughter Katherine was never conceived, never born. The universe was hanging on this moment—the possibility that Jake could turn out to be Katherine's father—but I have just given up the last part of Jacob Harker, a token breath. He no longer exists in any physical form and so cannot be Katherine's father. And so, when the Door weakens one generation after it was sealed, there will be no Hobarron blood to hold back the Demontide. What we are seeing here is that possibility played out. The demons rule and Rachel was never born. In that case, it is doubtful that Pandora or

Simon or Jake himself would have existed either.'

'So what can we do?' Pandora said.

'I can think of only one thing.' The Never Seen placed his right hand around the blade of his sword and his left around the handle. He pulled, and the weapon divided back into the Signums. 'We must resurrect the dead.'

In his mind's eye, Nightfall visualized the pale red cliffs of Hobarron Bay. Beyond the wolf-like jaws of a certain cave, he found an antechamber and a block of magically-frozen ice . . .

'I'm bending the laws of the universe here.' He felt Jake's old humour stir in his veins. 'Don't tell anyone, will you?'

He held the Signums aloft.

'Bring him.'

Rachel had almost disappeared when a huge block of ice materialized on the walkway. Immediately, her phasing began to stabilize. Nightfall refocused his magic on the ice itself.

'If you don't want to get your feet wet, stand back.'

He directed light from the Signums and the block imploded. Shards of ice flew into the air and freezing water rushed over the lip of the walkway and cascaded into the river. Simon dashed forward. He caught hold of the bearded, blue-faced man who had slipped out of the heart of the ice block.

Eleanor sank to her knees and took the young man's head in her lap. She brushed gentle fingers through his frozen hair and wiped crystals from his staring brown eyes. He wore the costume of his time and looked every inch a seventeenth century gentleman. Although a little older than Jacob Harker had been, there was no mistaking that face. Nightfall saw himself in the man and, by the tug of his soul, knew that part of him would always be Josiah Hobarron, just as part remained Jacob Harker.

At first, it looked as if Nightfall's spell had been for nothing. Josiah's eyes remained glazed, his lips unmoving. And then his left hand twitched. Air creaked into his lungs and a long shudder ran the length of his body. He blinked, focusing on Eleanor.

'My love . . . '

Before he could say any more, Nightfall came forward and pressed his fingers against Josiah's temples.

'Sleep.'

The man that some had called 'Witchfinder' sank into a happy slumber.

'He should wake up refreshed,' Nightfall said. 'After all, he's slept for almost four hundred years.'

'He's my Josiah?' Eleanor stroked the resurrected man's face.

'In every way. Josiah Hobaron carved out his own soul.' Nightfall leaned forward and kissed Eleanor's hand. 'See, my love? I kept my promise. I'll always be with you.'

Straightening up, he concentrated power into the Signums.

'And now I am sending you home. Eleanor and Josiah Hobarron will live together near the village that will bear their name. They will have a child and they will call her Katherine. The Elders of the village will keep the secret of

Josiah's return, and when he is old and grey and his long life is coming to its end, I will visit him. My magic will restore him to youth and I will freeze his body in a block of ice and place it in the cavern. In each frozen cell, Josiah Hobarron will carry my spirit with him. One day Josiah will be found by a noble scientist who will use those cells to create a child… The circle of time will start again.'

'But wait. That means . . . ' All eyes turned to Rachel, who had now ceased to phase. 'Luke Seward. Adam Harker's childhood friend. The kid who was sacrificed to stop the Demontide. He will always die. Can't we save him, too?'

'His is the only sacrifice that cannot be undone,' Nightfall sighed. 'It was his death that led Adam to create Jacob; it was Jacob who led us here. I'm sorry.'

Eleanor laid Josiah's head gently on the rooftop. She approached the tall figure of Nightfall and kissed his silver-green lips.

'Always remember who you are.'

Nightfall nodded. 'Are you ready?'

She knelt beside Josiah and took his hand.

'Goodbye . . . '

They vanished in a blaze of green and silver light.

The effects of the phantom Demontide disappeared with them. Despite being robbed of most of its monuments, London was no longer overrun by demons. The sky had cleared and whatever terrors might lurk in the Thames they were hidden again beneath the water. Time had been put right.

Nightfall listened to the Whispers of Oldcraft.

'Josiah and Eleanor had a child. They called her Katherine.'

'You always were a know-it-all,' Simon laughed.

To his surprise, Nightfall burst out laughing too.

People were moving in the streets, poking their heads out of doorways and sniffing the air like a pack of nervous moles. Nightfall wondered in passing how they would set about rebuilding their world. They had been shaken by the knowledge that things once discounted as myths really did exist. This knowledge could help them to embrace the unseen universe or it might drive them into undreamt of dangers. He had always believed in these people, and hoped that his faith in them was not entirely misplaced.

'Will we ever see you again?' Rachel asked.

'Never say never.'

'That sounds like a "no" to me, so in that case your celestial majesty will forgive me.' Pandora threw her arms around him. 'Your dad would be so proud.'

'I miss him, Pandora.' For the first time in history, Nightfall's magisterial voice trembled.

Simon came forward and hugged his friend tight. 'Wings, Jakey? Weird.'

Rachel took his hands. 'You really have to go?'

'I can't stay in this world. Already the atmosphere's burning me. I'm sorry.'

'You saved the world—probably the entire universe—don't start apologizing!' She stretched onto her tiptoes and kissed his forehead. 'This really is goodbye, isn't it?'

He bowed his head. 'I have the gift of Second Sight and

I . . . ' He struggled to find the words. 'I do not see us ever . . . '

The ageless, ancient Nightfall broke down. As Josiah Hobarron and Jacob Harker, he had suffered torture and grief beyond what most humans could ever endure. As Nightfall, the agony of the war against the demons had haunted him for millennia. To this store of pain and heartache he now added the loss of Eleanor and of his dearest friends, Simon Lydgate, Rachel Saxby, and Pandora Galeglass.

They gathered around him, held him close, whispered that they would never, ever forget him. That their hopes and prayers would follow him wherever he went. For a few minutes, they huddled together, human, dark creature, and Old One, speaking words of comfort, sharing memories and doing their best to mend their broken hearts. Finally, they had to let him go.

Nightfall spread his wings and soared into the light. The last farewells of the people he loved distanced and died as he climbed higher and higher, piercing the clouds, gaining the darkness. Just beyond the outer atmosphere of this world he had called *home*, two figures waited to greet him.

Nightfall smiled.

He had much to teach them.

NINE MONTHS LATER
A New Dawn

Roland Grype wandered aimlessly through the streets. Wherever he went, he could hear the sounds of the wounded city lumbering to its feet. At Westminster, the new Parliament building was springing up ahead of schedule. On Ludgate Hill, the framework of St Paul's dome was in place, and in Trafalgar Square a steel column was due to replace Nelson's old monument. After much public debate, it had been agreed that a new figure would stand on top of the pillar. A statue of the being that people had dubbed 'The Angel of London'. Thousands claimed to have witnessed this winged saviour as it battled dark forces in the skies above the city. A hero whose whereabouts were unknown . . .

It would take years to mend the devastation that the Demon Father had inflicted, and perhaps London and the wider world would never be the same again. Magic existed, and in the twilight places at the corners of reality, creatures of light and darkness waited and watched.

At Waterloo Station, a young woman wearing a fluorescent tabard shoved a collection box under Grype's nose.

'Spare some change for the Cyno Slaves?'

Grype frowned. 'I thought they'd all been cured. Made human again.'

After the destruction of the Door, Simon had managed to gather up all the surviving Cynos. It had then taken Pandora six months to reverse engineer Cynthia Croft's potion and come up with a remedy that broke down the demon blood and corrected the molecular changes. Now all four hundred and twelve Cynos had been successfully defanged. Only Simon remained resistant to the cure, the demon blood having had years to bond with his DNA.

'Most of them are still suffering from post-traumatic shock,' the girl said. 'They need psychological care, but the new government gives them only basic assistance. Oh, they've got money to rebuild London but can't spare enough to rebuild people's minds! How would you feel if you'd lived through that nightmare?'

Grype fished a pound from his pocket and received an 'I SUPPORT EX-CYNOS' sticker in return. *Where are the stickers for traumatized witches?* he wondered. *Who jingles the collection boxes for lost and lonely librarians?*

In this brave new world, no one seemed to reach out to Roland Grype. Only once in his life had he felt any sense of belonging. True, he had been the laughing stock of the

Crowden Coven, but he had also been given a role, a purpose, a place to call home. Where did he belong now?

He looked down at the scar on the back of his wrist. Transported from the bridge by Fletcher Clerval's Hand of Glory, Grype had materialized in a field just outside the city of Lincoln. The landing had been safe enough; the only problem was that most of the two hundred thousand protestors had ended up in the same field. The crush had resulted in some serious injuries, and now hundreds were suing Fletcher under the new Misuse of Magic Act. *And witches are supposed to be the bad guys,* Grype thought.

He had tried to make a place for himself among Jacob Harker's friends. After the battle on the bridge, they had all seemed friendly towards him . . . more or less. Pandora had asked for his help with the Cyno remedy; Fletcher had invited him to view his new laboratory (now sited in a hidden pocket of time-space beneath Buckingham Palace); he was guest of honour at the grand opening of Thaddeus Murdles's brand new 'Razor Club'; Joanna Harker had asked him to dinner at her renovated cottage in Hobarron's Hollow. And just this morning he had received an invitation . . .

Simon Lydgate and Rachel Saxby
request the pleasure of your company
at their wedding
in the grounds of St Meredith's Church,
Hobarron's Hollow
under the shadow of the Witchfinder's tomb

Despite all this goodwill, Grype knew that they did not really want him around. Even after he had helped in the search for Edward Rice, he could tell that Simon in particular would never completely trust him. His thoughts wandered back to that time just after the destruction of the Door. The way Rachel had told it, they were all together on the western walkway of Tower Bridge, watching as Nightfall disappeared into the heavens. Then Pandora had cast a glance at the other footpath—

'Where's Eddie?'

That was the question. When he'd returned to London the following morning, they had asked Grype to use his gift of Second Sight to locate the boy. All he could tell was that Eddie had used a powerful spell to transport himself from the bridge, and that dark magic was currently concealing his whereabouts.

Grype came to a halt. He had not intended to come here, and yet his feet had directed him along a well-trodden path. Behind him, the hubbub of the noisy street, in front, the eerie stillness of Yaga Passage.

Heart in his mouth, Grype plunged into the alley. It was all beautifully familiar—the dank, dripping walls, the deathly cold, the dusky light. Breathless, he reached the burned-out shop he had once called home and peered through the broken windows.

Voices came from the back of the shop. Murmurs emerging from the doorway of his old office. Grype was about to hurry away when a hand closed on his shoulder. He turned to find a lean-faced monster standing behind him.

'They've been waiting for you, librarian.'

The vampire lifted Grype over the sill and barged him through the shop. He was surprised to see the creature out in public. After their defeat at the hands of the trolls and the Cynos, the remaining bloodsuckers had gone to ground.

The vampire kicked open the office door and shoved Grype inside.

'Here he is, home at last!'

A voice as hard as iron cut the freezing air. 'Leave us.'

The bloodsucker retreated, closing the door behind him.

It took a moment for Grype's eyes to adjust to the candlelight. The first thing he saw was the boy. Filthy, lank hair dribbled down his brow and fell into his jet-black eyes. He was perhaps fifteen years old and yet, at a height of a little under six feet, he towered over Grype. The librarian had known many dark witches in his time: the malicious Mother Inglethorpe, the cruel Tobias Quilp, the malevolent Marcus Crowden, but he had seldom seen evil personified so completely as it was in this child.

Edward Rice stroked the head of the little demon at his side.

'Say hello, Mr Pinch.'

The demon snickered and made a mock bow.

'W-what do you want with me?' Grype garbled.

'It is time to begin again.'

'But how? The Door was destroyed, the Demon Father obliterated.'

'There are always other Doors. And as for the Demon Father, he plays the long game . . . '

Edward went to a curtained doorway. He motioned for his guest to follow him through the drape and into the emptiness beyond. Although Grype had served Marcus Crowden for many years, he had never become used to the desolation of the Veil. That inbetween place that straddled the worlds of the living and the dead.

'Roland has returned to us, my Mistress.'

Edward bowed before a woman dressed entirely in black. She had her back turned to them, and seemed to be studying the shadows that moved on the misty horizon.

'I'm so glad that you have seen the error of your ways, Mr Grype.'

There was no mistaking that cut-glass voice. Grype shuddered as Edward took him by the shoulders and pushed him forward.

'It was very bad of you to betray us as you did, but I am a forgiving woman. If you promise to tell us all you know about your new friends, then I will be merciful.'

'My friends?'

'One day they will pay for what they have done. When the Demontide dawns our enemies will feel our wrath, will they not?'

Grype bowed his head. 'Yes, my Mistress.'

Cynthia Croft turned to him.

Grype stifled a scream as he beheld what the mutant Cynos had made of her. A face beyond description. A horror that would haunt his dreams. A nightmare to take to the grave.

The Last Nightfall

In her arms, Miss Croft held a small ginger tomcat.

'Stay with us, Roland. This is where you belong.'

The Demon Father smiled down at Roland Grype, and the little librarian let go of his scream.

Simon found his fiancée on the cliffs overlooking Hobarron Bay. The moon had laid a milky carpet across the sea, a pathway that reached to the horizon and into the stars. Since returning to the Hollow, they had often come to the clifftops at night and stared up into the darkness. Both knew what drew them there, though they never spoke of it. They just stood, hand in hand, and contemplated the spaces between the light.

'Couldn't sleep?'

'Nightmares.'

'It's going to be OK, Rach.'

'You keep saying that. Are you trying to convince me or yourself?' She kissed the back of his hand. 'What would Adam have thought?'

'Things have changed. The world knows about magic and dark creatures. Someone has to keep an eye on it all.'

'As long as we don't get suckered in. I'm frightened, Simon. Frightened that we're going to make all the old mistakes again . . . for the greater good. Here, these came by courier.' She handed him a square of laminated card. 'Now we're all set for our first day at work.'

He looked down at the badge—

Simon Lydgate

Senior Adviser on Paranormal Affairs

THE HOBARRON INSTITUTE

It had all started the moment Dr Holmwood woke from his coma. Not only had the ever-resourceful Pandora managed to cure the Cyno-slaves, she had also found an obscure hoodoo potion that, with a little adaptation, had plucked Holmwood out of the Demon Father's nightmare. Faced with the aftermath of a near demon apocalypse, the new government had been keen to channel Holmwood's knowledge. The wily old doctor had agreed to advise them in their handling of the 'new world situation', on one condition. The re-establishment of the Hobarron Institute.

Like a phoenix rising from the ashes, Hobarron Tower was rebuilt within six months. A bigger, brighter, bolder institute, striding forward into an exciting and dangerous new age.

Twenty-four hours after the government go-ahead, Holmwood had made contact with Simon and Rachel. They had more field experience than any employee in the Institute's history; he would love them to come and work for him. After much debate, they agreed, but they had conditions of their own. First, no case of witchcraft was to be pre-judged as being of evil origin. Second, the torture and execution regimes were to end. Third, innocent dark creatures were not to be persecuted. Fourth, those who had fought against the Demon Father were to be offered roles within the organization—Pandora as head of magical healing, Olaf Badderson as security consultant, and Fletcher Clerval, head of mystic sciences.

All their demands were agreed to, but Rachel was right: this was the Hobarron Institute, an organization of questionable history.

'By the way,' Simon said, 'I reckon I've finally figured out why we weren't transported by the Hand of Glory.'

'It wasn't just a fluke?'

'I don't think so.'

'OK, brilliant husband-to-be, astound me with your deductions.'

Simon put his arm around her and drew his fiancée close.

'We're not human.'

Waves began to build and thrash against the shore. A cold wind ruffled the grass.

'Think about it,' he continued. 'Fletcher set the Hand to recognize human DNA. Well, I'm part Cynocephalus, and you, my angel . . .'

A white feather danced in the breeze, swooped over the cliff and raced along the moon-painted highway.

Rachel peered at the horizon. A brilliant light had crowned the world and thrown the stars into misty obscurity.

'Is that dawn?'

Simon's Cyno-senses flared. At the last moment, he threw

Rachel to the ground, covering her head with his arms and ordering her to shut her eyes. They heard a scream of air, the call of terrified sea birds, the crash of waves. Furious light burned against their closed lids.

Something hit the clifftop, and a minor earthquake rumbled across Hobarron's Hollow. Gradually, the ground settled and the light faded. Night reclaimed the world.

'It is safe. You may open your eyes.'

A figure stood silhouetted on the precipice—a beautiful, winged being with green and silver eyes. The creature smiled, although the expression looked a little forced.

'I am Dawn.'

It took a while for Rachel to find her voice.

'Why are you here? Is Ja—Nightfall. Is he OK?'

'My brother is very happy.' And now the smile seemed more natural. Radiant, in fact. 'Happy, because he is coming home.'

'I don't understand.'

The smile faded. 'I have had a vision. A new darkness is rising, and Nightfall must once again honour the promise he made.'

'A Demontide?' Simon said. 'When?'

'The powers of your enemies have weakened. It will take many years for the boy to reach his potential.'

'You mean Eddie,' Rachel said, her voice hollow.

Dawn nodded. 'He will be the one to raise the Door. I foresee the crisis arising twenty years hence, though the exact date is unclear. And so, I give you these weapons to hold in trust. Here is the Orb . . . '

She came forward and handed the dull green witch ball to Simon.

'And here is the Cup.'

The chalice looked far from brilliant in Rachel's hands.

'Give one to the child, but keep the other back until the time is right. He must not know his true identity until all hope is lost.'

Dawn spread her wings.

'Wait!' Simon called. 'What is this? What are we supposed to do?'

'Raise him,' Dawn smiled. 'He could think of no better parents.'

And with that, the Never Seen leapt from the cliff and soared towards the horizon. Just before she disappeared from sight, Dawn transformed into a silver blade, a meteor reaching into the heavens.

Rachel and Simon heard the sound of gentle crying. They turned to find a baby lying in the long grass. A blanket of tiny white flowers grew all around—hyacinths flourishing in the presence of a soul reborn.

While Rachel bent down and took the infant in her arms, Simon pulled off his sweatshirt and wrapped it around the child. They cradled the boy between them, keeping him safe and sheltered.

'What will we call him?'

Rachel smiled. 'Only one name I can think of . . .'

She kissed her baby son.

'Jake.'

About the author

William Hussey has a Masters Degree in Writing from
Sheffield Hallam University. His novels are inspired by
long walks in the lonely Fenlands of Lincolnshire and by a
lifetime devoted to horror stories, folklore and legends.
William lives in Skegness and writes stories about things that
go bump in the night . . .

www.williamhussey.co.uk

Acknowledgements

I would like to pay tribute here to the memory of two very special people, both of whom supported my writing—Colin Clarke and Christine Bettison. Kind, loving, generous souls taken before their time. Family and friends will never, ever forget them.

My eternal thanks go to the 'Three Good Witches', Jasmine Richards, Veronique Baxter, and Deborah Chaffey. Without these wise and wonderful sorceresses *Witchfinder* would never have been more than a whispered spell, a weak incantation lost on the wind. They are the *Three*.

Deep gratitude, as ever, goes to the Skegness librarians, especially Sue Coley, who has an uncanny ability to read minds and lay her hand on just the right research material. Spooky, Sue, spooky!

Over the course of these three books I have thanked most of the brilliant people who work at OUP Children's Books. It just remains for me to say huge thanks to Jennie Younger for all her marvellous and magical publicity skills.

And finally, a big, big thank you to each and every *Witchfinder* reader! It's been quite a journey! I'm sure we'll meet again, my friends . . . in the light and in the darkness . . .